John Whetham Boddam-Whetham

Roraima and British Guiana

with a glance at Bermuda, the West Indies, and the Spanish Main

John Whetham Boddam-Whetham

Roraima and British Guiana
with a glance at Bermuda, the West Indies, and the Spanish Main

ISBN/EAN: 9783337316716

Printed in Europe, USA, Canada, Australia, Japan

Cover: Foto ©Andreas Hilbeck / pixelio.de

More available books at **www.hansebooks.com**

RORAIMA AND BRITISH GUIANA.

RORAIMA.

RORAIMA

AND

BRITISH GUIANA

WITH A GLANCE AT BERMUDA, THE WEST INDIES, AND THE SPANISH MAIN.

BY

J. W. BODDAM-WHETHAM,

AUTHOR OF

'PEARLS OF THE PACIFIC,' 'ACROSS CENTRAL AMERICA,' ETC.

VIEW ON THE CURIPUNG RIVER.

LONDON:

HURST AND BLACKETT, PUBLISHERS,

13 GREAT MARLBOROUGH STREET.

1879.

PREFACE.

"WILL no one explore Roraima, and bring us back the tidings which it has been waiting these thousands of years to give us? One of the greatest marvels and mysteries of the earth lies on the outskirt of one of our own colonies—only not within British territory because the frontier line has been bent in at the spot, on purpose, it would seem, to shut it out—and we leave the mystery unsolved, the marvel uncared for."

The above words, together with a general outline of the wonders to be explored, appeared in a number of the "Spectator" for April, 1877, and aroused my interest to such a degree that I thought by day and dreamt by night of Roraima.

After reading Mr Brown's delightful book on British Guiana—which was referred to in the article from which I have quoted—I made up my mind to visit that colony, with the hope of at all events seeing Roraima and exploring its floral treasures, even if I should be unable to make its ascent.

The summit, Mr Brown says, is inaccessible, except by means of balloons. "According to the traditions of the Indians" says Sir Robert Schomburgh, "the summits of the flat-topped gigantic sandstone walls, which never can be reached by human beings, contain large lakes, full of remarkable fish-like dolphins, and continually encircled by gigantic white eagles—their eternal warders."

Full then, of curiosity, with a great longing to become better acquainted with this mysterious region, I arranged my plans so as to arrive in Demerara about January, paying a flying visit on my way to Bermuda *via* New York, and so on through the West Indies to Guiana. Fortune favoured me, inasmuch as on my arrival at Georgetown, Demerara, I found that the Colonial government was about to send an expedition to Roraima, for the purpose of trying to reach the top of that mountain. With great kindness, the authorities permitted me to accompany it, and I cannot let this occasion pass without expressing my sincere thanks for the opportunity thus afforded me of visiting the interior of British Guiana.

The following rough record of my journey is but a poor return for the many attentions shown me, but it may add its mite in attracting the notice of travellers to a country not often visited for pleasure.

J.W.B.W.

CONTENTS.

CHAPTER I.

CHAPTER II.

CHAPTER III.

CHAPTER IV.

CHAPTER V.

CHAPTER VI.

CHAPTER VII.

CHAPTER VIII.

CHAPTER IX.

CHAPTER X.

CHAPTER XI.

CHAPTER XII.

CHAPTER XIII.

CHAPTER XIV.

CHAPTER XV.

CHAPTER XVI.

CHAPTER XVII.

CHAPTER XVIII.

CHAPTER XIX.

CHAPTER XX.

CHAPTER XXI.

CHAPTER XXII.

CHAPTER XXIII.

CHAPTER XXIV.

CHAPTER XXV.

CHAPTER XXVI.

CHAPTER XXVII.

CHAPTER XXVIII.

CHAPTER XXIX.

CHAPTER XXX.

RORAIMA.

CHAPTER I.

OUTWARD BOUND—THE 'CANIMA'—A ROUGH VOYAGE—FIRST
VIEW OF BERMUDA — COASTING — IRELAND ISLE — COMMIS-
SIONERS' HOUSE—THE SOUND—HAMILTON—LANDING—AN INDIA-
RUBBER TREE—A BILL OF FARE—THE REGISTER—HAMILTON
HOTEL—PAPAWS—A SUGGESTION.

> " Under the eaves of a southern sky,
>   Where the cloud roof bends to the ocean floor
> Hid in lonely seas, the Bermoothes lie—
>   An emerald cluster that Neptune bore
> Away from the covetous earth god's sight,
> And placed in a setting of sapphire light."

" WELL, if we are going to a warmer temperature than this, few of us will return,'
was the remark made by one of the passengers
on board the little steamer 'Canima,' which was
rolling heavily in a perfectly smooth sea, past Staten
Island on her way from New York to Bermuda. It
was the month of November, but the sun was as hot
and the sky as brassy as though it had been August.
On shore we could see preparations being made for
cricket, lawn-tennis, and archery; and there were we

B

bound for a semi-tropical climate. It was one of those days with which the clerk of the weather favours New York in early spring, and sometimes even when the Indian summer is supposed to have ended.

I have said that the vessel rolled heavily, even in a smooth sea, and we were naturally anxious to know what she would do in rough weather; some thought that she would turn over altogether, others, that she would regain her equilibrium and keep it, but this latter idea was soon proved to be a fallacy, as the wretched ship had no more centre of gravity than a cherub.

Hardly had we entered the open sea when a change in the weather occurred. The sky was overcast, the waves assumed a threatening aspect, a cold drizzle set in, and general discomfort prevailed.

How gay and lively the scene on deck was when we started! how dull and quiet it suddenly became! just as I was imitating the example of the rest of the passengers by retreating to my cabin, an old gentleman who had made the passage to Bermuda thirty-two times spoke to me of

"The old green glamour of the glancing sea."

As I did not feel much inclined to listen to poetry, I merely remarked that I thought Lucretius was right when he declared that " the sea was meant to be looked at from shore," and then withdrew.

A less enjoyable voyage could not be imagined, and what with a head wind, rainy weather, the gulf-stream in a state of extra-roughness, and French-Canadian stewards, whose dirty appearance made the greasy food less appetising, if possible, than it other-wise would have been, a more ghostly, half-starved lot of travellers never arrived at their destination.

How many lines of steamers there are whose owners trade on the old Sanscrit proverb which they might adopt as their motto, "The river is crossed, and the bridge is forgotten."

Fortunately the passage only lasted four days, the advertised time being seventy-two hours; and glad indeed were we when we had passed through the narrow reef-channel, and were coasting along the western side of the main island of the Bermudas, and within the formidable chain of breakers which surrounds them.

The first view of the island is disappointing, as the low hills have a barren and desolate appearance, and the plain white cottages which are dotted about here and there stand in bare, uncultivated spots. Lower down, however, as we approach the central portion, the face of the island brightens. Old acquaintances of Bermuda point out the position of Harrington Sound, which they declare—and rightly as we afterwards thought—to be the most lovely part of the island; but from the vessel all we can see is a narrow inlet which one could almost jump across. The long lines of roofs which sparkle so in the sun on the hill yonder are the barracks, and the red coats of the soldiers make pleasant bits of colour, which contrast well with the gleaming sand and the deep green cedar-nooks in which the white houses nestle.

Farther on we pass Government House and the signal station, from which the arrival of the steamer has long been signalled; then Clarence Hill—Admiralty House—is left behind, and we round Spanish Point, with Ireland and other islands forming a semi-circle on our right. On Ireland Island is to be seen

as everybody knows, the famous floating dock which
was towed from England in 1869. At another time,
this would probably have been the centre of attraction,
but the eyes of our sea-worn passengers were directed
to a fine large building well situated at the extremity of
that island. "What a splendid hotel!" said one, and
"How delightfully cool it must be there!" said another.
It proved to be the "Commissioner's House," now used
as military quarters.

The history of this building is rather singular. A
certain Treasury clerk was appointed "Commissioner"
in charge of the dockyard, and, not being satisfied with
the house given him to occupy, received permission
from the Home Government to spend £12,000 in
building a new one. This concession appears to have
turned his head, for the house gradually assumed the
dimensions of a palace; marble chimney-pieces were
erected, and stabling built for a dozen horses, and this
in a country where fire-places were hardly necessary,
and where, at that time, horses were useless. Marble
baths and other trifles ran up the bill to over £60,000.
The gentleman for whom this expense was incurred
never occupied the house, as he went mad, and the
office of "Commissioner" was soon dispensed with.

Whilst an old resident was telling us this story, we
had entered the Great Sound, and we found ourselves
in a pretty land-locked harbour, on whose wonderfully
clear blue water floated numerous fairy islets—a scene
which reminded us of the words of Moore:

> "The morn was lovely, every wave was still
> When the first perfume of a cedar-hill
> Sweetly awakened us, and with smiling charms
> The fairy harbour wooed us to its arms."

Through these green islands we wound our way carefully, one channel being particularly narrow and dangerous. Beneath its transparent waters we could distinguish an old cannon ; and then a sudden turn brought
us into the pretty port of Hamilton, where we dropped
anchor close to the shore. But being on shore and
only near it are very different things, and it seemed
hours to us hungry mortals before the vessel was
gradually dragged to within forty feet of the quay.
Nearer we could not get, on account of a shallow.

Now to land in boats appeared too ridiculous for
such a short distance, but no other means were visible. A
bridge lowered by a crane would have landed us all in
a few minutes, but there was no appearance of such a
thing. Old-fashioned Bermuda wanted no new-fangled
notions, so we had to abide our time and wait until a
bridge had been manufactured in the following way :
Ropes were thrown from the vessel and fastened to the
outer ends of long beams, which were hauled on board,
their other extremities resting on shore. Then a
number of grinning darkies strided these beams, and
lashed cross-bars to them ; planks were laid on the
frame, and over these we walked on to the quay.

There were only two passengers besides myself for
the Hamilton Hotel, and these were a very charming
old lady and her son—a young physician from Boston
—who had been advised to spend the winter abroad.
A short walk brought us to the hotel, a good-sized,
comfortable building, commanding a fine view of the
harbour and port of the town. On our way up, we
passed a splendid specimen of the india-rubber tree,
whose luxuriant growth almost hid the broad veranda'd
cottage behind it. Speaking of this tree, Mark Twain

says that, when he saw it, it was "out of season, possibly as there were no shoes on it, nor suspenders, nor anything a person would properly expect to find there." This tree was the first sign of tropical vegetation that we had seen, which fact had rather surprised us, as on the cover of a " bill of fare," which had been shown to us in New York, was a picture of the Hamilton Hotel, with an avenue of palms and bananas leading up to it. The fine palms—mountain cabbage—we afterwards discovered about half-a-mile off, and not even within sight of the hotel. But one cannot expect to find everything one sees, even on a bill of fare. We were informed by the clerk that we were the first visitors of the season. " But somebody else is here," said I, pointing to a solitary name in the visitor's register. " Oh," said he, " that's me ;" and forthwith assigned us our rooms.

And now let me say a word about this hotel, which is notorious for having prevented many strangers from visiting Bermuda, and others who would have liked to return, from coming back. The rooms are simply but comfortably furnished, the situation is good, and the grounds might be very prettily laid out. The whole cause of discontent with the hotel has hitherto—that is, up to the winter of 1877-78—been with the management. The house had been leased to an American, a pleasant, agreeable person, but without the least idea of managing an hotel. People did not come to Bermuda for third-rate American hotel dinners, but there they got them, until they could stand it no longer. It was useless to speak to the manager ; no redress was obtainable. Everything was served at once ; an armada of little white dishes was placed before you,

in one a dry cutlet, in another a few dried pellets of
fried potatoes, peas like buckshot, boiled potatoes like
cannon-balls; here an inch of tough chicken, there a
slice of beef, baked until all its proper juices had been
extracted; heavy pumpkin pies, tea and coffee quite
undrinkable, butter that no one could touch; such,
with but little variation, were the component parts of
the three meals. Even the provisions of Nature were
not made as available as they might have been. In
the garden were two or three fine papaw trees, whose
insipid green fruit was sometimes given to us as a
delicious West-Indian preserve. It is said that the
leaves of this tree, if rubbed on a bull's hide, would
immediately convert it into tender beefsteak; now
our meat was always of the toughest description.

Day after day I used to see my two friends, fresh
from their home in Boston, rise from the table without
having touched anything, and I felt quite ashamed of
our English colony. Had the proprietor been English,
I think I should have run away. As it was, we limited
our visit to a fortnight instead of a month, the doctor
accompanying me to the West Indies, whilst his mother
returned home.

It seems a pity that quiet Bermuda should not attract
more visitors—Americans especially—than it does. A
well-kept hotel there would be very welcome to many
who now winter in Florida or Nassau (Bahamas).
The island is more interesting than either of those
places, and equally picturesque; and I have no doubt
that visitors, when they left, would carry away as
pleasant recollections as they would probably leave
behind.

CHAPTER II.

A WHITE TOWN—A CEDAR AVENUE—THE "DUCKING-STOOL"—
SEA ENCROACHMENTS—FERN PITS—SPANISH POINT—FAIRY-
LAND—THE ISLAND ROAD—AMUSEMENTS—A PAPER HUNT—
REEFS—SEA CUCUMBERS—THE SOUTH WIND—SAND-HILLS—
BOILERS—ARCHITECTURE—MUSEUM—A RARE SPIDER.

> " Pleasant it was when the woods were green,
>   And the winds were soft and low,
>   To lie amid some sylvan scene,
>   Where the long drooping boughs between,
>   Shadows dark and sunlight sheen
>   Alternate come and go."
>
> LONGFELLOW.

WHEN you first look out of your window over the town, you imagine that there has been a slight snow-storm, so gleaming white are the roofs of all the houses. But you soon learn that, owing to the absence of springs and streams, the roofs are white-washed, and kept scrupulously clean, as the rain-water is thence conducted into cisterns, from which it is drawn for use.

The roads are white, the houses are whiter, and the roofs are whitest; but what would otherwise be an unpleasant glare is modified by the foliage, which half conceals the houses, and by the green Venetian blinds, which shade all the windows.

Nearly every house has a garden, and passion-flowers, morning glory, and other vines creep up the pillars and over the piazzas in great profusion and brilliancy. " Pride of India " trees border the sides of the streets, but these fail to give the delicious shade which is obtained under the cedar avenue which lies on one side of the small public gardens. Here you can stroll in the heat of the day, protected from the sun by a green roof, and surrounded by roses,* heliotropes, lilies, great beds of geraniums, pomegranates, gorgeous blossoms of hybiscus, gladioli, and all sorts of lovely creepers. Then when the sun's rays have lost some of their power, you can prolong your walk along the winding road, past the pretty country church of Pembroke, and leaving Mount Langton (Government House) on your right, behold at the bottom of a shady lane spreadeth a golden network, like a veil of gauze, stretching far and wide. That is the sea, and in a short half-hour you have crossed this part of the island.

Better still is it to come here in the morning, and after a plunge in the deep blue water, sit on the "ducking stool," and meditate on the feelings of the poor wretches who, in days gone by, suffered the water punishment for witchcraft, sorcery, and other imaginary offences. A notice prohibits bathing on Government grounds, but down below the steep rocks there are plenty of nooks and hollows, sand-carpeted and as private as your own chamber. For myself, I never

---

* Some magnificent roses are grown near Hamilton, and one gentleman informed me that he had over two hundred varieties thriving luxuriantly ; not the over-blooming, straggling plants, whose blossoms are coarse, ill-shaped, and of faded colour, so often seen in hot climates, but beautiful bright roses with thick petals and rare symmetry of outline.

could make out where the Government property began or where it ended.

On this north shore a delicious breeze tempers the heat of the sun, and it is enjoyment enough to look at and listen to the sea, to watch the men collecting the seaweed for their land, or to read, and consequently fall asleep. No one will disturb you; there are no tramps in Bermuda, and your watch will still be going, even should you sleep for hours. To return to town two different ways are open to you; both are along the same sea-shore road, but lie in opposite directions; the one leads to the north-east, until you branch off to the right past the barracks; the other—and the one we will take—runs south-west towards Admiralty House and Spanish Point. All along this road you cannot help noticing the encroachment of the sea, and you wonder how long it will be before the road on which you are walking becomes the edge of a craggy wall for the waves to beat against and undermine. Here truly does—

> "The hungry ocean gain
> Advantage on the kingdom of the shore."

The hollowness of Bermuda is very remarkable, and in many places the cavernous ground gives forth very musical sounds when struck.

As we proceed on our walk, we see but few signs of cultivation; here and there are strips of garden running up into the ubiquitous cedar bush, but most of the land is used for grazing, and very indifferent grazing, too. One peculiarity amongst the four footed animals is that they are nearly all black and white; another is that they are all tethered; everything seems at anchor in Bermuda, cattle, goats, pigs, donkeys, even the hens are not at liberty. Occasionally one passes a deep well, originally dug out for the purpose of obtaining fresh water, but entirely lined with the lovely maiden-hair fern. This delicate species gives a special charm to the island, as it grows luxuriously on the walls and rocks, in caves and hollows, and drapes the numerous land-pits with its graceful fronds. Where the fern declines to grow, there the "life-plant" flourishes, and quickly covers up the bare places with its deep green, fleshy leaves. Of such vitality is this weed that a single leaf, if plucked and pinned to the wall, will live and send out shoots from its edges with perfect indifference as to its changed abode.

At Spanish Point the view across to Ireland Island is very picturesque, and one perfect horse-shoe bay, with white sandy shore, lingers a long time in the memory, not only on account of the peaceful scene of which it forms a part, but also for its own exquisite form. Near by is Fairy-land, well named, for it really is one of the most charming spots in Bermuda. The sea here runs far up into the island, forming a lake, with bays, islets, caves, isthmuses, and peninsulas. Just above one of the green bights stands a little nest called "Honeymoon Cottage," a gem of a place, where many a happy pair have passed the first week or two of their new life. The hall-door steps lead down to the bathing house, which, when I visited it, contained only one little shoe, but that worthy of Amphitrite herself.

Leaving beautiful Undercliff, our road now turns more inland, sometimes crossing a little hill, and sometimes running through a swamp with high reeds and

flags, and with its edges planted with potatoes and tomatoes.   Now it curves through a grove, anon it winds
past home-like cottages, whose black occupants grin
with delight at seeing a stranger, curtsey, and wish him
a pleasant walk; then once more the sea is in view,
pretty gardens line the road, life and activity betoken
the neighbourhood of the wharf, and you are again in
Hamilton.   Have you enjoyed your walk?   I must
not ask whether you have a good appetite for dinner!

There is no doubt that the scenery of Bermuda
improves on acquaintance.   At first sight the visitor
will probably be disappointed with the flat appearance
of the island and the apparently few possibilities for
the picturesque.   But in a very short time he will
discover that it is all hill and dale, on a minute scale,
it is true, as the highest elevation hardly exceeds two
hundred and fifty feet—but varied and even romantic.
Take, for instance, the view from the Barrack Hill.
Everywhere the coastland seems broken up in the
most capricious manner.   Deep bays, narrow promontories, and an infinite number of islands give to
the sea the appearance of a series of silver lakes, which
shine in the sun like the fragments of a broken mirror.
The undulating country is clothed with cedar-bush,
whose grey green is relieved here and there by the
brilliant flush of the pink oleander and the white perpendicular walls of a stone quarry.   Afar off a lighthouse is pictured against the sky, near at hand is a
white fort, and a church spire shows itself above the
trees.   But it is the beauty of the sea rather than of the
land that here takes the first place in one's affections;
and in after-time it is the memory of the molten silver
sea and its green islands that clings to one longest;

" Wherever you wander the sea is in sight,
With its changeable turquoise green and blue,
And its strange transparence of limpid light.
You can watch the work that the Nereids do
Down, down, where their purple fans unfurl,
Planting their coral and sowing their pearl."

Those who are familiar with the scenery of Puget Sound, or of Vancouver's Island, will recognise, I think, many points of similarity with that of Bermuda. The dense forests are wanting in the latter, but from a bird's-eye view the resemblance is striking. Above all there is the same air of absolute quiet and a subdued wildness characteristic of the two places. Certainly Bermuda is a quiet land ; so still a place, it seemed to me, I had never been in before. You are perpetually wondering why the church bells are not ringing for service, and I have heard people ask, " Did you hear the dog barking yesterday ?" But life here is by no means dull, a more friendly, hospitable, and fun-loving people you would not find, and what with military theatricals, croquet, cricket, lawn tennis, boating parties, and other amusements, time glides away very quickly.

There is little or no game on the island—one bevy of quails being the extent of my observations—but, as an Englishman must hunt or shoot something, a " paper-hunt" has been established. It may not be as exciting as fox-hunting, but, in a climate where you must take things easily, it affords capital exercise. The Bermudian foxes—or rather the Judases, as they carry the bag—are generally men from the garrison, and, with the thermometer 75 deg. in the shade, and 110 deg. or more in the sun, they have no easy task in giving a good run. Spectators are always invited to view " the

finish" at some previously selected spot, and there refreshments of all kinds are served, making a very
agreeable finale to an amusing day. A severe critic
might remark that the hurdles and other obstacles
placed near "the finish," were hardly worthy of the
excessive ardour displayed in overcoming them, but he
must remember that it perhaps makes up for a slight
failing off where the jumps were more formidable. It
is not only in Bermuda that the presence of a certain
pair of bright eyes has driven many a Nimrod to deeds
of heroism in the matter of hedges and ditches that
otherwise would have been neglected

For boating the Bermuda waters offer great facilities,
and, if you want to see how near to the wind's eye it is
possible to go, you cannot do better than hire one of
the native sailing-boats—one masted and flush-decked
—when there is a stiff breeze. You may get rather
wet, but you will spin along at a glorious rate, and you
certainly will admire the workmanlike way in which
your crew—a man and a boy—manage the rakish
craft.

Then, in calm weather it is delightful to pay a visit
to the reefs and gather for yourself the brain corals and
"sea-whips," specimens of which fishermen have
brought to the hotel for sale. In these water-gardens
may be seen all sorts of many-hued plants; crinoids
like palm trees, gorgonias, mosses, sea-feathers, coral
like creeping vines, sea-cucumbers,* and coloured weeds
waving to and fro over the brilliant fish. On bright,
sunny days, when the blue water sparkles, you may,

* A curious circumstance about these creatures is that nearly every
individual harbours in his stomach a large parasitical fish, that lies at ease
and feeds upon whatever comes in its way.

perhaps, in fancy, hear snatches of low music and gay
tones of laughter gurgling up from below, but, when it is
dull and gloomy, the sounds will be of sorrow, telling
secrets dire and tales of woe, wrung from restless spirits
buried amid wreck and ruin beneath the flood that
sweeps over those cruel, beautiful coral rocks.

We had heard so much of the disagreeable effects of
the south wind, which generates so much moisture that
everything is quickly covered with green mould, and a
general clammy feeling prevails, that we were continually running round the corner of the hotel to note
the direction of the wind by the flag at the signal
station. As we were constantly expecting it—the south
wind—the natural consequence was that it never came,
and we were very grateful. I think it was a French-
man who remarked that nothing happens except the
unexpected, and I have found this true in many cases.
For instance, when travelling in the tropics, if you are
continually on the look-out for snakes, you will rarely
meet them, and we all know that the best way to keep
off the rain is to carry an umbrella. The climate of
Bermuda is said to be capricious, but during our stay—
a short one certainly—we found the temperature very
pleasant, the thermometer seldom rising over 73 deg.,
and frequently a fire towards evening was very comfortable.

Small as Bermuda is—as the five principal islands
connected by ferries and bridges only form a chain
about twenty-four miles in length, and with a breadth
varying from a few hundred yards to about two miles
—it yet contains many points of interest. The splendid
light-house on Gibb's Hill is worth a visit for itself, and
for the fine view to be obtained from it ; the fortifica-

tions, too, which, together with the natural barriers, are gradually making a second Gibraltar, must be inspected. The Paget Hills on the eastern shore show how the drifting sand is elevating the land, and probably increasing it as fast as the western waves are washing it away. Unfortunately, this overwhelming mass of sand is steadily advancing over the cultivated land, and has already buried one cottage, whose chimney alone is visible above the surrounding whiteness. It is merely a matter of taste which is preferable—to be washed away or to be buried alive.

Near the beach, at the foot of these hills, may be seen, at low water, great circular masses of rock, hollowed out like huge cauldrons. Similar ones occur at intervals round the islands, and are by no means the least interesting of the Bermudian curiosities.*

However entertaining the country and sea-side may be, there is very little in the town of Hamilton worth noticing. With the exception of Trinity Church, the buildings are insignificant. The "Public Building" stands in an ill-tended garden and presents no inducement to the young Bermudian to prepare himself for the Legislature. But, perhaps, there will soon be no young white Bermudians, as the youths of these islands find the United States better adapted for their speedy advancement in life.

I had hoped to find in the museum a specimen of a

---

* In appearance these gigantic pots and cauldrons are similar to the large basin-shaped, or funnel-like holes made ages ago by the glacier on the sandstone ridge in the "Glacier garden of Lucerne," Switzerland. But there, lying at the bottom of the basins are the colossal balls, which once as hard blocks of stone had slipped through the icy fissures, and had then been rolled and twisted about by the action of water rushing down upon them until the deep holes were made. The Bermudian boilers appear rather to have been built up than hollowed out.

certain spider, concerning which an ancient chronicler of Bermuda has said: "They are of a very large size, but withal beautifully coloured, and look as if they were adorned with pearl and gold. Their webs are in colour and substance a perfect raw silk, and so strongly woven that, running from tree to tree, like so many snares, small birds are sometimes caught in them." The Museum consisted of a few South-Sea Island shells, some coral, some moth-eaten skins, three bottles of alcohol containing marine specimens, two butterflies, and no spider. I had a better ungathered collection of insects in my own room at the hotel. I must return there and see if I can find a mother-of-pearl spider.

CHAPTER III.

WE have not half exhausted the beauties of the neighbourhood, but, in case your patience should be at an end, please step into the carriage which is to take us to St. George's, at the other end of the island, whence we are to embark for the West Indies, and let us look about us on the way.

Three roads lead to our destination; we will take the middle one, which joins the ocean drive near Harrington Sound. Splendid roads these are, too! Bermuda may well be proud of them. Altogether there are more than a hundred miles of broad, white, smooth road. Sometimes the road-bed is so deeply hewn out of the white coral rock that Lilliputian canyons are formed with fern-hung walls, and capped with aloe or cactus. Several varieties of the latter plant grow in the islands, and a magnificent specimen of the night-blooming *cereus grandiflora* is to be seen in the small garden behind the Yacht Club in Hamilton. It runs in wild profusion over trees, walls, and bushes, and when in blossom is covered with hundreds of pale flowers, whose delicious perfume is quite overpowering. It may be inconvenient, perhaps, to visit it at the proper time—midnight—but it is necessary, as in the morning beauty and perfume have gone.

Dazzlingly white, but, fortunately, not dusty, is the road as we leave the snowy houses behind us, but soon we enter a stretch of cool forest. Here a deeper silence reigns than even on the sunny hill we have ascended, a melodious silence too, for the sweet note of the blue bird and the soft chirp of the "chick of the village" do not break the quiet, but rather adds to it. A crimson cardinal gives a rare flush to the grey cedar, and pretty little ground-doves sit perfectly unconcerned by the road-side as we drive past. Prospect is soon reached, and then we descend, again skirting a large morass, edged with cedars, mangrove, and palmetto. We see a new church, which makes a strong contrast with the old ruined one that stands farther on, near some really fine cedars.

Here we halt for a moment to inspect a natural curiosity, namely, a very ancient cedar, lofty and hollow, and in whose dead trunk is growing a young one, the green head of which appears high up, amid the dead branches of the old one. Patches of cultivated land with their great hedges of oleander were as common here as everywhere else, but, besides the usual tomato, onion, and potato, we saw for the first time that friend of our childhood—the farinaceous arrowroot. Could we do less than greet it with a friendly nod as we drove along? Alas! even the cultivation of this diminishes year by year; everything has to give

way to onions and tomatoes.—consequently, the
supply of other vegetables, cereals, and fruits is
extremely limited. With such a fertile soil the exports might almost equal the imports in value, but
I am afraid to say how many times the latter exceed
the former at present. No one would expect a black
man to work more than he is absolutely obliged,
and certainly in Bermuda he who can avoid doing
anything makes the best of his opportunities. Possibly
his nature is allied to that of the surrounding coral
formations, and he becomes a sort of human coral-
polyp, whose only labour of life is to get a little food
and to eat it; the rest he leaves to nature. Well,
who can blame him? he seems very happy and
contented, he sends his children to school, he is very
polite, and, if he is poor, poverty does not harm him,
and he is content.

Look at that merry group in the doorway of that
tumble-down old building! All smile at the strangers,
and the mother who has been plaiting away at some
palmetto work—which by the way is not half so fine
and pretty here as in Florida—leaves it, to gather
some magnificent roses we have stopped to admire.
But surely an earthquake has shattered this little
village; roofless cottages, mouldering walls, gardens
in which papaws, prickly pears, and lantanas form a
perfect jungle, everything has the appearance of
some such catastrophe. No, these ruins are the land
fragments of what was once an important harbour,
and the splendid sheet of water before us is Harrington
Sound. Very beautiful is this lake—as it may be
called—which at its junction with the sea is crossed
by a bridge a few yards in length, and only visible

when approached quite close; for it lies at the foot
of a circle of green hills, surrounded by cavernous
shores, and with islands dotting its green transparent
waters.

Taking the road to the right we pass some pretty
cottages, one of which has such a tremendous portico,
that we are reminded of the donkey that tried to convert itself into a deer by attaching antlers to its head.
Then we arrive at the Devil's Hole. Across the water
the Devil's Head rises up, its perpendicular cliff looking quite grand in miniature; there the tropic-bird
builds its nest in perfect security in some inaccessible
position. What the devil has to do with either place
I cannot say; both names seem singularly inappropri-
ate, and for the former "Neptune's Grotto" is more
suitable, and just as easy to pronounce.

There is frequently, I believe, a good deal of
difficulty in finding the proprietor of the pool in
question, but at the time of our visit he was standing
at the wooden door, and informed us we had come
at a good time, as he was just going to feed the fish.
Entering, we found ourselves in a pretty circular
grotto, lined with shrubs, ferns, and creepers. Steps,
cut out of the rock, led down to a deep pool of the
clearest salt water, in which were a number of great
fish called "groupers," gazing up with the most
expectant look—if a fish-eye can be expressive—and
evidently aware that feeding time was at hand. And
how they did eat! there was no dainty nibbling, no
coquettish trifling, a huge mouth opened and the
morsel was gone. "What does that great fellow
weigh?" "Oh, about two shillings," replied the
proprietor, whose idea of weight was a marketable

one, "and those angels will average one and six-
pence apiece." Well, those angels were worth it,
their exquisite azure hue vied with the wonderfully
tinted water, and, what with gold streakings, waving
plume-like fins, and really beautiful eyes, they well
deserved their name. If some clever soul could
discover a preparation for preserving the natural hues
of fish, what a benefactor he would be! At present,
the alcoholic collections of our Museums form a
ghastly contrast with the brilliant birds and insects
which surround them.

> " While blazing breast of humming-bird and Io's stiffened wing,
>   Are just as bright as when they flew their earliest voyage in spring ;
>   While speckled snake and spotted pard their markings still display—
>   Though he who once embalm'd them both himself be turned to clay—
>   The scaly tribe a different doom awaits—scarce reach'd the shore
>   Those rainbow hues are fading fast till all their beauty's o'er."

Right learnedly, and with the tongue of a gourmet,
did our fisherman discuss the habits and qualities of
the various fish that swim in Bermudian waters. Cow-
fish, porgies, hamlets, hog, grunts, bream, and many
others; a few he pointed out to us, amongst them a
squirrel with large eyes, of a blood-red colour and
peculiar shape; then he landed a "grunt," which
gave vent to sounds that would shame a veritable
porker. This natural aquarium is connected with
the sea by an underground passage, consequently the
water is always fresh ; formerly, we were told, it was
a cavern, but the roof had fallen in.

On emerging, we see eastward the pretty house and
grounds belonging to the American Consul. In his
garden is a salt-water fountain, in the basin of which
we, during a former visit, had seen many strange fish,

and also some good specimens of the sea-horse. On
that occasion we had been told of the terrible plot
concocted in these Islands by a Dr. Blackburn, for
introducing the yellow fever into the Northern part
of the United States, by sending thither boxes of
infected clothing. Fortunately—and I believe chiefly
through the instrumentality of our host—the plot was
discovered in time to prevent the shipment, and a
terrible calamity was probably averted. The worthy
Consul does not confine his attention to fish alone,
and his system of banana culture might be profitably
adopted in many other parts of the Island.

Continuing our drive round the Sound, we are more
and more impressed with its attractions ; the apple-green
water below us, the rocky inlets with white sandy
edges, here and there a stretch of shingle or a wooden
promontory, and, beyond, the blue sea with the foam
on its distant reefs, form a lovely picture, and we are
sorry when a turn in the road has shut us out from
such a wealth of colour.

Our next halting-place is at a farm house, near
which stands Moore's " calabash tree,"* beneath whose
shade the poet composed his verses, and wove his
amatory couplets addressed to " Nea, the Rose of
the Isles." The tree lives still, in spite of the severe
hacking it has received from tourists, whose carved
names are continually blurred out by time and the
hands of their successors. Even the seat under it
is the object of much curiosity, and as each new one
is placed in its proper position it is carried off piece-
meal by enthusiastic admirers, who must have a bit
of the chair the poet sat in. I never see the ravages

* Crescentia cujete.

made by relic hunters, or the desecration of historical places, without thinking of a certain tourist to whom an Italian monk was showing a consecrated lamp, which had never gone out during five centuries. Giving the flame a decisive puff, he remarked, with cool complacency, "Well, I guess it's out now." A few gourds are still left hanging from the topmost boughs of the tree, but the sable attendant will not allow any of these to be knocked down, so you must be satisfied with the one presented to you by the proprietor of the land at your departure. It may come from Moore's tree, but gourds are deceptive and much alike.

A short walk through tangled wild-wood leads to some limestone caves, which were also frequented by the poet. They differ little from other cavernous formations; there are vaulted arches, halls and aisles, gem-studded cornices, and upright columns; here there is a sheet of water so clear that the guide has to tell you that it is water; there, oozing stalactites embellish a Gothic temple, but the effect of brilliant crystallization is marred by the smoke of the bushes which light up the gloom of the interior. The visit is a scrambling one, but still worth accomplishing.

Shortly after leaving Walsingham we cross the causeway which connects the main island with St. George's; on our right, is the magnificent Castle Harbour, with numerous islands; on our left, a land-locked sound, with cranes and other birds fishing on the shallows and among the mangrove bushes, whilst in front, lying in the hollow of a curve under a hill, are the white houses of the town. Rapidly we drive along the fine causeway, the waves now and then almost dashing over us, so near is the sea; then, after

crossing a drawbridge, we are soon among cottages
and gardens. Here we see again potato fields and
patches of cultivated ground, apparently planted with
black bottles. These black bottles are quite a feature
in Bermudian cultivation during the sowing season;
they are not planted in the hope of their ever becoming
quarts or magnums, or even of their being refilled
by nature with their original contents, but, having
held the seed, they merely indicate the amount
sown.

A quaint old town is St. George's, with its high
stone walls and winding alleys. So narrow are the
streets that, if two carriages met in one of them, it
is difficult to imagine what would happen, as they
could not pass, and certainly could not turn back;
but two carriages in St. George's on the same day
would be an exceptional event. The whole place has
the appearance of having been cut out of a single
block of white limestone, rather than being built of
bricks of that material. It is not in many places that
a man can build his house from stone out of his own
quarry, on his own premises, but he can in Bermuda.
With a hand-saw he cuts out the soft stone, and the
blocks then harden by exposure to the air.

The numerous square cuttings in the hill-sides and
along the roads form a feature in the scenery, and by
no means an unpleasing one, as the new are snowy
white, and the old are generally draped with green
bushes and creepers. Walls are built of the same
material, and then receive, as the houses do, a coating
of whitewash, which hides the seams and joinings, thus
presenting a solid white mass. Over these walls, you
see broad plantain leaves and flaming poinsetties;

orange, lemon, and palm trees are more numerous here at St. George's than at Hamilton, and the tropical aspect of the town extends to its inhabitants. Of labour there is little or no sign, and what there is of life is hardly worth mentioning.

As St. George's is a garrison town—two regiments being considered necessary for the safety of Bermuda— it is probably gayer than when we saw it, which was in hot noonday, when all slept except one black man, who was shaving a white man under the shade of a tree in the square.

That evening the 'Beta,' from Halifax, left with us for the West Indies. Summer isles, in spite of that abused hotel, I would gladly revisit you; I carry away nought but a remembrance of white cottages and gardens, green islands, billowy masses of oleander, cedar hills, and coral rocks, and, above all, of a shining lake-like sea, as calm and restful as the happy homes which it surrounds.

CHAPTER IV.

HAD the passengers on board the comfortable 'Beta' been as poetical as Childe Harold was when in his clumsy brig he sang:

> " Four days are sped, but with the fifth anon
> New shores descried make every bosom gay,"

they might have said something less prosy than " Thank goodness, there's land !" when, precisely on the fifth morning after leaving Bermuda, a vision as of misty clouds grew out of the sea ! Then, as the yellow flush of dawn cleared the prospect, substance was given to the hazy outlines, and as the sun rose, touching the rugged peaks with gold and purple, the island of St. Thomas lay revealed before them.

As the vessel entered the spacious harbour and dropped anchor at some distance from shore, we thought we had seldom looked at a prettier scene. In front is a high, abrupt mountain range, from which three rounded spurs run down to the sea, and on these hills stands the town. On the right, a low, wooded savanna sweeps up to the hills which encircle the bay, whose mirror-like surface reflects the rocks and islands which close the entrance and almost join the promontory on our left. But it is the rich colouring that forms the striking part of the view. After demure Bermuda, with its white and grey-green, the bright red roofs and white, green, yellow, and blue houses are almost dazzling. There, clinging to the side of the hill, is a cluster of freshly painted cottages, looking very gaudy in the strong sunlight; nearer at hand are a few low houses, whose once brilliant roofs are now changed by time and weather to a golden russet-red highly picturesque.

The height of the dark mountains gives a diminutive appearance to the buildings, so that you imagine you are looking at a Dutch toy village—or rather three villages. This idea is enhanced by the toy fort which, with bastion, battlements, and barbican, is strongly suggestive of cake ornamentation. Commanding this Danish fortress are the two strongholds of those old pirates called Bluebeard and Blackbeard, which look feudal, and only want a few of Mr. James's horsemen slowly winding up the narrow causeway to be quite romantic. Over the trees of the toy public garden, which lies close to the landing, is seen a Moorish-looking structure, which proves to be the hotel, and gives promise of coolness and comfort, which I need hardly say is not realised. Behold, then, bright, cheerful little dwellings, with a prevailing hue of russet, perched on hills and nestling in the intervening valleys, amid tropical trees and flowering shrubs, forming the centre of a combination of mountain, sea, and island that is very pleasing, especially when seen in the soft golden light shining through the pearly grey mist of the rain storms which often sweep over the island—and such is St. Thomas.

The change of scenery from Bermuda is not greater than that of manners. There is no quaker-like simplicity in St. Thomas ; noise and clamour prevail. Hardly has the anchor touched the bottom before the ship is surrounded with dozens of boats, manned by sturdy negroes, anxious to take passengers ashore. Here we find among the boatmen the same names as those borne by Egyptian donkeys at Cairo and Alexandria—Derby winners, heroes of popular songs, &c. "Champagne Charlie" urges his cognomen as a special reason for your patronage, whilst another, blacker than the blackest of imps, claims the stranger's old acquaintance with "Remember Snowball, massa, last time you here !"

Just as we stepped into our boat, a young Canadian on board, who had been assiduously fishing ever since we arrived, and without success, suddenly called out that he had a bite, and triumphantly pulled up his line, to which a bottle had been attached by one of the little urchins when diving for coppers. This little incident reminded one of our party of the tricks which Antony and Cleopatra used to play each other by the aid of divers. In the play Charmian says to Cleopatra :

> " 'Twas merry when
> You wagered on your angling ; when your diver
> Did hang a salt fish on his hook, which he
> With fervency drew up."

"And thus history repeats herself," said somebody else, as we landed on the wharf.

The inhabitants of St. Thomas are apt to boast of their Hôtel du Commerce, and to inform the stranger that it is the best in the West Indies; all I can say is that out of the few I saw, it was by far the worst. It was kept by a Spanish family, each member of which was master, and each cared less than the other for the comfort of the guests. The beds were bad, the mosquito nets were full of holes, there was not a comfortable chair or table in any bedroom, dirt and uncleanliness prevailed everywhere; clean linen was at a discount, and the cook evidently thought that wretched food was compensated for by the fine, broad verandah in which it was eaten. My friend, the doctor, was so overcome by the heat and discomfort that he determined to return to Boston by the first steamer, which was not due, however, for nearly a fortnight. As mine, also, was not expected until about the same time, we determined to make the best of it, and try to enjoy ourselves. On looking back, we afterwards found that our enjoyment principally consisted in going from the reading-room to the club, and from the club back to the reading-room. It was too hot to sit down, and we found it necessary to keep moving in order to get a little air.

Main Street, which runs along the sea, is the only level piece of ground in St. Thomas; beyond that all is up-hill; it is here, therefore, that you see life in its busiest and idlest aspect. The shops and stores are prepossessing neither in their exterior nor in their interior. Straw hats, ready-made clothes, tawdry trifles, and provisions predominate; there is nothing to tempt you, nothing strange to invite a purchaser. But in the street itself it is more amusing; look at that stately woman in flowing white, with the bright turban, on which is poised a tray of cakes—she is a Haytian, those children sitting on the doorstep, and dressed in the suit they were born in, are evidently natives ; here comes a white horse, with a brilliant red saddle-cloth, followed closely by a sheep; is there a circus coming ? No; the patriarchal rider is only Mr. So-and So, and it is the fashion in many parts of the West Indies for sheep to accompany horses. They say it is healthy for sheep to live in the stables with horses, and they get so attached to one another that, out-of-doors, the former will not leave the latter as long as they can keep up with them.

Now groups of women pass ; surely they are real Amazons ! Jet black, and wearing only very short skirts, a twist of hemp round their heads, and with their woolly hair plaited in horns, or crowned with a half cocoa-nut by way of bonnet, they shout and sing like frantic Mœnads. They are coalers returning from their hard day's labour in the harbour. It is not in St. Thomas where " men must work and women must weep." That old negro who is declaiming with such vehemence in front of the hotel is a great admirer of Lord Beaconsfield, learns all his speeches by heart, and goes about reciting them. It is pleasant to observe this tribute of admiration to our great Minister, how-ever odd the expression of it may be. English, French, German, Dutch, Creoles, all sorts of nationalities, are met with here, but of Danes, to whom the island be-longs, there is a very limited supply. As for the Danish language, it is the only one not heard.

Of Danish rule the casual visitor can, of course, say very little. He sees clean, well-ordered streets, and evidences of continual improvements, sanitary and otherwise, although he cannot help thinking that the great open sewer, crossed by a bridge in Main Street, and down which, in the rainy season, come avalanches of dead cats, tin cans, and other despised articles, might be made less conspicuous, and answer its purpose equally well. He sees, also, a chain-gang on some public works, and the pitiful sight of women working with the male convicts; but the unfortunate creatures seem to care less about it than the spectator, and with a jaunty air shoulder their spade or pickaxe, and sing to a chain accompaniment.

The visitor to the island will probably hear—for at St. Thomas, as elsewhere:

> " There is a lust in man no charm can tame,
> Of loudly publishing his neighbour's shame—"

of the strange administration of justice (by the way, do we not, in our own neighbouring island of Tortola, present the strange spectacle of a president who himself combines the three functions of judge, prosecutor, and judge of appeal?), of harmless idlers being picked up by the police and exiled to the small island of St. John's, there to tend sheep and cattle; of theft being far more severely punished than murder, and of the general incapacity of the government. But the proverbial " grain of salt " must be taken with the tales, and I think the stranger will allow that things are carried on much the same as elsewhere; that harmony exists in spite of inharmonious elements, and that St. Thomas is not so bad as he had been led to expect.

The days here are monotonous, but variety cannot be expected in so circumscribed an area. In the early morning, just as you are about to drop off to sleep, after an intensely hot night, varied with earthquakes, and passed probably in opening and closing the shutters of your room—closing them against the driving rain, and opening them to get some air—the gun fires, and if that fails to waken you thoroughly, the negroes hold such a jubilee under your window that sleep is quite impossible.* A sudden screaming and wild vociferation makes you spring out of bed fearing an earthquake, but it is only the old black women having a "talk," or merely wishing each other "good morning." Then the men indulge in angry abuse, gesticulate madly, and just as you expect to see a knife plunged into somebody's bosom, the chief disputant walks off, singing the "Sweet by-and-by." There was no quarrel! You then go to bed again; but immediately bread and coffee are brought, and, as early rising is infectious, you go through the agony of dressing when, as Sydney Smith says, you would rather "take off your flesh and sit in your bones." St. Thomas is one of those places where, as the Irishman said, it is never cooler—it may be hotter, but it is never cooler. However, that is at last accomplished, and then comes a terrible gap of time until breakfast. There is little to explore, and ferns and shells are soon exhausted, so you ramble up Main Street, visit the much-enduring consul, or make one of the coterie in the grand réunions held in some store, where the affairs of the world are settled.

At last comes breakfast, which is dinner without

---

* Just before our arrival a case occurred in which a little urchin was sent on a similar expedition, his only offence apparently being that of running about the streets in a shirt which only extended as far as his breast-bone, and consequently was not regulation.

soup, and where quantity tries to make up for quality.

> " Such breakfast, such beginning of the day
> Is more than half the whole ;"

and very fortunate it is that such is the case, as until
the heat of the sun has decreased there is not much inducement for exercise. By that time dinner is ready,
and soon after—as early hours are the rule—you retire
to your room, to turn out the centipedes, which are of
enormous size in St. Thomas, from under your pillow,
and the mosquitos from out of the netting. Then you
perspire all night. And so passes hotel-life when there
are no dinner-parties, nor theatricals, nor excursions to
break its monotony.

One morning we took a boat to visit a very curious
place called "Krumm Bay." It was intensely hot, but
"Admiral Nelson" pulled away merrily across the
harbour, past the western suburb of the town, and in
among the islands and creeks, which in olden times
afforded good retreats for pirates. Here Blackbeard
was wont to retire after some filibustering expedition
and take in fresh supplies of wines and provisions. A
fishing boat sailed by, in which was an enormous Jew-
fish, at which the " Admiral " pulled a very long face,
and explained to us that, whenever a Jew-fish was
caught, some one of high position in St. Thomas was
sure to die, or perhaps was already dead. Strangely
enough, next morning we noticed that all the flags
were at half-mast, and heard that news had just arrived
of the death in England of the head of one of the
chief firms in the island.

The islets around were covered with thick under-
bush, out of which tall flowering aloes shot up like

telegraph poles, but on the mainland cacti predominated, with here and there masses of creamy blossoms of the fragrant Frangipani. I am at a loss to know how the latter plant gained its name, as its scent is by no means the same as that extracted from flowers by the great Roman alchemist Frangipani, and which as " a perfumed powder in a velvet bag," with

> " —— a cast of
> Odours rare—of orris mixed with spice
> Sandal and violet, with musk and rose
> Combined in due proportion,"

was considered a wonderful cure for the plague. High up on the arid soil rose a giant cereus, with arms like candelabra ; lower down were the round prickly forms of the echinocactus, looking like small hedge-hogs ; then there were numbers of the melocactus, which they here call the Pope's head, and which finds a ready sale among the shipping. We had noticed dépôts for shells and cacti at the other extremity of the town, and probably these are the only exports from the island. Those large trees near the water are manchineel, whose fruit is deadly poison to all but crabs, who esteem it highly. These crabs are themselves considered a delicacy, but are generally kept for a week, and thoroughly purged before being eaten.

But who are those light-complexioned men in that crazy canoe? The Admiral smiles disdainfully as he informs us that they are only " Cha-Chas," who live on the outskirts of the town, and employ themselves in fishing. We afterwards visited one of their little colonies, and found an industrious people—natives of small adjacent islands—living in huts made of the tin plates cut from kerosene cans and biscuit cases, looking not unlike extra large sardine-boxes, and as closely packed. There they raised some fruit and vegetables, plaited straw, and made ornaments of tamarind seeds.

At the bottom of a deep bay, we found the object of our visit, viz., an establishment for wrecks. Here, lying on the beach and stowed away under long sheds, were fragments of all sorts of vessels and their fittings. Long masts lay near rusty boilers, paddle-wheels were mixed with broken screws; a deck cabin half con-cealed a ship's boat; anchors, helms, poops, sterns, funnels, beams, all the makings of a ship were there, and a large workshop showed where the useless was made good, and the broken repaired. It was not a working-day, and the only sign of life was a large and hungry dog, whose appearance did not render a landing very inviting. We had, therefore, to be satisfied with an exterior view of this marine pawn-shop, where Neptune had got rid of some of his worthless lumber, perhaps only to retake it when it had once more been made serviceable.

And now, before taking leave of St. Thomas, let us ascend to the top of the hill above the town, and risk a hot walk for the sake of the fresh air and view. After passing the theatre, where a black troupe had lately performed "Macbeth," the road winds up and up, past cottages hanging like bird-cages to the hill-sides, and only waiting for a landslip to precipitate them into the valley—in fact, one house that now stands close to the town originally stood far up on a hill, but in 1877 it was carried down entire to its pre-sent position, after an earthquake, followed by a land-slip—and soon we were high above the red tiled roofs

The vegetation is of the scrub order, and among the

low bushes fly the repulsive " black witches," uttering
rich but melancholy notes. The yellow flowers of the
"cedar bush" sprinkle the mountain-side, and a species
of bitter aloe is common ; from the latter an old black
woman of the town makes a decoction which is positively declared to be a certain cure for lung disease.
The fleshy leaves contain a jelly-like pulp ; this, after
being extracted, is washed seven times in pure water,
and beaten up with eggs and milk. To effect a cure,
seven wine-glasses of it must be drunk. In Mexico I
have frequently seen the same medicine used, and have
heard wonderful stories of its power, but there the
number seven is not included in the recipe.

Continuing up the path, we do not see much animal
life ; occasionally a lizard runs across, or we meet a few
natives bringing down sugar-cane, and each carrying a
"sour-sop"—a large green fruit, with pulp-like cotton-
wool—or, perchance, a little donkey clatters down, so
loaded with grass that nothing can be seen of it except
the little hoofs.

The view from the summit is fine and contrasting.
On one side, far below, lies the busy town, with its
picturesque towers and harbour filled with shipping.
On the other, a silent waste of water, broken up into
fantastic bays and inlets, and with rocky islands
scattered over its face.

On the town side, hardly any cultivation is visible,
but on the other are long strips of cane-lands and
patches of garden, groups of fruit-trees, and grazing
pastures.

In the west, rises Porto Rico ; in the south, the dim
outlines of Santa Cruz are visible, and between the two,
like a ship under press of canvas, appears Caraval, or

Sail Rock, with its forked peak, white-shining in the sun.

To the east, lie the Virgin Islands in the midst of the "Grande Rue des Vierges," as the blue waters which surround them are called.   But we have not much time to admire the scene, already the rose-pink in the west is changing to gold, a metallic lustre dances on the water, the Virgin group is fading in the purple distance, and we must descend to the steaming town.

As we approach, a sound of music floats up to us, and we hear children's voices singing a Christmas carol. Can this really be December?   To-morrow we will go to Santa Cruz.

CHAPTER V.

SANTA CRUZ is situated about forty miles south of St. Thomas. To reach it, it is necessary to take the Government mail-schooner, which makes the passage generally in about six hours, though, with contrary winds, it has been known to take days, and even weeks. Nine o'clock in the evening was the hour for sailing, and precisely at that time we stepped on board. " Passports, gentlemen !" was the greeting we received. "What! passports to go from one Danish island to another!" We had none, so it was finally settled that we should pay the price of them —thirty-two cents. each—to the Commissioner of Police, who was expected on board to see his mother-in-law off. Ten o'clock came, and no sign of either Commissioner or his mother-in-law. The breeze was falling, and we began to doubt whether we should be able to get outside the harbour, but at half-past ten they appeared, and in a few minutes we were beating out.

When we gained the open sea, the north-east trade

wind blew fresh and strong, so that by four a.m. next morning we had passed through the narrow reef-passage, and had anchored in a picturesque bay at the fort of Bassin (Christianstœd), the capital of the island. The scene differed widely from that of St. Thomas. From the white beach backwards, acres of sugar-cane extended over the level land and swept up over the undulating hills and across to the mountain background in a waving mass of green, broken here and there by long lines of cocoa-nut palms, windmills, the white buildings of the planters, and the cottages of their labourers.

The town looked antiquated, but clean, and with ample foliage. Originally, the island was covered with forest, but the French burnt it, and now it appears like one vast sugar plantation. But the loss of its forests may prove in time the ruin of the island. Formerly its rain-fall was abundant, and its productiveness enormous. Now years of drought follow in quick succession, and it is said that the barren belt beginning at the sea-beach in parts of the island is annually spreading inland. Ruin is following closely in the path of the forest destroyer.

In former years Bassin was a place of great resort, but now visitors are scarce, and the wretched building near the wharf, although it still bears the name of hotel, is closed and receives no guests. We had been recommended to take rooms at the Widow Brady's. This we did, and had no cause to regret it. The widow herself met us before we reached her house. It was only a short distance, but, before we had accomplished it, we knew all the gossip of the island, the sugar prospect, the history of the poor deceased,

and had received a general sketch of past events, with
a few prophetic remarks concerning the future. A
refreshing bath made up for a sleepless night on the
schooner, whose night accommodation—unless you
preferred to stifle below—consisted of a few rabbit-
hutches, or dog-houses, as they are called, with a
mattress spread on the floor. After our bath we started
on a tour of inspection.

It did not require many minutes to find out that the
sleepy old town was not a success as regards its buildings, and that Santa Cruz rum was its chief article of
commerce, but its gardens and trees were delightful.
There were sapodillas, fine, lofty trees, with clusters
of leaves and brown fruit, avocados, trees of the mess-
apple, sour-sop, and other insipid fruits; then there
were mangoes, tamarinds, and guava bushes, overrun
with bright convolvoluses, and still more brilliant
ipomæas ; roses, jessamine, and honeysuckle grew
most luxuriantly, but they were overmatched in profusion, if not in fragrance, by the Mexican wreath
plant, with pretty pink flowers like clusters of coral,
and by the quiscualis, whose sweet jessamine like
flowers—white, pink, and red on the same stalk—
peeped out in hundreds from their glossy green hiding
places.

A pleasing feature in this island is the number of
good roads which run in all directions. On one of
these we drove over to Friderichstœd, or West End,
as it is called. I do not know why the latter name
should be used, but I suppose for the same reason that
Christianstœd is called Bassin, and Charlotte Amalia,
St. Thomas. During the drive, we saw to perfection
that system of cultivation which commencing in this

island continues all through the West Indies, with the exception now of Trinidad,—namely, the systematic neglect of all other products for one, and that one— sugar. There comes a drought, a deluge, or a blight, and great is the outcry of planters, who have nothing else to fall back upon. Here, outside the town, even the fruit trees had been cut down, because, as long as fruit is on a tree, the labourers instead of working will lie down and pick and eat. The same complaint exists everywhere against the fruit-loving workmen, whether native or imported, and it is said that the only way of stopping the evil is the ruthless cutting down of the trees.

Our road ran through a sea of cane, or an occasional acre of Guinea grass in different stages of ripeness, crossed at intervals by long rows of cocoa-nut palms, whose beauty was diminished by a blight which seems to have prevailed in all the West Indian Islands. Fortunately, it had not touched the mountain-cabbage palms, which rose straight and majestic, and with the greenest of plums, beside their faded brethren. These trees, although beautiful to look at, did not afford much shade, and as the sun was intensely hot, it was a relief occasionally to rest under the " Thibet," whose long brown pods made a strange rustling sound as they were shaken by the breeze. The branches and mimosa-like leaves of this tree make nutritious food for cattle, and it is therefore especially valuable in dry seasons. Now the planters were especially jubilant, as there had been an abundant fall of rain, and the prospect of good crops was cheering, after six or seven bad years. Rivulets trickled past us, and in the marshy ground small green herons peered at us inquiringly or plunged their bills into the soft earth.

As we approached the western side the scenery improved; high hills rose up on either side, and below us ran a mountain stream in a dell rich with mango and bread-fruit* trees, and gaily decked with heliconias, yellow cedar bush, and the crimson flowers of the "Pride of Barbadoes." On the high points of land, windmills stretch out their long arms, or, armless, resembled Martello towers guarding the cane valleys beneath. In the valleys, the smoke issuing from the tall chimneys showed that sugar-making was in progress, and at one of the plantations the owner kindly asked us in. Here they were ploughing, or placing the cane slips on the ridges ready for planting, there they were hoeing, and in another place, cutting the ripe cane or carrying it to the mill. The various processes were shown and explained to us, and then our host refreshed us with cane juice in different stages, from "sling," which was served in large jugs, to the material beverage—rum—which, as real old Santa Cruz, was drunk as a liqueur. We both agreed afterwards, that "sling" was the most unpleasant beverage we had ever tasted. The dwelling house was well situated for business and pleasure, as from one window the owner could overlook his workpeople on the plantation, and from the other he often shot the little Santa Cruz deer,

---

* The bread-fruit naturally recalls the "Mutiny of the Bounty," as it was for the purpose of introducing that tree into the West Indies that Bligh was sent to Tahiti in 1788. On the failure of that expedition he again set out for Tahiti in 1792, obtained his trees, and landed a number safely at St. Vincent. But in these islands it is not the grand tree which in the South Seas affords the chief sustenance of life, and the degenerated fruit is left untouched even by the negro.

which abound in the low underbrush of the uncultivated parts.

After a short visit we took our leave, and continued
our drive. At length, the hills were left behind, and
before us lay a flat rich country—cane-laden of
course—stretching to the sea. In the fine roadstead,
only two or three vessels lay at anchor, and we at
once exclaimed that surely this ought to be the
converging point for trade with the West Indies;
that instead of the small town of Friderichstœd there
were capabilities for a city. We were ignorant
perhaps, but we could not understand what advantages St. Thomas possessed over this pretty island.
True, its geographical position is not equal to that
of St. Thomas, but the very few extra hours taken to
reach it would be compensated for by its superior land
facilities and its healthiness. Possibly, shipowners and
merchants at home may say, what is health in comparison with three hours' extra fuel? but those who
live out here, and those who travel in ships, may
reverse the saying. Would hurricanes in the commodious roadstead be more dangerous than in the
harbour of St. Thomas? Well! in 1867, a tidal
wave at the latter place destroyed an immense amount
of property and lives, and swamped the shipping, and
to the present time particular prayers are offered in
the churches at the beginning and end of the hurricane season. It is said that, in a sanitary point of
of view, St. Thomas is very different from what it
was years ago, but of the two islands we certainly
preferred Santa Cruz.

Towards evening, after we had paid a very pleasant
visit to Major M—, one of the principal planters in the

Island—we drove back to Bassin by the central road, which was straight and flat in comparison with that of the morning. As before, cane and palms surrounded us, but many of the cocoa-nut trees had been robbed of their beauty and were headless; and, as the fresh breeze swept over the land, their bent shafts resembled the bare poles of a stricken ship scudding along through a waving green sea. At the corners of the different plantations by the roadside, were small white-domed buildings like Eastern sepulchres; these were watch houses, necessary to prevent stray passers-by from cutting the juicy cane. A steam plough next claimed our attention, and after that a Moravian* Church; then darkness closed in, and before long we were home again.

Another of our drives was to the new "Central Factory," about which Santa Cruz was then very much disturbed and divided into two factions. By a "Central Factory," the functions of the cane producer and the sugar-maker are divided, just as those of the wheat farmer and the miller. All the planter has to do is to grow the cane and take it when cut to the nearest dépôt belonging to the "Central Factory," and then his duty is finished.

The complaints against the one being erected in this island were many; among them, it was said that the Government—it was a Government project—had forced

---

* The Moravians here, as elsewhere, have schools judiciously administered, and these zealous people are still worthy of Cowper's eulogy when he said,

> " Fir'd with a zeal peculiar, they defy
> The rage and rigour of a polar sky,
> And plant successfully sweet Sharon's rose
> On burning plains, and in eternal snows."

the planters into joining the Company, most of the estates being in debt to the Government, owing to a series of bad years; that the planters had their own machinery and could make larger profits by manufacturing sugar themselves; that there was not enough sugar on the island to make so large a factory pay; that small farms and sub-lettings would spring up among the black population (which was already fast superseding the white), which would withdraw labour from the large estates and deteriorate agriculture. The "piping" was also objected to; miles of this had been laid down to convey the juice from the five dépôts to the Central House; up hill and down hill ran this piping, and its opponents declared that the means (pressure) adopted for its utility could never succeed. Nor was the price to be paid by the Company, viz., the value of five and a half pounds of sugar for one hundred pounds of cane, considered sufficient, and altogether so disheartened were the opponents that some of them who had one hundred shares in the Factory, and had paid up a half, were ready to give away the remaining fifty to anyone who would take them up. Whether the project has proved successful or not, I have never heard. To our eyes, the chief drawback seemed to be in the great cost of the buildings and machinery, which were on a far too magnificent a scale for the small island.

A cause of failure in the West India Islands has been the superabundance of central factories; where one would have been sufficient for the neighbourhood, three and four have been erected, to the detriment of all.* In Martinique, for example, there are no

* Among the important improvements, the factory intended to burn

less than thirteen, and out of these only six are profitable. Wages in Santa Cruz could not be considered excessive, the average for the negro labourers being ten cents per diem, with bread, sugar, and rum thrown in. But poverty was not noticeable, as it was at St. Thomas, and the number of plump, healthy-looking children was remarkable; when we wanted some memento to take away with us, and asked if they made nothing peculiar to the island, the answer might have been that given by an old lady at Martinique to a similar question :—" Rien que les enfants, Monsieur, en voulez-vous ?"

The vast preponderance of the black population over the white ought to be a subject of deep consideration to the island planters, and to us it appeared, from the rumours of discontent and negro outbreaks, that the very existence of the white property-owners was in danger.* Home we went by the beach, where the fresh-smelling sea-weed lay in great banks, and near us was a wonderfully bright colouring of green, blue, and yellow, as the still water lay over deep or shallow shoals, enclosed within circling coral reef, white with the foaming waves of the blue-black sea beyond.

When we re-embarked on the schooner for St. Thomas, we were delayed for more than three hours, which we knew would seriously imperil our chances of getting anything to eat on our arrival at the hotel. This time the delay was caused by the mail, and when it did arrive it consisted of one skinny bag, apparently

coal for fuel, thus saving the waste cane which it was customary to use for that purpose, for manure.

* Since the above was written news has arrived of a negro insurrection, and the destruction of nearly every sugar plantation on the island.

containing one letter. Fresh passports to take us back! truly there must be " something rotten in the state of Denmark." We lost our dinner by just half-an-hour, but were compensated in some degree by the arrival of our respective steamers, which were to sail on the following day. We had therefore to forego the pleasures of a shark hunt,* which had been arranged for us, and in a few hours the doctor was on his way to America, and I was bound South.

* A favourite amusement in St. Thomas; a dead horse is towed out behind a boat, and the greedy monsters, eagerly fastening on it, are then harpooned.

CHAPTER VI.

THE meeting of the steamers at St. Thomas brings together a varied company, and those on board the 'Tiber' formed no exception to the rule, clergymen, colonial officials, military officers, planters, engineers, commercial travellers, tourists, only a few of each denomination certainly, but those few all the more prepared to enjoy sea-life by having superior cabin accommodation.

Passengers just from England were of course well-acquainted with one another after a two weeks' voyage, and of the others even the most frigid had thawed out before we passed Saba. Strange little island! only a volcanic cone rising directly from the water. We glided by so close that we seemed to hear the lap of the waves as they gently kissed its rocky base, but no harbour, no habitation was visible. It must be an active volcano, for near the summit a faint blue smoke curled upwards and joined the floating clouds. No; that smoke is raised by human hands, for the crater

out of which it ascends is the home of a small colony.
A mixed population of Dutch and negroes live there,
raise fruit and vegetables, and build boats it is said,
though timber must be getting scarce in spite of the
trees that we see edging the crater's rim.

Some years previously I had visited a crater colony
in beautiful Apolima—one of the South Sea Islands;
there the whole of the interior had sunk, and we
paddled through a narrow opening into a lovely bay,
on whose bank stood the village. But here there was
no ingress, save by a rocky staircase leading to the
interior. I should much like to have gained an
insight into the life of the inhabitants, who may,
indeed, be said to "live with a volcano under their
feet," but time and opportunity were wanting, and in
a very short time we had lost sight of the green nest
in rough and rugged Saba.

Then another volcanic island, St. Eustatius, appeared.
The northern end is broken and rocky, with here and
there a ravine filled with trees, then a stretch of land
leading up to the crater. Unlike its sister isle, it is
the outside which is green and cultivated, and houses
dot the scene. It is picturesque, and, before we are
tired of looking at it, it fades like a dissolving view,
and, ere the accompanying music has had time to change
from a Dutch to an English tune, we are coasting along
St. Kitts.

Now we begin to realize the fact that we are in the
West Indies. The long promontory, which slopes up
to the chain of hills intersecting the island, is fresh and
green with sugar-cane; tall factory-chimneys and
planters' houses are scattered about, and the soft beauty
of the cultivated land contrasts with the bold moun-

tain heights which shoot up in culminating masses towards the centre.

Near the shore stands a lonely rock, huge and precipitous as if flung from the summit of Mount Misery, which, in the distant back-ground, towers above it to a height of nearly 4,000 feet. Brimstone Hill, as this imposing pile of igneous rock is called, is accessible only from one side; formerly it was the seat of the garrison and was fortified, the fortifications being still visible.

Further on, a shapely mount, flat-tipped and wooded, raises itself above a black ravine cut deep into the lower hills, which are cultivated in many parts to their tops. A white cloud floats across the volcanic chasm over which Mount Misery frowns, leaving the summit crag bare and distinct, and, for the first time since we entered the West Indies, atmosphere lends its charm to perspective.

Hitherto the clearness of the atmosphere had brought the island views strangely close, without a distance, and with a monotone of tint most unpaintable, but here there was cloud and mist enough to have satisfied Corot himself. It was pleasant to feel that there was a beyond that we could clothe with our own fanciful colours, and that our gaze did not enfold the entire landscape.

Basseterre, the capital, where we stopped for an hour, looked very bright and sunny. Red roofs, peering out of thick green foliage, a gleam of white among the palm trees, and a picturesque church-tower, formed the fore-ground to a valley of rustling cane, extending the circle of hills, whose links are here of a less elevation than in the other parts of the chain. To us, it looked a quiet,

fertile little place, and, no doubt, uncommonly dull.
Of its native products we only saw some very good
white grapes, and some very indifferent cigars which
were brought for sale. St. Kitts is the only one of the
Leeward* Islands that can be said to pay its way; the
others seem to retrograde year by year. Now, however, that the constitution of the islands has been
changed to the Crown Colony system, an improvement
may be expected, and the same progress looked forward
to as in the Windward group.

From Basseterre, the hill chain runs in a south-
easterly direction in a series of low ridges covered with
scrub mimosa, dwindling away until they reach the
"Narrows," as the two-mile stretch of sea is called which
separates Nevis from St. Kitts. A shallow dangerous
passage is this, full of shoals and hidden reefs, and
almost in its midst rises a sharp triangular rock.

Across the "Narrows," a long low plain slopes up
to a single cone, whose summit for ever sleeps in mist
and clouds. Much bush covers the lower lands, but
windmills here and there show that some cultivation is
carried on, and light green patches of cane are seen
divided by rows of cocoa-nut palms, which, in their
blighted state, alas! have more the appearance of
feather dusters. A dreamy-looking little island is this
Nevis, whose chief interest to a stranger lies in the
fact that here Nelson lived after his marriage with Mrs.
Nisbet for a few quiet years.

We sped along swiftly past the graceful southern
slope of old "Ben"—as the volcanic cone might be

* Leeward Islands consist of Dominica, Antigua, Montserrat, Nevis,
and St. Kitt's. Windward Islands consist of Barbadoes, St. Vincent,
St. Lucia, Grenada, and Tobago.

called—but he would not deign to lift his fleecy cap
to us, the shifty clouds merely paling or growing
blacker, until they were lost to view. The steep and
picturesque " Redondo " next claimed our attention.
It is only a cavernous rock rising out of the waves, and
sea-birds are its sole inhabitants. From it the eye
wanders off to the more distant island of Montserrat,
whose bold headland stands out in relief against the
thickly wooded gorges which traverse the broken uplands. In the centre, a three-headed mountain range,
like a crouching Cerberus, guards the fruitful lemon
groves and plantations that lie far below. How pleasant it would be to spend a few days on each of these
West Indian islands! to visit their *souffrières*, their
mountain forests, their wild hills, and their cultivated
estates! but, at present, to set one's foot on land
necessitates a two weeks' sojourn. Such being the
case, and with Roraima ever beckoning me on, I had
determined to halt only at Martinique and Trinidad
before reaching British Guiana, and therefore glimpses
—sometimes near and sometimes far—were all I could
expect of the Antilles.

It was night before we reached Antigua, but a full
moon rendered the coast scene as clear as day, and
added romantic effect to the lovely harbour. A bay
within a bay, a semi-circle of wooded hills and ravines,
a few white houses, lava cliffs which almost meet at
the narrow entrance, and a rampart-crowned rock were
the principal points in the picture. The basin in
which the vessel lay moored by hawsers seemed but
another sky, the stars scarcely quivering in the still
deep water; and, as the moon's rays silvered the sharp-
leaved aloes, or touched with a bright gleam the angled

fort, here softening the rough-edged tufa, and there defining more clearly the outlines of the palm groups, the whole scene wore a delightful aspect of unreality, which was heightened by the extreme quiet, broken only by an occasional plash of oars.

From Antigua we crossed over to Guadeloupe, whose broad and irregular heights were hidden by clouds; as it was night when we coasted along, we saw little except cliffs, green pasture land, and ravines leading up into the heart of the mountains. Next morning we sighted Mariegalante, far away on our port side, and then, in broad daylight, for several hours, beautiful Dominica sat to us for her picture. Up to this time the various island scenes had been pretty, but could not have been called grand, but now the first glance raised our expectations to a high pitch. Nor were we disappointed, for a more lovely island, a finer combination of grandeur and quiet beauty, could hardly be found in the West Indies.

Towards the north, the waves beat against a rock-bound shore, above which rise wooded hills, increasing in size until they join the seamed and contorted mountains. Here, in a retired village, dwell the Carib Indians, once the owners of the island. Reduced to a few score in numbers, these relics of a great tribe live peacefully under their own king, intermarry, hold but little intercourse with strangers, and seldom appear in the capital, Roseau, except now and then to sell their beautifully woven basket-work. On the western side, along which we coast, the sea-board extends further back; there is not much cultivation, but in the bush clearings are a few cane-fields, and beyond, out of the green sloping lawns, spring many hills, some bare and craggy,

others cultivated to the summit. Behind, rise the great
mountains in a thousand fantastic shapes, here buried
in forest, there frowning black and barren over some tree-
filled gorge. Everywhere there is a romantic mingling
of hill and valley, mountain and gorge. Lifting clouds
reveal wooded eminences crowning steep precipices,
from whose feet the green sward stretches down in
waves to the white beach, and, as the silver veil floats
higher and higher, still loftier ridges are unbared,
where the pale green of the sugar-cane is plainly distinguished against the dark setting of the forest back-
ground. So high and steep are the hills on which
many of these cane-fields are perched that the crop,
when cut, has to be let down in bundles by ropes

At Roseau, where we stopped for an hour, we were
gladdened by the sight of a river in which many washer-
women were at work. The scene was very pleasing;
in the midst of palms and verdure, stood a pretty
church and old grey and white houses with deep verandahs; on the right was Government House, with
diminutive fortifications, on the left, the land rolled up
in cultivated terraces, and a magnificent ravine behind
the town ran deep into the cloud-capped mountains.

If Dominica is celebrated for anything, it is for its
frogs, some of which are of enormous size. A curry
of frogs' legs is a very delicate dish, and we were in
great hopes that some *grenouilles* would have been
brought on board alive, but they only brought the
large *crapauds*, stuffed and varnished. A basketful of
them, together with some huge beetles, was quickly
disposed of, but a promised cargo of live ones never
arrived. Roseau appeared to be an interesting place to
pass a few days in, but we were assured by those who

knew, that the accommodation was bad in the extreme,
that there were no roads in the island, that it was difficult to obtain riding animals, and that, if we wanted
to carry away a pleasant memory of our English isle,
we had better be contented with its view from the sea.

So we sail on.   Still the same fair scenery ; mountains gathered up " like a woven garment, and shaken
into deep falling folds," here a velvet slope, there a
gigantic rib, sharp but forest-covered, or a bare perpendicular cliff with its feet bathed by the sea.   Now a
farm nestling in some winding glen, overshadowed by
brown-red rocks tipped with cane, and again a narrow
fissure feathered with evergreen foliage, and opening
into a deep bowl full of close and thick vegetation.
Clouds rest on the mountain sides, or hanging above
cast fitful shadows on upland and valley ; a hundred
varying shades give colour to the landscape, and, over
all, the blue sky, in perfect harmony with the green
tints of earth, blends with the sparkling sea into one
bright frame for the beautiful island.

The land ends abruptly in a mass of grey rock,
sparsely clad, which juts out into the sea.   On its summit stands a cross.   Passing this corner, we see palm-
covered slopes and gentle depressions, then a high
needle-like cone with perpendicular sides rising from
the ocean, and, beyond, the southern extremity of the
central mountain range.   Soon after, Dominica fades
from us in mist and rain.

CHAPTER VII.

> " Here the pilgrim may behold
> How the bended cocoa waves
> When at eve and morn a breeze
> Blows to and from the Carib seas,
> How the lush banana leaves
> From their braided trunk unfold ;
> How the mango wears its gold,
> And the sceptred aloe's bloom
> Glorifies it for the tomb."

THE above lines, appropriate enough for any West
India isle, yet for me associate themselves with
Martinique more than with any other. It may be because I lingered long enough to know that island better
than the rest, or it may be because the remembrance
of a certain ride across the rich country—a ride ever
memorable as the most beautiful I had ever enjoyed,
and which must be described later on—abides with me
as a practical lesson in botany by nature herself.

It was late in the afternoon when we anchored off
St. Pierre—the chief town in Martinique. The cha-

racter of the island had not seemed quite so broken and romantic as Dominica, there was more low table-land and more cultivation, but the mountain range, with its grand pitons looking out over the clouds, gave promise to the expectant imagination of many beautiful scenes.

From the roadstead, we saw in front of us houses thickly massed together and extending round the bay. Close behind the town, on the eastern side, rose a precipitous hill, crowned with waving sugar-cane, and its deep wooded side dotted with white villas. Towards the north, a broad ravine, through which a river ran, divided the town into two parts, and beyond rose the soft uplands, green with cane, and stretching to the delicately coloured hills which reached the high mountains in the background. On our right, the coast line was varied with rock, hill, and valley, and on one summit a large white statue stood out conspicuously against the green foliage ; on our left, the palm-fringed shore, with here a solitary house, and there a little white village, ran northwards in a gently undulating line.

On landing at St. Pierre the traveller finds himself the object of a popular demonstration; he is assailed by a swarm of stalwart women, some of whom dispossess him of his book, umbrella, or whatever he may be carrying, whilst others, after a short fight among themselves, seize on the luggage, toss great portmanteaus and boxes on to their heads with the greatest of ease, and amid shouts of laughter rush off with loud cries, " A la douane ! à la douane !" It is useless to protest that you want to carry such and such a thing yourself, you may recapture it for a second, but it is lost again ; everything goes aloft on female heads and shoulders, and to avoid a similar fate yourself you follow in the wake of the flying Amazons and arrive at the Custom House. Then a strict inspection ensues, after which the luggage is remounted and a procession is formed to the hotel.

We—one other passenger and myself—had been advised to go to the Hôtel des Bains, so when our porters said of course "les Messieurs" were going to the "Hôtel Micas," we answered of course not. Eventually we made out from the extraordinary Creole patois, that the former hotel was closed, and that its proprietor had opened the latter. We soon arrived there, and it looked clean and comfortable, but the landlord was "désolé," there was not a single vacant room ; " would the gentlemen be satisfied with a billiard table for to-night, then to-morrow——?" This offer was declined, and finally we found rooms in the Hôtel du Commerce, a place of very second-rate pretensions, but with a very obliging proprietor.

The first few days of my sojourn in this "Faubourg St. Germain of the tropics"—as the French love to call it—were certainly depressing. The heat was great, the food very indifferent, and the rain almost incessant. Much stress has been laid on the streams of clear, crystal water which here run through the streets. I should call them gutters, and, after one has seen the use to which they are put—the houses being entirely free from what we consider the most necessary requirements—the crystal romance is dissipated. Fortunately, owing to the slope of the streets and the ample supply of water which is brought down through fine aqueducts from the mountains, the flow is swift, and thus the gutters are kept pretty clean. Otherwise, the town of St. Pierre would be unbearable, as even now it rivals Cologne in the number of its smells. Under such conditions, it is not surprising that the stranger feels the effects of an "acclimatizing fever," as they here designate it.

Morning after morning I awoke dull, listless, and tired, and with all sorts of pains and aches in my limbs, but as the day advanced health returned and fever was forgotten.

St. Pierre is not a cheerful town even on its sunniest days; the streets are narrow, with side-walks of infinitesimal dimensions, the old stone houses, with heavy outside shutters, are gloomy and comfortless, no bright verandahs attract the eye, and the roofs are dingy with moss-covered tiles. But the outskirts are more attractive, and the road to the Botanical Gardens particularly so. Passing up the Grande Rue towards the north, we see shops and stores filled with gay-coloured foulards, straw hats, finery of all sorts, and an excess of gold ornaments. On the left is the Batterie d'Esnotz, with a few seats under the shady trees, and affording a fine view over the sea. Farther on, some fine mangoes overshadow a heavy fountain, and soon our road turns off eastward before reaching the bridges which cross the intersecting river. We follow its left bank under a beautiful avenue of tamarinds, whilst on our right is the Savanna or public park. And here commences picturesque Martinique. Down below in the wide rocky ravine flows the brawling stream, alive with dusky "blanchisseuses," whose methodical beat on the smooth stones with the clothes they are washing, keeps time with their patois songs. White houses rise in tiers over the opposite bank, their gardens filled with many bright flowers, and crowning

all are clusters of palms and ceiba groves. Across the
Savanna rises the mountain screen that shades the town ;
its steep side a perfect network of hanging vines. Here
and there a mango has gained a precarious footing, its
dark green dome contrasting well with the crimson
blaze of a neighbouring Bois Immortelle;* and these lofty
trees look like out-stretched arms on which is hung a
close-textured mantle of flowering creepers. Far up, at
the head of the cultivated river-valley, rise the mountains, whose dark gorges, veiled by almost constant
mist, are arched by the most brilliant rainbows.

In a few steps after leaving the Savanna, the Botanic
Gardens are gained. At the time of my first visit the
road outside was lined with cadets from the French
training ship "Flore," who were sketching a handsome Traveller's Tree—*Ravenala speciosa*—which grew
near the entrance. A crowd of little urchins hovered
about them, and it was very amusing to hear their
outspoken opinions on the efforts of the different
artists, who worked away with perfect composure.
Several times afterwards I met the young scholars
eagerly acquiring, under able tuition, that most desirable accomplishment—sketching from nature.

The Botanical Gardens are delightfully situated in a
wide ravine through which a stream flows. Terraces
have been cut out of the sides, and winding walks and
avenues lead to pretty scenes and charming outlooks.
Art here has done much in laying out the grounds and
forming the various rills, fountains, and waterfalls, but
nature has supplied a very beautiful site. Particularly
beautiful is one avenue of "Palmistes Royals,"†

* Erythrina umbrosa.
† Oreodoxa oleracea ; called the mountain-cabbage because within the

whose perfectly straight grey stems, ending in a light
green shaft and crowned with a leafy diadem of dark
green spreading leaves, form an aisle of living Co-
rinthian pillars, seventy or eighty feet in height. This
magnificent species of palm reminds me of an article
which appeared in the June number of "Belgravia,"
1878, entitled "The Great Tropical Fallacy." In it the
writer declares that "waving sugar-cane, graceful
bamboos, spreading tree ferns, magnificent palms, &c.,
may be found at Kew, but not in the tropics."
He also says "a true fern can scarcely be seen through
the foul mouldering fronds that cling around its musty
stem."

The amusing article certainly would dispel " The
Great Tropical Fallacy," if it was true, but it can only
have been written as a joke, as the writer adds that he
has "lived for years in the tropics, but never yet
beheld an alligator, an iguana, a toucan, or an antelope
in their wild state. Scorpions do not occur." It is an
undoubted fact that these creatures—with the exception
of scorpions—do not frequent the streets of towns or
villages, nor are they much addicted to highway travelling, but had the writer ever visited "the bush," or
walked in the "country," I think he would have hesi-
tated before making such a statement, that is, sup-
posing he has the full use of his eyesight and has lived
where these animals exist.

As regards the palm, it is true that cocoa-nut trees,
especially when blighted, are not very imposing; but

central spike lies concealed the cabbage, composed of white longitudinal
flakes forming a crisp compact body. When cut up into thin ribands and
boiled, it is served as a vegetable with meat. As all palm trees possess
this eatable spike, it is hard to tell why this species should in particular
be called the " cabbage."

there are many other splendid species, and to depreciate
the mountain cabbage-palms is to be guilty of high
treason against the princes of the forest. They are
simply wonderful. To admire them it is not necessary
to be a pantheist, or one of those to whom a forest is a
cathedral, each tree a missionary, and every flying
creature a sacred spirit ; one who bows down at the
sight of a daisy or buttercup, and kneels before an oak
as the wild Indian does before his ceiba. For these
palms are so matchless in grace, so simple and yet so
stately, that they lend an indescribable air of dignity to
auy spot where they may chance to grow.

To return to the garden. Leaving the palm avenue
one comes suddenly upon a beautiful waterfall rushing
down a steep rock amidst a mass of hanging grasses,
ferns, and waving cannas. A little way below it runs
into the heart of a garden-wilderness rich with bamboos, plantains, thickets of tangled vines, and fragrant
coffee trees. Here shrubs and trees are more cultivated
than flowers, but the former with their brilliant blossoms save the place from the monotonous effect of a too
prevailing green. Gloxinias and primulas are scattered
over the sloping banks, and overhead are interlaced the
branches of various trees. The bright flowers of the
" Flamboyant,"* form a red canopy which vies in rich-
ness with the large crimson blossoms of the mountain
rose.† Here may be seen South Sea Island bread-fruit,
cinnamon from Ceylon, and sandal-wood from the
Marquesas. That tree with bunches of wax-like and
pear-shaped fruit is a Eugenia ;‡ its trunk is a perfect
fernery, and its branches are hung with parasites.
Next to a stilted pandanus rises a tall " poui " with

* Carolinea.   † Brownea   ‡ Eugenia Michellii.

saffron flowers, and beyond are the long white trumpets of a datura. Close at hand is the much prized persimmon of Japan, having a wood like ebony, and a reddish-yellow fruit. The ground is everywhere strewn with the red beads of an erythrina, and occasionally the large uneatable fruit of a species of inga comes down with a thump, that a passer by, if hit, would not soon forget.

Perhaps the prettiest spot in the garden is a small lake fed by a slender fall, whose water trickles down a moss-covered rock through ferns and drooping grasses. The three tiny islets are fringed with arums, heliconias, and bamboos, amongst which are scattered dark glossy green and gold-marbled crotons, purple dracœnas, and crimson hybiscus blossoms. In the centre of each stands a " Traveller's Tree," like a gigantic fan, surrounded with a few flowering shrubs and graceful plantains. But here as elsewhere, there is an air of neglect, the shady walks are full of weeds, the stone seats under the trees are damp and green, a broken canoe half full of water lies on the yielding bank, the few remaining tree labels are illegible, and, in a word, the gardens are not tended as they deserve. Their charm seems to have vanished with their novelty, as they are seldom visited by the inhabitants, and the funds granted for their maintenance are insufficient.

Within the grounds there is a building which contains a small natural history museum, and the native products form a very interesting collection. There is also an interior nursery-garden, where some delicate orchids and rare exotics are reared.

A primitive people these French Creoles must be, as a printed notice strictly prohibits bathing in the small fountains in this inside garden. Unhappily the people appear disinclined even to walk in the pleasant grounds, and the casual visitor feels that a time may come when the few labourers will be withdrawn and a " Forsaken Garden " realised :

" Not a flower to be prest of the foot that falls not ;
  As the heart of a dead man the seed plots are dry ;
  From the thicket of thorns when the nightingale calls not,
  Could she call, there were never a rose to reply.
  Over the meadows that blossom and wither
  Rings but the note of a sea-bird's song,
  Only the sun and the rain come hither
      All year long."*

One of the pleasantest drives from St. Pierre is to Morne Rouge. The village is situated high up in the hills, and near it and cut out of a rocky wall is a celebrated grotto dedicated to " Our Lady of Lourdes." Morne Rouge is one of the localities which the negroes say is at certain seasons visited by the celebrated Dominican Friar, Père Labat, who arrived in Martinique in 1693. He is said to appear in the guise of a lambent flame.

The road thither passes the Botanical Gardens, and for some distance is lined with country houses standing in pretty grounds. It was in one of these villas that the Empress Joséphine was born. The hedges and banks are covered with blue flowers of the " ipomæa " and the buff-coloured "thumbergia," whose dark brown eye attracts the attention of numerous humming birds.

The houses for the most part look cool, but comfortless and devoid of privacy. The foliage of the tall trees shades them, but the bare trunks leave an

* Swinburne.

F

uninterrupted view into the interior. Here, one sees Madame in a very airy costume enjoying her early coffee; there, Monsieur in his dressing-gown lounges on a long cane chair.

Grass is conspicuous by its absence, but rich and gaudy flowers are in abundance. Tall yuccas guard the entrance, and the lavender spikes of the " petrœa" cluster over the verandahs. Many varieties of "dracœna" are scattered about, their slender stems and bending blades contrasting well with the showy hybiscus and the bright green bananas. In each garden one sees a tall clavija, like a giant papau, and with panicles of the fragrant white flowers beloved by Creoles. Thick stone walls surround some of the villas, but tropical nature heeds no such barriers. Creepers of every hue fling themselves over, then catching the hanging air-roots scramble up to the tree-tops and mingle their blossoms with those of their more lofty brethren. Among the numerous trees with hanging pods, the " rosary bean "* is very prominent, as the curled and split pod displays the bright red seeds within. Gradually the houses are left behind, and the road becomes more steep and winding. The high banks are thickly carpeted with begonias, both pink and white. From a neighbouring hill a high waterfall—caused by a deflected stream—descends and turns the wheel of a sugar-mill situated at its foot.

At last we reach the village of Morne Rouge. A long straggling street with pretty cottages and gardens. From trellis-work hang great granadillas, fruit which is only palatable when cunningly compounded with sugar, ice, and wine. The life around is simple, but

* Abrus precatoria.

full of colour, and picturesque. Old women spin in the doorways. Mothers, with bright kerchiefs round their heads, watch their children playing in the road. The children themselves, often only dressed in a plain suit of gold earrings, have fresh, happy faces, brighter and ruddier by far than those in the hot town below. Round the fountain are groups of girls with water-jars poised on their heads, and in the bright sunshine each touch of red and blue in their dress shines out clearly and effectively. From this fountain a beautiful view is obtained seaward, but from the higher Calvary there is a more extended landscape. The prayer-stations leading to the chapel stand between hybiscus hedges, and are surrounded with roses, lilies, azaleas, and palms. The little shrines contained terra cotta representations of the Passion, but the protecting glass was broken and the figures were defaced. Within them green lizards played at hide and seek, and humming birds searched the flower-offerings that had been thrust through the torn grating.

The view from the top is worth the climb. On one side a mass of undulating hills sweeps off to the sea; through the intervening pasture land a winding stream threads its way, and here and there a cottage is seen half buried in clumps of palms and bamboos, and with its cane patch or banana grove. The lofty "pitons" form the background. Below us lies the village, and extending westward towards St. Pierre are cane-covered hills, fertile valleys, and a broad cultivated plain, squared like a chess-board by the dividing palm rows. Beyond rises the glittering blue sea far into the sky, white sails catch the sunbeams, and nearer is the dark line of anchored ships. On rare occasions

—one of which favoured me—rounded masses of
fleecy clouds of intense brilliancy float over land and
sea, and pour down such a flood of light that the
panorama is illuminated.   The white glare is almost
painful, but the strong sea-breeze soon drives the
wandering rain-heralds back to the mountains, where
they wreathe themselves round the higher peaks and
lie like snow-drifts in the hollows between the summits.   And thus the scene changes from sunshine to
shade, from rest to storm, and from light to darkness,
each a life-phase typical in itself, but not more
significant than the solemn Calvary above us in its
bright frame of green trees and flowers.

CHAPTER VIII.

ON Sundays and gala days St. Pierre brightens up. The band plays in the Savanna, and thither the inhabitants flock. In the matter of carriages and horses, Rotten Row would certainly outvie this favourite drive, but in brilliancy of colour the latter would carry the day. On ordinary occasions the Creole woman is content with a simple long-flowing dress of light material, but on state occasions her costume is bright and picturesque. Then you see a bewildering display of silk or satin skirts, short enough not to hide a daintily shod foot; embroidered bodices and gauzy scarfs, a profusion of necklaces and bracelets, all of plain gold—for precious stones are never worn—and jaunty turbans ornamented with gold pins and brooches. But the most striking as well as the commonest feature in the national costume of Martinique is the quaint earrings—cinq-clous. These consist of five gold tubes welded together at the sides into a circular form, not unlike the barrels of a revolver, and vary in size from

the dimensions of a toy pistol to those of a full grown
Colt's.   Many girls carry their entire future in their
ears.

Those splendid beds of tulips were not in the
Savanna when we last passed through!   As we
approach, we see they are not composed of flowers,
but are merely gorgeous head-dresses.   Another trait,
and a charming one too, of Martinique costume.   Here
you see no dyed feathers, or artificial flowers and fruits,
decorating the flashy hats and bonnets so dear to the
negro soul.   Bright coloured foulards, twisted into
various pyramidal, circular, and oval shapes, crown
every head with rainbow hues.   There are ten
different ways of tying these kerchiefs, and the
initiated can tell by the twist whence the wearer comes

Near the band is a motley group.   Two or three old
negresses dressed in flowered chintz, and with trimly
turned head-dresses gossip over the last scandal ;
slowly sweeping along comes a majestic creature, her
long white dress hitched up on one side and displaying
a foot neatly blacked by nature ; in that family coach
are some white Creole ladies with charming faces, and
tastefully dressed in the latest Parisian fashion, while
the youngsters who force their bouquets on them are
habited in little else than " native " worth.   The excitement is of the mildest kind, but enjoyment is universal.
Here and there some little maidens dance to the music,
boys run races, the elders give the prizes, handsome
carriages and wretched *fiacres* continue their monotonous
round, and meeting is so perpetual that everybody
smiles at everybody else, till at length the sun goes
down.   Then the vehicles are turned towards home,
dandies prance off on their rocking horses, old ladies

put up their umbrellas against the dew, peasants take off their shoes preparatory to their homeward tramp, and very soon the Savanna is deserted.

Wonderfully clear are the nights in Martinique. You see distinct shadows, and on looking up for the moon you find they are cast by a star (Venus probably) shining with a radiance of most remarkable power.

From the Batterie d'Esnoty you look down on a sparkling sea in which every vessel stands out distinctly. You can almost count the piles of merchandise and barrels on the wharf. It is so quiet that you can catch the words of the song that the black crew are singing as they pull to shore from some outlying ship, and their strange rising and falling to each stroke is plainly visible. Suddenly a hideous bray rings out close beside you. It comes from one of three buglers who make this their starting point, and in turn repeat the discordant sounds until they reach their distant barracks. This is the Martinique tattoo. The stranger in St. Pierre will notice the quantity of thin white cakes about the size of a cart wheel. These are made from cassava* which here, as in many of the islands, and in parts of South America, affords the chief sustenance of the poorer classes.

We drove out one day to a farm to witness its manufacture. We soon came to fields covered with the plant, which grows to a height of about four feet. In appearance it is a slender-knotted grey stem, with branches at the top from which spring red stalks of broad digitated leaves. The root, which is cylindrical and about a foot long, is a deadly poison in its natural state, but by a simple process it is converted into

* Jatropha manihot.

nutritious food. As we approached the wattled shed
in which it was being prepared, we heard sounds of a
veritable pandemonium. On looking in, we saw thirty
or forty jet black Africans stripped to the skin and
furiously grating the white roots against a rough board,
the meal falling into great tubs.

The exertion was apparently immense, as they
steamed with perspiration, and, as if the fumes of the
poison got into their heads, they would every now and
then utter yells or bound into the air. To this wild
scene there was a musical accompaniment. The instru-
ments consisted of tom-toms, pipes, chac-chacs, and
long bamboos, struck by pieces of wood, and a strange
concern made of cane-work, from which issued a
grating sound by drawing a stick quickly up and down.
Music from such sources was not likely to be of a high
order, but it was conscientiously gone through at all
events. All that lungs could blow was blown; all that
fists could do to break a drum skin was done. White,
eyes rolled, black lips blew, and black fists struck.
The " grater " sounded worse than the grating, and the
monotonous chant of one of the performers was more
horrible than the howls of the workers. Never had I
heard a like " charivari." " Ils ont de la couleur," said
the pleased proprietor, as he rubbed his hand and
glanced at the rapidly filling tubs. The next operation
is to get rid of the poisonous juices. Here, as the
factory was on a large scale, the meal was put into a
great sort of oven and the poison extracted by heat or
pressure. But the usual mode, and the one invariably
applied by the Indians of Guiana, where in after-days I
many a time witnessed the operation, is as follows:
A long plaited tube—matapi—made of a certain reed is

filled with the grated meal; its upper end is
fastened to a beam so that its lower end, which possesses a loop-hole, hangs a few feet from the ground.
A pole is then passed through the loop and the shorter
end firmly fixed so that the longer, when pressed down,
serves as a lever; the elastic tube presses the meal
together, and the poisonous juice escapes through the
interstices. The flour is then dried and sifted. When
required for use, a handful is baked over a fire on a flat
plate, and in a few minutes "cassava bread," resembling
an enormous oatmeal cake, is ready. If required for
a journey, it is thoroughly dried in the sun until it
is as hard as a nail, and will then last for months; if
not properly dried, it quickly gets mouldy and uneatable. Cassiripe, which is the extracted poison-juice of
cassava, is the foundation of the well-known "pepper
pot," which is an "olla podrida" of meat and peppers
cooked in an earthen pot, and always on hand in the
West Indies. Fortunately, the deleterious principle of
the juice is so volatile that it is entirely dissipated by
heat, and it then becomes a wholesome seasoning;
and thus the good is extracted from the evil in this
strange blending of life and death, as exhibited in the
cassava root.

That evening, before we reached home, we witnessed
a scene of excitement. As we drove along the sea-
shore there was a sudden rush of people to the beach,
boats were pushed hurriedly out, men jumped into the
water and swam out, women waded up to their knees
and ran back again, and children did their best to get
drowned. Presently, a series of long nets formed a
semi-circle and enclosed a large shoal of sardines
which had been the cause of the uproar. Gradually

the nets were drawn in, and so large was the haul that in a few minutes five boats were filled with the little silvery fish. Buckets, barrels, baskets, and cans were then put into requisition, and, even after every article from the neighbouring cottages that could hold a fish had done its duty, there were still sardines enough left on the beach to have stocked a market.

Next morning I started for a ride across the island to Trinité, a distance of about thirty miles. The scenery on the road had been so extolled that I attributed enthusiastic descriptions of it to patriotism, and was prepared for a disappointment. When I returned, I acknowledged it was the most beautiful ride I had ever taken, and one whose like I should probably never see again.

It was dawn when my mule drew up at the hotel door, and we were soon clattering over the rough cobble stones which pave the narrow streets. We passed the Promenade, which was deserted by all save a solitary sentry, who slept in his box under the Palace of the Archbishop, and then the road commenced to wind up the hill under whose shadow the town lay, dark and quiet. Before we reached the top it was broad daylight, the great crimson blossoms of the hybiscus and the fragile bells of the abutilon, which we had left sleeping below, were now unfolded, and the white flowers of the night cereus and of the ipomæa, had already drooped and faded. For some distance beyond the summit the road is walled in with sugar-cane, then bends inwards towards the mountains by a gentle acclivity. Here and there, one passes a little *cabaret de ferme*, where the market people are drinking coffee, or, more probably, rum.

Down in the valley lie cottages and farms, and the hill-sides are flecked with groups of trees, whose light and dark green foliage is very conspicuous. Fine mango trees are dotted about here and there, and fringing rocky heights, or clustered in hollows, are aloes in various stages of their growth; some fully flowered and rapidly collapsing, others whose tall stalks are covered with fresh blooms, and more still whose rich green expanding heart is suggestive of a thyrsus—"thro' the blooms of a garland the point of a spear."

On approaching a small and picturesque village, cane culture is superseded by cassava, and the country becomes more rugged and grander. Cottages are perched upon jutting cliffs, and immediately above the road is situated a delightfully quaint old church, which is reached by a flight of rough stone steps. Near this, a large wooden cross overlooks the valley. The view looking west is lovely. Afar off is the bright blue sea, to which extend the mountain arms and the undulating hill spurs. The valleys between are partly tilled and partly bush-covered, and the few houses stand in garden patches high up on the hill slopes. Through the central valley a twisting thread of green, darker than the surrounding foliage, marks the course of a stream, and clumps of trees of a similar contrasting hue, above and around us, show where orange groves and mangoes lie amid the paler green of cane fields and bananas. Behind rise the forest-clad peaks of the mountains, through which runs the road to Trinité.

Up to this point we had enjoyed a very beautiful morning. Here spring was in the air, and we had

left hot summer below. There was such fulness of
life in the cool air that all nature seemed affected by
it.   The flowers looked brighter, the birds sang
sweeter, and even the running water seemed to tinkle
with a more silvery sound than in the valleys.

A simple circumstance, but one that impressed me
very vividly, occurred as I was looking over the blue
shadowed valley.   An old peasant woman, very brown
and wrinkled, laid a bunch of flowers on the cross, and
as she knelt at its foot an oriole flew on to one of its
arms and poured forth such a trill that it seemed as if
the bird-voice was carrying aloft her mumbled prayers.
When she entered the church a few minutes later, tears
were in her eyes, but she looked so happy that I am
sure the bird had not sung in vain.   The romance of
the little episode was injured by an unsentimental goat
who completely demolished the flower-offering, and
then tried to butt some children who had done nothing
to offend it.   They, however, did not seem to mind
it, and laughed merrily at the antics of the creature.
These children's voices were just what was wanted to
give a charming finish to the bright picture.   What
the flowers were to the garden, the stream to the
valley, the birds to the air, and the sun's rays to
all, were the happy child-tones to the surrounding
scene, gladdening everything in accord with each,
and freshening with rippling music the fragrant uplands :

> " Ah, what would the world be to us
>   If the children came no more ?
> We should dread the desert behind us
>   More than the dark before."

I had hardly whispered these lines to my mule before

the last two words sounded ominous. The animal showed signs of uneasiness which could not be attributed to the verse; for among his many faults a mule cannot be accused of sentimentality, and he cares as little for poetry as he does for a stick. He is so stubborn and self-willed, and yet carries it off with such a nonchalant air, that there is no way of knowing what may be passing in his mind, except by watching his restless ears. Fortunately, these appendages are so expressive—more so in fact than some human faces — that they explain his feelings and foretell his movements. On this occasion they were suddenly pointed straight forward, and as suddenly laid limp on his neck, then pricked again.

The air grew hot and still, a black mist was descending on us from the now hidden mountains, and it was plain that a heavy storm was about to break. On looking round, I saw a hand beckoning to me from a door, and in a few minutes my mule was under cover, and I found myself in a clean room drinking coffee with the kind hostess. Then the rain came down in torrents, and held me prisoner for some time. Here I saw one of those terrible snakes known as the "Fer-de-lance," which had been killed not long before on the road to Trinité by the old lady's husband, who had preserved it in a jar of spirits.

At the first lull we started again, and soon reached a stream spanned by a stone bridge of a single arch. This we crossed, and in a few minutes entered the forest ravine. Turning in the saddle, I was dazzled by a brilliant rainbow, which in a broad band struck the bridge at a right angle. It was so close that I could not resist the novelty of riding back into the

middle of it. Then it danced off up the deep bed of
the river, and before I re-entered the forest it had
formed a bow, stretching across the mountain sides
like a grand triumphal arch. A last look from the
wooded portals revealed a bright blue sky and the
sun shining over the lowlands, whilst around us the
rain still fell, and through the dripping branches of the
trees that met overhead only dull grey clouds were
visible. Here commenced a series of mountain pictures
in bewildering variety. For almost all the rest of the
journey the path runs up and down hill, with a deep
ravine sometimes on one hand and sometimes on the
other Through the ravine runs a stream, on the other
side of which the mountain rises in a grand and almost
perpendicular wall. On the near side the path is
edged with banks which slope away to the higher
hills, and diversified with glens and hollows, and an
occasional overhanging rock.

The vegetation is of the most luxuriant description,
as numerous waterfalls descend from both the mountain sides, here crossing the path in a broad stream,
and there trickling down in a slender thread, which
loses itself in thick ferns and grasses. Each turn in
the road presents some new combination of rock, tree,
and falling water. You emerge from an avenue of
bamboos, to enter another arched over by the fronds
of magnificent tree-ferns. The latter grow everywhere; you look up at their rough fibrous stems,
and you look down into their very hearts. The banks
are covered with begonias and primulas; above these
rise the dark green blades of plantains, or dark green
heliconias, with their red and yellow flowers. Then
come the great forest trees, such as the locust,

the angelim, the bois violon (fiddle wood), the bois immortelle, &c. Of begonias I counted four varieties, one of which was sweet-scented. For some time I searched, wondering whence the delicious fragrance—very like that of the lily of the valley—came.

I had never heard of a sweet-scented begonia, but at last I discovered one, and gathered a large bunch of the delicious blossoms. The flowers of this variety were very small and of a pink colour, but the elephant-eared leaves were as large as those of much finer flowering species. I regret much that I did not endeavour to transplant some specimens, as I have since heard that a scented begonia is unknown. The extraordinary wealth of tropical vegetation was such that, in spite of heavy rain, I constantly stood for many minutes lost in astonishment. And there was no questioning the down-pour; sometimes a perfect stream would enter the sensitive ears of the mule, and the poor animal would actually squeal and kick, and then droop, until he presented a spectacle of abject misery. Thoughts of fever hovered about me, but I had a change of clothes in my saddle-bags, and even without it I doubt whether I could have hastened my steps, so fascinating was the scenery.

Our progress had been so slow that it was noon before little more than half the distance had been accomplished. Then a certain spot offered such irresistible attractions for a halt that I picketed old Solomon—as the mule had been named—under a hanging rock, and lunched. There could not have been a prettier place, with its rich banks of flowers, feathery bamboos, and silvery fall, trickling down through a fernery of frail, shivering beauty. Across the wild ravine rose a perpendicular mass of black rock, hung with long waving grasses and tufts of green. Large trees clung to its side where there was, apparently, no root-hold, and their branches were loaded with orchids and red-spiked bromelias. The only sounds were the pattering of the rain-drops and the murmur of the rapids below, which foamed over the rough stones that were hidden by the fringing arums, bamboos, and branching ferns.

Suddenly a whirring sound broke the silence, and I immediately saw a " Purple Carib "* humming-bird, hovering over a flowering vine. It was the first time I had ever seen one of this beautiful species alive, and he seemed determined I should not forget him. After every plunge into a flower, he retired to a favourite branch and preened his velvet black feathers and shook his wings, until their metallic green and the deep purple of the throat flashed again and again. His resting-place was a magnolia tree—numbers of which line this woodland path—and the dark, shining wet leaves formed a lovely frame for the dainty *oiseau-mouche.* He looked like a living gem, set in green enamel, and diamond sprays. I saw no other birds, and the silent woods raised in me a fancy to pull the long bell-ropes hanging from the trees, and thus set the forest chiming. I did so, and got nothing but a shower bath ; and the falling leaves and sticks stilled for a moment the melancholy croak of the frogs, in their perpetual lament for the departed Indian race, "Ca-rib, Ca-rib." Then I saddled Solomon, and we resumed our journey.

* Eulampis Jugularis.

There is little more to describe. Everywhere beautiful scenes, and blending of loveliness and grandeur. Sometimes from the overhanging cliffs a landslip, caused by the heavy rains, rendered the path—which, with a very little trouble, might be made good enough for a carriage—almost impassable; otherwise, the road is remarkably easy and free from obstructions.

The finest view remains for the last. When the highest point to which the road ascends is reached, a narrow ridge, with a deep ravine on each side, commands a magnificent prospect over Trinité to the sea. Near by are rocky gorges, mountain peaks, and half-hidden glades. The rank vegetation forms green vistas above the descending terraces, and through them shines the deep blue water, out of which rise the bold outlines of Dominica on one side, and St. Lucia on the other. That these islands are visible, I only know from hearsay, as mist and clouds enshrouded so much of the landscape that I could only form an idea of what its beauty would be on a clear day. In rain I went to Trinité and in rain I returned. No feeling of ill-will towards the weather was felt by me, but rather one of gratitude, as, had it not been for the rain, I might never have torn myself from those enchanted grounds. It was my last and pleasantest excursion in Martinique.

CHAPTER IX.

"YEO-HO, boys, ho, yeo-ho," rang out merrily from the crew, and before the last notes of "Nancy Lee" had died away, the 'Eider' was slowly steaming from Martinique on her way to Barbadoes. A slight delay had been occasioned by the prolonged absence of one of the passengers who was an enthusiastic curiosity hunter, and who, having rifled the other islands and bought up all the frogs and beetles at. Dominica, had gone on shore to buy Eau de Cologne, dolls in native costume, and the various liqueurs for which Martinique is celebrated.

Soon we pass Fort de France—the Fort Royal of Imperial days—which is nominally the capital of Martinique, though far inferior in size and population to St. Pierre. A small steamer runs daily between the two places, and Fort de France is well worth a visit. The fine harbour and the pretty town, backed by the great Piton, are more thoroughly tropical in their surroundings than is St. Pierre. In the neighbourhood are some picturesque walks, and the "Baths of Didier," where there are some mineral springs, is a very favourite resort. In the outskirts dwell a few of the Carib Indians, who occupy themselves with their peculiar basket work. It is a quiet little town, but gains an air of industry and life from the freighted wharfs and the busy dockyard with its spacious floating dock.

From the deck of the 'Eider' all eyes are centered on a steep island pyramid, which rises out of the water to a height of about five hundred and fifty feet. This is the celebrated "Diamond Rock," whose history forms a memorable page in the annals of the West Indies, where nearly every link in the chain of the Antilles has been the scene of England's naval warfare.

The well-known story may be briefly related as follows. In 1804, the English admiral determined to prevent the escape of French ships, which hitherto had baffled him by running between this rock and the opposite Diamond Point into Fort Royal harbour. The deep water that surrounded the almost perpendicular rock permitted an anchorage within a few feet of its side. The admiral therefore laid his ship, the 'Centaur,' close alongside, and performed the surprising feat of hoisting heavy guns from the topsail yard-arm, and mounting them on the summit of this improvised fortress. Here Captain Morris was established, with men, ammunition, water, and provisions, and the rock was recognised at the Admiralty, as His Majesty's ship 'Diamond Rock.' For months the gallant captain and his crew defied the exertions of the French to dislodge them, destroying their merchant

vessels and gun-boats, and harassing them to despera-
tion. Finally, want of water and ammunition necessitated a surrender, and the rock-ship was once more
untenanted.

On approaching Barbadoes, it is surprising to see
the vast shoals of flying-fish. Like flights of silver
arrows they shoot over the water on all sides, and
just as you are beginning to think they must be birds,
down they drop into the waves. No wonder that the
catching of them is a trade in that island, and that
flying-fish in Barbadoes is the staff of life—and a very
delicious one. No time is lost in their pursuit, nets
surround them by day, and at night, by means of an
attractive lantern, they fly against the outspread sail
and fall victims by the hundred.

After Martinique and Dominica, the appearance of
Barbadoes is flat and tame. One misses the central
hill range, which is so marked a feature in the other
islands. The wide-stretching fields of bright green
cane, and the windmills, recall Santa Cruz. Like that
island, Barbadoes, when discovered by the Portuguese
in the early part of the sixteenth century, was covered
with thick forest. From many of the trees hung the
beard-like Tillandsia, whence arose the island's name.
In the present day there is no forest, and the one little
wood, with its boiling spring, is reckoned among the
" lions" of Barbadoes.

But if the island is devoid of great physical beauty,
it is interesting, as being the most ancient colony in
the British Empire, one also that has never changed
hands, and the only one which thrives—or shall I
say has thriven—without foreign labour.

From Carlisle Bay, the harbour of Bridgetown,

which is the capital of the island, the view is one of bright colour. One sees gleaming sands broken on by blue water, and edged with deep green avicennias, with here and there a bending cocoa-nut palm. From the busy wharfs white houses extend back into the country to a limestone ridge, and to the undulating hills which are covered with sugar-cane and dotted with lines of palms, leading to the planters' houses. White roads wind through the green fields, and a church tower peeps over the shady trees; a windmill rises above a cluster of cottages, and near by is the tall smoking chimney of a sugar factory. There are no clouds in the intensely blue sky to cast their shadows, and the breeze rushes across the cane slopes in white green waves. On all, the sun pours down with a pitiless glare, and its strong light brings to full view the finished cultivation and well-to-do aspect of the island.

"Passengers for Bimshire all aboard," was the cry, as the ship's cutter pulled for the shore, thus disappointing the clamorous native crews of several expected fees. Presently we landed in Bimshire—as Barbadoes is sometimes called—and were at once surrounded by an agitated crowd of "Bims," both black and white. As there are no hotels—properly so-called—our luggage was carried to "Hoad's," the best boarding house; and after escaping numerous blind beggars who pursued us from the wharf, we were soon ensconced in clean lodgings. Here we found small but comfortable rooms, good food— flying-fish served in two or three different forms being particularly tempting—and indifferent bathing accommodation.

After Martinique, where there are no mosquitoes, one looks disconsolately at the stuffy nettings, and cannot help wondering why the detestable insects should patronize the English islands and not the French. The Barbadian mosquito is of an exceptionally dissipated disposition, as it keeps up its revels far into the morning, and with the heat increases the misery of the late as well as of the early riser.

As may be expected in an island whose population averages a thousand to the square mile, Bridgetown swarms with negroes, whose high-pitched voices and incessant "talk" effectually relieve the streets of any air of dulness. The town is not imposing. Its architectural features are collected in Trafalgar Square, where are situated the Government Buildings. Their style, though striking, is a marvellous blending of Gothic and Venetian architecture, mixed with bow windows and Moorish arches, and as much out of keeping with the adjacent Cathedral as the National Gallery in London is with its neighbouring Church of St. Martin. The statue of Nelson, which stands in the centre of the square, cannot be considered as complimentary to the great admiral, and in its present condition fairly represents "the triumph of Nature over Art." Shops, stores, and warehouses are good and thriving, and, last but not least, there is an excellent tea-house, which is an institution peculiar to the West Indies. It vies with the club as a place of resort, contains a restaurant, and a well-kept bar, provides the latest papers, and disseminates the freshest news.

In the matter of ice, which is of no small importance in hot climates, the English are ahead of the French.

Here it is admitted free, I believe, of duty, whilst in
Martinique it is heavily taxed and monopolized.

Most of the white inhabitants live in the suburbs
of the town, and in a drive one passes many pretty
villas and pleasant gardens. The roads leading to
them are lined with negro huts and cabins, shaded by
flowering trees, and now and then surrounded by an
ill-tended garden plot. On some of these abodes we
noticed hanging-boards, on which quaint greetings had
been written; one of these bore the words, "A mery
Krismas and a hapy New ear to everybody;" on
another was printed, "Welcum home 1 and
all."

Towards evening carriages wend their way past the
seaside villages of Hastings and Worthing, or, when
the band plays at St. Ann's, stop there to listen to it.
The latter appeared to me to be the most agreeable
place in or around Bridgetown. The barracks are
situated there, and fronting them is a fine savanna,
surrounded by shady avenues. Here there is the
race course, the cricket ground, a ball court, theatre,
and opportunity for the various amusements which
relieve the monotony of life in the tropics, and which,
fortunately, are always to be found where England
has established her garrisons. I should have liked to
have visited "Scotland," as the northern part of the
island is called, for it is said to be picturesque and
interesting, but time would not permit. Mount
Hillaby, which has the highest elevation, is not quite
1200 feet in height, but the scenery is bold and
mountainous, though of course on a small scale.

About twelve miles from Bridgetown is Codrington
College, and above it, near the edge of a cliff, stands

the old St. John's Church, celebrated for containing in
its churchyard the tomb of a Palæologus, supposed to
be the last descendant of the Christian Emperors of
Greece.

At the time of my visit, the island was somewhat
excited over impending Government changes, and the
"storm in a tea cup," raised by the late Governor,
Mr. Pope Hennessy, had not subsided. The scheme
of confederating it with Tobago, St. Lucia, St. Vincent,
and Grenada met with strong opposition. The Leeward Confederation had not proved a success, and the
Barbadians objected to having the Windward group
joined to them in the same way. Very conservative
in their manners and customs, the white inhabitants
look with no friendly eye on change and innovation;
but I have heard it said, by some whose opinion was
valuable, that the Crown Colony system would eventually prove the saving of the island. There were
rumours too of fresh negro disturbances; provision
grounds were pillaged daily, and the already incredibly
conceited blacks were growing more and more pre-
tentious. No other negro can come up to a Barbadian
in impudence. If in any of the other islands you meet
or hear of a case of peculiar insolence, the offender is
sure to be a Barbadian. "You do not like me," says
the deservedly-rebuked servant, "find one more bettar,"
and then walks off.

In Barbadoes, you hear that only the worst negroes
leave the island, as their love for it is so great that
few can be induced to emigrate, in spite of small
wages. In time, however, even the most home-loving
may find himself compelled to agree with the African
philosopher, who, when asked what he thought of

freedom, replied, "Well, sir, freedom is a mighty fine thing, but I can't eat freedom, and I can't wear freedom, and now I'se got to export myself." Two days were all that were allowed us in Barbadoes, and then the steamer arrived to carry us to Tobago and Trinidad.

On approaching Tobago from the north, the island presents a mass of high hills, terminating in abrupt precipices. Heavy forests clothe the central ridge and the hill spurs which spring from it. There is hardly a break in the luxuriant vegetation, and except here and there, where a patch in the valleys or on the hill sides has been cleared for cultivation, not a single bare spot is to be seen. We skirt the small island of Little Tobago, the haunt of boobies and tropic birds, and then come in sight of a pretty estate on the main-land, which greatly brightens the wild and gloomy scenery. Soon we round a point, and anchor in Scarborough Bay.

On the right rises a hill, crowned by the dismantled fort of St. George. Below it, and forming the central feature, lies a cluster of grey, steep-roofed houses, grouped on a low conical hill which slopes towards the water, and ends in a steep bank fringed with bamboos.

On the left, cane-fields extend from the shore far back over the undulating land to the hill-range, which curves round in a southerly direction towards a long, low promontory, called Sandy Point. Government House is prettily situated on the rising ground at some distance behind the town, but there is nothing of the slightest interest to induce a passenger to land for the short time during the exchange of mails. For a longer stay, that is if you have a friend's house to go to, Tobago is very interesting, both to the geologist and naturalist.

Up to the present, over one hundred and thirty different species of birds have been discovered there, among which a " Penlope" is peculiar to the island, and is known as the Tobago pheasant. A bird-seller, who came on board, had some fine skins of trogons, jacamars, humming-birds, manakins, and others. It is to be hoped that the bird laws which have been wisely established in Trinidad will be adopted in Tobago, as at present the bird-killers from the former island gain their supplies from the latter.

A curious circumstance in connection with the fauna of the West Indies is the number of species of birds, animals, and reptiles peculiar to certain islands, and those islands actually within sight of others. For instance, the Santa Cruz deer is distinct from the deer of St. Vincent or Tobago. The frogs of Dominica and the snakes of Martinique differ from those found elsewhere. The "Imperial Parrot"* from Dominica, is unknown in the other islands. Regarding humming-birds, Wallace says that "the West Indian islands possess fifteen distinct species, belonging to eight different genera, and these are so unlike any found on the continent that five of these genera are peculiar to the Antilles."

The cave-haunting Guacharos are found in Trinidad, as well as on the main-land of South America, but they have not reached the more northerly islands. It may be that the isolation of species is not so in reality, but owes its apparent existence to a want of know-

* Chrysotis Augusta.

ledge, as the recesses of many of the densely wooded islands have still to be explored.

It was with no regret that we left Tobago, as the heat was intense, and we could sympathize with a certain officer, who, when quartered here, was once found sitting in his tub, uttering the most vehement denunciations, with the invariable refrain, "D— Columbus, confound the fellow! why did he discover this rascally island?"

CHAPTER X.

A S Tobago and Trinidad are little more than eighteen miles apart where nearest, we were soon coasting down the latter island. The scenery was bold and picturesque, and the richly clad mountains were of a deep green, flushed in spots, with the crimson canopies of the "bois immortelle." Fertile valleys gently opened to the sea, which here dashed angrily against the caverned limestone walls, and there rippled to the feet of the cocoa-nut palms which encircled the bays.

On reaching the "Boca de Monos"—monkey's mouth—the mountains of Cumana on the main-land of South America loomed up before us. Stretching far out into the sea, these mountains resemble islands similar to those which form the different entrances to the Gulf of Paria, and so near do they appear that it is hard to believe that they are really part of the main-land. As so often happens, whether travelling by sea, lake, or river, the finest scenery is sure to present itself at dinner time. I regret to say that, in our case, enthusiasm was damped by the thought that the soup was getting cold, and that probably the "pepper-pot" would be finished before we got through the "mouth." The scene was striking, as must be the case where wild woodland, reaching to the water, and bold mountain cliffs combine with steeply rising islands, fringed with palms and mangroves, and covered with a thick vegetation wherever a plant can cling. As if the passage was not narrow enough, a rocky islet, tufted with cactus and draped with euphorbias and cistus, stood in the way; but we slipped past it, and soon sailed into the broad gulf. On we went, past wooded islets crowned with white houses, to which the Trinidadians retire in hot weather, and at last anchored off Port of Spain at a long distance from shore.

The view from the water can hardly be called picturesque, the flat shores stretching on either side of the town in a long line hardly above the level of the sea. But the town itself is prettily situated in a profusion of foliage trees and feathery palms, which half conceal the white houses and graceful church towers. Higher up lies a green savanna, with the handsome "Queen's House" on its outskirts, and close behind rise the forest hills of Montserrat.

At a short distance from the wharf, the main street is entered. A broad shady avenue runs up its centre, terminating with the mosque-like Roman Catholic Cathedral. Half way up, a break in the avenue is caused by Marine Square, with a fountain in the middle, and two of its angles occupied by boarding-houses. The nearest of these is known as Emma Clark's, and is supposed to have the best accommodation in the town. Here, we accordingly entered, and were received by the hostess, a Creole lady, of ultra Junoesque proportions, and of renowned verbosity. Good-tempered beyond measure when not annoyed, but terrible in her wrath when aroused. I shall never forget her sublime indignation and torrent of words once, when one of her guests had the temerity to ask for an extra pillow. He did not get it, nor did he even repeat the request. Altogether, Miss Emma did not treat us so badly. Certainly, some people did say that her food, though good, was very limited as to quantity, that the wine and beer she supplied were execrable, that the solitary bath-room might have been kept cleaner, and that the apartments might have contained a little more furniture. But then somebody is always sure to grumble about something, and those who were not satisfied had the option of leaving—only there was nowhere else to go. What a benefit it would be to travellers, and probably to the entire West Indies, if the Government—Home or Colonial—were to erect suitable hotels in the different islands, and lease them to competent persons who would render a sojourn among them more attractive than at present!

The town of Port of Spain is not very interesting. Stores and shops are good, and Brunswick Square is adorned with a handsome cathedral and a curious old Government building. Beyond the latter are the new Court Houses, of massive and striking design, and large and expensive enough to satisfy the requirements of the entire West Indies. It is a handsome town, and with that all has been said. Its chief features, irrespective of Emma Clark, are buzzards*

* Cathartes aura.

and smells. Of the birds there are an immense
number; they line the roofs of the houses, perch on
the fountains and wade in the basins, blink at you
from the trees, and refuse to get out of your way
in the streets. Alive, the noisome creatures sweep
close to your face when you look from a verandah;
and dead, they greet your nostrils in your walk, as
they generally choose the centre of a road as a
suitable place to expire, and where they fall, there
they lie.

In smells, Port of Spain vies with St. Pierre. Our
rooms were sometimes unbearable from the odour of
salt fish, raw onions, potatoes, and coffee, which
ascended from the provision stores underneath, and
equalled in intensity the fumes from the small court-
yard in which a cow, goats, pigs, a sheep, puppies,
naked black children, and parrots wandered at liberty.
Often did we exclaim with Mrs. Partington, "How
flagrant it is!" Perhaps these odours account for the
number of chemists' and druggists' shops that exist in
Port of Spain. But the outskirts of the town are
fresh and bright. Pretty houses and lovely gardens
line the approaches to the park-like savanna. The
only blot on the fair scene, is an unsightly building—
originally erected for the Duke of Edinburgh—which
stands in a conspicuous position, unrelieved by a tree
or flower.

On approaching Queen's House, which is situated
in the Botanical Gardens, the eye rests on, what to me,
was the most charming sight in or around Port of
Spain. Grand clumps of the most magnificent
bamboos here line the roadside. Splendid ceibas,
tamarinds, and samans are dotted about close by, but

to my mind, could not compare with the bamboos,
whose feathery arches and drooping boughs seemed
like a "forest fit to fringe fairy land." The gardens
disappointed me, perhaps from over-expectation.
Unlike those of Martinique, nature has not here
granted a picturesque situation. Art has only partially
succeeded in rendering the grounds attractive. There
are many beautiful varieties of palms, deep-green nut-
meg groves, towering erythrinas, ceibas, and various
rare shrubs and trees, but there is something wanting
to make up an effective whole. The gardens are of
small extent and are deficient in any leading feature
of special interest. There are no fountains, no pieces
of water, no falls, no rockeries, and the only flower-
garden proper is a small one under the windows of
Queen's House. Great care and attention are bestowed
on the gardens, and in the nurseries I saw some rare
orchids, luxuriant ferns, and many species of begonias,
caladiums, and morantas. I was also shown some
Liberian coffee trees, whose berries were far larger
than the common. Formerly, there was a small
Zoological collection here, but that is of the
past.

The drive round the savanna in the cool evening
is a very pleasant one. Here a black game of cricket
is going on, amid much laughter and noise ; there a
white one is being conducted, in a very sedate and
orderly fashion. Near the ugly Prince's building
is a croquet lawn, and close to the opposite Grand
Stand an impromptu race has been organized. Moon-
eyed Chinese trot along, with a basket of vegetables
slung at one end of a long bamboo and a bundle of
clean clothes at the other. Delicate-looking cattle are

being led to water by still more delicate-looking
Indian coolies, and scattered over the grass are brilliant
patches of colour, caused by the gay robes of Hindoo
women, whose arms and ancles, heavily hung with
bangles, glitter brightly as they milk soft-eyed cows,
to the music of laughing babies riding astride their
hips.

Coolie immigration from India has been very
successful in Trinidad and Demerara, and speaks
well for the system of labour which has been adopted
in those places. And, certainly, the coolies have no
cause for complaint. From the time they leave India
until they return there—that is if they choose to
return—every suitable provision is made for their
comfort. Unlike the Chinese, whose only object is
to make money and get back to the Celestial Empire
as soon as possible, the Indian coolies become attached
to their new home, and in Trinidad a great number—
nearly three thousand—have obtained grants of land
instead of " return " passages, and have settled down
as colonists. Many of them possess sugar estates,
and one owns several good race-horses.

Hindoo villages are seen in many parts of the
island, and near Port of Spain, on the road to St.
James's Barracks, is a coolie village, so oriental in
its character, even to its native priests, charmers, and
prayer-house, that, if an aeronaut suddenly descended
there, he might readily imagine himself near
Calcutta.

From the moment a stranger sets foot in Trinidad,
he recognises that he is in a flourishing island ; and the
more he sees and hears of it, the more convinced does he
become of its prosperous future. In the large and busy

town, he can form some estimate of its resources, but, when he visits the interior and more distant regions, the fertility of the soil speaks for itself. To use one of Jerrold's witticisms, the land is so fertile " that, if you tickle it with a hoe, it smiles with a flower." Though sugar is the chief produce, there are other staples to which Trinidad directs her attention in a greater degree every year. The chief of these is cacao, which is a product continually increasing in value, and which is admirably adapted to the soil. Apart from the ease with which it is cultivated and prepared, a cacao plantation is a very desirable one, on account of its beauty. It has none of the monotonous stretches of a sugar plantation, as cacao has to be protected from the sun.

In some picturesque valley, or on undulating slopes, with a forest back-ground, and probably with a glorious sea view from a neighbouring hill, you see a dwarf forest whose trees are about the size of apple-trees, and on whose stems and red-brown branches grow hundreds of pods like great golden lemons. Through this forest, run rows of " bois immortelles "—Madres del cacao—tall, elm-like trees, with bright flame-coloured canopies which afford a complete shade. On an eminence stands the white house of the planter, and near it a few rustic cottages and provision grounds; there is no tall smoking chimney, no din of machinery, no mingling of negro and molasses, all is cool and quiet, and you feel that, out of the few agricultural pursuits in the tropics, that of cacao-growing, must be the pleasantest.

Around Port of Spain the absence of bird life makes a sad void in nature ; one misses the humming-birds, which in Martinique dart from every shrub, and even visit the balcony-flowers in the town. Even at a distance inland, it is only occasionally that the yellow "sucriers" are met with, or that the amusing, glossy brown "trembleurs" are seen bowing and scraping to one another in their usual polite fashion, but in some other islands these birds are very common. The "Wild Birds' Protection Ordinance," which was passed in 1875, has hardly had time to bear fruit as yet, but before long the feathered tribe may once again abound. Especially rare is that most beautiful of all humming-birds, the "Tufted Coquette," —Lophornis ornatus—and once the species was as numerous as the "Ruby-crested,"* the "Savanna Sapphire,"† and the "Snowy-throated Emeralds,"‡ which are still abundant in Trinidad. Some lovely specimens of the above-named were offered me for sale, and I doubt whether I could have refused them, even without the assurance that they all came from the "Main." I must have made a mistake in thinking that the "Snowy-throated Emerald" was peculiar to Trinidad!

From Port of Spain there are many delightful excursions to be made. There is the Blue Basin, at the head of the Diegomartin Valley, and above it is the Signal Station, from whence the land and coast views are very beautiful. Then there is the celebrated Maracas waterfall, the road to which affords an opportunity of seeing the most picturesque plain, forest, and river scenery in the island. Besides the mud volcanoes, there is also that natural phenomenon, the Pitch Lake

---

* Trochilus moschitus.   † Chlorostilbon atala.
‡ Thaumatias chronopectus.

of La Brea. A weird, uncanny, intensely hot locality is that in which this strange lagoon is situated. The lake itself, which is nearly three miles in circumference, is surrounded by wood and jungle, growing luxuriantly from the pitchy soil. Out of the black sea rise little green oases covered with flowering shrubs, and occasionally lines of grass streak the surface. In the asphalte, which is hard in some places and soft and sticky in others, are numerous cracks and channels, often filled with clear brown water. Here and there a massive tree trunk or tapering pole protrudes through the pitch, like the hull and masts of some wrecked vessel sinking gradually out of sight.

Charles Kingsley has already fully described the sights and wonders of Trinidad, and since " At Last " was written the face of the country has little altered. Civilization of late has progressed, a railroad and coast steamers now connect different parts of the island, plantations have increased in number, and trade is augmenting annually. But Trinidad is still in its infancy, as by far the greater part of the island is still unreclaimed and unopened forest.

When Trinidad is traversed by proper roads, it is hardly too much to say that her prosperity will outrival that of Jamaica in her palmiest days. On this subject a good authority has recently said :

" Unfortunately, the same conditions of soil, &c., which render Trinidad a very productive country, make the construction of roads, which are essential to the prosperity and advancement of a country, very difficult and expensive, and the peculiar conditions of the colonial community allow of little interest being manifested in the well-being of the island, beyond the immediate concerns of the moment. Thus it is that our highways, such as they are, are mostly very narrow, devoid of footwalks, and for many weary miles without a single tree which might afford shelter to man or beast, who are thus exposed to the fierce rays of a blazing tropical sun, the direct effects of which are heightened by the scarcely less pernicious ones of reflection and radiation from all the surfaces around. The correction of these and other evils can hardly be be expected, unless there should arise a spirit of enlightened public feeling which at the present time does not exhibit itself."

Let us hope that the writer is too severe on the community of Trinidad, and that the road-making difficulty will soon be overcome. I ought to add that in the neighbourhood of the capital the roads are remarkably good, but glaring.

From Trinidad I proceeded to Demerara, and there found, as I stated in the preface, that the Government was about to send an expedition to Roraima, and with great kindness allowed me to accompany it. As it was not to start until the end of February, I determined to return to Trinidad, and from thence ascend the Orinoco. In the next chapter I must describe that trip.

CHAPTER XI.

THE "HEROE DE ABRIL"—APPROACHING THE ORINOCO—MOUTHS
OF THE ORINOCO—THE MACAREO CHANNEL—MACAWS—WATER
LABYRINTHS — GUARANOS — INDIAN CAMP — TROUPIALS — BAR-
RANCAS—LITTLE VENICE—LAS TABLAS—CARATAL GOLD MINES
—VENEZUELA—THE CARONI—ROCKS OF PORPHYRY—CIUDAD
BOLIVAR—PIEDRA MEDIO—ANGOSTURA BITTERS—UPPER ORI-
NOCO—FEATHER HAMMOCKS.

BEFORE a traveller can ascend the Orinoco, it is
necessary—or said to be necessary by the
steam-ship company—to obtain a passport. It is, I
believe, quite unnecessary, but as the salary of
Venezuelan officials depends in a great measure on
perquisites, it is an act of charity to purchase your
passport from the consul at Trinidad. This is the
first of the many blows which go far to destroy the
romance of the great river. At least we—my companion being a master from the college at Barbadoes—
had an idea that the Orinoco must be a romantic river,
for had not Raleigh cruised about it in search of
golden palaces and of El Dorado!

We obtained our passports and tickets, and at the
hour of sailing were informed that our vessel—the
" Heroe de Abril "—was in the hands of the sheriff and
could not leave. The following day, however, we
received notice to be on board at a certain hour, as
the steamer was to be allowed to depart on this occa-

sion only. The owners chuckled over this, as, owing to defective boilers, neither she nor any of the passengers were expected to return at all. The "Heroe" proved to be an old Hudson River tug-boat, with sufficiently comfortable cabins on its upper deck, whilst its lower deck was open and crowded with second-class passengers who slung their hammocks wherever they could find space. Nearly all on board were bound for the gold mines of Caratal, and a very motley crowd it was.

Regarding the food and service, I will merely say that both were of the worst possible description. Those who had made the trip before had brought their own provisions, and were kind enough to share them with the novices. Without this aid, it is doubtful whether some of the passengers would have arrived at their journey's end.

It was late at night when we left Trinidad, so that early the following morning we found that we had crossed the Gulf of Paria, passed through the "Serpent's Mouth," and were approaching the gruel-like water of the Orinoco. On either side, but many miles apart, stretched two long, low lines of trees, which extended from the equally low coast line in front. To all appearance it was a deep ocean bay, but the colour of the water and the fact that there was no longer any heaving of the lead, told us that we had crossed the bar and had entered the Macareo channel of the Orinoco. Of the numerous other mouths which form the enormous delta of this river, but two are used by vessels, and of these two the "Boca de Navios" has fifteen or sixteen feet of water on the bar, while the "Pedernales" has barely six feet.

On nearing the mainland, we saw numerous islands covered with bush and shrubs, and on one, which looked like a floating mass of weeds that might be swept away by the waves caused by our paddle-wheels, an Indian fisherman had established himself. Two sloping sticks covered with leaves formed his shelter, which was half concealed from the prying eyes of fish and birds by a wide-meshed net. A little bark canoe showed that, in case of inundation, means of escape were at hand. Gradually the channel mouth narrowed, and the dense mangrove thickets which line the banks became more and more conspicuous. It is chiefly to these ever-extending mangroves that the great delta of the Orinoco owes its development. The twisted and matted roots stem the tide, retain the soil, and gradually raise the surface. Year by year the mangrove increases its dominions, and, judging from its present wide extent, it seems that ere long the smaller delta mouths will be choked.

All we saw was a low but vast expanse of bright green foliage. At one spot the mangroves appeared to be mingled with large bushes of hybiscus, covered with enormous crimson blossoms. Suddenly the blossoms took wing, and we recognized a flock of scarlet ibises. At length, we were fairly in the river channel, with a width across of less than a quarter of a mile. Various shrubs were now mixed with the mangroves, and at some distance from the banks tall clumps of trees, with masses of creepers, fringed the outlying lakes and open swamps. From these arose clouds of wild-fowl, which, after a look at the steamer, returned to their feeding-grounds, or in endless strings took long flights to more distant solitudes. There was no scarcity of birds here; there were geese, ducks of various sorts, bitterns, spoonbills, crested pheasants, herons, egrets, water-turkeys, and many specimens of the huge tantalus.

After a time the vegetation assumed a forest aspect, and we entered a palm region. Here we were greeted by the harsh cries of the blue and yellow macaws, which in numberless pairs flew overhead, and in flocks rose screaming from lofty trees. The scenery was very tropical, and we began to think that perhaps a trip up the Orinoco was not the mistake that it was said to be by a gentleman on board, who had made the voyage before. Palms predominated, but there were also splendid trees, from whose branches the hanging creepers formed a perfect wall. Here and there these green curtains lifted, and disclosed an aquatic maze threading its way deep into the wild forest. The monotonous green was varied with white-plumed ingas, crimson poivreas, and yellow bauhinias, which overhung the arums, the thick-veined caladiums, and the bamboo-like grasses growing on the banks. White egrets stalked along, tortoises flopped into the water from the branches, water-turkeys dived and always came up just ahead of us, and solemn cranes with one eye on the stream and the other on a fish, did not stir from their one-legged position as we puffed past them.

Only on the beautiful little Ocklawaha River in Florida, have I seen such lovely vistas as here penetrate the recesses of the border forests; each one, in fact, was a tropical Ocklawaha. Once, on turning a bend in the channel, we came suddenly upon a canoe whose occupants had not time to disappear in the side labyrinths, as they had done previously. It was evidently a family party of Guaraños or Kirishana Indians. The poor creatures looked terribly frightened, and the trembling women turned their faces towards the forest. Such modesty was hardly to be wondered at, seeing that the only clothing of any description that one of them had on was a baby, which she hastily caught up and wore as an impromptu apron.

It was with no small interest that we gazed at these few members of an almost extinct tribe, whose home is—or used to be—for the greater part of the year in the tree tops. For this Delta, which is always wet, is for several months inundated. The swampy soil is then many feet under water, and, therefore, high up in the trees, the Indians build their houses. If it was on account of its freedom that they selected such an unpropitious spot for habitation, they chose well and were certainly safe from intrusion, as none but an Indian could thread in his canoe the water-paths of the dismal forest. But probably their choice was determined by the extraordinary abundance of a certain palm called the "Mauritia" or "Ite."* This has been well named *arbol de la vida*, for it supplies the Indians with food, drink, clothing, habitation, canoes, and hunting and fishing implements. Food is made from the scaly fruit, which resembles pine cones hanging in clusters, and also from the soft pithy substance contained in the trunk; the two are treated like cassava and mixed into a cake of the consistency of sago and called "yaruma." From the juice of the flower-spathes toddy is made, and from the sheaths at their base sandals and girdles are manufactured. Hammocks,

* Mauritia flexuosa.

nets, and lines are woven from the fibres, canoes are fashioned out of the trunks, and bows and arrows from the leaf-stems.

Besides these necessaries of life, some luxuries are also supplied, as from the pith of the large arm of the leaf, split longitudinally, a sail is made for canoes, and by raising the fibres of the arm and placing a bridge under them, a rude kind of musical instrument is formed. To make their domiciles, four suitable palm trees are selected, notches are cut, and beams, stretched from trunk to trunk, are lashed together with fibre. A layer of mud, which hardens and is capable of bearing a fire, is then spread over the flooring, a roof of trees is added, and the dwelling is complete.

Whether these Indians still take to the trees in the wet season, or whether they find more comfortable lodgings on the ground, I know not. Higher up the river we passed one or two small Indian settlements, where the huts, pitched on elevated ground, consisted merely of a thatched roof supported by poles, but whether the inhabitants were Guaraños or not we could not say. They were better dressed than our old friends, as each individual was provided with fully six inches of cotton girdle. But their attire did not prove that they were not Guaraños, as it may be that they only put on their Sunday best on the approach of the steamer. Nature has admirably assisted these beings in their hiding propensities, as the reddish brown colour of their skins assimilates with that of the bush stems and tree trunks, among which they conceal themselves. In one place where we had seen a canoe enter, we saw a camp with hammocks slung and fire burning, but not a trace of the occupants, although they were probably looking at us from out of the bushes a very short distance away. They must have been close, as the canoe was there and empty.

It is not surprising that these timid savages consider everyone who does not belong to their own tribe as their natural enemy. At a " wooding " station where we had stopped, a canoe hovered about for some time but would not approach. At last, just as we were starting, it came alongside, and we found that it contained several cages of black and yellow troupials. The owners would not come on board, and could not be induced to hand up their birds for inspection until they had received payment, and then they paddled hurriedly away. On inquiry, I heard that the ship's company (Venezuelans) made a good deal of money by the sale of these beautiful birds in Trinidad and other places, and it had been the practice to obtain them from the Indians and delay payment until it was too late. Thus the unfortunate natives lost their birds and their money.

Besides the sight of an occasional Indian, we had no other excitement. Once in the night the steamer came to a halt owing to a thick fog, and at another time a loud crash preceded the stoppage of the engine; loud cries of "Has the boiler burst?" came from different parts, in various languages, but we had only run ashore, and soon steamed off again.

On the morning of the third day after leaving Trinidad, we arrived at Barrancas, where the mouths of the Orinoco separate. We did not anchor, but sent off the mails in a small boat to the little town

which stands on the left bank of the main river, and
then proceeded on our way. Here the scenery changed
completely. The forest had disappeared, there were
no more palms, no bright creepers, even the mangroves
were absent. Macaws, parrots, troupials, all were left
behind, and we looked over a river some miles in
width, with sandy banks and low, dry, unprepossessing hills in the distance. It was a barren, desolate
scene, and even a great, lean heron sitting on a
withered branch, with his long neck sunk between
his shoulders, seemed to think that life with such
surroundings was not worth fishing for. We were
certainly in Venezuela, but "Little Venice," with
its water lanes and streets, lay behind us.

After several hours of slow steaming we arrived
at Las Tablas, which is the nearest port to the mines
of Caratal. It was a dreary-looking place, consisting
of a few houses and one large tree. No one was
allowed to disembark as there is no Custom House,
consequently passengers for the mines have to proceed
on to Ciudad Bolivar and wait there some days, until
the steamer returns to Las Tablas. Thus, for want of
a Custom House, passengers, as well as goods, have to
travel nearly two hundred miles out of their way.
The mines of Caratal are taking a very conspicuous
position among the gold mines of the world, and
already there are over 4,000 British subjects—mostly
natives of the West Indies—at work there.

Strange to say, we have no representative at Bolivar.
Some years ago our Consul was dismissed by the
President in the most arbitrary manner, and no notice
was taken of the insult, neither was the office re-filled.
The need of a representative is very great in a country

where the authorities are in the habit of raising troops
to suppress perpetual insurrections, and where they
seize on anyone without regard to nationality. I
have heard it hinted that, were the boundaries of
Venezuela and British Guiana properly assigned, it
would be found that the valuable mines of Caratal
belong to the latter. This, however, is by no means
the opinion of Venezuelans, and as these boundaries have
been of late under much discussion, I have appended
the translation of some official reports which have
lately been published on the subject in Carácas. The
Venezuelan idea of the correct boundary line—that
of the Essequibo—is so different from our own, that
a perusal of the papers may be interesting.

Close to Las Tablas the Caroni joins the Orinoco,
and a curious effect is produced by the differently
coloured waters running together for a long distance
without mingling. This was the farthest point
reached by Raleigh in his search for El Dorado
in 1595, when, finding that his men were discouraged
and nothing was to be gained by remaining, he
returned to England. From Las Tablas upwards,
the scenery was almost identical with that from
Barrancas. Here and there on the banks stood a
cottage and plantation, beyond stretched wide plains
edged by green slopes and woods, which imparted a
brighter aspect. Soundings were continually taken,
and in many places there was barely sufficient depth
of water to carry us over. From the waste of waters
rose numerous islets of porphyry as smooth as glass,
and which, being covered with a crust of oxide of
manganese, sparkled in the sun and formed remarkable objects in the scene. Sand-banks were frequent,

and on one a brig bound for New York lay stranded,
and had been there two weeks, owing to the captain's
refusal to pay a steam-tug from Ciudad Bolivar the
enormous sum demanded for towing her off. As
she was in the same position when we returned, it
is probable she remained there until the rising of the
river in the wet season.

Animal life was reduced to a few cranes and some
enormous alligators, which basked on the sand in utter
indifference to the noisy anathemas heaped on them
by the black crew, who yelled again whenever they
caught sight of the scaly bodies.

On the day after leaving Las Tablas, we anchored
off Ciudad Bolivar, the capital of Guayana, which is
the largest state in the Republic of Venezuela. The
town was built in 1764, by Mendoza, who named it
Santo Tomas de la Nueva Guayana, which was afterwards changed to " Angostura," and then to its present one, Ciudad Bolivar. Angostura—the Narrows—
was a very appropriate name, as here the Orinoco,
whose breadth above and below averages about two
miles and a half, contracts to less than half a mile. In
the middle of the river stands a famous rock, called
" La Piedra del Medio," which serves as a metre to
gauge the rise and fall of the flood, which at its
highest rises no less than sixty feet above its summer
level. As our visit was during the dry season we
had to land in a boat, struggle over a sandy beach,
and then clamber up a high bank, whereas in the
wet season you step from the vessel on to the
Alameda.

From the river the town looks picturesque, as it
is situated on a conical hill, with the houses rising in

tiers and crowned by the cathedral. The streets are narrow and steep, with the exception of the principal one, which skirts the river, and which is partly shaded by a double row of fine spreading trees called "mamon." The most prominent building is the market-place, which stands on a rocky eminence overhanging the river.

After a strict inspection of our luggage at the Custom House, we went to the only hotel in the town which the two Germans who keep it call "the Club." Here we found clean rooms without furniture of any kind, but the proprietor promised to give us canvas cots, and, if possible, two chairs. We were glad to sit down to breakfast after our long fast on board the "Heroe," but alas! the food was almost as bad as that on the steamer, and, as we were informed that it was impossible to cook any dish without garlic, we had to live chiefly on bread during our stay. Some claret that we ordered was so bad that we sent for another and much more expensive brand; finding it equally bad we complained to the servant, who laughingly informed us that it all came out of the same cask.

A more uninteresting town than Ciudad Bolivar it is impossible to imagine. In half-an-hour you can see the whole of it, including the cathedral, a bronze statue of "the Liberator"—Bolivar—and a very tall pillar with a small bust of Guzman Blanco—the late President—on the top of it. The cemetery contains the monument of the first Dr. Siegert, of "Angostura Bitters" celebrity, and, when you have seen that and the two above-mentioned statues, you have seen the "lions" of Ciudad Bolivar. Apropos of of "Angostura Bitters," the manufactory is no longer carried on here owing to its exorbitant taxation by the Government, but has been removed to Trinidad.

Near the cemetery are the barracks, and these are buildings worthy of their occupants. We were told that the soldiers collected here were not good specimens of the Venezuelan Army, and we hoped not. In Carácas I afterwards saw some troops that were well equipped and presented a soldier-like appearance. But here half-starved, ill-clad, of a wretched physique, in height averaging about five feet, and with miserable arms and accoutrements, the troops that we beheld presented a sorry spectacle. Their pay is hardly worth mentioning, but they are fortunate when they receive it. This circumstance reminded me of a distribution of pay that once occurred in a certain town in the United States.

A number of Pinte Indians had been brought in to take part in a 4th of July procession, and after the parade each man received a dollar. It had been customary to hand over the entire amount to their chief—Captain Bob—for distribution, but the fact had become known that coin did not readily leave his grasp. The captain observed this new method of paying with more complacency than was anticipated. He was out-generaled, but not beaten. Being a great poker player he took his men to one of his favourite haunts, and before sunset had cleared his entire army out of the last cent.

From the pitiful condition of the troops when we saw them, it was difficult to imagine what the state of the private soldiers must have been in 1822, when

I

hundreds of officers were seen begging from house
to house in the streets of Carácas. Even as late as
1862, the army was in want of the necessaries of life.

It is not from a lack of generals that the troops are
uncared for and ill-disciplined, for the supply is unlimited.   Two boatmen, who once rowed us over
from Ciudad Bolivar to the opposite shore to visit
a cattle ranch, were both generals. The butcher who
supplied the hotel was a general, and, if his military
tactics were as good as those he exhibited in his
steady resolve not to furnish good meat, he ought
to have been a success. But in Venezuela it is not
necessary either to be, or to have been a soldier, to
become a general.   The title is distributed indis-
criminately, and sent about like a bouquet of flowers
or a box of cigars, with the compliments of so and
so.   A late aspirant for the Presidency intimated
that he would abolish this distinction, by making
everybody a general.   Needless to say he lost his
election. In more recent times, did not the son of
Prince Bismarck lose his nomination to the Reichstag
by a premature declaration of his policy?

At Carácas, one day, I was looking over a book
called *Cervantes y la Crítica*, by Urdaneta. In it was
a list of subscribers to the volume, and out of four
hundred names I counted two hundred and seventy-
eight generals, and all the rest were doctors. Well
might the Irishman exclaim in Venezuela, as he did
upon his arrival in the United States, "What a divil
of a battle has been fought near here, where all the
privates were kilt!"

Finding so little to see or do in Ciudad Bolivar,
we were anxious to ascend the Upper Orinoco, but

heard to our dismay that the small steamer "Nutrias"
no longer went up the river. We therefore had to
pass a week in the town until the "Heroe" returned
to Trinidad. Formerly, the trade with the Upper
Orinoco was very considerable, and four steamers
used to ply on the river, bringing down coffee,
indigo, hides, cotton, &c. Revolutions have destroyed
that, and now almost the only trade is with the mines
of Caratal. Now and then large Indian canoes from
the Rio Negro descend the river, bringing birds,
hammocks, and curiosities, which they exchange for
necessaries, and then return. Some of their feather
and grass hammocks that we saw were marvels of
skill, and must have been highly remunerative to the
merchants, who demanded from one hundred to one
hundred and fifty dollars apiece, having probably
obtained them for ten or twelve dollars worth of
goods.

It was excessively hot during our stay, but fortunately a dry heat, and there were no mosquitoes,
although a lagoon on one side of the town gave
promise of an abundant supply. In the wet season
the heat is almost unbearable. As our hotel was
close to the river—in fact, just outside the door was
the hull of a vessel which had been left there high
and dry when the water fell—we generally had a good
breeze, and the verandah was the coolest place in the
town. Few of the other houses possessed verandahs,
as in Ciudad Bolivar the roof is the favourite family
resort in the evening. Some of the roofs are prettily
laid out with flowers and shrubs, and there the ladies
sit and talk, receive visitors, promenade, and enjoy
any breath of air that may relieve the stifling heat.

Ciudad Bolivar used to be a very hospitable town, but that was in the good old days when Señor Dalle Costa was President of Guayana, and there seemed a fair chance of good government. Then there was a good deal of amusement; travellers, English officers from Trinidad, and others were gladly welcomed and entertained, puma and jaguar hunts were organized, and a trip up the Orinoco was a great pleasure. Now trade is depressed, the town is woefully dull, and I doubt whether any traveller would visit Ciudad Bolivar for pleasure a second time. Whether the community—which numbers 7,000 or 8,000 souls—is an intellectual one I do not know, but I do know that I was unable to obtain a book in any language or of any description—except grammars—at any store or shop in the town. After a long search in stores that contained a little of everything, from pomatum to ship's cables, I was told that I might find some books at the chemist's. His stock consisted of a few grammars, very useful in their way, but hardly entertaining enough to wile away the hot hours. It must be remembered that this was in the capital of the largest State in Venezuela, a republic whose area is larger than that of France, Spain, and Portugal taken together.

Trinidad is very little better off for books than Ciudad Bolivar, as the only bookseller there has very few works except an old collection of volumes of Tauchnitz—an edition, by the way, which I think is " particularly requested not to be introduced into English colonies." A collector of coins might visit Ciudad Bolivar with advantage, as a more miscellaneous currency could not be found. Not only do you receive in change coins from every country in the world, but also chips of silver and blocks of copper that would be utterly valueless anywhere else. The scenery around the town was flat and tame, but it acquired a charm from the great river and the wonderful transparency of the atmosphere.

From the Calvary behind the town, easy of access, but fruitful in rattlesnakes, the eye embraced a vast extent of country. For the most part it is covered with thick *chaparro*, with here and there an undulating line which marks the course of a rivulet. Dotted about are what look like specks of pasture, but which, when approached, prove to be wide savannas, which afford grazing for countless cattle. Dark masses of trees show where virgin forests lie, and on the verge of the horizon the hills rise, looking pink and purple in the brilliant sunlight. The environs are dry and uncultivated. A few Indian huts and cottages with plantain patches are all that are to be seen.

Every evening we used to go to the old fort near the market and watch the sunset, and the last we saw surpassed in colouring any that I have ever witnessed. We looked up the river towards the west, and were fairly dazzled by the rich lights in sky and water. An arch of dead gold spanned a dip in the distant purple hills; below it was a crimson disc, and above a clear blue expanse. Radiating from this arc were bars of distinct shades, which shone for a few seconds and melted into a sheet of yellow and rose. The light was continuous from the sky far down the river, where it touched with pink the great cross on the black rock " del Medio." Turning from the rainbow-tinted water to the north-east we looked down the river, and, though a rose flush still tinged the horizon, the broad flood flashed like burnished steel as the rays of a full moon fell directly upon it. After the glare of the sunset, the change was as sudden as from noon to midnight. But gradually the eye became accustomed to the chastened silvery light as it touched the dark green foliage and brought into clear relief the houses and cottages on the bank, and, when once more we turned towards the west, it was there where the seeming darkness rested. Only for a moment though, and then we discerned a beautiful olive-green horizon, which gradually faded in the clear silver moonlight. For sharp, decided colouring, we had seen nothing like it, and in spite of our anxiety to leave Ciudad Bolivar we regretted that we should not witness one more sunset there.

Before we left our rocky standpoint, a loud exclamation from some bathers below us drew our attention to a black object floating down the stream. It proved to be an alligator, who would, doubtless, have made short work of anyone who ventured beyond the shallow pools that bordered the river. When the river is high, it is not an unfrequent occurrence to see one of these monsters in the very street. Waterton says: "One Sunday evening some years ago, as I was walking with Don Felipe de Yriarte, Governor of Angostura, on the banks of the Orinoco: 'Stop here a moment or two, Don Carlos,' said he to me, ' while I recount a sad accident. One fine evening last year the people of Angostura were sauntering up and down in the Alameda. I was within twenty yards of this place, when I saw a large cayman rush out of the river, seize a man and carry him down before anybody had it in his power to assist him. The screams of the poor fellow were terrible as the cayman was running off with him. He plunged into the river with his prey; we instantly lost sight of him, and never saw or heard of him more.'"

Humboldt also saw an alligator seize an Indian by the leg, while pushing his boat ashore, in the lagoon behind the town. He was dragged into deep water, and his cries collected a crowd, who saw him search for his knife. Not finding it, he seized the reptile by the head and pressed his fingers into his eyes. But the creature held on and disappeared with the unfortunate Indian.

Our descent of the Orinoco was as uneventful as our ascent. The only change was a substitution of cattle for our former second-class passengers. Freight, human and mercantile, was discharged at Las Tablas; we were stopped by frogs and impeded by shallows, but the boiler did not burst, thanks to the untiring watchfulness of the Scotch engineer, and we arrived safely at Trinidad. Soon afterwards I proceeded to Demerara.

CHAPTER XII.

A DARK thread stretching across the horizon, only a faint streak, which thickened into a fringed skein as the tops of cocoa-nut trees came in view, told us that we were in sight of British Guiana.* Soon the blue water assumed the hue and consistency of pea-soup, as we approached the mouth of the Demerara river. A pilot came on board, but for six hours we had to await the pleasure of the tide before crossing

---

* This, the largest of our colonies in the West Indies, and the only one in South America, comprises the three counties of Demerara, Essequibo and Berbice, which derive their names from the three principal rivers which border them. Georgetown, the capital, and seat of Government, has a population of 37,000 inhabitants, whilst the total population of the colony approaches 240,000. The coast line of British Guiana on the Atlantic is about 280 miles in length, and in breadth the country varies from 200 to 450 miles, the total area being estimated at 76,000 square miles. Its boundaries inland may be said to be Venezuela, Brazil, and Dutch Guiana, but the precise limits of the two former are still undetermined. Cultivation is restricted to a long narrow strip of the coast and along the banks of the rivers for a few miles. The whole of the cultivated area is under 80,000 acres, and the greater part of that is in sugar cane alone.

the shallow bar that guards the entrance to the river.

The first impression on beholding Demerara is that a wave of moderate proportions would submerge the country. You see no background, no hill or rising land, nothing but a thin coast line of avicennia and mangrove bushes, above which rise cocoa-nut palms and high chimneys. Presently you discover that there is land behind the coast line, as beyond a fine sea-wall on the left you can see the barracks, fine spacious buildings with deep verandahs, and several white houses. A fort is passed, and a goodly array of shipping at anchor in the river, and lying alongside the wharfs, betokens a busy town. Groups of royal palms, spires, and steeples rise up in the rear of large warehouses and go-downs that line the bank, and before the vessel anchors you recognize the fact that Georgetown is the first and most promising town in or near the West Indies.

We anchored in the river, but now the steamers run alongside a wharf, which is a comfort that cannot be too highly estimated. A hundred voices greeted us on landing, with offers to convey our luggage to the hotel, and " Kerridge, sir, kerridge," resounded on all sides. Not only were there " kerridges " of different descriptions, but there was actually a " hansom " in waiting. Had it not been for the numerous black faces, we might have landed on the coast of England, but, then again, the numerous bangled women and turbaned men suggested India.

We were quickly driven to the new " Tower " Hotel, which looked clean and comfortable, but not a room was vacant. In Georgetown, house-rent is so exorbitant that many resident bachelors, and occasionally families, live together at the hotels; consequently, strangers often find accommodation unobtainable or indifferent.

Across the road was the "Kaieteur Hotel," a large, rambling, wooden structure, but with the prestige of antiquity, and kept by Captain Holly, the American consul at Barbadoes. Here we found rooms, and the worthy proprietor did his best to make us comfortable, but it must be allowed that, with all his kindness and attention, he had not then attained the art of keeping a good hotel. But as the two I have mentioned are by far the best hotels in the West Indies, allowances must be made for a few short-comings. There is one item though for which no allowance ought to be made, and in the tropics it is a most important one. In the matter of baths and bath rooms the hotels and boarding houses in the West Indies are disgracefully negligent.

At St. Thomas, to reach the cobwebby and tarantula-occupied bath room, it is necessary to descend a flight of dirty stone steps and to pick your way across a court-yard which is never swept, and which is a repository for old boots, rags, banana skins, and fowls. At Martinique there were no bath rooms in my hotel, and I had to hire a tub; I was told that even in the best hotels—the Hotel Micas—there were no baths. At Barbadoes, one very small shower-bath taken on the bare bricks did duty for the whole establishment at Hoad's. At Trinidad, a green, slimy tank into which fresh water ran, but which was never emptied or cleaned, was the sole bathing accommodation for Miss Emma Clark, her boarders, and servants.

And here at the " Kaieteur," the two bath rooms—one on each floor—were not fit for sculleries, a use by the way to which they were frequently put. Their size was such that they barely held a small tub, and it was difficult to stand upright in them ; as for a chair, there was not room for one, and, what with the intense heat and the want of space, I have frequently seen people come out of the wretched hole streaming with per-spiration after their bath. The supply of water, too, was very limited, as in Demerara rain water alone is used, and when we arrived there the long continued drought had nearly emptied the tanks.

The average rain-fall in Demerara is estimated by feet instead of inches ; but last year (1877) had been very dry, and now the absence of rain in the usual short wet season—December, January, and February—had already created more loss to the planters, and as it was too late to expect rain before May, a water famine was anticipated. It used to be positively asserted that the year was divided into two wet and two dry seasons in British Guiana, but it is gradually dawning on the public mind that no uniformity in weather ever did, or can exist, and that, though the climate remains, the weather changes.

Georgetown is a handsome, well-built town, with broad streets, avenues, excellent stores, and shops of all descriptions, and with a lively, well to-do air that is as invigorating as the heat is depressing. In the streets, besides the white race, you meet sharp-featured Madrassees, Hindoos of various castes, Parsees, Nubians, and half-breeds. Stepping timidly along may also be seen two or three " bucks," as the natives from the interior are called, dressed—if dressed at

all—in a motley suit of old clothes, and only anxious
to sell or exchange their parrots and hammocks, and
then return to their wilds. From a merchant's store
filled with European goods, you step into a little shop
redolent of the East, and stocked with bangles and
silver ornaments worked by their Cingalese proprietor.
There stands a Portuguese Jew, ready to fleece the
first "buck" whom he can entice into his cheap
general-store, and here sits stolid John Chinaman,
with his pigtail wreathed round his head, keeping
guard over his home-made cigars.

The Government Building is a large, fine-looking
structure, the numerous churches are graceful and
picturesque, and everywhere there is a home look
about the town, without pretension, that is very
attractive. The reading-room is cool and very comfortable, the library well managed, and the museum in
the same building is likely, under the care of Mr. Im
Thurm, the new curator, to become a very valuable
acquisition to the colony. Under his superintendence,
a very interesting exhibition of native produce and industry had been held previous to my arrival, and I
was sorry to have missed it.

It has been said that hospitality is on the wane in
the West Indies; well, if that of Demerara may be
taken as an example, may it always be on the wane!
A kinder, more hospitable community I never met. It
seems to be the object of the residents to make a
stranger's sojourn among them as home-like and agreeable as they can. Some one once remarked, and it has
been the fashion to repeat, that the French alone in the
West Indies make the land of their adoption their
home, and that the English make it merely a place

of business, from which they hasten at the earliest
opportunity. This may be so, for the English of all
others are a home-loving race, and "the old country"
is more, I think, to them than "fatherland" to the
Germans, or "notre pays" to the French. But, whilst
they are in exile, they, at any rate in Demerara, surround themselves as far as possible with home comforts
and home reminiscences, and infuse something of the
far off country sweetness into the inner circle of their
lives. No heart—no, not even a Savoyard's—feels
expatriation so deeply as an Englishman's, and none,
save those whose lot has been to sojourn far from
home, can imagine the intense longing to see again
the native shores. Do you remember that old poem
called "The Home Fever: A reminiscence of the West
Indies?"—the first verse is—

> "We sat alone in a trellised bower,
>   And gazed o'er the darkening deep,
>   And the holy calm of that twilight hour
>   Came over our hearts like sleep,
>   And we dreamed of the banks and the bonny braes
>   That have gladdened our hearts in childhood's days.

and the last,

> "Oh! talk of spring to the trampled flower,
>   Of light to the fallen star;
>   Of glory, to those who, in danger's hour,
>   Lie cold in the field of war;
>   But ye mock the exile's heart when ye tell
>   Of aught save the home where it pines to dwell."

It will be asked, where do these good people of
Georgetown dwell?

Opposite the "Kaieteur" hotel is the Club, which is
the pleasantest resort in the town, as it receives the full
benefit of the trade wind, which on certain occasions

by-the-bye wafts other zephyrs than those fresh from
the beautiful hybiscus hedge in front, and is much frequented by its members. Stretching far away from
this club towards the sea-wall is Main Street, and there
and in the neighbouring parallel one the principal houses
of Georgetown are situated. Main Street is broad
and picturesque ; a series of wide trenches* with green
sloping banks divides it, and on each side runs a fine
road. The residences which line it are all detached,
and of various styles of architecture, from a three-storied
edifice with towers and cupola to a low wide-spreading
structure with but one floor above the basement. But
all are built for coolness as well as comfort, and their
wide shady verandahs are the favourite resorts of the
family. Many of the gardens are brilliant masses of
colour, resembling a rich oil-painting, rather than a
delicate water-colour of those of European lands. The
tints are so gorgeous and heavy ; there are bushes of
the crimson hybiscus, scarlet cordias, flaming poin-
settias, trailing corallitas, the bright flowers of the bois
immortelle, the drooping clusters of the red quiscualis,
the vermilion blossoms of the flamboyant, all vying in
splendour with saffron petrœas, deep blue convolvuluses,
abutilons, and the white trumpets of the datura. In
one garden I remember seeing a resplendent mass of
Bougainvilleas, and on a neighbouring tree some equally
showy blossoms of a magnificent crimson orchid —
Cattleya superba ; between them crept pale clusters of
English honeysuckle, not a bit abashed by their grand

---

* As there is no natural fall of water, these open trenches, which are
seen everywhere in the country as well as town, are necessary to carry off
surface water to prevent flooding in the wet season. By sluice-gates the
town trenches can be flooded when required.

neighbours, but rather exulting in the fragrance denied to their bright-coloured companions.

Marbled crotons and purple dracœnas are tipped by strange-looking papaws, whose wax-like blossoms grow direct from the trunks and branches, and above these tower shade-trees and tall palms. Very conspicuous are the royal palms, standing either singly or in groups, and near them bend the cocoa-nut trees, as if in acknowledgment of the superior majesty of their kings. Besides the houses, some pretty churches, half-hidden in trees, give a finish to this the most picturesque street in Georgetown.

In the adjacent street are also some neat houses, and on one side of it are the Public Gardens with the small but ever hospitable Government House opposite. In the gardens are some specimens of the Victoria Regia —the lily which was discovered by Sir Robert Schomburg on the Berbice river—but in size they are not to be compared with some in other parts of Demerara; for instance on one of the plantations, Leonora, is a plant whose leaves are over six feet in diameter, and strong enough to bear the weight of an average-sized man when a board has been placed across to distribute the weight properly. There is also a fine cannon-ball tree,* under whose shade the weary traveller may experience sensations similar to those of Damocles, as the huge fruit, which is as big as a twenty-pound shot and nearly as heavy, seems always ready to fall from its slender hanging stem. The gardens are not very interesting, but afford a pleasant playground for children, and a delicious gossiping ground for their attendant nurses.

* Couroupita Guianensis.

Let me now recall the usual daily routine in Georgetown. A little before six o'clock tea and toast; after
that I never knew for certain what anyone did up
to breakfast at half-past nine, probably because my
time till then was entirely taken up in getting a bath,
dressing, and trying to keep cool. I believe though
that business was the occupation. As for riding or
early walking exercise, I saw none of it, but then again
that may have been through my own dilatoriness,
although I doubt it. Breakfast was a very substantial
meal, too substantial in fact at the " Kaieteur," and not
tempting enough for a hot climate.

Long before the traveller reaches Demerara, he will
have discovered that no meal in the West Indies is
without salt-fish from Newfoundland ; that and pepper-
pot are standard works. Good fresh fish in Georgetown is something of a rarity—at least it was with us
at the hotel—and when Jew fish is in the market a
bell-man goes round proclaiming the fact and the price
per pound. The flesh is coarse, but appreciated by
the poorer class when it is cheap. Housekeepers also
complain of the scarcity of good meat, and certainly
the beefsteaks and mutton chops furnished to us were
poor.

After breakfast, business is attended to with de-
creasing energy up to luncheon, and then dies a natural
death in the course of the afternoon. About five
p.m. all the world—with the exception of the steady
whist and euchre players at the club—takes an airing.
Those who have carriages drive out to the sea-wall,
which is the promenade, and those who have not walk
there. Nursery maids take their charges to the public
gardens, coolies lead out cows and oxen to graze, black

boys exercise their masters' dogs, horsemen ride out
to the race-course, and unfortunate cripples—chiefly
Chinese—in all stages of terrible disease, come forth and
beg. A late dinner, followed probably by some delightful music—as Georgetown boasts of a very excellent
Philarmonic Society—winds up the day.

I must not forget to add that it is just possible that
its interludes have been filled up by a certain institution
of Demerara known as "swizzles." Most cities and
towns have some small peculiarity, for which they are
as well remembered as for their greater. Demerara
and swizzles are inseparably connected in my mind.
The exact recipe for a swizzle I cannot give, although
I have seen it concocted not unfrequently ; but it is a
deliciously cold drink, of a delicate pink colour, and
when lashed into a foam by the revolutions of a peculiar
instrument called the swizzle-stick, and imbibed out
of a thin glass, it makes a very pretty drink. By a
wonderful provision of Nature the tree which furnishes
the pronged stick, without which the beverage
would lose much of its charm, grows abundantly in
Guiana. The exact time for indulging in a swizzle
has not been clearly defined, but as a general rule in
Demerara it is accepted whenever offered. It is taken
in the morning to ward off the effect of chill, before
breakfast to give a tone to the system, in the middle of
the day to fortify against the heat, in the afternoon as
a suitable finale to luncheon, and again as a stimulant
to euchre, and a solace for your losses. Before dinner
it acts as an appetizer, and it is said that when taken
before going to bed it assists slumber. And very frequently in Georgetown anything to induce sleep would
be welcome, as the incessant "dignity" balls of the

negroes are fatal to slumber. The noisier they are,
the better they are enjoyed, and a lull of a few minutes
only gives fresh energy to subsequent demonstrations.
Verily the coloured folk give a literal interpretation of
their own proverb, that " what you lose in de jig, you
gain in de reel."

Even the guttural notes of the frogs, of which there
are an extraordinary number in the trenches, are preferable to the negro discord. When Bacchus was
rowed along the Styx he could not have been greeted
with a more varied frog's chorus than that which day
and night salutes the inhabitants of Georgetown.
" Awnk, awnk, awnk," roars the bass, " week, week,
week," pipes the tenor, " cru, cru, cru," screams the
soprano, and then the full choir joins in a refrain which
swells and falls with the breeze. One quaint little
fellow has a peculiarly sweet note, so exactly like a
whistle that I have frequently stopped in my walk and
turned to see who it was that wanted to attract my
attention. Just as plentiful and more amusing are the
crabs which frequent the dykes and mud flats around
the town. The " calling crabs "* are especially entertaining, as they wave and beckon with their great claw,
and then scurry away at the least attempt to approach
them. Often in their fright they miss their holes,
then in despair place themselves in fighting attitude,
and dare you to the attack. Another common and
very hideous creature is the little fish known as " Four
Eyes,"† which takes amusement in shooting along the
water and stranding itself at every opportunity.

The feathered tribe are not strongly represented
around Georgetown, but, as a " Birds' Protection

* Gelasimus vocans.   † Anablaps tetraophthalmus.

Ordinance " has lately been passed in Guiana as well as in Trinidad, they may have a chance of multiplying. The commonest bird is a species of flycatcher called " Qu'est-ce qu'il dit," which are the exact words it utters ; it is pretty and sociable, and its querulous notes are heard from many a tree and house top. It will be interesting to learn after a lapse of time whether the bird-law has tended to the increase of birds in towns and settlements. Of bright-plumaged birds the hum-ming-birds alone frequent habitations, and it will be chiefly their increasing numbers that will tell the tale. The brilliant family of chatterers, the troupials, the cocks-of-the-rock, the trogons, toucans, the tanagers, fire-birds,* macaws, manakins, and other gay denizens of Guiana live so far from the haunts of white men that any increase in their numbers can only be assumed.

It is singular to note the constant development of the feather trade ; the day is long past when every fine gentleman, king and commoner, decked himself with plumes, but now, when fashion requires them for ladies alone, the demand is far greater. Forests, mountains, and swamps in all parts of the world are ransacked to supply the dealers, and probably, not before the last bird becomes as extinct as the dodo, will the mania for feathers have died out. And it cannot be denied that the plumage of birds makes a most beautiful adornment, and, though in dress, a head here, a wing there, and a bit of the breast somewhere else, is not the most advantageous mode of showing off the glistening beauties, yet even the dismembered parts shine with matchless and inimitable tints. In the

* Phœnicircus carnifex.

present day there is little that cannot be imitated; artificial flowers, stones, plants, fruit, fish, and human limbs are so skilfully fashioned as sometimes to deceive the sharpest eye. It has been said, too, that glass eyes have been made so perfectly that even the wearers themselves cannot see through the deception. But birds and their nests defy imitation.

A short time before my arrival in Georgetown, the community had been much amused by the advent of a series of commissioners who had come from the United States to inquire into the manufacture of "coloured" sugar. Some cargoes of this sugar had been detained at the custom-house in one of the American ports, under the impression that the sugar had been "artificially" coloured, thereby avoiding the high duties on light sugars.

Duly furnished with Government credentials, they came, saw, and departed, fully convinced, I believe, that the "coloured" sugar outcry was what is vulgarly called a mare's nest. One of the commissioners—a very pleasant young fellow—on finding, when he arrived, that he had been forestalled by others, wisely relinquished his sugar researches, and instead established the first telephone in British Guiana between Georgetown and Berbice. The last I heard of him was that he was about to be appointed consul either in British, French, or Dutch Guiana. The versatility of the true American is indeed wonderful.

Sugar-making has been so often described that I must refrain from giving an account of a visit to a Demerara plantation, much as I should have liked it. It must suffice to say that there you see the latest improvements in machinery, the latest scientific appliances for vacuum pans, centrifugals,* &c., and in fact sugar manufacture on a grand scale.

You also see a veritable "little Holland," as water forms the boundaries of estates, and by water the produce is transported to the mills. Dams and canals intersect the estates, and the navigation system is complete. You see, too; how the welfare of the coolie is attended to, his hospital, his home, his provision grounds, and how much better off in every way he is than in his native land. I once saw a coolie vessel arrive in Georgetown, and though her passengers wept and embraced the captain and officers in their sorrow at having to leave, yet they looked very lean and emaciated in comparison with those I afterwards saw working on the estates. The ships which bring them over are well regulated, and as comfortable as circumstances will admit, but the voyage is trying for a non-sea-going race. One of the mates, in answer to a question, told me they were "a docile, uncomplaining lot, but dirty, as they were always using water."

The visitor to a Demerara plantation is sure of a hearty welcome, that is always fresh and invigorating, however hot the day or tame the scenery may be. And even in the scenery there is always something interesting besides sugar, some strange fruit-bearing tree, some flower or bird, and the cane-laden boats, with a brightly clad figure among the green blades, are always picturesque The country is flat certainly—the only hill I ever found about Georgetown was on the cricket ground—but it is not monotonous if one chooses to look about and

---

* Centrifugals are open round boxes of metal, pierced like gauze. These are whisked round and round at a tremendous speed, and the molasses flying out through the gauze leave the sugar white and dry.

enjoy it. Even the muddy river has its attractions, as the last time I crossed it after a visit to a plantation it was covered with hundreds of Portuguese men-of-war[*] whose large air sacks and vertical crests shone resplendently in every shade of purple and blue.

I must not conclude this sketch of social Demerara without alluding to a certain distribution of the government of the colony which, I believe, is peculiar to British Guiana. Besides the Governor, there is what is called a Court of Policy, and also the Combined Court, which consists of the members of the Court of Policy together with six financial representatives chosen by the people for two years. The Court of Policy is composed of ten members, five of them being Government officers, and five elected from the college of Keizers or Electors. This college is a body of seven members chosen for life by the inhabitants who possess the suffrage, for which an annual income of six hundred dollars qualifies. The Court of Policy carries on the general legislative business, whilst taxation and expenditure are in the power of the Combined Court. Every member of the Combined Court has an equal vote, and also the power of rejecting, if he thinks proper, a bill passed by the majority. Thus Kings, Lords, and Commons rule in Demerara, and to their enterprise and liberality I owe my visit to Roraima.

Mr. McTurk a Government official, who was experienced in bush life, and possessed of qualifications well suited to the purpose, had been commissioned by the Governor to superintend the expedition, and towards the end of February I received intimation to join him at the settlement near the junction of the Cuyuni and Mazaruni rivers, where he awaited me with his boats.

* *Physalia atlantica.*

CHAPTER XIII.

EARLY on the morning of the 23rd of February the steamer, which was to take me part of the way to the settlement, started from Georgetown. The wharf—or stelling, as the wooden pier is called—presented an animated scene as the fruit-boats were being unloaded, and the vast quantities of pine-apples and mangoes, especially of the latter, were surprising; some of the canoes were actually overflowing with the golden fruit, and were weighed down to the water's edge. Mangoes form no inconsiderable item in the food of the blacks of Demerara.

We were soon clear of the native and foreign craft, quitted the Demerara river and proceeded in a north-westerly direction towards the Essequibo. To the mouth of that river from Georgetown is only about five and twenty miles, and so in spite of one or two delays at different landing-places on the west coast, it was not long before we found ourselves in a vast island-dotted expanse that suggested a lake rather than a river. From one side of the mainland to the other, the embouchure of the Essequibo is seventeen or eighteen miles in width, and is divided into four separate channels by islets and sandy shoals.

At Wakenaam, one of the largest of these islands, we changed steamers, as from that point a smaller one alone runs up to the settlement, fifty miles further on. Then we were fairly in the Essequibo River, whose breadth here is about eight miles. Of the mainland, we could only see now and then the fringing line of courida* bushes and the chimneys belonging to the plantations, but the island scenery was pretty and varying. In places the luxuriant vegetation had been cleared and plantain farms were seen extending far back into the surrounding bush, with a few tumble-down but picturesque huts in the foreground. These farms are chiefly owned by Portuguese, who make considerable profit out of them. Here and there in the open spaces were ovens for burning charcoal, and their proprietors—Chinese—were busily employed cutting down trees or planting rice and other vegetable products.

Mingled with the bamboos and larger trees were several varieties of palms, of which the most prominent were the Mauritias—Ite—easily recognised by the bunches of red fruit, and the dead drooping fronds which give an untidy aspect to the useful tree. There were also specimens of the jagua and numberless fan palms,† whose leaves furnish a sort of wax, but the most graceful of all were the manicoles, very straight and slim, and rising to a height of about forty feet.

At last, after some hours, the monotonous green of

* Avicenna nitida.   † Coryphæ cerifera.

the land scenery was broken by a narrow promontory, on which stands the small village of Bartica Grove, which is situated at the junction of the Essequibo and the Mazaruni. This little settlement is a favourite resort of the Indians from the interior, who come down to trade with the few Portuguese who live there. Besides the latter there are but few whites, the greater number of inhabitants being river-men, who, as their name implies, pass their lives in navigating the waters, their principal occupation being in carrying timber from the various wood-cutting locations. They are a strange race, a mixture of Dutch, Indian, and negro descent, and though skilful and hard-working in their own vocation, yet possess in a marked degree, it is said, the attributes of the half-breed, *i.e.*, all the vices of civilization and none of the virtues of the savage.

Leaving the Grove on our left, we proceeded up the Mazaruni, and in half-an hour arrived at the settlement. The view here is fresh and charming. On land the rising ground is planted with mango, palms, and shade trees, behind which are seen the neat prison buildings— for it is a Penal Settlement—and the houses of the Superintendent and other officers. Across the river some houses are situated on the bank, and also on the cleared sloping forest land, which is diversified with pasture and huge granite boulders. Below, at Bartica Grove, the mighty stream of the Essequibo is joined by that of the Mazaruni, and higher up there is another meeting of the waters, as there the Mazaruni is joined by the magnificent Cuyuni, whose mouth is nearly a mile in width.

About thirty miles up the Cuyuni is an abandoned gold mine, the sole spot in Sir Walter Raleigh's "El

Dorado " where gold has up to the present been discovered, and even here in such small quantities that
the working of it did not pay. Since the days of
Raleigh, Guiana has earned a fictitious fame, chiefly
through the extraordinary stories set abroad by that
adventurer. Historians differ regarding Sir Walter's
own belief in the existence of " El Dorado," but
it seems probable from his writings that he was
capable of believing anything. For instance, he says,
" A similar people were said to live in Guiana, on the
banks of the Caora; this may be thought a fable, yet
for my own part I am resolved it is true, because every
child in the province of Arromaia affirms all the same ;
they are called Ewaipanomi, and are reported to have
their eyes in their shoulders and their mouths in the
middle of their breasts, and that a long train of hair
groweth backwards between the shoulders." Again,
in speaking of the supposed city of El Dorado, he
says that, " for greatness, riches, and the excellent
seat, it far exceeded any city in the world, and founded
on an inland sea two hundred leagues long, like unto
the Mare Caspium."

The historian Hume says : " So ridiculous are the
tales which he tells of the Inca's chimerical empire in
the midst of Guiana; the rich city of El Dorado or
Manoa, two days journey in length, and shining with
gold and silver; the old Peruvian prophecies in favour
of the English, who, he says, were expressly named as
the deliverers of that country long before any European
had even touched there; the Amazons, or republic of
women; and in general, the vast and incredible riches
which he saw on that continent, where nobody has yet
found any treasures !"

As regards the Amazons and the Ewaipanomi, there are plenty of civilized Indians who still assert the existence of a wonderful race of beings who inhabit certain portions of Upper Guiana, which as yet have been untrodden by white men. Concerning the golden city on the inland sea, it is not improbable that the origin of the romance arose from the fact that the low alluvial lands around Lake Parima were inundated every year to such an extent that the natives navigated the forests in their canoes. The chief of a certain tribe who inhabited this locality, is said to have indulged in the luxury of a golden shower-bath every morning, that is, he powdered himself with a glittering but valueless substance called golden sand, which is merely iron ore in minute particles. Hence his cognomen, El Dorado, or the Golden Man. His palace was found to be a natural grotto, the walls of which were formed of micaceous rock that shone with a yellow metallic glitter. It may be that the glittering mica, derived from the granite which is prevalent in Guiana, deluded Raleigh into the belief that it was gold, for he says, when speaking of a ledge of " white sparre or flint," that he endeavoured to break it by all the means that he could, " because there appeared on the outside some small grains of gold . . . . of which kind of white stone (wherein gold is engendered), we saw divers hills in every part of Guiana wherein we travelled."

To return to the settlement. Immediately on landing I was met by McTurk, who, in spite of the day being far advanced, wisely determined to start at once ; and so, throwing aside those trammels of civilization, coat, collar, and waistcoat, we stepped into our boats

and were ready for our trip of two or three months
into the interior.   Two ordinary-sized boats—or
bateaus, as they are called—and a strong well-built
canoe composed the fleet.   In colour they had been
respectively painted red, white, and blue, and each was
named after a certain species of frog; the largest was
the " Bura-buraloo," the next was the " Adaba," and
the canoe was the " Akoora."   The crew consisted of
fifteen civilized Indians—Arawaak and Acawais—good
and tried men, most of whom had been on short expeditions with McTurk, and who therfore understood
his ways and were aware that when he said a thing he
meant it, that faithfulness and good conduct would be
rewarded, and laziness and bad behaviour as surely
punished.   They nearly all understood a little English,
but they preferred a sort of "pigeon" English peculiar
to McTurk, and which always reminded me of a stage
Dutchman's language.   The strongest and most intelligent Indian in each boat is the captain, who, seated in
the stern, uses his paddle to direct the course.   Next
to him in rank is the bowman, who has to keep a sharp
look out for rocks and shoals.

Each boat was laden with provisions,* which were
limited as far as possible to absolute necessaries, as
after leaving the boats we knew that the difficulties of
transportation would be very great.   In addition, there
was our own clothing—a very slender supply—guns,
ammunition, trading articles, pots and pans, &c.,

* Provisions intended to last for three months.   Six barrels of flour, one
and a half boxes of cod fish ; three bags of brown rice ; three barrels of
ship's biscuit ; one hundred and forty pounds of bacon ; seventy-five
pounds of coffee ; one barrel of sugar ; one case of brandy ; fifty pounds
of onions ; twelve gallons of split peas.   Also a small quantity of canned
provisions.

everything, certainly, reduced to a minimum, but nevertheless, forming sufficiently heavy loads.

Before starting, I cast longing eyes at two or three luxurious tent-boats, provided with awnings, lockers, and curtains, all of which were denied us; but before many days I recognised the superiority of our own, as the long drought had shallowed the river, and it would have been impossible for the deep tent-boats to have ascended some of the cataracts. Taking our seats in the centre of our respective boats, McTurk gave the word, and in an hour the strong paddles of our crews had placed a considerable distance between us and the settlement, and we were really on the way to Roraima. At one time we feared that our start would prove inauspicious, as the strong wind blowing up the river raised such waves that once or twice we were almost swamped, but gradually we gained the opposite coast, and under the lee of the land entered comparatively smooth water.

Owing to the lateness of our departure we soon had to camp, and spying an old shed near the water's edge, we landed, slung up our hammocks, and there passed the night. To a traveller, I know of no cheaper luxury than a hammock. On a former long journey through the tropics I had burdened myself with a folding bed, thinking from very slight experience that to sleep in a hammock would be impossible. But now I discovered that a well-slung hammock, in which you have placed yourself diagonally, not parallel, so that your head and feet are too elevated, is a very delightful place of rest. By day a pleasant lounge, by night a clean bed even in dirty hovels, unscalable by insects, light and compact, easily put up and easily taken down, a hammock becomes an indispensable companion, especially dear when travelling in countries where even the most necessary articles have to be limited. We could hardly have selected a more likely spot for those pests of Guiana, namely, vampires and jiggers. The former frequent the clearings around sheds and houses, and in the dead of night when all are asleep—they never pay their visits as long as even one person in a party is awake—they fasten on an exposed toe or some part of the foot and cup the sleeper, who awakes faint and exhausted. Horses and cattle suffer equally from their attacks, and fowls frequently drop dead from their perches, their life blood drained to the very last drop. As a provision against these unpleasant visitors I had provided myself with a long double blanket, so that under no circumstances could a forgetful toe exhibit itself outside its covering.

A jigger (*Pulex penetrans*), as everyone knows, is a toe-loving creature, and makes its nest under the nails, and, if allowed, lays its eggs. As they swarm in every deserted hut and in every old Indian shed, and in sand, it is impossible to avoid them; morning and evening a strict examination of the feet by a competent Indian is absolutely necessary when travelling in the interior. In spite of great care and watchfulness on our part a search was seldom unrewarded, but we never approached the number once collected by Sir Robert Schomburgh, of whom it is related that a negress once extracted eighty-three from his feet at one sitting.

But, notwithstanding jiggers and vampires, the nights on the Mazaruni are always enjoyable because there are no mosquitoes; in many parts of Guiana, especially on the Pomeroon River, these plagues are so bad that cattle have been driven wild by them, and

are always obliged to be shut up at night in mosquito-
proof sheds; there, also, a mosquito net is invariably
included in the agreement between master and labourer.
Here we were free from them, and a patent hammock
mosquito netting that had been given me by a kind
friend in Georgetown was devoted to other uses.

Next morning we made an early start, and soon
passed Coria island, on which a Dutch fort once
stood, and the last that we saw of civilization was the
little mission-house of St. Edward's, picturesquely
situated on the opposite bank of the mainland.
Above this point we entered that labyrinth of islands
which, together with the innumerable rapids and
cataracts, form the chief features of the Mazaruni River
for nearly one hundred miles. Only one of our crew
had ever ascended the river before, and, as he did not
appear to remember much about it, we determined to
keep to the main channel, as being the safest, out of
the numerous ones into which it was divided. This
was no easy matter, as, on account of the lowness of the
water, and the great breadth—between three and four
miles—of the river, it was often very difficult to decide
which was the main channel, and sometimes we found
our passage barred by shallows and had to return and
seek another.

We ascended two rapids, and then came to the rather
steep falls of Kosterbroke. A sad interest is attached
to this place, as it was here that in 1863 seven young
men lost their lives. A pleasure party, consisting of
visitors from Trinidad and others who had been
engaged in a cricket match at Georgetown, visited the
settlement and ascended the Mazaruni as far as these
rapids; whilst descending them, the tent-boat capsized

and seven of its occupants were drowned. Report says that a midshipman, who formed one of the party, was swept away and given up for lost, but was discovered later on sitting on a rock in mid channel, drying a five-pound note in the sun.

The ascent of these cataracts affords a very lively and exciting scene. All hands, except the steersman, leave the boat, a long stout hawser is fastened to her bow, and by sheer strength she is hauled up through the rushing waters. Some of the crew wade by the side of the boat, to keep her from the rocks, others swim or dive across from adjacent points to where the best purchase can be secured, and the rest, holding the rope, pull with might and main straight up the current. A charming variety exists in these rapids; sometimes they may be ascended by taking advantage of the different currents and paddling with great power diagonally across the channel; others have short but steep falls, and others again extend for a long distance in a series of steep inclines, whilst the volume of pouring water in a few is so great that boats have to be carried round them overland. At the Warimambo Rapids, which we reached soon after passing Kosterbroke, we had to unload the boats and make a portage of about two hundred yards. A lot of negro woodcutters, who sat grinning at us on the rocky banks, informed us that it would be impossible for us to haul the boat up those rapids, but our men worked splendidly, and in about two hours we had loaded the boats and were off again.

The river here presented an extraordinary appearance from its great breadth and the innumerable rocks which cropped up in every direction. Many of these

rocks were covered with the pretty pink flower of
some water-plant. The islands and the low mainland
were covered with virgin forest, whose intense green
was relieved at intervals by the blazing crimson spikes
of the kara-kara* or the various tinted canopies of
the giant moras. The mora† may be termed the
oak of the tropical forests of Guiana, as it far exceeds
other trees in dimensions; its lofty wide-spreading
branches, with glossy foliage changing from purple to
red, add a distinctive charm to the scenery, but a
deceptive one, as frequently we would exclaim. "At
last there is some rising ground," which on approach
proved to be only two or three moras towering above
the rest of the forest trees. Besides the moras, we
were continually passing many varieties of the valuable
timber with which Guiana is so plentifully supplied.
Now a green-heart‡ or a splendid purple-heart, occasionally a "letter-wood" tree and numerous "ballis,"
such as mora balli—balli meaning wood, and when
attached to a word signifies akin to: itaballi, hubaballi,
silverballi, &c.§

McTurk from practical experience in superintend-
ing Government wood-cutting was quite an authority
on timber, and cast many longing eyes on grand trunks
that would have squared from twenty to twenty-eight
inches, with a length of from seventy to eighty feet.
Overhanging the river, were also many shrubs of the
"mahoe,"‖ whose bright yellow flowers contrasted
with climbing purple petrœas and crimson passion-
flowers. But the bright colours were mere islets in

* Chaconia Calycophyllum.   † Mora excelsa.
‡ Nectandra Rodiei.   § Oreodaphne sp
‖ Hybiscus elatus.

L

the surrounding sea of green, and it was necessary to
observe closely in order to note the varying forms of
vegetable life.

After the Warimambo, we came almost immediately
on some very steep rapids, but which fortunately had
sufficient depth of water to allow of the boats being
hauled up without unloading. Here one of the crew
nearly lost his life, as he was swept off his feet by
the strong current, and only just caught the rope in
time to save himself from being carried over a
dangerous eddy, in which, as he was a weak swimmer,
he would probably have been sucked under and
drowned. He attributed his safety to the strictness
with which the Indians had observed the proper respect
due to a trogon that had flown over our heads in the
morning; they have a superstition that, if on setting
out on a journey they should turn their backs to
this species of birds, ill luck will surely follow.

That evening we camped under some fine green-
hearts that grew on the banks, which were here
higher than we had hitherto seen. At this period
camping was a very short business with us, as
owing to the prevailing fine weather no shelter
was necessary. On landing, some of the crew collected fire-wood and the cook prepared his provisions; two or three cut away the underbrush and
slung up our hammocks on suitable trees apart from
the others, and after they had hung their own the
camp was finished. As McTurk had been unable to
obtain at Georgetown a cook who was willing to work
and carry loads like the other men, we were entirely
at the mercy of the Indians, whose ideas of cookery
were of the most primitive description. To them their

rations of salt fish, rice, and fat bacon were luxuries, and a small alligator they considered a prize, but McTurk and I often agreed that our very plain fare would have been improved by even moderate cooking. Of canned meats and relishes, we had to be very sparing, but of flour we had an unlimited supply. But here again we failed in having any means of rendering the flour palatable, although it perforce formed the chief item of our meals. It was prepared in two ways; in the first, the flour was kneaded into a cake of dough, roasted on the embers and called a "bake;" in the second it was kneaded into a ball of dough, boiled in a pot and called a "dumpling;" under either name it was equally leathery and indigestible, and only with butter, of which we had a very small supply, and brown sugar, was it possible to eat it. Later on in our journey we made a slight improvement in the bakes and dumplings by adding some of "Eno's Fruit Salt," which had been recommended to us as containing valuable properties for a cooling drink in case of fever, thereby causing the flour to rise and the cakes to become lighter. It was certainly a novel baking-powder, but it succeeded. In future years should a traveller discover one of these "bakes" on the banks of the river, he will be puzzled about its origin, and will probably conclude that it is the fossil remains of some extinct species of shell fish.

The crew took it in turns to cook for themselves, whilst the smartest of them became our own particular "chef," and a strong active young fellow, called "Charlie," acted as our trenchman. Charlie could turn his hand to anything, from building a house to making a basket, and was always ready and willing; he and his duplicate, Sammy, were the ones who worked hardest in and out of the water ; they carried the heaviest loads, they shot the most game, were most skilful in raising shelters, and were the two who were never ill. Sometimes in the night a rain storm would come on, and Charlie was always ready with tarpaulins to stretch over our hammocks.

The nights were usually warm, but the mornings were chilly, and an early plunge into the river was like a warm bath, so great was the difference between the temperature of the air and water. And those morning and evening swims in the clear brown water —brown from the colouring matter of the wallaba* trees—of the broad Mazaruni were delightful, especially when contrasted with the tiny bucketful and the narrow bath-room of the hotel at Georgetown !

* Eperua falcata.

CHAPTER XIV.

"THIRTEEN o'clock," was the extraordinary and invariable announcement with which McTurk roused the slumbering Indians at daybreak. The origin of such an unwonted hour has always been wrapped in mystery to me, but it sufficed that the men understood it, and, a few minutes after the cry had resounded through the camp, coffee was ready, hammocks taken down, boats loaded, and we commenced another day of river travel. Our nights under the purple-hearts had been cool and pleasant, and had prepared us for a day which turned out to be one of incessant falls and rapids. The crews were hardly ever out of the water, and the sun poured down with such power that even the well-tanned backs of the Indians were scorched and blistered.

Between the wooded islands acres of rock rose two or three feet above the water, revealing the most curious formations and indentations, varying in size and shape from perfectly rounded bullet moulds to smooth oval cauldrons. About half-past ten we stopped for breakfast, and whilst it was being prepared I wandered around the island with my gun in search of game, but found nothing. I was not quite unrewarded however, as on passing under a low-hanging bough I received a sharp and painful nip, as if a pair of red hot pincers had taken a piece of flesh out of my back. At first I thought a snake must have stung me, but to my relief on looking back I saw it must have been done by a "marabunta," whose nest was hanging near.

The sting of these Guiana wasps is extremely painful, and it was predicted that fever would probably set in ; although it caused a good deal of inflammation, however, I was none the worse, but avoided marabunta nests in future. When paddling, the Indians were continually annoyed by large bumble-bees, which buzzed about their heads, and sometimes followed the boats for more than a mile ; I do not know what attracted them, but as they did not trouble me I could afford to laugh at the frantic efforts of the men to drive them off.

That evening we camped on the left bank of the mainland near a creek, whose cold stream was very refreshing after the warm river water we had been drinking. Here McTurk and some of the crew suffered from slight feverish attacks, but a good dose of quinine set them up again, and next morning they were ready to proceed. On this day we met with an accident which might have occasioned a very serious loss. Two of the boats had been hauled safely up a long rapid, down which the water was rushing with great velocity, but the large one—the Bura-buraloo—was struck by a wave and commenced to sink ; the crew, instead of slackening the rope, held on, and only loosened it when it was too late, as the boat drifted a short way down and sank. Fortunately it was not deep, and in less time than it takes to relate we had reached her, and rapidly unloading conveyed her contents to the neighbouring rocks. Then commenced such a drying as probably had never been witnessed on the Mazaruni before. Tarpaulins were laid, and the wet rice, soaked biscuit, and drowned peas spread over them.

The flour was not much damaged, as the water had made a cake round the inside of the barrel which kept the rest dry. The greatest loss we sustained was in the brown sugar, as not more than half was saved, and that in a semi-liquid state. This was a misfortune, as the Indians were intensely fond of sugar, and it formed part of their daily rations; indeed without it their wretchedly made coffee would have been barely drinkable. Knives, forks, and spoons were swept away, and had I not had a small travelling case with another set we should have been badly off. Our guns, clothes, and hammocks happened to be in the boat, and all were in a sad plight, but the sun shone so hot and strong that, though it drove us from the rocks to the shade of an island, everything gradually dried, and after a detention of about four hours we were enabled to proceed. Our camping ground that night was near some rocks whose formation was more extraordinary than that of any we had hitherto seen, resembling the bones of mammoths, and the fossil teeth and jaws of gigantic animals of the old world.

The following day, after ascending a few rapids and traversing the wide stretches of almost still water that lay between them, we stopped for breakfast at a pretty spot where a dry water course between two islands formed a dark cool lane, overhung by the meeting branches. Wandering up this I disturbed a beautiful Ara humming-bird,* which I recognised by its two long tail feathers, and the flash of red and golden green. He flew from a dead tree—which had been split down the middle, probably by some wandering Indians to obtain honey, as I found the glutinous remnants of an enormous comb—and then returned to it, but I could not catch another glimpse of him, although I searched long and ardently, as I was anxious to obtain a specimen of this gorgeous little creature.

Near this place we shot some fine macaws, whose long scarlet and blue tail feathers were quickly made into head-dresses by the crew. With the exception of parrots and cranes, we had not seen up to the present time a great variety of birds; the most numerous were orioles, trogons, and toucans. The latter were a never-failing source of amusement, as, with slow and jerky flight like that of a woodpecker, the ungainly birds crossed and recrossed the river, uttering their monotonous cry, " Tucáno, tucáno." The commonest of this species was the large one called by the Indians " bouradi," whose enormous bill is of the most brilliant and variegated tints of red, yellow, blue, and black. The crested cassique† was another common bird, and the only one which uttered musical sounds; it was very delightful to hear one of them pouring forth his rich and ventriloquial notes, and with raised crest and outspread golden tail singing love-songs to his mate as she swung in her aerial hammock.

Some of the pouch nests of these birds that we saw

* Topaza pella.   † Cacicus citrius.

must have been nearly three feet in length, and, as they are invariably suspended from the ends of most slender boughs, they are safe from the rapacious maws of monkeys and other marauders. As a further pre-caution against danger, it is said that they always build on trees where the the dreaded marabuntas have their nests, and in return for the protection thus afforded feed their young on the larvæ of their patron insects.

We were now approaching what we had heard were the most formidable cataracts in the river, namely, those of Yaninzaec, and hardly had we with difficulty dragged the boats up one set of rapids before we heard a roar of water that betokened a great fall. A turn in the river then brought us in full view of a most pictu-resque scene. Forming a crescent were five separate cataracts, fifteen or twenty feet in height, and divided from one another by wooded islets. The river rushed with great force over the rocky barriers, and the foam flakes were carried past us in large white masses, or before reaching us were caught in the back eddies and lay like snow-banks under the green bushes.

When we first appeared, a great jabiru*—or negro cap, as it is sometimes called on account of its black head and neck—was stalking about under the falls; and above, on a ledge of rock overhung by the golden flowers of the cedar-bush, three white egrets stood and looked in amazement at our unexpected intrusion, then gather-ing up their long legs flapped off to a distant tree.

After a lengthened investigation as to how we could reach the top of the falls, we discovered the Indian "portage;" so, after landing, we unloaded the boats, carried the baggage over the rocks for a distance of

* Mycteria Americana.

about one hundred yards, and then camped. That night I was awakened by the patter, patter of heavy rain on the leaves overhead, and discovered that McTurk—who always provided for my comfort before he thought of his own—had stretched the only available tarpaulin over my hammock, and that he himself was crouching under a tree trunk trying to keep his hammock dry. On these journeys a dry hammock is of the utmost importance, as, if it once gets wet, it takes a long time to dry, and fever is the inevitable result of sleeping in a damp one.

The rain forced us to commence our day's work even earlier than usual, and so by seven o'clock we had carried the boats over the " portage " on our shoulders, had loaded them, and were again wading through the rapids above the falls of Yaninzaec. Shortly afterwards we passed on our left the Cabuni River, which here empties itself into the Mazaruni, and then another baggage portage became necessary. Then two more cataracts were overcome, and on the following day we arrived at a fine stretch of river comparatively free from rapids. On that day we were gladdened by the first sight of hills, but still the scenery remained tame and monotonous. Only here and there was the all-pervading green, stained by the young dark-crimson leaves of the wallaba trees, and but for the slim matapolo palms scattered in places, and the hot sun, we might have been anywhere rather than in the tropics.

Only when we landed and on penetrating the forest could we appreciate the strange forms and luxuriant growth of the tropical vegetation. Then we saw the great moras and Bertholletias strangled in the folds of some gigantic creeper, and with their branches laden with arums and the curiously indented leaves of the pothos family ; twisted bush-ropes and lianes of all de-scriptions linked the trees together and chained them to the earth, and while the ground was free from heavy growth, a chaos of intermingling plants and foliage formed a dense canopy overhead. In many places on the river, and especially near the rapids, we had seen the dams which the roving Indians had made for the purpose of catching fish, but we had not seen any of the natives ; now, however, we knew that we were at last approaching them, for on the rocks around one of the dams we discovered some freshly beaten hai-arí roots which had been used for poisoning the water.

Fishing with poison is a favourite method with the Indians, as they thereby obtain the greatest quantity of fish with the least possible exertion. Dams are built on the rocky ledges with loose stones, and with spaces left open for the fish to enter ; the roots of the hai-arí—a leguminous creeper—are beaten on the rocks with heavy clubs until they are in shreds, which are then soaked in water ; the yellow acrid juice thus obtained is finally poured into the ponds after the inlets have been stopped. In a few minutes the fish appear on the surface, floating aimlessly about as if intoxicated, and are either shot with arrows, or knocked on the head with clubs. Enormous numbers are some-times killed in this manner. The flesh of the fish so destroyed, receives no more deleterious qualities than does that of the forest game which the natives shoot with arrows poisoned with the deadly " wourali." For preservation, a barbecue is erected, and the fish are smoked over a fire.

In the open river, other means have to be adopted for obtaining fish, and the usual method is with the bow and arrow. Indians are not only wonderfully quick in seeing fish, but also possess great skill in shooting them, and, when it is remembered that allowance has to be made for refraction, the resistance of the water, and the movements of the fish, it is surprising how successful some of them are. McTurk, who was no mean performer himself with the bow, told me of most extraordinary shots that he had witnessed. Amongst our crew we had no very brilliant marksmen, and we had to depend in a great measure for our supplies on the Indians whom we chanced to meet. Seven or eight different kinds of arrows are used, and each has its own particular name. One of the most curious has its iron or bone point only slightly fixed to the shaft, and to it is attached a long string which is neatly wound round the stem. When the fish is hit the point detaches itself, the line runs off, the floating arrow shows the position of the fish, and the Indian at once gives chase. All the arrows are very long, some that we used being between five and six feet in length, and made from the stem of a certain reed.*

Several delicately flavoured fish are found in the Mazaruni, but the most delicious of all is the pacu,† which feeds on a species of lacis that grows abundantly near falls and rapids. They are very shy, but their red gold colour renders them easily discernible in the clear pools. Owing to the extent of water-poisoning which had preceded our ascent of the river, we had only obtained one of these fish, but now, as we were

---

* Gynericum.   † Myletes pacu.

approaching the Indian camp, we hoped to obtain a
good supply of both fresh and smoked.

Suddenly we espied a solitary Indian paddling with
might and main to get away from us; we gave chase,
but in his light wood-skin he speedily distanced us.
Then at the end of a long stretch of river we saw
what appeared to be a line of animals swimming across.
It proved to be a string of canoes, whose occupants,
frightened at the appearance of the white men's boats,
had left their fishing ground and were making all
haste to their camp. This we soon reached, and found
about twenty men, women, and children squatting on
the rocks like brown monkeys, and evidently very
nervous about the strangers. They proved to be
Acawais, and could certainly not be complimented
on their good looks. They were short of stature,
had olive complexions, and hair like a black mop.
The women added to their charms by a few pot-hooks
tattooed into the corners of the mouth, and by staining
their limbs with blue stripes, which at a distance gave
the idea of tight-fitting drawers. But their dress was
strictly one of imagination, a few square inches of bead
apron—queyou—taking the place of the old original
cestus. The men were attired in the buck-skin
suits in which they were born, with some pieces
of straw in their nose and ears, and instead of
a bead apron they wore a strip of calico called a
" lap."

The poor things looked very thin and half-starved,
and we learn that owing to the drought the cassava
crop had been a poor one, and they had been reduced
to eating a wretched sort of bread made from the
grated nuts of the green-heart, and now had descended

the river on a fishing expedition. Moore in one of his poems asks:

> " Know you what 'midst such fertile scenes
> That awful voice of famine means ?"

To such a question these Indians might answer "yes." A more improvident race does not exist; as long as they can satisfy their immediate wants they are content. They seldom live on the banks of the large rivers, but build their huts—two or three of which often constitute a village —near some retired creek. There they plant a little cassava, and when that is exhausted they pack their household goods on their backs, and, as they express it, "walk" *i.e.*, they wander about wherever fancy leads them, pitching their camp sometimes for a day, and sometimes for weeks in one place. In an indolent fashion they will hunt and fish, and, when they have no game, live on wild berries; occasionally when they have anything to sell they will paddle leisurely down to the Settlements and paddle back in the same easy manner. Time is no object to them, except when a paiworie* feast and dance are on the *tapis*. To be present on such an occasion they

---

* Paiworie is a drink made from cassava bread, which is prepared in the same disgusting way, viz.: by chewing, as is the "kava" of the islanders of the South Seas. When a drinking feast is at hand the women are occupied for several days in chewing cassava, which with the addition of hot water gradually fills an enormous wooden trough, shaped like a canoe, and capable of containing a hundred and fifty gallons. On the appointed day, the invited guests dressed in their best feathers and decorated with teeth and beads in the latest styles, assemble round the trough. A preliminary song and dance are indulged in, then the calabashes are dipped into the intoxicating beverage, and the orgie commences. It does not finish until the paiworie is exhausted, or not a soul is left with a leg to stand upon. The scenes incident to such a performance need no description.

will travel great distances, in an incredibly short time, they will ascend and descend rivers, cross mountains, penetrate forests, and die from exhaustion rather than forego the effort necessary to obtain a drink of paiworie. Our friends had no fresh fish, but we obtained a few dried pacu, averaging five or six pounds each, and some fish arrows, of which we were in want, in exchange for fish-hooks and a little salt. Indians are very fond of salt, and as they can only obtain it in trade it forms a good article of barter.

We did not camp that evening until we had placed some distance between ourselves and the natives, as, when the latter think that anything is to be obtained from white men, they will follow and keep near them as long as they can, although the direction may be the opposite to that in which they themselves were originally travelling.

The next day the river was freer than usual from rapids, and we were enabled to replenish our larder, which up to the present had been sadly deficient in fresh meat. Some golden red howling monkeys—baboons the men called them—were our first acquisition, and the chase they gave us through the forest, though very amusing, covered us with garrapatas—large ticks—and the equally annoying bête rouge. The latter insect is of a bright scarlet, and so small as hardly to be distinguished, but it causes great irritation, and if the skin is scratched it ulcerates, and like all other sores and wounds in the tropics is difficult to heal. Then we shot two young alligators each about three feet in length ; it was strange that although on the Mazaruni we saw several baby alligators, yet we never saw any large ones. Of game birds we bagged a paui, curassow,* and two maroudis, a species of wild turkey. The Indians say that the maroudi obtained its bare red throat by swallowing a fire-stick which it mistook for a glow-worm.

Two sorts of water-birds, were very plentiful, namely: ducklars† and curri-curris.‡ We did not often fire at the former, unless we were very badly off for fresh meat, as, irrespective of their ability to carry off an incredible amount of the largest shot, they are fishy, ill-flavoured birds. But the curri-curris, so called from their peculiar cry, are by no means to be despised, and probably being aware of their eatable properties generally disappeared into the thick bush, just out of range. These birds are of an olive and bronze colour, feed snipe-like on worms, and have a heavy flight, similar to that of an owl.

Sometimes we startled a little sun-bittern, and occasionally we crept near enough to watch him in his motions whilst fascinating an insect; then his body would writhe and twist, his slender neck undulating like a serpent's folds, but all the time with head quiet and eye steadily fixed on his victim; finally there was a quick darting movement, and there was no more insect. Our day's sport was brought to a conclusion by spearing a very large electric eel. It was Saturday night, and according to custom McTurk's cry of " Grog-oh" speedily brought the crew to receive their weekly glass —dose they called it—of brandy, and this well-earned medicine infused such life into their tired bodies that we were kept awake for a long time by the monotonous strains of an old fiddle with which they were " making dance."

* Crax alector.　　† Plotius anhinga.　　‡ Ibis infuscata.

The next day we remained in our camp below Turesie cataract, and as somebody shot a deer, and somebody else a maroudi, we had a grand Sunday dinner consisting of:

SOUP.
Macaw.

FISH.
Smoked pacu and Electric eel.

SIDE DISHES.
Curried monkey, Maroudi à la Turesie.

JOINT.
Haunch of Venison.

BAKES.
Dumplings, Sea biscuit.

—

Coffee and Eno's Fruit Salt *ad lib.*

M

CHAPTER XV.

TOWARDS midnight I was aroused by a low
rustling sound in the bushes; as I
glanced around, my eye fell on an old mora tree just
opposite, and at the foot of my hammock, there on
the grey trunk I plainly saw the shadow of a
snake's head and neck. From its position, there could
be no doubt that it was close beside me, and almost
over my head, its body being half hidden by the
branches of one of the trees in which it was coiled.
As I watched, the head and neck moved towards me
and drew back in slow undulating movements, the
forked tongue shot out and seemed almost to touch
me. I did not dare to move, and hardly to breathe,
as the reptile seemed only waiting for my slightest
motion in order to strike. The minutes that I lay
there with my eyes fixed on the horrid shadow seemed
like hours; all sorts of thoughts passed across my
brain; had I the night-mare? could the curried monkey have disagreed with me? I was wet with per-
spiration and at last could stand it no longer, but,

slowly disentangling my feet from the blanket,
threw myself forward and sprang to the ground.
Seizing my gun, I pointed it to where the snake must
have been, but there was no appearance of one, and a
careful search revealed nothing. Then I went to bed
again, and there in front of me, on the tree, was the
same writing form and shooting tongue. I put up
hand, and its shadow almost grasped the neck of the
creature ; then I raised myself, and looking up saw my
enemy. A projecting twig and a few leaves gently
swayed by the breeze were all that remained of my
snake, but the shadow they cast was so exactly that
of a serpent that when I pointed it out to McTurk he
fully believed for a moment that it was one.

The forests of Guiana are well furnished with everything that a traveller can want in the shape of beast
or insect, and in snakes they are especially prolific. Of
these, the "bush-master"* is the most dreaded, and
as its name implies, is lord of the woods. In colour it
is as brilliant as its bite is venomous. The "labarri"†
is equally poisonous, but is not so aggressive as the
"bush-master." The "camoodi"—a boa-constrictor—
is the largest of all the snakes, and the stories of their
enormous size and strength would be incredible to any
one who had not travelled in Guiana. A gentleman
in Georgetown solemnly assured me that once when he
was out shooting in the interior, with a party of seven
others, they stopped to rest after a long walk and all
sat down on a falling trunk ; all at once it began to
move, and what they had imagined to be the trunk of
a tree proved to be an immense "camoodi," which
glided slowly into the forest without being fired at by

* Lachesis rhombeata.   † Trigonocephalus.

any of the amazed spectators. The "water-camoodi"* is even larger and more dangerous than the land species.

It was destined that our night after the shadow-snake incident should not pass wholly destitute of the pleasures of camp life, as, on putting on my hat before starting, I found that it was wreathed round and round with the clay tunnels of the wood-ant, thousands of which had taken advantage of its position, at the foot of a tree, to erect on it their covered ways before they climbed up aloft. Charlie was highly amused at the appearance of the hat, but soon rid it of its inhabitants by holding it over a fire.

After ascending the fails of Turesie we noticed a long reed performing strange evolutions in the water ; this the Indians knew to be an arrow with a pacu at the end of it, which had been shot and then lost by a native. We at once gave chase, and a most amusing hunt followed. Whenever we approached it, one of the crew plunged into the river, and immediately the arrow disappeared to come up again fifty yards off in another direction. This was repeated until the poor fish was tired out and at last landed. Another excitement was in store for us, as hardly had the pacu been caught before we saw in the distance a deer swimming across the river. Away went the three boats in full cry, but the light canoe soon led the chase, and it was a pretty sight to see her shoot through the water amidst a shower of rainbows raised by the splendidly sweeping paddles. Now she gains on the deer, no, the animal will reach the shore; to shoot would be useless, as the body would sink ; now he

* Eunectes murinus.

flags, as the distance he has already swum is great, the "Akoora" flies through the water, the crew are near enough to hear the panting of the victim, and the next minute is his last. He proved to be a fine young buck, and was a great acquisition to our stores. I am afraid I did not want him to escape, until he had been captured; but I did then, it seemed so hard that he should have chosen the moment of our arrival for his swim.

Soon after our deer chase we saw a splendid cashew* tree loaded with purple-red fruit. This was a treat not to be neglected, and so in a quarter of an hour the tree was down and stripped. The fruit was tart, but extremely refreshing and of a pleasant flavour Near this place I took a shot at a parrot, and brought him down so little hurt that by the evening he had quite recovered his spirits, and in two days was perfectly tame. He became a great pet, and, as he called himself "Pourri," we christened him so. Later on, when one of the boats was sent back to the settlement, he accompanied it, and there I found him well and happy on my return.

The river now was freer from impediments than it had been hitherto; the islands were fewer, and occasionally we were in sight of both banks. Owing to its shallowness, sand-banks were numerous, and we frequently were obliged to get out of the boats and push and lift them over. We camped that evening in sight of a range of hills near the Issano river. An Indian who had been following us at a distance in his woodskin,† since the previous day, here came up to

---

* Anacardium occidentale.

† A woodskin is constructed out of a single piece of bark of a tree—

us. He was skinny and shy, but as berries and cashews had of late formed his chief support, hunger overcame his timidity, and he was thankful for some venison. A few matches pleased him highly, as he had never seen any before, and the small fire which was burning in his boat must have been a continued source of trouble, as if it went out, the relighting of it was a laborious process.

Before sunrise next morning we were afloat on a beautiful clear expanse of water, with a white sandy beach under the trees on both sides. A silvery haze lay over the silent river, and the western hills were seen as if through a filmy veil. As the sun rose, the silver changed to gold in a flood of light that touched the hill crests, and then pouring over the strange, peaceful land, cast rare tints and shades among the drooping trees and into the forest depths. Our painted boats were quite in accord with the bright scene, and the gay feather ornaments of the crews and the gleam of the paddles were strikingly effective. The sky was of a frosty blue, unrelieved by a single cloud.

Near where we stopped for breakfast was an Indian shed—banaboo—and there we found numerous jaws of the pirai, and we were thankful that in our morning bath we had escaped these voracious fish.

---

generally the purple-heart. After the bark has been removed from the wood it is kept open by cross sticks, and the extremities are supported on beams so as to raise those parts. A more cranky affair cannot be imagined, and even to step into one required the greatest care ; and if upset it sinks instantly, owing to the great specific gravity of the bark, which is hardly one-eighth of an inch in thickness. Its great advantage is that it can float where no boat or canoe could possibly pass Some of the large ones will carry six or seven persons and their effects.

The pirai* is not large, but its jaws are so strong
and teeth so sharp that it can take off a finger or
a toe at a bite. It will attack anything, even an
alligator, and ducks and geese seldom have any feet
where this species of fish exists, but a man bathing is
an object of peculiar attraction to it. Its flesh is coarse
and bony, but the Indians eat it.

Several times that day our attention was directed to
a peculiar humming noise, like the distant burr of
machinery in motion, proceeding from the water over
which we passed. McTurk and the Indians, who had
heard similar sounds on the Pomeroon and other rivers,
said that they were uttered by singing fish. That it
was fish-music there was no doubt, as the nearer we
placed our ears to the water the more distinct were the
sounds, and on dropping a stone they ceased for a
moment and then re-commenced. The tone was by
no means inharmonious, and resembled the hum of a
busy city heard from a high church steeple, or the voice
of Saint Francis reading prayers to the fish, to which
they were repeating the responses.

As we approached the Teboco hills, one of our
Acawais said that he had an uncle who lived in a
village not far from the river, and asked permission to
visit him. This was readily granted by McTurk,
and on finding the landing we all went ashore, and
the Indian, quickly dressing himself in a clean shirt
and an old hat, evidently with the intention of
astonishing the natives and showing them what
civilization had done for him, started off with two
companions on a two-mile walk through the forest.
On the high bank near where we had landed we found

* Serra salmo.

an old shed, and near it, not in it, as it probably contained a rich entomological collection, we prepared breakfast, and then awaited the arrival of the absentees.

After a delay of nearly three hours our Indians arrived, and they were quickly followed by the strangest procession I have ever seen. Along the narrow forest path, which led from the clearing in which we were seated, stalked in single file, noiselessly and solemnly, the whole of the inhabitants from the Indian village. There were only twelve or thirteen altogether, men, women, and children, but their slow march and the long intervals between each gave magnitude to their number. As they arrived they touched our hands, and then retired to a short distance, the children trying to hide themselves behind their mothers, but with little success. It was with the utmost difficulty that we could refrain from loud bursts of laughter, so utterly ridiculous was the appearance of the natives. The men were short, but stoutly proportioned, and wore the customary "lap" and bright feathers in their hair. A few had little patches of white fluff stuck about their faces, and all were freshly painted. Their heads were got up in a very elaborate style; the parting of their long black hair was dyed vermillion, and a Vandyck pattern of the same brilliant colour ran round the forehead. Through the nose and ears of each were passed yellow straws or strips of wood, those of the ear resting on that of the nose, and giving a most humorous expression to their pathetic countenances. Some carried a blow-pipe, others a bow and arrows. In addition to their bead aprons, the women wore broad armlets and anklets of beads, and their bodies and limbs were

stained and painted in stripes with crimson "arnotto"*
and blue black "lana."† They were tall in propor-
tion to the men and had well-turned limbs, but in
features were coarse and plain.

We were anxious to secure the services of a man
who was acquainted with the river and its tributaries;
so, selecting the strongest, we found he was willing to
accompany us, and at once sent his son for his hammock.
In the interval, the ladies and gentlemen entertained us
with a dance. Placing their hands on each other's
shoulders, they formed into line, and advanced and
retreated in a kind of jig. As there were only two
or three steps in it, it became monotonous to all but
the dancers, who continued their amusement until the
arrival of the hammock. The wife of our late acquisition then bitterly lamented the departure of her
husband, and seemed inclined to accompany us herself, but as there was no room for her we had to
decline her offer; then she burst into tears and would
not be comforted. As a last resource we produced
some beads, and immediately tears were dried and the
mourning wife was changed to a merry coquette, whose
only anxiety was concerning the colour of the ornaments. Shakespeare says:—

> " Win her with gifts, if she respects not words,
>   Dumb jewels often in their silent kind,
>   More than quiet words, do move a woman's mind."

Fashion reigns in the wilds of Guiana as it does in the
regions of civilization, and it is of no small importance
to a traveller that his *negotia*—beads, knives, &c.,—
should be of the proper colour, shape, or description.

We christened our new hand "Mazaruni," not

---

* Bixa Orellana. † Genipa Americana.

because his name was William—he said he had been
called William during a visit he had paid to the settlement—but because we already had most of the common
Christian names among our crew. Paiworie and fresh
cassava had been the cause of our delay in the first
instance, and a bowl of that unpleasant beverage was
brought for the entertainment of our Indians, who
thoroughly enjoyed it. Two woodskins, containing
friends of Mazaruni, accompanied us as far as the
Teboco hills, and there left us, as our course was
deflected due south for some distance. This part of
the river was very pretty, as from each bank numerous
points ran out, all thickly wooded with trees of various
shades. Before we reached the southern extremity of
of this river-bend we obtained a beautiful view of the
Karanang Hills, and beyond them, to the south, we saw
in the far distance a high table-mountain, and behind
that again a lofty peak, dim and hazy, but standing out
in clear outline against the pale blue of the evening
sky. This sugar-loaf peak was said by Mazaruni to
be that of Illuie, but on our return another native
who was with us gave it a different name.* After
passing the mouth of the Semang River on our left,
we rounded the Teboco promontory by ascending the
pretty falls of Teboco, and continued on our way in a
northerly direction. That evening we camped, during
a rain storm, on the left bank of the Mazaruni, opposite

* We found it very difficult to determine with any exactness the names
of mountains and falls, not only on account of the names themselves, but
also from the Indian habit of slurring over the last syllables. Then again
different tribes have different names for localities, and not unfrequently
the various parts of mountains and even of rapids are called by various
denominations. By constant repetition we approached as nearly as we
could to the names uttered.

the Karanang River. Next day we varied our game-
bag by shooting some snipe, and the numerous fresh
tracks of tapirs gave us hopes of obtaining large game,
but a small accourie* was the only four-footed creature
we got. This little rodent figures prominently in Indian
mythology.

One of the legends runs thus; the inhabitants
of the sky once peeped through a hole that they had
been told not to approach, and on looking down saw
another world. They therefore cut down long bush-
ropes and let themselves down. After wandering about
they became frightened and began to ascend the ladder,
but an old lady of too ample proportions stuck in the
hole, and, during the fighting and scrambling that
ensued the rope broke and many had to remain on
earth. Then, as they had no provisions they became
very lean, but noticing that the accourie was always
plump they set the woodpecker to watch its feeding
ground. But the woodpecker betrayed himself by his
tapping. Then the alligator was told to watch, and he
found out, but came back and told a lie, so they cut
out his tongue.† Then the rat was sent off, but he
never returned and the people starved. They wandered
off and left a little child behind, and when they returned after a long time, having lived on berries, they
found the child alive and well, and surrounded by
Indian corn cobs that the accourie had fed it with.
Then the child followed the accourie after its next

---

* Dasyprocta agouti.

† The Indians to the present day do not recognise in the alligator that
shapeless fleshy mass, which is incapable of extension, as a tongue.
Herodotus, too, who was a keen observer of the crocodile, repeats the
idea that it is tongueless, and for that reason was regarded by the
Egyptians as an emblem of mystery.

visit and discovered the maize field, and the people were saved. In gratitude, they kill and eat the delicate little animal whenever they have the opportunity.

In their tradition of the Deluge, maize takes the place of the olive branch. They say that only one man was saved in his canoe, and when he sent out a rat to discover land, it brought back a head of Indian corn. The Caribs, in their account of the Creation, say that the Great Spirit sat on a mora tree, and picking off pieces of the bark threw them into the stream, and they became different animals. Then the Great Spirit—Makanaima—made a large mould, and out of this fresh, clean clay, the white man stepped. After it got a little dirty the Indian was formed, and the Spirit being called away on business for a long period the mould became black and unclean, and out of it walked the negro. All the Indian tribes of Guiana— Acawais, Arawaaks, Arecunas, Warraus, Macusis, &c.—rank themselves far higher than the negro race, and the Caribs consider themselves the first of the tribes, calling themselves "the" people, and their language " the " language.

Ever since our departure we had regretted that we had brought no dog with us, as without one it was almost impossible to drive the labba* or the great pig-like water haas† from their lair amongst the reeds and moco-mocos‡ that lined the banks. The labba and tapir being nocturnal in their habits were hardly ever seen by us, and it was only occasionally that we chanced to see the day-feeding animals. We fre-

* Paca caligenis.   † Capybara.
‡ Caladium arborescens.

quently tried to buy an Indian dog from the natives, but they invariably declined to part with them.

After leaving Teboco, we encountered no more falls or rapids of any importance, having up to that time ascended about thirty and gained an elevation above the sea of about two hundred feet. Continuing our northerly course, we saw towards the north-west a long table mountain known as the Comaka, which was much broken and very jagged at the northern extremity. On our left was the precipitous hill of Tamanua, wooded far up its sides and then presenting a massive face of rock, seamed and scarred in places with ravines and crevices. Over the strange mountain crests rain clouds continually came and went, and storms which never failed to deluge us in their progress hurried past on their way to the hill regions.

At last from north our direction changed to west, and after about six miles of this westerly course we arrived at the mouth of the Merumé river. Twenty miles to the south lay the Merumé mountains, in which the Mazaruni has its source. The course of this river is a very singular one, completely enclosing a great area of country, with the exception of the narrow strip of land, twenty miles in breadth, between its source and the mouth of the Merumé.*

* In speaking of the course of the Mazaruni, Mr. Barrington Brown in his " Geology of British Guiana," says that it rises in the " Merumé -mountains, part of the Pacaraima group, at a height of 2,400 feet above the sea, near the 60th degree of west longitude ; it runs eastward for some miles, curving round to the south in 68° 8′ 30″ west longitude, and 5° 34′ 23″ north latitude, and descends to a level of 2,000 feet. From this it flows in a tortuous course in a west-north-west direction to the Cako river mouth, in 60″ 44′ west and 5° 47′ 11″ north, being joined on the way by numerous large tributaries, and descending by a set of high falls at Chi-chi to a level of 1,400 feet above the sea. Flowing smoothly along

It had been our intention to ascend the Merumé as far as possible, then, striking across the mountains, to cross the head waters of the Mazaruni, and reaching the Oweang river, down which we could travel in woodskins, again meet the Mazaruni in its course westward. Owing to the shallowness of the Merumé, we found it would be impossible to ascend that river in our boats, and there were no woodskins to be obtained. We therefore determined to continue our course up the Mazaruni, until we reached the Curipung river, which our new hand, Mazaruni, assured us would have a sufficient depth of water as far as the commencement of the overland path. Within three days we expected to arrive at the mouth of the Curipung.

at this altitude in a north-north-west direction to Sericoeng, it is precipitated down a succession of lofty falls, occupying a distance of eight miles to a level of 500 feet. Passing along at this level with a north-north-east course, it plunges over two more sets of falls to a height of 150 feet, and, emerging from the sandstone mountains in 6° 26′ 14″ north latitude, turns suddenly to the east-north-east for a distance of 105 miles to Teboco cataract, passing on the way near the foot of the Merumé mountains, 20 miles to the northward of its source.

CHAPTER XVI.

IT has been well said that mountains are privileges, blessings ; Ararats whereon the dove of thought may alight when weary of the deluge around. And truly after the level country we had been traversing, it was an unutterable relief to gaze on the strange forms and picturesque colouring of the cliffs and crags that rose up around us. Though in height they did not approach the sublime order of mountains, yet their forest slopes, broken with clefts and chasms, and their perpendicular flat-topped walls, streaked here with clinging shrubs, and there glistening with falling water, were more suggestive of the wonderful land changes, yet more mysterious than the rounded and lofty forms of some grand Sierras. They resembled Cyclopean monuments scattered through the grave-yard of a universe.

On the day after passing the Merumé river, we saw two natives carrying some large fish ; as soon as they caught sight of us, they took to their heels and fled over the sand-bank on which they had been walking towards the bush. As we were in want of fish we called to them, but the more we called the faster they ran. Then Mazaruni gave evidence of his value, as with a grunt of indignation at the silly fear of his countrymen, he jumped into the water and speeded after the fugitives. It was a most laughable chase and won eventually by Mazaruni, who returned triumphantly with his heavily-weighted captives. They gladly sold us two of their pacus, but would not part with more, as they required them for their own camp, which was pitched somewhere up the Cabeparu creek, near which we were. Shortly afterwards, we captured two more pacus that had lately been shot, and they afforded us a more amusing hunt than even those of the previous week.

On account of the number of electric eels and sting-rays it was dangerous work jumping carelessly out of the boat, and in the last hunt one of the crew touched a ray with his foot but fortunately without receiving any injury. In appearance a ray is rather like a frying-pan, and its lance-like tail, fringed with a series of barbs, is a most terrible weapon. The wound it inflicts causes great agony and is always followed by severe inflammation. It frequents shallows, where it lies half buried in the sand, and its yellow colour renders it difficult to distinguish. The flesh is eatable, when you can get nothing else, and we speared many of them with a bayonet fastened to a long pole, or shot them with arrows. Some were of enormous size and defied both arrow and spear.

The next day we met a party of Indian hunters dressed in the costume of the chase, *i.e.*, in feathers, and armed

blow-pipes and bows, but they had no game. We
found out from them where we could obtain a certain
liane called "mamurie," which we were in search of
in order to make "quakes" for our overland journey.
We therefore camped early that day on the left bank
of the river, and the men were sent into the woods to
look for the required vine. As we ascended the river
from Teboco, we had noticed in some distant hills a
remarkable rocky peak which is called " the Caribisce,"
from the legend stating that it is an Indian hunter who
was turned into stone for daring to ascend the mountain. To-day from our camp, we saw in the direction
from which we had come, east, another curious peak
rising like a gigantic thimble from a flat table-mountain. The name of this is Sororieng *i.e.,* Swallow's
Nest, and it is an object of much dread to the superstitious Indians. Not far from it was the rugged outline
of Ishagua, and far away in the south-west we saw the
misty range of the Curipung mountains.

We had chosen a pretty spot for the camp, where
on the high bank big moras and solemn ceibas cast a
pleasant shade over rocky pools, deep and clear, in
which small and large fish played near the surface.
Among them McTurk thought he recognized a
lucanani* and fished zealously for a couple of hours,
but without success. I suggested that perhaps the fish
saw him; he was dressed in scarlet flannel knicker-
bockers, and in his Scotch cap he wore the macaw's tail
feathers, that even the greediest fish could hardly have

---

* The "lucanani," or sun-fish, so called from a golden ring in its tail,
weighs five or six pounds, and its flesh is by many preferred to that of the
pacu. A peculiarity in the habits of this fish is that, when the young
—which always swim near the mother—are in danger, the mother opens
her mouth and they all rush in.

mistaken for a fly—at all events we got no lucanani
that day.   But the fisherman was delightfully picturesque.

Then we strolled through the dark forest, where
great butterflies, with wings whose outer side was of a
dull brown, whilst the under part was of metallic blue,
flapped heavily along.   Blue morphos, too, of a most
lustrous sheen glanced here and there, and danced
through the foliage like the will-o-the-wisp. Besides these
there were not many other species, some pretty
swallow-tails and heliconias being the chief representatives of the diurnal lepidoptera.*

Under the fallen trees were several species of
brilliant beetles, and occasionally a great golden green
buprestis† whizzed past us. This beetle is very
common, and its wings are used by the Indians for
armlets and anklets.   The few flowering plants that
we saw were yellow; an oncidium, the mahoe, cedar-
bush, ginger-wort, and other cannas, all were yellow.
The prettiest leaf was that of a crimson-veined cala-

---

* During our journey the principal butterflies that we noticed were as
follows :—

"Morpho Adonis," of the most brilliant azure blue.

"Urania Leilus," with black velvet ground and golden green bands of
a silky lustre, and black tail.

"Marius Thetis," tawny, with narrow black lines.

"Erycina Octavius," dark bands and crimson spots, long black tail
with crimson patch.

"Papilio Æneas," velvet black wings, with red patch in middle of
hinder wing, upper wings with large green spot.

"Papilio Sinon," black wings with pale green bands.

"Callidryas Eubule," surface of wings a fine yellow.

"Vanessa Amathea," dark brown surface, with broad band of deep
red across centre of wings, which are edged with white spots.

"Heliconia Cynisca," surface deep black, red at base of upper wings,
under wings with red stripes.

† Buprestis gigas.

dium, the bulb of which had probably been dropped by
an Indian on his way through the forest. The natives
are fond of this plant, often bringing it back with
them from their journeys to the settlement and using
it medicinally. When the crew returned they
brought a good supply of " mamurie," and in addition
one had a large land· tortoise, another had some toucans,
whilst a third had seen some wonderful animal or other,
but of course had no gun with him. The rest of the
day was spent in basket-making.

Just before sun-down the noisy monkeys commence
their usual chorus ; cranes and egrets betook themselves
to their resting places ; macaws and parrots crossed the
river, uttering their harsh good-nights, and were
answered by "pourri," who had not forgotten when
they, too, wended their evening flight over the waters ;
and finally, with a rush of wings and with weird minor
cries, the green ibises—curri-curris—flew by and disappeared in the gloom—

> " And far away in the twilight sky
> We heard them singing a lessening cry,
> Farther and farther till out of sight,
> And we stood alone in the silent night."

When we left next morning, the Giant's Thimble was
just touched by the rising sun, and after we had
crossed a fine reach of river, we had a fresh mountain
view. In the distance it looked like a single mountain,
much broken and castellated in the centre, and with
table ends. Mazaruni informed us that the central
position was called Tapusing and the flat Aricanna ;
so probably they were two mountains, one standing in
front of the other.

Soon afterwards we passed a peculiar rock in the

middle of the river, somewhat resembling a human figure; the Indians thought it was a river god watching for pacu. Strange rock formations had been the rule rather than the exception in all parts of the river, and owing to its unusual shallowness, we had been able to notice the action of the water on the various developments, such as granite, porphyry, green stone, gneiss, &c., below the ordinary low-water mark. Hitherto we had seen no Indian village on the banks of river, although we had passed the sites of several deserted settlements, which were easily to be recognized by the forest-clearing and the new growth of bush. To day we were glad when Mazaruni told us that we were approaching the village of Masanassa, and soon, on the left bank of the river and opposite a small island, we saw a number of woodskins and evident signs of habitation. Long before we reached the landing we had been descried by the natives, who flocked to see us and escorted us to the principal house, which stood on a high bank, with a neat approach of flowering shrubs, plantains, ochro, peppers, papaws, cotton, and fruit trees. The house was merely a large shed with wattled walls. From the beams were suspended twenty-five hammocks, so that it was evident that three or four families occupied the same house. In the centre were two large paiworie troughs, and scattered about the floor, or resting on a platform overhead, were the various cassava-making implements, calabashes, tastefully fretted " pegalls "—covered baskets in which the women keep their paints and knick-knacks—quaint, low stools, parrots, accouries, and a few snarling dogs.

In appearance and dress the inhabitants were the same as we had before seen, only the men had put on their finest and largest necklaces, made of the teeth of monkeys and peccaries, and of wild-boars' tusks. To some of these necklaces were attached long cords with tassels of toucans' breasts, and various bird-skins. Some of the women were engaged in chewing cassava, whilst others were occupied in the pleasanter employment of cotton-spinning and hammock-weaving. The villagers were not particularly enthusiastic in their reception of us, and one man, with a fierce countenance horribly painted in red, lay in his hammock in an open shed outside the house, and scowled ferociously at our intrusion, but it was plain that his enmity arose from a too copious indulgence in paiworie. The chief of the house was named Lanceman, and though his knowledge of speaking English only amounted to "yes," yet he understood a few words, and seemed an intelligent man. To his care McTurk confided the baggage—tin boxes, &c.,—that would be troublesome to carry during our overland journey, and also sufficient provisions to last us on our return from his house to the settlement. He also promised to accompany us himself to Roraima, and on the following day to bring to our camp, on the Curipung, as many men as were willing to assist us as carriers.

In two hours after we left we arrived at the Curipung River, in whose broad mouth the water had shrunk to one narrow channel, just deep enough to admit our boats. Just above, however, it widened out into a stream of about fifty yards in width, and on its left bank we camped. On the other side of this creek, and bordering the Mazaruni, was a large stretch of white sand, and on its edge a number of Indians, who had come down on a fish-poisoning excursion, were

encamped. Above all other localities, an Indian is
fond of an open, sandy beach whereon to pass the
night. In the ground he sticks a few poles from
which to suspend his hammock, and if the weather is
rainy, a few palm leaves form a sufficient shelter.
There in the open, away from the dark, shadowy forest,
he feels secure from the stealthy approach of the dreaded
" kanaima ;"* the magic rattle of the "peaiman"†
has less terror for him when unaccompanied by the
weird rustling of the waving branches; and there even
the wild hooting of the " didi "‡ is bereft of that intensity with which it pierces the gloomy depths of the
surrounding woodland. It is strange that the superstitious fear of these Indians, who are bred in the forest
and hills, should be chiefly based on natural forms and
sounds. Certain rocks they will never point at with a
finger, although your attention may be drawn to them
by an inclination of the head. Some rocks they will
not even look at, and others again they beat with green
boughs. Common bird-cries become spirit-voices.
Any place that is difficult of access, or little known,
is invariably tenanted by huge snakes or horrible four-
footed animals. Otters are transformed into mermaids,
and water-tigers inhabit the deep pools and caves
of their rivers. Yet with all their superstition, I
doubt whether any of them would object to set out on
a journey on a Friday, or whether any would place
faith in " lucky numbers," and I am sure none would
refuse to join a dinner party of thirteen.

* The " kanaima" is a secret murderer who performs his work generally by poison.

† The " peaiman" is the sorcerer and doctor of the tribe.

‡ The " didi" is supposed to be a wild man of the woods, possessed
of immense strength and covered with hair.

We passed a whole day at our camp on the Curipung, and completed as many "quakes" as we could
out of the material, in all numbering forty-two,
each capable of holding about fifty-five or sixty
pounds. Here we shot a "great mâam,"* whose
flesh proved superior to anything we had tasted.
The anatomy of this bird is peculiar, as it may be said
to be nearly all breast; the flesh before cooking is of a
light green, and when cooked is white and delicate. In
size it is about the same as a pheasant, and its shrill
plaintive whistle, which gradually increases in volume,
is a never-failing forest-sound both night and morning.
There is another but smaller bird of the same species.
We also bagged two or three "duraquauras"†—
partridges—which were almost as good on the table
as the "mâam." The notes of this bird, from which
it takes its name, are usually the first heard in the
morning and frequently before dawn.

In spite of repeated assurances from Lanceman that
he and his Indians would be ready to accompany us
early on the following morning, they failed to appear
at the appointed time. Some of the natives from the
sand-bank encampment were willing to join us, so we
accepted their services and loaded one of their woodskins, so as to lighten our own boats, and then started.
Soon after we left the river widened considerably,
but became so shallow that for over an hour we had
to walk and drag the boats, and even the woodskin.
Then it became deeper, and maintained an average
breadth of sixty or seventy yards. The banks were
thickly clothed with a jungle growth, above which
locust and cork-trees reared themselves. Here and

---

* Tinamus Brasiliensis.   † Odontophorus Guianensis.

there a great Brownea,* with brilliant red flowers or
fiery legumes, stretched out, Briareus-like, a hundred
arms wreathed with deeply cut arums and parasitical
plants, and over the water drooped the feathery foliage
of an amherstiæ, with beautiful rose-tinged flowers
having long crimson stamens. Sport was easier to be
obtained here than on the large river, and we had
plenty of amusement spearing rays and shooting sun-
bitterns, hanuras,† white egrets, and sometimes a
beautiful Quaak heron.‡ The latter is a very graceful bird with plumy crest, and curly neck and breast
feathers of a lovely lavender colour. Nothing was
wasted, for most of our civilized Indians found no
flesh amiss, and apparently enjoyed the leg of a heron
as much as they did the breast of a mâam. But two
of our Acawais would not eat the delicious pacu,
although they did not refuse the ray, or the electric-
eel. In North America, too, the Comanche Indians
will not eat fish that have scales, but are fond of those
that have none.

The different tribes of Guiana have various ideas
regarding what food is fit and what food is unfit to be
eaten. For instance, the Caribs will not touch large
fish, nor will they eat pork. The Macusi consider the
flesh of cattle unclean, but do not object to that of
peccary and wild boar. The Warraces think roast dog
a great delicacy, therein resembling the Cheyennes of
North America. On this river we missed the little silver
fish running swiftly over the top of the water, the bats
that flew out of every dead tree near the water's edge
as we passed, and even the bumble bees that had been

* Brownea racemosa.　　　† Ardea cocoi.
‡ Ardea myrticorax.

our constant companions on the Mazaruni. But their
place was supplied by sociable king-fishers, many of
which kept in our society for hours, awaiting our
approach on some bare bough, and then skimming
over the water just ahead of us. Ducklars, too, and
curri-curris stood less on ceremony, and scarcely waited
for an invitation to dinner. We stopped for breakfast
near a village—two houses—where fifteen or twenty
people assembled to look at us. A successful wild-pig
hunt had just provided them with a quantity of meat,
a small portion of which we wished to purchase.
They, however, declined to part with any of it, unless
we gave in return a much larger supply of salt than we
could afford ; so we had to go without it. "Gentle
hospitality" quoth the Sanscrit sage, "dwelleth not in
palaces. Rather seeking, shall ye find her in the tent
of the desert." Before we left, a woodskin, containing
Lanceman and six other Indians caught us up, and we
proceeded together.

The river scenery was now more picturesque, and
mountain forms, with outlines ever changing as we
moved, gathered round us. Our course was so winding that sometimes the same mountain appeared on
one side of us and sometimes on the other. Towards
evening we obtained a very pretty view. Beyond
where the river narrowed a little, two mountains stood
almost together, the nearer—Wattaparu—flat-topped,
and with bare, perpendicular walls, loomed up grandly
and in striking contrast with the other—Aricanna—
whose rounded base was crowned with a curious
pinnacle, the whole being thickly wooded from top to
bottom. The one was all shining silver-grey, the other
of a rich purple bloom. But with the mountains had

come the rain, and it was as much as we could do by perpetual bailing to keep the boats above water. At length we camped on a sand-bank, and for the first time since we left Georgetown built a house.

As we might now expect constant rains, in all our future camps the building of a shelter was our first care. The huts were necessarily substantial, in order to sustain the weight of our hammocks. Four stout forked poles were worked into the ground, and formed the corner posts; these were connected by strong poles, and in the centre of the narrower ends of the parallelogram two more thick forked poles were erected high enough for the tarpaulins, which were thrown over the connecting beam to form a sloping ceiling. All the fastenings were made with bush-rope, which was as pliable as cord. Rafters placed across the connecting side-beams formed a dry platform in wet weather for the "quakes," guns, &c. After a little practice, it was astonishing how quickly the shelter was set up. In spite of our house the night was not a pleasant one, as owing to our exposed situation the rain beat in terribly through the open sides. It passed though, and before day-break the tarpaulins were down and the boats reloaded. The course of the river was more tortuous than on the preceding day, and it seemed as if we should never reach the other side of Wattaparu, so frequently did we pass and repass it. In some places fallen trees obstructed our passage, and these had to be cut away; and in others enormous boulders, formed of coarse conglomerate and diorite rising from the bed of the river, gave us but scanty space to squeeze through.

At last we reached a mountain triangle. In front

was Wairinu, a splendid table-mountain with bold perpendicular wall, and castellated like some gigantic fortification of the most perfect stone masonry. On our
left was Pacaru, surmounted by a high cone and with
massive slabs of rock jutting out from its side. On
the right rose Wuruima with its outline similar to
Pacaru. Everywhere there was a beautiful blending
of rock and forest, the rocks varying from red overhanging buttressess to grey perpendicular heights,
furred at intervals with shrubs, and the forest which
covered every available spot with dark green foliage
was brightened in places with a few patches of colour,
and the lighter tints of palm and wild plantain leaves.

On reaching the Seroun creek, near which the Indian
path leads across the country, we found the water too
shallow for an ascent, so crossing to the right bank of
the Curipung, we camped on some high ground below
the falls of Macrebah. Nowhere had we found so
picturesque a camping ground. Under the trees was a
broad beach of the whitest sand, at whose foot ran the
dark river, foam-flecked from the beautiful falls over
which the water rushed in three successive cataracts,
flanked and broken by enormous boulders. Mountains
surrounded the little valley through which the river
flowed, and their wonderful precipices and curious
forms were a never failing source of attraction. As this
was the terminus of our river travel in boats, we soon
set to work filling and weighing the "quakes;" the
weight assigned to each man being forty-five pounds of
provisions, which together with his own bundle and a few
et ceteras altogether amounted to about sixty pounds,
no inconsiderable weight to carry, when the temperature
and the difficulties of the route are considered.

For our future progress McTurk arranged the following plan. All the hands, except two, who were unwell and were to be left at Macrebah in charge of the boats, were to take part in the overland journey to where we rejoined the Mazaruni. Then all the original crew, except six of the best men, were to return to Macrebah, and with the two sick ones make the home journey to the settlements in two of the boats. The other boat, "the Adaba," was to be left on a raised platform, which was built under the trees, to take us back on our return from Roraima. As we had forty-two quakes and only twenty-two men to carry them, Lanceman started off in a woodskin to a neighbouring Arecuna village, to try and get more. He succeeded in obtaining five, so we saw that we should be compelled to make short daily journeys, and after each to send back relays of men to bring on the extra quakes.

Our preparations occupied us for a day and a half, during which time our Indians also cut a short track through the woods from the opposite bank of the river to join the Seroun path, thereby avoiding a tedious and rock-encumbered walk up the shallow creek. As it would require two trips to remove all our baggage to the first day's halting place, McTurk started early in the morning with the intention of sending back the necessary number of men for the remaining quakes on the following day. I remained behind, so as to superintend the departure of the second detachment, and guard against any unnecessary delay.

CHAPTER XVII.

IT was a dismal morning when McTurk set out on
his tedious march; the rain fell in torrents, and I
congratulated myself on being under shelter, and hoped
that by the morrow the weather would have cleared.
At intervals during the day the rain ceased, and I was
able to ramble about the falls, where there were many
botanical treasures in the various agaves, yuccas, and
ferns. Wherever a gleam of light shone across the
forest border, there the little sun-hairs—as the
humming-birds are well named by the Aztecs—
darted among the blossoms, and often poised themselves for a minute at a time close to my face, as if
wondering to what class of vegetable I belonged.

Under our house was a fine dacana-balli tree,
whose large white blossoms lay strewn on the ground,
and weighted the green foliage like a snow-fall; in the
forks and on the branches were some orchids and pretty
pink and white euphorbias, and amongst these flowers,
also, humming-birds loved to revel. In the white sand

were numerous tracks of wild animals that daily came
from the forest to drink, but none ever appeared when
I was on watch.   Towards evening the atmosphere had
cleared, so that I anticipated fine weather, but one of
the Indians said it would surely rain again, as the
toucans cried so loudly.   The birds were weather-wise,
as in the night the rain recommenced, and when the
carriers arrived next day it was still pouring.   There
was no time to be lost, so after the men had break-
fasted we set off.

After crossing the river, the first part of our journey
was to ascend the slopes of the Seroun mountains.   As
soon as we joined the old path above the creek, difficulties commenced.   The narrow trail wound in and out,
and up and down, and over and under enormous masses
of conglomerate rock, whose smooth and shapely sides,
rising perpendicularly for sixty or seventy feet, were
crowned by grasses and ferns.   Under some of these
were flowers and green branches that had been offered
to the rock spirits by the superstitious natives; others,
with their overhanging crags, formed natural shelters
which had served for a night's resting-place to the less
timorous Indians.   Between these boulders were deep
pits, which were hard to avoid, and into which a false
step would have given a drop of thirty or forty feet.

Over rocks and streams, and through quagmires, we
made our varied way, and at last caught sight of the
Curipung River above Macrebah, far below us.   Soon
after we reached the top of the hill range, having
ascended nearly one thousand feet.   Here the path
ran through a level forest, but, instead of by boulders,
the walking was henceforth made exceedingly fatiguing
by the countless roots which composed the track.   No

ground was to be seen; it was simply a net-work of
roots from which all earth had been washed away, and
which varied in size from a sharp thin blade that cut
like a knife, to a rounded, full sized limb, over which
you slipped, with every probability of straining your
ancle even if you did not break your leg. I wore a
pair of moderately-sized shooting boots, but to my unaccustomed soles the proceeding was most painful; a
pilgrimage on peas to Rome would have been nothing
in comparison. The resemblance to a pilgrimage was
rendered all the more striking by the perpetual tolling
of the bell-birds,* which in spite of the pouring rain
uttered their wonderful notes from every part of the
forest. Sometimes the ringing sounds produced by
these birds resemble "quâ-ting," at other times you
hear a drawling "kóng, kóng, kóng" at intervals, and
then the full notes "kóng-kày." In each case, the last
syllable is a note higher than the first, and the tone is
more that of an anvil when struck by a hammer than
that of a bell. The sounds are remarkably clear and
resonant.

The campanero is pure white—strange colour for a
tropical bird—and from its forehead extends a long
tube which it can inflate at pleasure, and which is
covered with small white, downy feathers. Its belfry
is generally the topmost dead bough of some lofty tree,
and even if in spite of its ventriloquial notes you have discovered its whereabouts, yet its colour renders it extremely
difficult to distinguish. Our Indians, and others that we
met, did not object to shoot one occasionally, but in
Brazil the campanero is greatly dreaded, as its toll is
believed to be the cry of a soul condemned to perpetual

* Procnias carunculata.

torments. The American poet Whittier has made this belief the subject of one of his poems, entitled

THE CRY OF A LOST SOUL.

" In that black forest, where, when day is done,
  With a serpent's stillness glides the Amazon,
  Darkly from sunset to the rising sun,
  A cry as of the pained heart of the wood,
  The long despairing moan of solitude,
  And darkness and the absence of all good,
  Startles the traveller with a sound so drear,
  So full of hopeless agony and fear.
  His heart stands still and listens with his ear;
  The guide, as if he heard a dead-bell toll,
  Starts, drops his oar against the gunwale's thole,
  Crosses himself and whispers ' A lost soul!'
  No, Señor, not a bird, I know it well,
  It is the pained soul of some infidel,
  Or cursed heretic that cries from hell.
  Poor fool! with hope still mocking his despair,
  He wanders shrieking on the midnight air,
  For human pity and for Christian prayer."

After six or seven hours of the weariest walking we arrived drenched to the skin——by the way it does not take much to wet the Indians to the skin——at our camp. There I found McTurk footsore, but energetic as usual, and happy in the addition of a few more Indian carriers who were "on the walk," and willing to accompany us. The chief of the party was an old fellow with streaming black hair and of fierce aspect. He did not know his proper name, but produced a small package in the folds of which was a card with " Isaac " written on it. As there was already one Isaac in our party, we christened the new man "the Pirate." Among his most cherished treasures was a large parcel, which he opened with much ceremony. It contained five or six other palm leaf packets, from the last of which he drew a printed tract in the Acawai language, which he had obtained from one of the missions near the coast. The tract was composed of a few prayers and Bible extracts, which he requested McTurk to read aloud. It was a curious scene ; a few fires threw a glare over the dark forest outside, and clustered round the shelter, under which we lay in our hammocks, were the Indians listening with the deepest attention to the reading, and now and then repeating to each other in a low tone some word that was better understood than the rest.

The Pirate, although he could not read, knew many of the lines by heart, and made an admirable clerk, although I much doubt whether his knowledge was more than that of a parrot. Our friend lived on the Cako River, and together with the rest of his party was on his way down the Mazaruni to sell birds and hammocks. Thinking that on our arrival at the Cako the assistance of these men in obtaining woodskins might be valuable, we easily induced them by the promise of food and a few knives, &c., to retrace their footsteps, and aid us in carrying our quakes.

When we started next morning it was still raining, but the ludicrous appearance of the Pirate made us for-get all discomfort. On his head, shoulders, back, and perched all over his quake were a number of parrots ; we saw nothing of the man but his legs, he was literally clothed with parrots. These birds were not in the least alarmed at the brown-skinned Indians, but whenever McTurk or myself approached they uttered their harsh cries, and whilst some in terror ran their claws deep into the poor man's flesh, others fluttered off into the bush and caused much loss of time before being recaptured.

Our path differed but little from that of the preceding day; we hardly ever touched the ground, but limped painfully over the matted roots. We continually crossed small streams and creeks, whose water ran fresh and sparkling over the stony beds, except when we were hot and thirsty, and then it generally lay in tepid, stagnant pools among the rocky basins. These Indian paths are not always easy to follow, so little do they vary in appearance from the surrounding bush. The original picking out of such a path must have been of considerable difficulty, as in the dense forest there are few landmarks to steer by, nothing in fact but the sun. A track once made, however, even by a single Indian, is easily recognized by the sharp-eyed natives, to whom a broken twig, or a scratched root, tells the story of a previous traveller. So exactly do they follow the narrow trail—always in single file—that often for miles the very footsteps of the explorer are trodden by his successors. I think paiworie has much to do with the generally true direction of these paths, as if you were to place a trough of that liquor on one side of a trackless forest twenty miles in breadth, and an Indian on the other, the two would meet in a very short space of time.

The vegetation which surrounded us was not of a very interesting nature, as the soil was often poor and stony, and frequently covered with a carpet of selaginella or other lycopods. A pretty little dark blue and white gloxinia was very abundant, and in swampy places grew yellow lilies and various cannas. The dakama trees strewed the ground in every direction with their brown nuts, of the size of an orange, and having a pink and white core. These are uneatable, and it was only occasionally that we found the delicious Souari nuts, whose

finely grained kernel rivals the most delicate almond.
Besides the buttressed forms of the bombaceæ, there
were strange-looking trees whose trunks were made up
of a number of thick stems joined together at a height
of ten or twelve feet from the ground. One that I
measured had eight separate supports, and above where
they united the trunk had a circumference of over
twenty-five feet. We saw no game birds, although
we sometimes heard the drumming of a "pani"—
curasson—or the shrill notes of a mâam. In addition
to the tolling of the bell-birds, we frequently recognized the harsh peacock cry of the "cock of the
rocks"—Pipra rupicola—and near one of their dancing
places we shot three specimens. The colour of the
Guiana species in the male differs from that of Ecuador
and Peru in being much lighter; instead of crimson
it is a splendid orange on the body, and the wing
feathers are brown instead of black and silver grey.
The short square tail is ringed with reddish yellow,
and the orange crescent-shaped feathers placed on the
head like a cocked hat are edged with black.

In Australia the bower-birds—Chlamydoderæ—build
their galleries and cabins, and in New Guinea the
gardener-bird* not only builds a house but also arranges

---

* "Amblyornis inornata." Dr. Beccari, the well-known Italian
naturalist, in describing the home of this species of paradise-bird says:
"Directly in front of its cabin is a level space occupying a superficies
about as large as that of the structure itself, which has a diameter of about
a metre. It is a small lawn of soft moss, all transported thither, kept
smooth and clean and free from grass, weeds, stones, and other objects not
in harmony with its design. Over this graceful green carpet are scattered
flowers and fruit of brilliant colours in such a manner that they really
present the appearance of an elegant little garden. After these objects
have been exposed for some time, and have lost their freshness, they are
taken from their abode and thrown away, and are replaced by others."

pleasure-grounds around it, and here in Guiana the
"cock of the rocks" has his dancing place. The spot
chosen is a mossy level, which is cleared of stones and
sticks, and surrounded by low bushes. The assembled
birds form a circle, and presently an old cock walks into
the ring and with spreading tail performs a series of
steps, which from the Indian account of them must vary
from those of a stately minuet to those of the "Perfect
Cure." When he is tired, he receives the applause of
the hen-birds and retires, another taking his place.
Some of their upward leaps are said to be astonishing,
and are repeated in rapid succession until the bird is exhausted. It is during these antics that the natives shoot
them or capture them alive, as so absorbed are both
the spectators and the performers that they pay no
attention to the stealthy approach of the Indian. In
captivity these delicate birds soon languish, and out of
two that I sent home from Georgetown, one died on
the passage, and the other only lived about a month in
spite of great care and attention. The dancing grounds
of the "cocks of the rock" are unadorned with flowers,
fruit or shells ; as long as they are smooth and free
from stones, the birds are satisfied and apparently
believe that their own bright plumage is a sufficient
ornamentation, and that they can afford to turn their
attention to the study of graceful accomplishments.
Also among the birds of Paradise, the beautiful plu-
maged species do not construct bowers or gardens, a
gift which is possessed only by their more intellectual
but less ornamental brethren.

We camped after our second day's tramp near a
stream called the Lamung, and at once sent back to the
old camp a sufficient number of men to bring on the

remaining quakes the following day. The good temper and cheerfulness with which all the carriers, and especially the new contingent, performed their double journeys was really remarkable; and, though these forest journeys were to most a natural part of their lives, yet we could not help feeling sorry for the great but unavoidable labour. We remained in camp all next day, but sent forward a number of quakes, the carriers returning, so that the entire number might be ready to depart with all the remaining baggage when we again set out. Besides the palm-leaf covering of each individual quake, those that were sent forward or left behind were ranged by the side of the path on poles, and well protected from the weather by broad leaves and branches. Naturally they formed very conspicuous objects, and though they must continually have been noticed by several parties of Indians that passed on their way to the Curipung River, yet nothing was ever touched or in any way disturbed.

In one of our rambles around the camp we killed a beautifully marked boa-constrictor, about nine feet in length and very thick. Another disagreeable visitor we had was an enormous hairy monkey-spider (araña monos) six inches long and with two formidable nippers like a bird's talons. On touching it with a stick it threw itself back into a fighting attitude, clashed its nippers and twined its long legs about the wood in its efforts to break it. We saw no wild beasts, but the Indians reported having seen a large tiger,* which walked slowly along the path in front of them, close to the camp, and disappeared in the bushes. One of them had a gun, but he was too frightened to fire.

* Felis onca.

A circumstance, trivial in itself, here very nearly put an end to my journey. Charlie, whose zeal had outrun his discretion, in drying my boots had placed them so near the fire that they were roasted; consequently when I put them on the following morning, they literally came to pieces in my hands, and during the day the heel of one of them dropped off. As I knew that without them it would be impossible for me to reach Roraima, for with our limited luggage one pair of thin canvas shoes was all I had besides, my future occupation whenever we arrived at our camping ground was that of a cobbler. McTurk and Charlie first of all cunningly re-attached the heel, and ever afterwards I managed by the aid of string and bush-rope to keep the different parts together. So carefully did I nurse and mend them, that they actually brought me back to Macrebah, which was as far as necessary, but the anxiety caused by so simple an accident can hardly be imagined.

During that day we shot a pani, for which we were duly thankful, as good fresh meat had of late been very scarce. Game was not plentiful, and as McTurk was extremely anxious to complete the expedition as quickly as possible—as the men were paid by the day —we wasted but little time in looking for it. In many parts the bush growth was ill adapted for game of any sort, and in the likely places, though we heard panis and duraquaras, yet we could not get a shot at them. Seldom had the truth of the old proverb " a bird in the hand, &c.," been more forcibly presented to us.

We passed through one very pretty silvan scene, where the path came out on to an open mossy glade surrounded by a perfect circle of grand old trees, whose grey buttressed trunks contrasted vividly with the green-robed stems of the slender plants in the background. In other lands it might have been a temple grove dedicated to the old Druid worship, and Hellenic belief would have peopled it with Dryads and Oreads, but to the Indian mind no dancing fay or wood-nymph would step from the opening trees, and only the terrible Didi could inhabit the mysterious circle. Soon afterwards we crossed the Stenaparu River, and then commenced a very steep ascent, which we climbed by the aid of rocks and roots.

When we reached the summit we were at an elevation of 2,600 feet above the sea, and the forest plateau extended for miles before us. The fatiguing ascent had made us very thirsty, and from passing Indians we heard that we should not find water for a long time. The sight of several " swizzle-stick " trees added to our thirst, and recalled the iced pepper-punches and cooling drinks of Georgetown. At length, after passing a branch path on our right which led to Camarang, on the Upper Mazaruni, we arrived at the brink of a great precipice. At first it was difficult to imagine how we were to descend, but by following a zig-zag trail, and aided by bushes and stony juttings, we gained a ravine about 700 feet below, through which flowed a delicious stream. From here the path ran along the mountain side, and though we should have been glad to halt, the absence of water prevented our doing so. At length we saw a few Manicole palms, a sure sign of the vicinity of water, and in a few minutes we found a small rivulet, where we erected our house.

The night was wet and stormy, and when we started next morning in the rain, one of the Indians who was lame and feverish had to be left behind, with the understanding that he was to overtake us with the rest of the party, who had gone back for the extra quakes. On this day the path gave signs of being almost untravelled, and in many places we had to search diligently before we could pick up the lost thread. By continually bending a twig here and slashing a branch there, we left sure indications of our line of travel for those who were behind, but in order that all should overtake us, we shortened our arduous day's march over hill and creek, and camped near a stream called Cariapu, *i.e.*, mora. From the father of an Indian family encamped near, we found that we had followed an unused trail, but that by retracing our steps for a short distance we should be able with his assistance to strike the new path, which would bring us to the Mazaruni by the middle of the next day. Our party was now at three different points, but as our new friends had of course established themselves beside us, we formed a small though very picturesque camp, under the fine moras from which the stream took its name.

As the rain never ceased to pour, one of the men thought he would improve the occasion by setting fire to a gigantic mora, whose trunk was hollow throughout. From the inclination of the tree, we thought that in the event of its falling the direction would be away from the camp. Still, as it looked dangerous, McTurk gave orders that the fire which, apparently, grew less and less, should not be relighted, and after our usual game of euchre we stretched ourselves in our hammocks quite ready for a good night's rest. Before midnight there was a cry that the tree

was falling, and springing up we found that the
draught had so fanned the flames that the entire tree
was ablaze, sheets of fire and smoke rushing from all
the apertures, and from the very summit.   It was a
magnificent sight, but from that moment sleep was
banished, as had the mora fallen towards us, we should
inevitably have been crushed.   As the rain fell in
torrents we could not change our shelter, so we had
to pass the rest of the night staring at the burning
tree, and ready at a moment's notice to rush to a
place of safety.

Dawn found us still watching, but the mora had not
fallen, and as far as we know never did fall ; still it
had caused us to pass a very uncomfortable night.
When we departed the rain ceased, but the dripping
bushes supplied us with abundant moisture, and we
soon forgot that the storm was over.   The new path
was but little better than the old one, and was very
intricate, now crossing swamps, or running over steep
hills, and now making us wade through creeks, or
traverse a slippery bog for fifty or sixty yards.

Snakes were plentiful, but two duraquaras were the
only birds we obtained.   Owing to our anxiety to
reach the big river, this last day's journey, although
the shortest, seemed longer than any previous one, but
at length we arrived at a dry creek called the Asima-
paru, and after following its muddy bed for a short
time we again found ourselves on the banks of the
Mazaruni.   We had left it flowing east, at an elevation of less than 200 feet above the sea ; here it was
flowing north, at an elevation of 1,300 feet.   On the
high bank we made a clearing, cut down the trees that
intercepted our view of the river, and built the usual

shed. Before night the Pirate, Lanceman, Mazaruni, and the rest of the Indians had all arrived with the baggage, and the tired party enjoyed a well-earned rest.

The next day our original crew, with the exception of the six best men, set off on their return journey to Macrebah on their way home, accompanied by the other Indians, with the exception of Lanceman, Mazaruni, and two Arecunas, who remained with us. In order to send news of our progress to our friends at Georgetown, McTurk loaded an empty cartridge shell with the letter he had written, the novel envelope ensuring its arrival in a clean and dry state, if ever it reached its destination. The Pirate went away in a canoe to obtain woodskins for us from the Indians who live near the mouth of the Cako, from which we were only a few hours distant; but long before he returned our arrival had been discovered by natives whilst passing up and down the river, and we soon received a number of visitors.

When the Pirate returned, he brought with him the chief inhabitant of that part of the river. He called himself Captain David, and having once been to the coast, understood yes and no, wore a shirt and an old black hat, had only two wives, and considered himself a white man. He graciously accepted a cigarette, and after critically examining our baggage promised to send woodskins on the following day to take us to the Cako, from which river we had determined to find our way across country to Roraima. He himself had never been to Roraima, and thought we were insane for wishing to go there, but said that perhaps he might find somebody who could guide us. Owing

to the influx of visitors, who as a matter of course
established themselves in close proximity to us, our
narrow camping limits were inconveniently crowded.
But want of space was atoned for by the picturesque
scene, which, when darkness fell, was very curious.
Our own white-roofed habitation overlooked the silent
river, and behind it were slung the twenty red* hammocks of the Indians, some under palm-leaf shelters,
some covered with broad uranias, and others merely
suspended from tree to tree. Here and there little
fires were scattered about—as Indians are particularly
fond of sleeping close to or over a fire—and from one
nook a burning lump of the hyawa† resin sent up a
fragrant smoke. Through the dark background of
trees the fire-beetles flitted, and the occasional nocturnal
forest-sounds only rendered the silence more complete.
Once a loud rustling overhead brought some of the
Indians to their feet, but it was only caused by a species
of the harmless lemur, and the camp was soon wrapped
in sleep.

* The hammocks of Indians are invariably of a greasy red colour from
contact with their painted bodies.

† Icica heptaphylla.

CHAPTER XVIII.

AS the Captain did not arrive at the appointed time with the woodskins, we amused ourselves with some amateur hair-cutting, which so delighted the natives that many of them insisted on being shorn of their long black tresses. These they carefully gathered, and after wrapping them in leaves buried in some retired part of the forest, so that no Kanaima should get hold of them and exercise his incantations to the destruction of their late owner. Here we discovered that Mazaruni, who was extremely plain, was excessively conceited, and was never tired of gazing at himself in a small hand-glass, and arranging the straw ornaments in his nose and ears in what he considered the most becoming fashion. Whenever a woodskin appeared in which there were any ladies, he would immediately retire to his hammock and change his dress, *i.e*, take out the old straws and insert new ones, carefully placing them at the proper angle. Then with a few fresh touches of blue and vermillion he brightened himself up, and felt that he was a dandy of the first water. By the time the barber's duties were completed the Captain arrived with his woodskins, which were quickly loaded, and we proceeded up the river.

Stepping into a woodskin for the first time is a delicate undertaking. If the foot is placed on one side a capsize ensues, and in the exact centre the bark bends so that the feeling is that you are trusting yourself to a sheet of brown paper. The only safety is in stepping in lightly and quickly, and at once sitting down in the bottom of the boat, breathing only when you are perfectly balanced in the middle of it. A little practice, however, soon gives confidence, and you are able to use your gun as well as in an ordinary-sized craft. The paddlers sit one at each end, the man in the bows having to keep a sharp look out for rocks or snags, which would pierce or upset the frail shell in a moment.

In about three hours we reached the mouth of the Cako, and looking up that river saw in the distance a fine table-mountain called Carotipu. We found the Cako to be a fine river, about one hundred yards in width, and with moderately high banks. We ascended a short distance, and then camped on the left bank—the Venezuelan* side—in order to be free from several Indian parties who had erected their " banaboos " on the opposite shore. But our precaution was of no avail, as when we were comfortably settled and had cleared the bush around, over came the Indians and

---

* I use the expression " Venezuelan side" because of our own idea of the national boundaries, but the Venezuelans claim as theirs the territory stretching east as far as the Essequibo river, and south to Brazil almost to the River Parima.

quietly established themselves in our midst. One or
two of the women had pleasing countenances, but
their striped and too sturdy limbs and sack-like
forms entirely destroyed the first impression of femi-
nine beauty. I think it was Alphonse Karr who
said, " La nature a fait la femelle, et la civilization
a fait la femme !"

Most of the men were powerfully made, but their
painted and unintelligent faces were not improved by
the black pellets which, according to custom, they all
held between their lips. This vegetable pellet—I do
not know what it is composed of—is the Indian sub-
stitute for the betel-nut of the Malays, the cocoa-leaf of
the South Americans, the opium of the Chinese,
the tobacco of Europeans, and in outward appearance
is not an improvement on any of them. When the
natives heard that we wished to buy provisions, they
brought us all they could, but it only amounted to a
small quantity of cassava bread, a few pumpkins, and
three or four roots of sweet cassava.* The latter not
being poisonous require no special preparation, and
when the roots are roasted they are very palatable.
Our next object was to buy some woodskins, as the
owner of those that had brought us from the Mazaruni did not wish to part with them. On the day
after our arrival five were offered to us, and these we
purchased for four small flasks of powder. As ten
shillings was not much to give for five boats, we
promised the natives that on our return they should
receive them back again.

Powder is eagerly sought by the Indians, as many
of them have long single-barrel guns—buck-guns they

* Janipha Cœflingo.

are called in Demerara—that they have obtained in
trade, and their opportunities of getting ammunition
are exceedingly limited! They are very fond of fire-
arms, and our breech-loaders were a never-ending
source of wonder to them. Of late, we had heard
the most appalling sounds issuing from the forest;
sometimes they resembled the bellowing of a cow who
had lost her calf, and at others were like the howls
of a wild animal. At last one of the perpetrators was
shot, and it proved to be a small bird known in Guiana
as the "calf bird," which has a bald head and
plumage of an olive colour.

McTurk told me that these birds are common on
the Pomeroon River, and that once a newly arrived
Englishman, who had been out shooting one day, returned in haste to camp, with the intelligence that he
had heard such a terrific bellowing and roaring that he
was certain a band of tigers were fighting with some
other animals. McTurk and others hastened to the
scene, and shot three calf-birds. Considering that it
comes from a bird, the noise is certainly the most
astounding I have ever listened to. We shot some
trumpeter* birds, which also make a very peculiar
sound. They live in flocks, run swiftly over the
ground, and look like a number of diminutive ostriches.
They are graceful creatures, with long velvety necks,
beautiful blue and purple breast-feathers, and back and
wings of a silver grey. The Indians call them Wara-
cabas, from a fanciful resemblance in their notes to
the cry of the Waracaba tigers, which hunt in packs.

Having spent nearly two days in camp, with the
vain hope of securing a guide to Roraima, we deter-

---

* Psophia crepitans.

mined to start early on the following morning. The
natives promised to bring more cassava on the morrow
if we could only wait another day, but with an Indian
the morrow is as indefinite a period as "mañana" with
the Spaniards, or "bookra" with the Arabs. The five
woodskins—the two largest each containing three
persons, and the smaller, two—were loaded down to
the water's edge when we set out, but we soon reached
Captain David's house, and there we left the three
quakes of provisions for our return journey. The
course of the river was pretty and very winding, continually opening out fresh views of distant mountains.
We rounded the northern extremity of Mount Carouta
which was thickly wooded, except under its high
central dome, where the precipitous rock was quite
bare. Nearly all the mountains that we had hitherto
seen, were extremely precipitous on the northern and
eastern faces, but on the western side there were
generally patches of heavy forest even where, to the
eye, it looked most perpendicular. We hoped that
Roraima would present the same forest growth, and by
ascending the Cako River we thought we might arrive
opposite the western slope of the mountain.

We knew little about the course of the river, as no
information could be obtained from the Indians, and
we were probably the first white men who had ever
ascended it. As it was probable that the river rose in
the mountain range near Roraima, we intended to
follow it as far as we could, and then strike off across
country. From what Captain David told us, we were
much afraid that owing to the scant population along
the river banks we should be unable to find a guide.
Still we determined to push on, and in the event of

failure, to return to the mouth of the Cako and make
another attempt to reach Roraima by the Cukuie River.

After passing Carouta, we saw in our front the flat-
topped mountain of Ibropu, and soon after we camped
on the right bank of the river, opposite a path leading
to Camarang, on the Mazaruni. We erected our shed
on a high jutting promontory above a white sand beach,
and after unloading the woodskins carried the quakes
up the bank. It was fortunate we did not leave them
below, as in the morning there was no sand to be seen;
the river had risen, and the beach was covered to a
depth of three or four feet. As we approached
Ibropu, we caught sight of a fine waterfall that descended from its eastern slope, and the stream which
it formed entered the Cako near a very pretty
island. Here, two fine Muscovy* ducks flew over our
heads, and, as they ran the gauntlet, each boat in
succession greeted them with a volley, but unsuccess-
fully. Shortly afterwards, I discovered five more
swimming near the shore, and by dint of quiet
paddling and taking advantage of a bushy point we
crept within range, and with two barrels I bagged
four of them. They were very large and heavy birds,
differing from the tame Muscovy only in having less
coral about the bill. They are difficult to approach,
and though we frequently saw them alight on the
high trees, and from afar distinguished them by their
white wing-coverts, yet by the end of the day we had
only obtained six. It is said that these ducks build
their nests on lofty trees, and, when the young ones are
sufficiently grown, the parents carry them down to the
swamps to educate them. Those we shot were uncom-

---

* Anas moschata.

monly tough, but duck and pumpkin were such rare
delicacies that, had the former been of cast-iron, I
think we should have enjoyed them.

We passed along the east side of Ibropu, then the
ever-winding river turned south, and we saw a high
table-mountain which we fancied must be Roraima,
but the view was only for a moment, and then a veil
of clouds concealed it. Afterwards we found out that
the mountain we had seen was Marima, which is
situated to the north-east of Roraima. We paddled
along fine stretches of river, here getting a snipe, there
a duck, and sometimes a curri-curri, and at last camped
on the left bank. Before it was dark we heard the
sound of a horn blown lustily from the river, and
soon a woodskin appeared containing a man, woman,
and child. It turned out that they lived near Roraima,
and having heard from Captain David that we wanted
a guide had hastened after us. The man's name was
Abraham, which was about the only common biblical
name that we had not encountered among our various
crews at some time or other. He declined to camp
with us, but preferred going farther on, as he said that
close by was the cave of a celebrated " water-māmā,"
near whom it was dangerous to sleep.

The Indians firmly believe in the reality of these
mermaids, or " water-māmās," as they are called in
Dutch Creole ; and where they are supposed to have
their caves or nests, there great danger awaits the
traveller. Some are related to be extremely beautiful
and possessing long golden hair—like the Lorelei—and
whoever casts his eye on them is seized with madness,
jumps into the deep water, and never returns. Others
are hideous, snakes being twined about them, and with

their long white talons they drag boats under the water and devour their occupants. On the Orinoco and Amazon similar creatures are supposed to exist, but these are capable of drawing their prey into their mouths at a distance of a hundred yards. In order to avoid such a calamity, the natives always blow a horn before entering a creek or lagoon in which one of these monsters may be living; if it happens to be there, it will immediately answer the horn and thus give warning to the intruder.

When we awoke in the morning it seemed as if the " water-māmā " had indeed bewitched us. The river, which on the previous night flowed quietly beneath the bank on which we were encamped, had disappeared. The woodskins were high and dry on a ledge of rocks that extended for some distance up and down the bed of the stream There, on the other side of the rocky plateau we discovered the lost river, which had fallen three feet during the night, and had lost nearly the same volume of water that it had gained after the recent rains. About a mile farther on we found Abraham waiting anxiously for us, and glad that we had survived the perils of the night. On this day we caught some beautiful views of Roraima whenever the clouds lifted, and towards noon we left the Cako and turned into a broad creek on its right bank called the Aruparu. By so doing we feared—as eventually proved to be the case—that we should not reach Roraima from its western flank, but as our guide assured us that it was the only way he knew of, we thought it best to follow his advice.

The creek scenery was pretty, but monotonous ; the clay banks were clothed with thick bush, with here

and there masses of yellow blossoms and the pink
tassels of the Brownea.   There were also many shrubs
known as the "witê," whose long velvet pods contain
beans covered with a very sweet but insipid pulp.   A
drawback in picking them was that every pull brought
down showers of stinging ants, which, as well as parrots,
are very fond of that fruit.   Sometimes we passed an
Indian banaboo that had lately been occupied, and at
others the new jungle growth showed where a small
village had once existed.   At the mouths of the smaller
streams, which flowed into the creek, there was generally
a barricade of sticks and poles made by the natives for
securing fish, but most of the streams were dry and the
barricades of ancient date.   In the mud and sand were
endless tracks of tapirs and the "water-haas"—capybara
—and occasionally a splash and rustle told where we
had disturbed one of the latter, but we were seldom
near enough for a shot.

Ducklars were very numerous, and as we turned
each corner, there they would be sitting in rows on the
branches of fallen trees awaiting our approach ;   then
a dive and an ungainly flutter to start them, and away
they would go to the next bend in the river.   But
after the Muscovy ducks the men looked with disdain
on the fishy ducklar, and those that were shot that day
remained uneaten.   On many subsequent occasions they
looked back with regret on the despised and wasted
ducklars.   Now and then we heard the "kwet-kwet"
of the beautiful scarlet cotinga, and once the brilliant
but harsh-voiced pompadour* flew across in front
of us.   Not seldom the narrowing stream was over-
arched by the bending trees, and under their dark

* Ampelis cotinga.

shadows the splendid blue morphos and still more lovely butterflies of a sparkling violet hue floated lazily. At one place where the forest seemed clearer we ascended the bank, and were gratified by the sight of a savanna, which with a diversity of wood and hill stretched off to some distant mountains.

Owing to the muddy nature of the banks and the thick bush, it was late that night before we could find a camping ground, but at last we came to a spot where some Indians had already erected their sheds. They were wild-looking creatures, hideously painted and stained, and the hair of the men was longer than that of the women. They were stalwart and tall, and had come from their homes in the savanna country to this fashionable watering place for fishing and bathing. They shook their heads and groaned when they heard that we were going to Roraima, and recommended us to turn back and not act foolishly.

An amusing incident occurred here. Our primitive acquaintances kept us awake for some time with their monotonous sing-song talk, and shortly after I had dropped asleep McTurk awoke me with the intelligence that he was going to have his bath, as day was breaking. I got up at once, as it appeared to be getting light, and we bathed and dressed, and sat in our hammocks waiting coffee. After some time day did not appear to advance much, and to our astonishment we saw the moon slowly rising over the trees. In our anxiety to make an early start we had mistaken moonrise for daybreak, and had got up at about half-past twelve a.m.

Hitherto the creek had been free from all impediments and was deep enough to float large boats, but

soon after we left our sleeping quarters the ominous
stroke of an axe told us that Abraham was cutting a
passage through a fallen tree.   For the rest of the day
our journey was like going in a canoe through a forest
that had been cut down and left.   Here, a great tree
trunk permitted the passage of the woodskins underneath, but without their loads ; there, an enormous
limb necessitated the unloading and lifting over of
the boats ; in some places a sunken log had sufficient
water flowing over it to float the woodskins, but only
after their contents had been discharged ; in others an
opening had to be cut through tangled branches and
stems.   We were never in the boats for five minutes
at a time ; it was a perpetual jumping in and out,
loading and unloading, lifting and hauling, pushing
and carrying, cutting and squeezing.   Frequently, the
arch formed by the overhanging trunk seemed high
enough to allow the woodskin and its contents to
pass under, but when well in the centre a jam would
occur, and we would find ourselves crouching in the
bottom of the boat unable to move hand or foot, and
water rapidly coming in over the sides.   It was most
amusing, and I never enjoyed a good laugh at McTurk's
expense without immediately finding myself in a similar
position.   The great strain on the woodskins caused
two of them to split, and only by rapidly conducting
them to shore did we save them from sinking.   By
filling the cracks with bark, linen, and paper, they were
soon made serviceable again.

The windings of the creek were extraordinary ; often
after following a southerly direction for a mile or more,
we would turn north for the same distance, and come
out on the other side of the narrow promontory

only a few yards from where we had started. The same thing would be repeated east and west, and the patient stream seemed never tired of twisting itself into a hundred folds and then untwisting.

Just before dark, we arrived at a place past which it would be impossible to proceed, and Abraham informed us that we had reached the end of the creek journey. So we landed and built our house.

CHAPTER XIX.

ABOUT half a mile higher up the creek lived Abraham's mother, and there we intended to leave sufficient provisions for our return journey and whatever articles we could not carry with us.

Our first care on the day following our arrival was to hide the woodskins in the forest, so that they should not be appropriated by any passing Indians. Then we followed a trail through the bush which brought us to the hut. A very old lady with long white hair received us, and began to moan and beat her breast wildly. We asked what she was doing, and discovered that she was relating the difficulties of the path to Roraima. Over level country she travelled smoothly and in low tones, but when she came to the mountains that had to be crossed, then her voice rose, she shrunk to the ground, raised herself on tip-toes, waved her arms, struck her chest, uttered strange cries, and the higher and steeper the mountain the louder and shriller became her screams.

Already our superstitious carriers had lent too ready an ear to the terrors of Roraima as depicted by the son, and now the mother seemed disposed to add her store of legends and tales of witchcraft for general information. We therefore arranged our quakes as quickly as possible, rethatched her crazy shed so as to preserve from the weather the numerous articles we deposited on fresh rafters and were ready to start. Before we left she made the entire party blow three times on her back for good luck, but whether the luck was for her or for us we never found out. It was an odd farewell, but as it pleased old granny—as we called her—we were content.

Our path did not differ much from that of our previous foot-journey, but the creeks and streams were more numerous and the crossings often extremely difficult. Our bare-footed and trained carriers walked easily enough over the narrowest logs, but for us, with boots and weighed down with gun, bag and cartridges, it was different. Generally the water was too deep to wade through, and the only way of crossing was by means of a slippery trunk as narrow as a tight-rope, and many feet above the stream. Sometimes when the slender bridge was suspended at an angle, the crossing was more dangerous than amusing, as a fall would probably have been on to the sharp snags and branches that threw their points out of the deep pools underneath. As in our former walk, the ground was covered with dark blue gloxinias and a pretty creeping plant whose glossy leaves were delicately veined with pink; near the streams grew cannas and thick masses of the umberilla grass* varied with soft-textured marantas.

* Cyperus alternifolius.

Palms were more plentiful than before, and we saw
varieties that we had not previously met with. We saw
also the curious "monkey-pot" tree* with its strange
bowl-shaped fruit and wooden covers. Purple-heart
and the crab-oil tree† were not uncommon and strange
nuts constantly fell around us.

Many of the bush-rope forms were very curious,
differing in size and shape from a boot-lace to a ship's
cable. Here, like the strangling serpents of Laocoon,
they hold a great tree in their huge folds, and there a
delicate vine had formed a complete network around
some forest giant until it was as helpless as a fly in a
spider's web. Very terrible are these lace-like parasites
which cling at first in their helplessness to some lordly
trunk and then slowly extend their treacherous embrace until their support is shut up in a living grave.
The poor tree dies, and its destroyers live and thrive on
the dead body of their benefactor. Few flowers relieve
the monotony of these dark forests, and it is strange
that here, where birds have such brilliant plumage,
flowers should be almost unnoticeable. Nor do they
atone by perfume for their want of colour, as with the
exception of a faint breath of vanilla, or of the fragrant
blossoms of a lecythes, no odour of flowers greets the
senses.

The forest was not dull, as besides the tolling bell-
birds, numerous kites and hawks added their harsh
cries; nearer at hand little humming-birds were perpetually lisping "tweek-tweek" or a gay fire-bird
calling out "quark."

Once we heard a flute-bird,‡ whose mellow ventri-

---

* Lacythis ollaris.   † Carapa Guianensis.
          ‡ Cyphorinus cantans.

loquial notes were of wonderful sweetness, and as they floated around the sound was that of an Æolian harp struck by the wind on the tree tops. The exquisite tone reminded me of the "Siffleur montagne," which I once heard singing in the woods of Martinique. But in the forest all birds' sounds are pleasing, and even the harsh-throated parrots and macaws are pleasant to listen to. What does the bell-bird say when he tolls out "quiâ-ting" or the pompadour cotinga when he screams "wallababa" or the duraquara when he greets the dawn with his own name? Something surely, and though we cannot understand it, it is clear to the initiated. Those two parrots holding such confidential intercourse must understand one another, and that touching monologue of the flute-bird cannot be uttered in vain! Forest music must be, like Tzigane music, without laws and dogmas, and though subtle and mystic, yet distinct and easily comprehended by those who utter it.

After some hours of steady walking, during which we had been gradually ascending, we arrived at a small clearing in the centre of which stood a circular house, thatched and wattled. A fine cashew tree shadowed it, and in a twinkling we were enjoying the refreshing fruit which an agile Indian who had climbed up, shook down for us. Cashew Cottage was unoccupied, the family being in town or at some watering place, or more probably "on the walk." Abraham conducted us to a point which was a little way off the path, but from which we obtained a fine mountain view.

We were facing the west, and close in our front ran the Marima* range, sloping and forest-clad for the

---

* I have adhered to the spelling of Roraima as laid down by Sir R. Schomburgh and Mr. Barrington Brown, but the natives certainly pro-

greater part, but towards its southern extremity was an enormous square pile of sheer rock without even a shrub on its smooth sides. Behind this and in the far blue distance another perpendicular wall of rock was just visible; this was the northern end of Roraima. Stretching far away to the north were other mountains, the most conspicuous of which were the dome-shaped Serāpi and the flat-topped Ilotipu. As far as the eye could reach the violet tinted ranges rose one above the other, and threading its way between them we could trace the course of the Cako River. As usual Roraima only showed itself for a moment, for the white clouds fell slowly down and hid its sharp profile. Then we resumed our journey, whose direction was now towards the south-eastern end of Marima.

From Cashew Cottage two paths branched off into the forest. Abraham chose the one to the right, and in about four hours we emerged on to a high savanna plateau. In the centre of it were two conical huts, old and deserted. Close to them lay several large troughs hollowed out of tree trunks, but whether they had originally been intended for canoes or to hold paiworie we could not determine. Not far from here we built our shelter, as Abraham said that a stream ran through the forest below us. When we sought it we found it was dry, but as McTurk was unwell and feverish, owing to the numerous cuts, bruises, and sores gained during our hard tramps, we thought it better to remain where we were and send back for water to the nearest brook.

---

nounce the "ai" in the same way that they pronounce the i in Marima, *i.e.* Mareema. It may be, as in other cases, that different tribes have different pronunciations of the same name.

From the savanna we had a fine view all round. On one side were the Marima mountains, and a picturesque fall which proved to be the head waters of the Aruparu; and on the other, from the foot of a steep precipice, a broad valley bounded by wooded hills extended far away to the east in one unbroken surface of foliage.

In the evening a party of Indians arrived. They were on their way to the Mazaruni, but some of them agreed to accompany us, and others said that if we waited for a day they would bring us some cassava from their home in the forest. We therefore promised to wait, and early next morning despatched three men to bring some more quakes of flour from old Granny's house. Like other Indians we had met and questioned, these people beat their breasts and uttered various cries when they told us of the mountains to be crossed, and added their testimony to the spirits of Roraima. Besides cassava, they brought us some cobs of Indian corn and green plantains, which we paid for in small silver coins, as they said if ever they went to the coast they should require money. They were an inquisitive set, and our clothes and shoes astonished them beyond measure. I admit that at that time my boots certainly were curiosities. When we went to perform our ablutions in the rain water that the troughs held, we were always followed by a squad of sight-seers who had never seen soap or sponges, and who stood at a distance and laughed.

At this period Mazaruni was in his glory, for besides Sarah—Abraham's wife—three more women were added to our party by the arrival of the new comers, and as they carried burdens as well as the men, he was always on hand to assist them in any difficult

places. And the difficulties were many, for we found
that the hardest part of our journey was before us.
Directly after leaving camp the path descended through
the forest, over the usual terrible but unavoidable roots,
and in the course of time we arrived at the Owtaro River,
which we crossed just above a splendid set of falls
that were precipitated over a rocky wall, between
two hundred and three hundred feet in depth, into the
valley below.

Soon afterwards we reached the foot of the Opuima
Mountain,* and commenced an ascent which fully
accounted for the breast-beating and wild outcries of the
natives. By root-ladders and with the aid of trees, which
were themselves clinging with difficulty to the precipitous side, we slowly wended our way to the top. The
ascent seemed interminable, and from sheer exhaustion
I was frequently on the point of throwing away my
gun and cartridges. At length the struggle was over,
and we sat down on the summit to await the arrival
of the plucky carriers. I should not have been at all
surprised if none of them had reached the top, as I am
certain that with the same weight they carried I should
have been totally unable to make the ascent. But
they all arrived safely, not quite so light-hearted as
when they started, but ready to proceed after a short
rest. In many places the ground seemed covered with
snow, from the whiteness of a pretty lichen† which
was specked here and there with a yellow flower
growing from the end of a long stalk.

---

* Most of these so-called mountains are little more than high hill ranges,
but their excessive steepness and the difficult nature of the ascent render
them far from despicable.

† Cladonia reticulata.

On the hill slopes were many magnificent palms, one species of which was finer even than the royal palm. The shapely stems were of great height, and the beautiful fronds were over twenty feet in length. McTurk had never seen the species before, but probably it is the Ceroxylon Andicola, which is found high up on the Andes. Scattered about at their feet were delicate ferns whose tiny pinnules quivered at the least breath, whilst the huge fronds above them were unmoved by the passing breeze. It was a rare treat to behold these two singularly contrasting examples of the most exquisite grace and beauty known in the botanical kingdom. Here were also shrubs of the Bixa orellana, whose seeds furnish the "arnotto" paint so much used by the Indians.

At length we came to the Cotinga River, or, as the natives call it, the Quiâ-ting. It is curious that both the English and Indian name of this river should have reference to the bell-bird, although it is common in the locality. Here the stream is deep and about thirty-five yards broad, and a canoe which we fortunately discovered took us over in relays. On the opposite side was an unoccupied shed and a provision ground, which gave evidence that the desertion of the house was only temporary. Here were some blocks of red jasper of a very smooth and delicate grain.

On re-entering the forest, our path ran parallel to the river, but at some distance from it. Presently a bend in the river brought us to the side of a very pretty fall, where the water swept over a long and deep dyke, whose stones were as smooth and regular as if chiselled by hand. The name of the fall was Ookootawik, and there we intended to camp, but

Abraham assured us that a large village was very
near. So on we went, terribly fagged and tired,
and at last reached a scene of desolation. In North
America a similar scene would be called a "windrow,"
for the appearance was that of a forest overturned by a
whirlwind or tempest. Tree lay piled on tree, the
roots of one interlaced with the branches of another;
there were ladders of trunks stepping up and up, and
topped by the gnarled branches of some great tree,
which seemed to have been whirled down from a height
and to have lodged there. Many were black and
charred, and others snow-white and barkless, throwing
up their scraggy arms like skeletons. Of course all
signs of a path had vanished, and over this forest wreck
we had to scramble and pick our way, trusting to the
horn of Abraham for the right direction.

Horn-blowing was a very useful accomplishment of
our guide, as it kept us straight and frightened away
the various evil spirits, from a water-māmā to a wood-
demon.

Another stretch of forest and then we came out
on to a savanna, across which we saw the dome of
Waëtipu—the sun mountain. Four hours after
Abraham had told us the great village was close
at hand we arrived there. The first house that we
came to belonged to the head of the village; he seemed
highly delighted to see us, said his name was Captain
Sam, that he had been to Georgetown, that his house
and everything in it was at our disposal, but that we
would be more comfortable in the stranger's house,
which was on the other side of the savanna. Thither
we hastened, and found a very large, lofty, and well
built open shed, and we were soon more comfortably

housed than we had been since our departure. Around us were a few more houses, but they all had wattled walls, and none looked so cool and clean as ours. Close by, at the foot of a sugar-loaf hill, flowed the Quáting, and never was bath more enjoyed than ours that night in its cool, clear water. The name of the village was Menaparuti, and numbered probably about fifty souls.

Next morning we only waited long enough to buy some cassava, and then started off again. On clear days Roraima is in view from the village, but the morning was wet, and clouds covered all the mountains. We commenced with a short but very steep ascent, and after following a wretched path came to a mountain called Marikamura. Then we had a climb which, in length, far surpassed that of the previous day; the rocky steps were steeper, the root-ladders longer, the trunks which here and there formed the path more slippery, and the ascent altogether more fatiguing. About half way up we met an unpleasant-looking Indian who informed us that he was a great "peai-man," and the spirit which he possessed ordered us not to go to Roraima. The mountain, he said, was guarded by an enormous "camoodi," which could entwine a hundred people in its folds. He himself had once approached its den, and had seen demons running about as numerous as quails. We asked him if they would be good broiled on toast, and though he did not understand, he made an angry gesture and soon disappeared. The tale of this monster carried us back to old classical days, when the famous python hindered the march of Regulus.

From the summit we descended a considerable distance, and at length camped on the right bank of the Marika River. This was a pretty stream, the water foaming here among great boulders, and there flowing dark and smoothly over slabs of stone. The high banks were clothed with helianthus and cannas, and some beautiful ferns threw a green mantle of the most delicate point-lace over the moist earth. Away from the streams the soil was stony and poor, and the trees, instead of taking root, balanced themselves by great buttresses and numerous stilted stems of the most fantastic forms.

In the course of the day we had crossed many little savannas, strewn with small hard pebbles, which so hurt the feet of our Indians that most of them were compelled to make and wear bark sandals. On these savannas grew a very peculiar grass which bore a strong resemblance to miniature mops, as from the top of each stem fell a thick crop of hairy fibres. There was also a very pretty flowering grass, like a half-opened snow-drop, with its white outer petals extended to a long pale green point.

A wet evening made us retire early to our hammocks, and soon after, a few shrill cries were heard issuing from the forest, and presently with hair streaming wildly and shaking a rattle, the old sorcerer, whom we had met on the mountain, passed hurriedly along the path towards Roraima. He looked neither to the right nor left, and quickly disappeared in the gloom. Then Abraham once more dilated on rock spirits and sorcery to the timorous Indians, and the night passed slowly away in storm and rain.

CHAPTER XX.

AVANNA—RORAIMA AT LAST—APPEARANCE OF THE MOUNTAIN—
WATERFALLS—HEAD OF THE QUATING—TRIBUTARIES OF THE
AMAZON AND THE ESSEQUIBO—KUKENAM—ITS FALL AND RIVER
—THE "PEAIMAN" AGAIN—FALLS OF EKIBIAPU—A CELEBRA-
TION.

THE sun was fiercely bright when, after an early
start from our camp on the Marika, our
straggling party issued one by one from the dark,
shady forest on to an open savanna. A glad shout
from the foremost announced that our goal was in sight.
Hastening up an intercepting hill we looked down on
an undulating savanna country, streaked here and
there with forest belts. On our right towards the
north were the craggy heights of Marima; on our left,
beyond the terraced side of Waëtipu, the table-land
faded away in the silver-blue mountains of Brazil; and
in front of us, at the distance of a few miles, " walled
round with rocks as an inland island," stood Roraima.*

At the foot of the mountain the hilly ground lay in
patches of yellow stony savanna, and dark strips of
woodland rising in elevation as they approached its base.
Then came a deep forest-clad ravine whose farther side
sloped steeply up to a distance of about three thousand

* The height of Roraima above the sea is about 8000 feet; the table-
land from which it rises being about 3,500 feet above sea level.

2

feet, and springing directly out of this sea of green rose
a perpendicular wall of red rock, fifteen hundred feet in
height.   Hardly a shrub broke the sheer descent of the
shining cliff; scarcely a line of verdure marked where
clinging grasses had gained a footing on its smooth face.
The south-eastern corner was slightly rounded, and its
tower-like appearance increased its general resemblance
to a Titanic fortification a few miles in length, rising
from a forest glacis.

The glancing rays of the sun struck the red sandstone layers which shone like glass, and stood out in
bold and bright relief above their green base. A fly
could hardly have rested on the slippery slabs, and this
was the mountain we had come so far to scale!   The
level summit-line was backed by forest trees, which to
us appeared like bushes, and from their feet, like skeins
of floss silk swaying in the wind, three waterfalls
descended and were lost in the woods below.   But
towards the northern end of the mountain, a magnificent
cascade, whose lip seemed to be below the summit,
sprang in a broad silvery arch right down into the
green depths, barely touching the rocky wall in its
descent.   This is the source of the Cotinga River, or as
the Indians call it Quáting-yama *i.e.*, head of the
Quáting.   Eventually this river falls into the Amazon
after mingling with the Rio Branco and Rio Negro.
Still farther north was another fall whose waters formed
one of the principal tributaries of the Cako River.

To the north-east of the mountain, and close to it,
was a miniature Roraima, and towards its south-western
extremity was another mural precipice, apparently just
as impregnable.   The mountain was Kukenam, and
from our position it seemed to be part of Roraima, but

afterwards we found that they were separated by a wide and wooded valley. From this mountain, too, a splendid waterfall makes a clear leap of fifteen hundred feet before it disappears in the green wilderness at its base. It issues from the forest as the Kukenam River, and after joining the Yuruarti, which also rises in the Kukenam mountain, forms the Caroni River, which flows into the Orinoco below Ciudad Bolivar. Thus this extraordinary group of mountains becomes the watershed of some of the tributaries of three great rivers, viz.; the Amazon, the Orinoco and the Essequibo. No wonder that the Indians named it "the ever-fruitful mother of streams." No wonder, too, that such a spirit-dreading race should regard the weird and mysterious mountain with an awe which might almost be called reverential, were it not entirely inspired by fear. They believe that the magic circle which encompasses their "red-rocked night mountain," cannot be approached without danger, that he who enters it will never return, and that the demon-guarded sanctuary on the summit will never be gazed on by mortal eyes.

It is impossible to behold these smoothly chiselled mountains without wondering how they have been shaped and moulded by Nature into their present uniformity of feature. It could not have been by fire, as no trace of volcanic action exists in them. Were it possible that the present equatorial regions had passed through a glacial period, one would think that by the polishing and grooving of glaciers alone could the planed and sculptured rocks have attained their massive and perpendicular outlines. But it is supposed that South America, in ages long past, was divided into island groups, indicated as Wallace says, " by the great area and low elevation of the alluvial plains of the Orinoco and Amazon. A subsidence of less than two thousand feet would convert the highlands of Guiana and Brazil into islands separated by a shallow strait from the Andes."

Hence it must be that the action of water has carved the island sides into smooth perpendicular walls. For my own part, the idea would cling to me that in the untold past the surrounding region was a high plateau which by earthquakes and convulsions had been so shattered and broken that nothing was left in its original position save these mountain-monuments that lie scattered over its surface. It is also a matter of no little surprise that in a country of almost perpetual rain and moisture, which usually tend to produce rounded and broken hills and mountains, the predominating features should be the perpendicular cliffs and plateaus of dry and arid climes.

Our first full view of Roraima did not last long, for thick fleecy clouds gradually rolled over its flat top, and then slowly unfolded themselves down the red sides until they rested on the green slopes, presenting the appearance of a carefully spread damask table-cloth. Near where we had halted, we found the " peaiman" looking very disconsolate under the shelter of leaves. For a consideration, he offered to charm away the evil spirits that would beset us, and declared that without his assistance we should be unable to cross the river that we saw below us. Not desiring his society, we declined his aid and continued our walk.

In an hour we reached the river, and crossed it just above some fine falls where it was about forty yards in breadth. The water was not deep, but its red sandstone bed was as slippery as the smoothest ice, so that it required much caution to avoid falling, and being swept over the cataract, which was between forty and fifty feet in height. Where the river was dry, a curious appearance was presented by the sandstone which lay in perfectly even blocks like large red bricks. Abraham said that the name of the river— Eki-biapu—was derived from these singular slabs which are supposed to resemble the stones on which cassava is baked. In the savanna, on the other side of the stream, we erected our shed, a neighbouring grove supplying poles and the necessary fire-wood.

We celebrated our arrival by a grand clothes-washing, Charlie being chief washer-man, whilst I did the ironing by placing the articles between flat-stones and sitting on them. The day was finished by a grand banquet, consisting of rice, " Worcestershire " sauce, and " bakes." In bumpers of sparkling " Eno's Fruit Salt," we drank to the successful issue of our undertaking, and retired soberly to our hammocks for our first night's rest under the shadow of Roraima.

CHAPTER XXI.

FROM the ridge above our camp, we saw a long tongue of savanna running up through the forest belt, almost to a level with the base of the moun- tain wall. To this clear spot we bent our footsteps, taking with us provisions for three days, and leaving all the men except two in camp. To avoid the wooded ravines, we followed the undulating savanna for a long distance in a south-westerly direction. The path was well trodden and distinct, but there were no signs of habitations, and, indeed, the arid appearance of the country gave but little promise of support. The ex- ceptional drought which prevailed in the lowlands of Guiana prevailed also in the mountains, and no water flowed over the beds of many of the rivulets that we were constantly crossing. Wherever streams ran, the hollows and ravines were clothed with a bright green foliage; beautiful ferns grew on the banks, and among them was a grand species, which, in growth, resembled the sago palm. There were clusias too with pure wax-like flowers, and innumerable trees of a species of Melastomacea, whose large white blossoms unfold themselves with a rare tinge of pink which fades as day advances.

In the larger forest belts, the trees were chiefly of the chinchonea* and laurus; but their pale flowers were varied with yellow gomphias and crimson befarias. Slender palms and quaint cecropias added their beauty to the woodland edges, and the rough-leafed curatella mingled with the fragile mimosas. Over the savannas large kites hovered, and occasionally small parrots flew from one grove to another; white-throated swallows, of a reddish brown colour, dashed here and there, and a few long-tailed fly-catchers† balanced themselves on the thin stems of a rubus whose berries we often found very refreshing. I recognised some old friends, too, in meadow larks,‡ with their pretty black horse-shoe marked throats. But birds were not numerous, with the exception of a little brown species like a linnet which was continually rising from under our feet, and settling again a few yards off. In the wooded dells and ravines were pigeons, and from the thick bush came the unceasing frog-like croaks of the fringed chatterer.

On all parts of the savanna were dotted pyramid-shaped ant-hills, many of which had been freshly torn open by the great ant-eaters.§ These curious animals as well as the smaller tamanduas are very common in Guiana, though on account of their nocturnal habits they are not often met with in the day time. They are slow clumsy creatures, peaceable and harmless, but

* Ladenbergia densiflora.   † Milvulus forficatus.
‡ Sturnella magna.   § Myrmecophaga jubata.

formidable when attacked, as their hug is almost as
deadly as that of a grisly bear. Their skin will
resist the bit of a dog; but the snout is their weak
point, as a sharp blow on it from a stick will kill them.
When an ant-eater throws itself back and extends
its powerful claws, it will seize the first object within
reach and hold on to it, so they are often killed by
throwing some article into their embrace, and then
tapping them on the proboscis. The tongue of the
animal is very long and round, and can be lubricated
at pleasure from two large glands below the roots;
when with its strong claws it has opened an ant-hill,
it thrusts in its tongue which sweeps around and is
quickly covered with the insects which must, one would
think, be swallowed in enormous quantities to afford
sustenance for so large a body. The wonderful me-
chanism of an ant-eater's tongue calls forcibly to mind
the extraordinary muscular flexibility of all tongues,
from that of a giraffe, or snake, or bird to our own.
The tongue is so familiar an organ that we are apt
to overlook its varied offices, and its power and motion.

At last we turned off the Indian path, and soon
reached a delicious mountain stream which flowed at
the foot of the slopes, directly below Roraima. A
thick grove on the other side of the rivulet formed a
sheltered nook, and as the position seemed an admirable one from which to attempt an ascent, McTurk sent
back one of the men with instructions to move camp
to the present site. We then continued our climb
towards the south-eastern extremity of the mountain.
The higher we mounted, the more tedious became the
walking, owing to the boulders and débris which lay

hidden under the long grass. Sometimes a ravine had to be crossed, or our way pushed through a narrow belt of woodland.

On all sides were flowering shrubs and trees whose blossoms were not only brilliant but extremely fragrant. A more sweet-scented region than that around Roraima cannot be found. Eugenias, aromatic lantanas, ericas, genipas, a species of salvia, gesnerias and many other plants were as abundant on the mountain-savanna as the bignonias and passion-flowers which draped the forests.

After copious rains this district would be a perfect El Dorado for botanists. Even after the drought which had preceded our visit there were still many rare blossoms to be seen, and, though often faded or withering, we could form from them some idea of the floral wealth of Roraima. There were orchids, too, both tree and terrestrial, and of the latter a lovely crimson cleistes* bore off the palm. Wherever it was damp panicles of golden oncidiums drooped from the tree branches, but they as well as the odontoglots and epidendrons were dead or dying. One species—a Stanhopea†—seemed to set the dry weather at defiance, and its dark purple cup and bright green petals always looked as fresh as though they had been watered daily.

At length we arrived at a point almost on a level with the perpendicular wall of Roraima, but with a vast forest-clad gulf intervening. It had been evident to us from the first that our best method of proceeding would be to choose from one of these open savanna ridges any point in the straight-cut rock that appeared at all practicable for an ascent, and then by the aid of

* Cleistes rosea. † Stanhopea oculata.

a compass to make our way direct to that spot across
the wooded ravine. We afterwards found that the
passage of this deep and precipitous ravine presented
difficulties which were second only to those of the wall
itself. The north wind swept so keenly over our
elevated position that we were glad to seek shelter for
a time under one of the great black boulders that lay
around.

Our climb had made us thirsty, but we had to content ourselves with the water contained in the sheath
bases of the leaves of the wild pines,* which grew in
great numbers on the surrounding trees. These
natural reservoirs contained a good supply of rain-
water, but it was very old and full of insects.

Looking back over the country we had traversed, we
saw a picturesque landscape of mountain and plain.
Far below, the undulating yellow savanna was pierced
at intervals by tongues of green forest; beyond, a
few silver flashes marked where a stream ran through
a narrow valley, and on its left towards the east rose
the Sun mountain—Waëtipu—in a series of wooded
terraces, and with its southern extremity crowned by a
high sugar-loaf. From here, far away to the south,
stretched a chain of blue hills with flickering spaces of
shadowed sunlight between them, and on the edge of
the horizon towered the great table mountains of
Brazil, which, like colossal monoliths, contrasted with
the peaks and domes of the adjacent ranges in Guiana.
The scene was by no means grand but acquired a certain charm from the variety of colour diffused by the
western sun. The arid savannas which had seemed so
barren and dreary were now tinted with a soft green

* Tillandsia lingulata.

paling to silver-grey; the purple film of distance, which
we knew was only the parched foliage of some forest
belt, was streaked with golden lines, and the hard red
rock shingle over which we had painfully trudged,
gleamed and sparkled like early dew. Colour brightened the landscape, but life was wanting. No bird
sang, no hut was visible, no wreath of smoke curled
up from wood or plain, no moving object caught the
eye as far as it could reach. Cows in the green valley
by the river, a goat clambering about the rocks, or
even an Indian banaboo would have relieved the lone-
liness of the picture. Once we thought we could distinguish a cluster of huts in a distant vale, but the
sweeping shadows hindered any close observation.

From the open country we turned to the giant
fortress which rose sternly above us. The contrast
was sharp and decided. From the heights on which
we stood, the wide-stretching savanna land seemed a
grassy country over which a good horse could galop,
jumping with ease the narrow forest belts which inter-
sected the plains like hedges. But nothing less than a
winged Pegasus could expect to attain the summit of
the bare red wall that raised itself for hundreds and
hundreds of feet, unrelieved by aught save a few tangled
bushes and tasselled bunches of some wild grasses.
Carefully we scanned every ledge and crevice, seeking
some practicable spot to which we might direct our
steps on the morrow. At the southern extremity of
the eastern side, which we were facing, a ravine near a
rounded tower-like rock, draped with grass and lichens,
which recalled to my mind the Metella Tomb of the
Roman Campagna on a gigantic scale, gave better promise of a foot-hold than anywhere else. But a closer

examination showed that this fissure only separated the
rounded mass, at about two-thirds of its height, from
the rest of the mountain which then rose as perpendicular as in other places.

The following day when we resumed our explorations the results were similar. Near one of the falls
an angle in the rock, and a fringe of shrubs running
up for some distance along a deep crack, held out
hopes of a practicable ascent, but they vanished in a
plumb-line of wall without ridge or chink. Upon the
elevated ridges we were not troubled by animal life,
as besides a large rattlesnake, which one of the men
killed, we found nothing except two goat-suckers' nests,
each containing a young one. But down on the
savanna we were so plagued by a small black fly
that life was almost insupportable. These insects
attacked the eyes and ears, and bit severely, leaving
a bright red mark with a black centre. Even the
Indians were obliged, when in camp, to sit all day
surrounded by dense volumes of smoke.

It was therefore with no regret that, after finding
the ascent of the eastern side of Roraima impracticable,
we left camp one day with hammocks and provisions—
the latter now unfortunately reduced to little except
flour, of which we had far too much—with the intention of exploring the south side. The nights were
very cold, as the thermometer generally fell below 60
degs., but the days were intensely hot, and in walking
over the open savannas we were much blistered by
the sun, a circumstance which rendered the incessant
attacks of the black flies more aggravating. As we
crossed over the ridges, before turning towards the
mountain, we passed a very pretty tree-filled hollow

with precipitous sides and very deep. At one end of this chasm a fine stream emerged from underground, and after falling over the rocks in a picturesque cascade, wound round the base of the cliff and disappeared through a narrow outlet.

To reach an open point suitable for a survey, we passed over ground very similar to that on the eastern flank. There were the same steep spurs, the same widths of jungle, and the same black boulders, grass-covered and so slippery that the greatest caution was necessary in placing the feet, for a sprained ancle or a broken leg would have been of serious consequence in these wilds. At last we stood above the great ravine that surrounds the mountain, and commanded a near view of the southern wall. This side of Roraima is, if possible, even more precipitous than the eastern. The outline is similar, except in the centre, where it is wonderfully turreted and shaped with battlements. Here and there enormous black slabs appear to be let into the red stone as smoothly as if by hand, and in other spots quaint mosaic patterns can be traced. There were no water-falls from the summit, but in three or four places the dark shiny lines showed where water had only recently ceased to flow. A fine cascade issued from the forest slope near the smooth western extremity, but we could not tell whence the water came. This we imagined must be the second fall of the Kamaiba, mentioned by Schomburgh as having a breadth of seventy yards. Although when we saw it we estimated its width at barely that number of feet, yet its diminished size could readily be accounted for by the exceptionally dry season.

From this point we had a splendid view of the

eastern side of Kukenam, which projects beyond, and runs up parallel with the western flank of Roraima. Its steep wall, though seemingly perpendicular, did not present the same inaccessible front that Roraima did. North of its great water-fall, we could trace ledges covered with trees and bush, which to us seemed contiguous and continuous enough to reach the top. But Roraima was our goal, not Kukenam, and even to reach its base across the broad, dense forest valley that intervened, would have been the work of days. These southern slopes are actually more prolific in floral treasures than the eastern. The great fantastic black rocks which lie scattered about in infinite variety, are all clothed with agaves, cactuses, bromelias, gesnerias, mosses, and orchids. Every step reveals some new charm, every breath of air seems laden with a fresh sweetness; now it is the delicate fragrance of a yellow melastoma, and now the heavier odour of a chocolate-tinted odontoglot.

The soil on the southern side of Roraima was more moist than on the eastern, the plants were brighter, and the blossoms more abundant. In one place, which in our excursions we continually had to cross, there was a broad swamp, which was the last thing we expected to find on such elevated ground, traversed apparently by no stream. Here, grew a beautiful utricularia with dark blue flowers, a nepenthes, and various cœlogynes. There were also numerous sobralias,* but none were in flower, which was a great disappointment to us, as Schomburgh has pronounced this variety of orchidea to be the most fragrant and beautiful of its class. Near this swamp and hovering over the bell-blossoms of a

* Sobralia Elizabetha.

thibaudia* we saw the only humming-bird that we met with in the locality ; from the quick glance we obtained of it we could see it was not one of a very brilliant species, the plumage being of a reddish bronze.

It was always a relief to emerge on to this flowery marsh from the thick forest entanglement of the craggy ravine, and one day, after repeated failures to trace out the smallest likelihood of a possible ascent, we sat down on a rock near its edge, and agreed that the southern flank of Roraima was as impracticable as the eastern. One thickly-bushed crevice near the south-western end had cheered us with a prospect of success, but alas! between the wooded ledges were impassable walls of sheer rock, which neither man nor monkey could ascend. At another place the bush connection up to a certain point was only interfered with by an over-hanging slab, but that projection was an insuperable impediment. Gradually the conviction was forced upon us that the Indians were right, and that Roraima was impregnable. That the north side, even if it were approachable through the wide-stretching primeval forest, was impossible of ascent we had no doubt, on account of the stupendous wall of rock we had seen—though at a distance—from Cashew Cottage. So now it only remained for us to see what we could of the western side. Of this flank we could only get glimpses by retiring towards Kukenam, and from savanna hills obtaining our view up the dividing valley.

Owing to the clouds which almost incessantly filled this gorge, it was seldom that we could enjoy a satisfactory view, but what we did see only convinced us

* Thibaudia Pichinchensis.

R

that the western side was a repetition of the others.
To thoroughly examine that side of the mountain,
it would have been necessary to make a journey
round Kukenam, with the hope of finding high, open
ridges, from which we could have made a close inspection.   But this would have been a work of many days,
and, as we felt, a fruitless labour.   Irrespective of my
expressed opinion—when asked by McTurk—of the
futility of further efforts to ascend Roraima, I was
influenced by two other unexpressed considerations.
One of these was my firm conviction that my unfortunate boots would not stand a longer sojourn in the
neighbourhood, and I did not wish to pass the rest of
my days in the wilds of Guiana, and the other a
desire for something to eat.   For the fact was that our
provisions had run short ; rice, bacon, coffee, sugar,
mouldy biscuits, all had vanished except several great
quakes of mildewed flour, and it was beyond human
nature to return to camp day after day, hungry and
tired, and sit down with any enjoyment to cold water
and " bakes " or dumplings.   In theory the carrying
of a great quantity of flour may have been good, as I
suppose—although I am by no means certain of it—it
would have warded off actual starvation, but in practice
it was bad.   May future visitors to Roraima take
plenty of flour, but also may they take other things
to render it eatable !

On the day after our last view of the western wall
we turned our steps homeward, that is to the camp
under the eastern slopes, where our Indians awaited
us.   Before dark, we arrived at a circular hut which
stood alone on the top of a barren hill.   It was
deserted, so we took up our quarters in it for the

night. As daylight faded, the mountain fortress loomed more and more mysterious; the battlements were touched with a light rose colour, and the clear-cut summit was sharply defined against the purple sky. For a short time the mists rolled away, and this great "sermon in stone" stood out in vivid, faultless accuracy, all the more impressive from the perfect stillness of the scene. Then darkness fell; but presently the moon arose, and lo! the recent rich colouring gave place to a fretwork of pure frosted silver. The edges of the woods and the pencilled lines of the delicate foliage were burnished with the soft rays, and then, indeed, Roraima looked weird and solemn.

We were destined to see the mountain under many aspects, as whilst the clouds were enveloping it for the night, a pink reflection in them made us look for the cause. Then we saw that all the country to the south and east was illuminated by fire. We knew that probably the savanna grass around our camp had been set on fire by the Indians, but had the design and direction been arranged by an experienced pyrotechnist the effect could not have been finer. As if by art, the flames kept in accord with the hill outlines, here rising in long lines one above the other, and there encircling the oval peaks as with coronets of fire. The exhibition did not last long, for a storm, whose approach had been signalled by a few thunder-claps, broke with great fury and a deluge of rain descended. It continued all night, and we were very thankful that we had a roof— although a leaky one—over us.

Next morning the face of the country had changed, the parched appearance had disappeared, and all was green and fresh. The great Kukenam Fall, which of late had been growing more and more attenuated was now a splendid body of water, and three or four fine cataracts dashed down the side of Roraima where previously there had only been the faintest indications of moisture.

On our way back to camp, rivulets whose thread of water we had before stepped over, were so swollen that we were forced to wade through them, and in one or two cases we had to seek a place where a ford was possible. Our Indians were rejoiced to see us back again, as they had not expected that the mountain-demons would allow us to return. They were very glad to hear that on the following day we should prepare for our departure towards home. During our absence, they had transformed an open shelter into a picturesque little house with door and walls formed of palm leaves; a similar one, but made entirely of boughs, gave them a comfortable lodging. Thus warmly housed, our last nights at Roraima were pleasanter than the previous ones, and the smoke-filled apartment proved a successful remedy for the poisonous flies.

CHAPTER XXII.

WHEN engaged in repacking our diminished baggage, we were visited by a hunting party of Arecuna Indians. They were taller and fiercer looking than our Acawais who shrunk timidly away, and it was with difficulty that we could induce our own Arecunas to approach the strangers and interpret their language. Their long black hair was cut short and combed over the forehead, and the part thus "banged" was painted red. Their feet and knees were also painted red, and their faces were striped. Some of them wore cross pieces of steel wire as a lip ornament, and one was contented with a couple of common pins crossed in the same way. The chief wore a peculiar bell-shaped and tasselled ornament in his under lip, which he gave to me in exchange for two or three charges of powder. For his necklace of teeth I offered him a very good hunting knife; this he declined, but intimated his willingness to part with it for an old cutlass whose value was about one-third of the knife.

McTurk offered them two guns if they would show us how to reach the top of Roraima, but they beat their breasts, grunted, and with wild gesticulations declared that there was no way of ascending to the summit of the cloud mountain. If they had known of any way, the promise of a gun would certainly have induced them to point it out. The chief had a miserable "buck" gun, but the rest carried only bows and arrows and blowpipes.* The only bird they had shot was a duraquara which they had obtained near their own village, that was a few miles off in the savannas towards the east. We had noticed a few deer tracks, and once McTurk had seen a large animal cross slowly over an opening in the high ridge on Roraima, but he was unable to make out what it was. But game was scarce, and the Indians said they could not get any before we left next day, but they would return to their village and meet us on our journey with vegetables and cassava.

True to their appointment, we found them waiting near our former camp at Eki-biapu Falls, but the provisions they brought only consisted of some old cassava as hard as rock, and a few unripe plantains. We had started before sunrise in order, if possible, to reach the village of Menaparuti on the same night; it was a long march, but with our lightened loads we hoped to accomplish it. Before entering the forest we

---

* Waterton, in speaking of the blow-pipe says that this extraordinary tube of death is, perhaps, one of the greatest natural curiosities of Guiana. The amazingly long reed of which it is composed grows hollow without knot or joint. This is called the Ourah. Being of itself too slender to answer the end of a blow-pipe, a species of Palma is used as a case in which they put the Ourah. This outer case is called Samourah. The arrow—poisoned—is from nine to ten inches in length.

turned for a last full view of Roraima. " Parting looks," says the old Welsh proverb, " are magnifiers of beauty," and to us the grand red walls looked more perpendicular, stiller, and more solemn than ever. Against the pure blue sky the sharp outlines of the softly-coloured mountain stood out in perfect relief, and the atmosphere was so clear that we fancied we could hear the roar of the falls. What messages were those waters carrying to earth ? They alone knew the secret of Roraima, but their language, like that of the birds, is understood only by themselves. They could tell what we had vainly tried to find out, for we most assuredly failed to tear the veil from the head of this mysterious Sphinx. We were disappointed—who would not be ? —at the time. But we did not regret those Roraima days ; to others, perhaps, we had apparently laboured fruitlessly ; but not to ourselves, for we had learnt far more by Nature's lessons than can be taught by books, had witnessed scenes that well repaid some weariness of body, and had so enjoyed them that the spell of the mountains lingered long after we had left them. It is far from an unpleasant reflection to think that there are still a few unvisited spots in the world, and as the summit of Roraima is one of them, it may be that before long the fascination of travel will induce some toil-loving mortal to again attempt its exploration.

If I have dwelt too long on the various points of our journey, it has been with the idea that a knowledge of the difficulties to be overcome and the assistance to be gained *en route* may be of use to future travellers. I do not think it possible to make the ascent of Roraima except by a balloon, and the novelty of such an

exploring tour would give additional zest to the undertaking.

And now let me atone for my tiresome details by a
quick journey home. We reached the village of
Menaparuti late at night, after a very long day's walk,
and once more slung our hammocks in the fine open
shed. Here we rested a day in order to obtain a supply
of cassava, which the villagers prepared for us in
abundance. They had no fresh meat, so a hunting
party went off to the woods in search of game. All
they brought back was a small mâam, and a large
striped coatimundi,* whose flesh was so pungent that it
completely spoilt the bird which was cooking in the
same pot. The favourite beverage among the inhabitants was a disagreeable-looking compound called
cassiree; it was of a pink colour, and being prepared
in the same way as paiworie it was highly appreciated
by our men.

We were much amused by a number of village
children who used continually to pass our house on
their way to the river. Slowly, in single file, they
marched past, the tallest leading, and the sizes
diminishing until the last was not the height of his
bow. They never smiled, and were so grave that they
impressed one with the idea that they were little old
men starting on some dangerous expedition. Once we
followed them, and directly the small troop was out of
sight of the houses, its members changed immediately
into children. They shouted and laughed, pushed
each other into the river, jumped into their tiny canoes
and raced one against the other, swam about and were
as happy as schoolboys on a half holiday. After their

* Nasua.

fun had lasted some time they all crossed the river, resumed their solemn air, and disappeared in single file up a forest path on a shooting foray. About an hour afterwards they returned triumphantly, dragging another coatimundi which the little imps had managed to kill, probably with a poisoned arrow.

From childhood to old age male Indians are seldom without a bow or a blowpipe in their hands, peccaries, pumas, and panis falling as easy a prey to the man as toucans, pigeons, and small birds to the boy. To get food is their principal object in life. They have few pastimes, but enjoy a dance, or the " ha-ha " game.* In some tribes, when a youth wishes to show his courage and powers of endurance of pain, he is shaken up by his friends in a bag filled with Monouri† ants, which are the most dangerous of their kind, the sting of one being sufficient to cause fever. This is almost their only amusement. I do not think they were much impressed with the intellectual recreations of the white men, as when McTurk and I were playing our usual evening euchre, they could not understand the object of throwing down pieces of painted paper only to pick them up again. They thought the picture-cards were wonderful, and that they were the portraits of foreigners.

We obtained a good many teeth necklaces from them, as they were inclined to sell anything they possessed for powder or knives, but they had no other curiosities worth the trouble of carrying. There was great com-

* The " ha-ha " is a wicker shield, with which the opponents try to push each other down.

† The Monouri ant is used by the Indians as one of the ingredients in preparing the deadly Wourali poison.

petition amongst the women as to who should dispose
of the most cassava ; in fact they brought a great deal
more than we could take, and much of what we did
pack soon became mouldy and uneatable, in consequence
of insufficient sun-drying.

The evening before we left, some natives from the
Mazaruni spread a report that we were to be attacked
and killed by the Cako Indians, as soon as we reached
that river. We paid no attention to the rumour, but
our men were evidently much disturbed. We thought
it highly improbable that the timid and peaceful people
we had seen should suddenly become hostile ; still the
idea of an ambushed river and poisoned arrows was
not a pleasant one. It was just possible that traders in
Venezuela, hearing of our expedition, and being ignorant
of its import, had instigated the Indians to take offensive
action, but it was very improbable, and we soon forgot
all about it.

Before dawn we were up and away, and ere the last
house in the village had disappeared, we heard the
crowing of a cock. Had we heard it sooner what a
dinner we might have had ! Indians never eat eggs or
poultry, and only keep hens as pets. On leaving the
savanna, Abraham conducted us by a different path from
that by which we had come, stating that it was a much
shorter one, but he had not known of it before. In an
old cassava field, there were some beautiful golden red
blossoms of an amaryllis, evidently a garden-flower
run wild.

We crossed the Quáting much higher up than previously, near a small village called Nimapi. It was a
pretty place, the houses being perched on the side of
the high hill on the left bank of the river, and

surrounded with plantains and fruit trees. There were
also a few huts on the right bank, and as in one of
them there was a trough of paiworie, we had to sentinel
the door until the last man had crossed in the cranky
canoe which we used as a ferry-boat. From this
village commenced an ascent which equalled, if it did
not surpass, in steepness any that we had accomplished.
The damp and slippery ground made it all the more
difficult, but in time we reached the summit. The
path afterwards branched into our old one near the
Opuima mountain, which we descended in wonderfully
quick time. So long and rapid was that day's march
that we slept that night at Cashew Cottage, having
made the distance in half the time that we had previously taken.

A large family party was assembled at the cottage,
and from them we received the intelligence that three
of our woodskins had been taken from their hiding
place. This was worse news than the other, and when
about the middle of the next day we arrived at old
Granny's, a man was at once despatched to find out the
truth. He returned with the joyful intelligence that
all the woodskins were perfectly safe. Several parties
of Indians had stopped at the old lady's hut during our
absence, but nothing that we had left had been
touched, and the rice and coffee were very acceptable
to us.

After the late rain, the water in the Aruparu creek
was deeper and our descent was not so much impeded
as our ascent had been. On the way down, we reple-
nished our larder with a fine water-haas, which was as
large as an ordinary pig. At last we arrived at the
house of Captain Sam on the Cako River, and there

found that the story of the attack was an entire fabrication, probably invented to induce us to remain longer at the village, or to proceed by another—the Cukuie—route. Then again we entered the Mazaruni River and landed at our former camp. Our old friend the Pirate, who was cruising about in his canoe, came to bid us farewell, and in his charge we left the woodskins to be returned to their owners.

Before starting on our last walk through the forest, we saw a woodskin approaching, its paddles being plied vigorously by a man and a woman. Mazaruni, at the prospect of another conquest, immediately began to adorn himself, and as the boat drew near, our amusement was great at recognizing old Granny and her son, Abraham, whom we had left at their home on the Aruparu creek. The paddles, under the strength of the skinny arms of the old lady, swept the water as powerfully as did those of her robust son, and she did not appear to mind in the least the physical exertion for which we pitied her. Indian women, although well treated by their husbands, are so accustomed from their girlhood to the exercise of physical endurance that what we consider must be a sad strain on their powers is but a second nature to them even in old age.

Our friends had brought with them much of the flour and salt, and some of the various articles that we had given them, and intended to proceed farther down the river on a trading expedition. We gently blew on the old lady's back for good luck, and with a farewell to Abraham set off through the dark forest.

CHAPTER XXIII.

IN order to reach Macrebah before our hands and
feet were quite worn out, we determined to waste
no time but to proceed by forced marches. Poor
McTurk, in addition to injured limbs and feverish
attacks, was worse off as regards foot covering than I
was, as he was reduced to three pair of india-rubber
shoes, which he wore one over the other on account of
the holes.

With our thin soles, the sharp-ribbed roots made our
movements as delicate as walking over eggs, and it was
very ludicrous but rather painful to find ourselves now
on one leg and now on the other, vainly endeavouring
to escape the knobs and pointed projections which thrust
themselves against our bruised feet. I could not help
thinking of the grasshopper when he said to the bee ;

> " There's a time to be sad,
> And a time to be glad,
> A time both for working and stopping ;
> For men to make money,
> For you to make honey,
> And for me to do nothing but hopping."

During this walk we saw for the first time the great
" bird's nest" fern, adapted for the purpose its name
implies. Numbers of these plants grew on the trunks
and low branches of the trees, and in many instances
they had been made the nesting places of ground-doves.
No other species of bird occupied them, but we invariably
discovered one or two eggs of the dove, and in one instance the mother allowed us to look at her as she sat
on her nest.

Concerning the rest of our foot-journey, it suffices to
say that in three days we arrived at Macrebah and
there found our boat, the Adaba, all safe. My wonderful boots would certainly not have lasted another day ;
but I had no further need of them, and in gratitude I
hung them to a high pole driven into the sand, and
after tracing underneath the well-known words

> " Whoever dare these boots displace
> Must meet Bombastes face to face !"

I abandoned them as an offering to the Spirit of
Macrebah Falls.

The large dacana balli, which we had left covered
with white flowers, had now fruited, and the great green
nuts fell heavily to the ground. The Curipung River
was but little affected by the recent rain, and its claret
coloured water reflected the white sand in as clear a
purple as when we first saw it. Here we rested for a
day and dismissed all the Indian carriers, with the
exception of our own six, who formed the crew of the
Adaba, and Lanceman and Mazaruni, who accompanied
us, when we departed, in a woodskin. "Master will
no take boot," said Charlie with a mischievous grin, as
he pointed to the two skeletons swinging near the
water's edge, when we started.

A long day's journey brought us down to the Mazaruni River. There was little current in the creek, and in some places so little water that there was scarcely sufficient to moisten the throats of the disconsolate herons which, like lone fishermen, moodily gazed at the shallow stream from the pebbly shore.

The sun was just setting when we arrived at the mouth of the creek, and never before had the scenery of the great river appeared to us so picturesque as it did then. The black water stretched away north and south-east to the wooded hills, whose sides were first a a rose colour, then crimson, then purple. Above the dark forest, across the river, a golden green haze expanded itself up and up until it touched the pink and pearl clouds in the east. The sharp promontories of silver sand sparkled as they caught the expiring rays, and stood out so clearly that even on the most distant could be seen the shadowy forms of the egrets or cranes. Then, as the colours all faded into a slowly darkening purple, a mysterious silence prevailed; the cries of the monkeys ceased, the toucans had called "tucano" for the last time, and the ibises no longer screamed "curri-curri" as they flapped by. The sombre jungle grew blacker, the sky clearer and the thin vapour which stole up from the water's edge crept along the forest-crest and spread a film over more distant objects. Then on noiseless wing the night-hawks floated past looking like great butterflies, bats skimmed through the forest openings, and fire-beetles suddenly started into life.

Presently the breeze brought faint sounds from the river, a frog croaked, again we heard the fog-horn notes of the howling monkeys, and then the "brief

twilight in which southern suns fall asleep" was over.
When the full moon rose, the scene might have been
in Greenland. The river changed to a sheet of silver-
blue ice, the vapour-clad trees sparkled like dew, the
sky and stars were brilliantly clear, and the great sand-
bank was a drift of the purest snow. On this white
bank some travelling Indians had encamped, and their
dark figures stood out in as bold relief as those of
Esquimaux on a snow-field. The illusion was heightened by the sleigh-like appearance of a woodskin
which had been drawn up from the water, and at
whose side three dogs were lying asleep.

The night sounds which issue from the forests of
Guiana are singularly strange and weird. Whether on
broad river, narrow creek, or out in the lonely woods,
the traveller is greeted with unearthly sounds that
utterly banish sleep. Scarcely had we ensconced ourselves in our hammocks, which had been slung to the
trees bordering the sandbank, when the " voices of the
night" broke forth. First, the night-jar ran down its
scale " ha, ha-ha, ha-ha-ha," each note lower than the
preceding, and each the acme of the most hopeless
sorrow. The utter misery told in this bird's voice
must be heard to be believed. Next a mâam uttered
its shrill plaintive whistle, whose volume increased
until the whole forest resounded with it. Then, as if
a warning to the noisy reveller, a loud rattle, like that
of a night-watchman, sounded close by. This was the
music of a night-hawk. Immediately after came the
melancholy cries of a pigeon, like a human voice calling
for aid. These sounds were hushed by the dismal
wail of a sloth, which, in its turn, gave place to a series
of sharp clucks like those of a hen, and which were

produced by some winged creature of darkness. After a moment's stillness a stealthy rustle in the leaves betokened the neighbourhood of a snake or lizard, and, farther off, a breaking branch told where a larger animal was pushing its way.

These sounds continued until nearly midnight, that hour when, as Cotton says:

> " The goblin now the fool alarms,
> Hags meet to mumble o'er their charms ;
> The nightmare rides the dreaming ass,
> And fairies trip it o'er the grass."

Suddenly the Indians commenced to whisper, for even their sleep had been aroused by the wild screeching of the terrible didi, whose dreaded notes ended in a prolonged and mournful crowing This unearthly sound seemed to be the climax, and soon the real silence of the night settled down.

> " Now night it was, and everything on earth had won the grace
> Of quiet sleep ; the woods had rest, the wildered waters' face ;
> It was the tide when stars roll on amid their courses due,
> And all the tilth is hushed, and beasts and birds of many a hue,
> And all that is in waters wide, and what the waste doth keep,
> In thicket rough, amid the hush of night-tide, lay asleep."

For three or four hours the silence lasted, only broken occasionally, and for a few minutes at a time, by the moan of a jaguar, or the fierce snappings of the small hunting tigers on the track of some peccaries, or of the night-loving tapir. Before dawn the concert was renewed; the monkeys howled, the mâams whistled piercingly, the honoquas and duraquaras gave endless repetitions of their own name, and with the first streak of day-light the parrots chattered from the tree tops. Day broke, and the camp was again alive.

Bird cries are imitated to perfection by Indians, and

we not unfrequently obtained a pani, or a duraquara,
by such means. At night they would note the position of the roosting bird by its notes, and then in the
early morn proceed in its direction, attract it by their
imitative cries and shoot it.

Amongst the Indians encamped on the sandbank
was a family which was on its way to Georgetown,
with hammocks and birds for sale. We christened
its members the Cowenaros, *i. e.*, cocks of the rock, as
they had a fine specimen of the bird in their possession. They were good-looking people, and as the
father was the only one who had ever visited the coast,
there was considerable excitement with the younger
members, especially on the part of Miss Cowenaro,
who was going to celebrate her début into society by
a new dress—the first she had ever worn. By some
means she had obtained some pink calico, and out of
it she had manufactured an extraordinary robe which
she was always trying on, or, perhaps, accustoming
herself to wear. At any rate, on our way down the
river we never arrived near a prominent rock without
seeing the young lady perched on the top of it, and
evidently lost in admiration of herself.

After leaving Lanceman's house at Menaparuti where
we found all that we had left, the rain, which we could
see by the heightened river had been falling heavily
in the mountains, burst upon us. The fine weather
which had favoured us for so unexpected a length of
time, broke up and rain set in. Sometimes the squalls
were so severe that the waves almost swamped our
boat, and the woodskins, containing Lanceman and
Mazaruni, who accompanied us to the Settlement,
were only saved by a quick run to shore.

Our journey up the river had by no means been a slow one, in spite of the delays at the cataracts and rapids, but now with the swift current in our favour and the speed with which we shot the falls, up which we had toiled wearily on foot, our progress was extremely quick. Shooting the falls was splendidly exciting, and not unaccompanied by danger. I had once employed a spare afternoon in Ottawa by accompanying the rafts in their descent of the " timber shoots," and great amusement it was, but devoid of the inspiring element of danger. There the descent was swift but smooth, steerage was unnecessary, and no impediment barred the narrow, wall-edged current. Here it was different, conflicting currents seethed in all directions, broken rocks and half-hidden projections cropped up all around, and nothing but the strong arm and steady eye of both the man at the prow and the man in the stern could save the boat from being dashed to pieces.

To those unaccustomed to it—as I was—the novel sensation of fall shooting is delightful. Choosing the long smooth tongue of water which indicates the safest passage, the words " Give way all !" are spoken, and though the paddles work with intense vigour, and the foaming water is pouring madly at your side, the boat seems to stand still; the rocky walls rush up to you, the waves dash at you instead of from you, the the roar increases, the drop looks perpendicular, and still you are apparently not moving ; there is a plunge, a wave or two shipped perhaps, and the next moment the boat is floating quietly in the smooth back-water below the falls. Sometimes the difficulties of the descent are much increased by the twists and turns which have to be made in the very middle of the fall itself. Our Indians, who had been rather nervous at the first few cataracts, soon recovered their self-possession, and were so elated at their skill that once or twice their valour almost overcame their discretion.

When we reached the Falls of Yaninzaec, the rising water had so altered the appearance of the river that we could no longer recognize our old landmarks. In the island labyrinth we lost the channel which led to the " portage," and it was in vain that we tried to regain it. All our efforts only brought us to one or other of the great falls, a safe descent of which could no more be accomplished than that of Niagara. Darkness at last came on, and we had to encamp on a small island.

Next morning we were fortunately discovered by the two woodskins—containing Lanceman and the Cowenaros—and under their guidance we reached the portage; passing on our way a curious rock called " the Cabuni"—near the mouth of the river of that name. After carrying the boat over the portage, and reloading it, it was McTurk's intention to proceed a short way down the river and camp early, so as to replenish our larder with fresh meat. It was many days since we had tasted meat, and our appetites told us that game would be very desirable.

" I shoot and eat one pani," said Sammy.

" Pani!" said Charlie indignantly. " I eat one maipurie myself."

Now as a pani is nearly as large as a turkey, and as a maipurie, *i. e.*, tapir, is about the size of a small donkey, the speakers must, indeed, have been hungry. For ourselves we had arranged quite a little banquet with the remnant of the provisions that had been left at Lanceman's house. There was a tin of mullaga-tawny soup, a pot of marmalade, a tin of biscuits, and besides a bottle of brandy which we had been treasuring for weeks, there was still a small supply of Seidlitz Powders, which had of late superseded Eno's Fruit Salt on occasions of great jollification. In order the better to enjoy our intended repast, we had refrained from breakfast on that day, but "*l'homme propose, Dieu dispose.*"

Having safely descended several cataracts after leaving Yaninzaec, we saw in the distance a pleasant spot for camping, and from the same direction heard a great howling of monkeys which promised sport. We rapidly approached a fall, the roar of whose waters seemed unnecessarily loud. This we descended, but a sharp turn that had been hidden by a high rock revealed another and steeper fall, which it would be madness to attempt to shoot. But it was too late, no power could stop us; we were already in the long swift current which swept down to the deep drop. "Give way!" shouted McTurk, as a glance showed that there was no chance of escape except by the mere possibility of speed; then there was a sweep of paddles, a plunge, a wild swirl of waters, wave after wave rushed over us, and the boat went down. The whole affair had happened so quickly that, almost before I could realise it, I found myself under water and powerless to rise to the surface, as my legs seemed to be entangled in something—probably the framework of the awning we had lately put up as a shelter from the rain. The idea flashed through me that this surely could not be the end of my long looked for Roraima expedition, and giving a great struggle up I came to the surface.

The first thing I saw was the Adaba, bottom upwards, floating down the river, and McTurk and two of the crew clinging to her. I soon reached them, and in about thirty minutes, by gently guiding our support towards a rocky island, our feet touched the ground. Higher up the river, in a different direction, we saw that what we thought were the remaining four of the Indian crew, standing on another rocky islet. Almost immediately afterwards the woodskins appeared; having descended on the opposite side of the river, where there was a moderately easy passage unknown to us. They at once unloaded, and pushed out into the river to try and save whatever happened to be floating.

Suddenly the cry was raised " Where is Charlie ?" Then we saw that only three men stood on the far rock, and that what we had at first taken for a figure was only a barrel. We never saw him again. Sammy, who sat next to him in the bow, said he saw him spring clean out of the boat before she went down, and strike out for land. No cry was heard ; we on the boat thought he was with those on the barrel, and they thought he was with us. As he was a very strong swimmer, we could only suppose that he had been sucked down by the terrible undercurrent, or that he had been dashed against a rock. It was very, very sad, and for a time we could not believe that he was really drowned. For the rest of that day and next morning we searched long and carefully in the hopes of recovering the body, but uselessly. The Indians said that two years ago three natives were drowned in the same place, and their bodies were never found. The poor fellow had only been married a month before we left Georgetown, and among the crew were two of his wife's brothers. One of these had a very narrow escape as he was not a good swimmer, and was just sinking when he caught at a pillow floating by, which supported him until he reached the flour barrel that saved the other two. Everything was lost, with the exception of a few hammocks and a tin canister of mine, which, besides Indian curiosities, fortunately contained shirts and other clothes. For the crew had divested themselves of everything when in the water, and not one of their bundles was picked up. Guns, ammunition, field-glasses, provisions, plants, boxes of clothes, in fact almost everything we had, and alas! a human life—the only thing that could never be replaced—all lay in the deep water under the falls of Tebucu.*

When we continued our journey, we took Lanceman as a guide to guard against any future catastrophe, and no other accident occurred, with the exception of a hole which was knocked into the side of the boat whilst being let down a fall by means of ropes. From the woodskins we had received paddles to replace those we had lost, and urged on by hunger we made rapid progress, and at last issued from the island-dotted river into the large lake-like expanse of water near the junction of the Cuyuni.

After we had passed the neat houses of the Caribs, the island church came in view, cottages appeared, people with clothes on were seen walking about, there

---

* The names of these and the other falls marked in the map were given to us by Lanceman, who claimed familiarity with all of them.

were ducks and geese, and the different signs of civilization. We soon rounded Palmer's Point, and after a
tremendous squall of rain and wind, arrived at the
Settlement, where we received a hearty welcome from
the Superintendent and his family. And thus ended
our expedition to Roraima, a journey which we had
accomplished in a little more than two months.

CHAPTER XXIV.

WHEN, on our way back to Georgetown, we saw the waters of the Mazaruni mingling with those of the Essequibo, it was like parting with a human friend whose career we had watched until its close. We had seen it, or its great tributaries, at its birth, spring from its cradle in the broken mountain tops into the green valley below, and in that one great leap for life rush blindly into the big world that lay before it. Not an easy-going, quiet life—not a gentle, cared for one, but a life from first almost to last of strife and battle. Occasionally, in its school days, checked and restrained, and forced into channels that it spurns, only to dash more impetuously than ever against the rocks and crags that beset its path. Sometimes its smooth, shining face rippled only with a smile, and the tremulous music of its voice as it flows softly over its pebbles, tell of peace and rest, but such expressions are but minutes compared with the years of its more troubled life. Not until its youth and middle age are long past, does this turbulent river exert its powers for the benefit of mankind. Wearied with strife, it now sweeps on with deep and silent current, bearing contentedly on its bosom the joys and sorrows of others, and rendering fruitful the land through which it courses. Older and older it grows, but persevering to the end, until at last it slips away from us, and the course of the tired river is ended in the grey sea.

At Georgetown, we heard that the drought had continued until very recently, and had caused much suffering among the poorer classes. The public tanks had run dry, and water brought from a long distance was sold in the streets by the bucket. But now the long looked for rain had come, much to the satisfaction of everybody—even of the planters—and as an old black lady said, " It was indeed a cause of great 'tank'-fulness." With the rains had also come the annual visitation of " hard-backs," great beetle-like insects, that flocked in myriads to the gas-light, and literally enveloped tables and chairs in a coat of living mail.

We arrived just in time for the races, and for the two days they lasted the town presented an unwonted scene of excitement. The road to the d'Urban race-course was alive with a laughing, pushing crowd of various nationalities, in holiday garb. Vehicles of all descriptions, heavily weighted, plodded to the course, or empty rattled back at full speed, eager for another load. The days were hot but the distance short, and the broad road lined with pretty gardens and cottages, half hidden in green shrubbery, formed a pleasant and animated drive. Some of the buildings, too, were worthy of notice, especially the handsome Roman Catholic Cathedral, the Orphan Asylum, and the

Almshouses. A gateway and avenue of palms marked the entrance to a wide-spreading grass-land, round which the course ran. A dividing road led up to the circular grand-stand, which was not a very picturesque building, as its architecture was something between that of an umbrella and a band stand; but it was cool and suitable to the occasion. The surroundings differed but little from those of most race-courses; tents, booths, sheds, and structures of more or less pretension, varying from the well carpentered stand, admission to which was four "bits"—a bit in Guiana is fourpence—to the slender structure composed of a few boards and a roof of leaves, where the entrance fee was theoretically a "bit" but practically nothing.

Of the races themselves there is not much to be said. As nearly every event—as was expected—was won not only by the same stable, but also by the same horse, the meeting could hardly be termed an exciting one. To stimulate competition and to avoid disappointment, a certain gallant major entered his carriage horses, but as I do not think they ever got round the track, their entries were not altogether a success. Still the intention was laudable, and if others had been equally public-spirited, the racing would have been far from tame. The winning horses were undeniably good, and were the love of sport as widely diffused as cane, the Georgetown race-meetings would compare favourably with those of any colony. At present the inhabitants, object to an annual presentation of cups, plates, stakes, and purses to one stable, but as long as the races are kept up, it must continue until enterprise claims a division.

To the coloured population the races were a source of unmixed enjoyment. From the rude Barbadian to

the peaceable Mongol, all were bent on a day's diversion.
When the inevitable dog ran down the track, they
howled and screamed with delight, and when the horse of
the mounted policeman ran away with its rider, joined in
the race, and came in a good third, the enthusiasm was
unbounded. After each race the crowd was permitted to
rush into the space hitherto kept clear in front of the
judge's stand. Then as many as could approach swarmed
round the box, eagerly demanding a piece of paper with
the name of the winner written on it. The numbers
posted up were nothing to them, they had probably seen
a wide difference between the first and second horses, but
nothing could satisfy them except a written statement ;
a " bit " depended on the result, and oral testimony
was valueless. Such laughter and shrieking would
follow ! Those who had lost would try to defer payment
until the next race was over, and those who had won
would loudly demand their money. Angry gesticulations would succeed to wordy warfare, and just as a
free fight seemed inevitable, the band would strike up
and the whole crowd, without exception, would
commence to dance. Then, until the course was again
cleared, nothing would be visible but a mass of parti-
coloured heads bobbing up and down.

With the exception of the brilliant head-dresses,
white predominated too much in dress for much effect,
but here and there might be seen Indian coolies in
cardinal red or mazarine blue, and others who had not
been afraid to risk the union of green, orange, pink
and purple. But from above, one saw only the bright
turbans and twisted handkerchiefs keeping time to the
music, and it was very amusing to witness the transformation when, during a passing shower, the animated

poppies were replaced by a dense mass of dancing umbrellas. No drunkennness nor any unpleasant incident marred the enjoyment of the meeting, and not until the roses of the setting sun had all faded, did the merry crowd wend its way back to the duties of every-day life.

Very soon after the race meeting I took leave of kind and hospitable Georgetown, and proceeded to Trinidad on my way to Carácas. A few days after our arrival in Port of Spain, I heard that the French mail-steamer "Cacique" was about to sail for La Guaira, and so instead of waiting for the monthly English mail-boat, I secured my ticket by the former and hastened on board at the appointed hour.

As the " Cacique " lay at anchor about two miles from the wharf, and besides a heavy surf running the rain poured in torrents, the little open boat that conveyed two or three of the passengers—myself included—was almost swamped, and we were thoroughly soaked before reaching the steamer. After the well-appointed vessels of the Royal Mail, with their disciplined crews, ad-mirable attendance, and officers who spare no pains to make their passengers as comfortable as possible, it was with some dismay that we saw the little tub in which we were to continue our voyage. A closer inspection was not more cheering as the cabin accommodation was wretched, and the tiny upper deck unpleasantly crowded. I must add that this was not one of the regular French Mail-steamers, but only an inter-colonial vessel running between Martinique, Trinidad, and La Guaira.

Our fellow-passengers were nearly all Venezuelans; the ladies were extremely pretty and graceful, but a

little over-dressed for a sea-voyage, and not being good
sailors they soon presented a very dishevelled appearance. The men, as usual dreadfully vociferous, in
their shouting, stamping, and gesticulations reminded
me of my late friends the Arecuna Indians. They
mean nothing, it is merely their mode of emphasizing
their expressions, and though they shake their fists in
each other's faces, and contradict one another flatly, no
insult is intended or received as such. They all wore
long black coats, tall hats and high-heeled boots, a
dress which they thought quite appropriate to the
deck of a ship. Fortunately, except for the invalids,
there was no necessity to go below, as all the meals—
and very good they were—were served on deck, which
also answered for sleeping quarters. In the matter of
ice, there was not much on board, and no one was
allowed any except the captain. I once drew his
attention to that fact, but he only shrugged his
shoulders.

It was dark when we left the Gulf of Paria and
sailed through the Dragon's Mouth, and then turned
west towards the mountains of Cumana. Next
morning we found ourselves at some distance from
shore, but moving parallel with the Venezuelan coast,
which looked high, grey and arid. After passing
Caribe there were a few signs of habitation; stretches
of white sandy beach were backed by groves of palms,
and in the bright green wooded ravines, which inter-
sected the cactus-covered hills, a hacienda peeped out
here and there.

Our first halt was at Carupano, which is said to be a
rapidly progressing town. There is certainly room for
improvement. In the centre of the bay rises a high

rock covered with different species of cereus, and on it stands a lighthouse. On the beach is the custom-house, and a collection of low yellow mud huts surrounded by brown rocks and bare hills. The town itself is situated farther back, and a river flowing through the neighbouring palm groves gives a fresher aspect to that part of the withered scene. Like most ports on this coast, it is excessively hot and unhealthy.

Early next morning we entered the Gulf of Cariaco and anchored off Cumana the capital of the State of that name. Here, as at Carupano, the town is situated at some distance from the coast, and at the foot of a brown hill crowned by an old fort. Between us and it is a broad sandy plain, dotted over with mud huts of the most unprepossessing appearance. There is little to interest the spectator in the arid scenery, except its colouring, and that is of the brightest and most varied description. The intense light, the excessive radiance of the sun, and the clearness of the atmosphere—Cumana is comparatively healthy—produce an astonishing effect of colour that would not be possible if vegetation predominated.

Here and there glistening points of white sand run out into the water, and behind them are undulating grey hills which end abruptly in low walls of red rock. Through the yellow plain the Manzanares winds its way from the town, and its banks are covered with a growth of dark green verdure. The hill of San Antonio above the town looks white and shining. Nearer to us, a long promontory is covered with a broad belt of palms, among which some red-roofed houses are seen. Beyond, across the gulf, is a red, rocky shore, which fades away in a russet brown; and over the coast-range, which is almost crimson in its rich tints, rise the purple peaks of distant mountains. Sky and sea are of the purest blue, and the snowy sails of the fishing boats, that skim over the latter, are only matched in whiteness by the gossamer shreds of cloud that float above. To what extent modern conveniences are carried in the capital we could not tell, but the canoes that brought us Muscat grapes were only hollowed tree-trunks, and the vehicles on shore that conveyed passengers to the town were donkey-carts.

From the number of nets which we observed, it was evident that fishing was the chief occupation, and the continuous strings of pelicans showed that there was an abundance of food. These ungainly birds were a great amusement to us as we basked in the intense heat of the powerful sun. Sometimes they flew past in long lines on heavy wing, with their long necks doubled over their backs, and with no other thought than that of regulating their movements with those of their leader. At others, they approached singly or in pairs, each one attending to its own business. Here one falls like a bullet, but diagonally, and disappears under the water. In a second it re-appears, and disgorging the fish from its capacious pouch swallows it whole. That one must have missed his aim, as he sits gazing with an air of astonishment, as if such a thing was impossible; and his mate who alights behind him and slides along the water to his side, reproves him with a look as comical as it is expressive. The graceful man-of-war "hawks" appeared to be much more expert than the pelicans, and though they did not dive so frequently, yet they seldom missed their fish.

Around Cumana the dry plains and barren rocks,

the stunted vegetation, the roofless walls and shattered buildings are suggestive of the earthquakes and tidal waves which have desolated this as well as other parts of this region of South America. Only now is the town recovering from the shock of 1854, which in twenty seconds reduced it to a heap of ruins.

After leaving Cumaná the scenery was more picturesque. Deep bays ran in between rocky headlands, at whose feet were islets as white as if they had been salted. Crags and bare hills, varied with tree-clad promontories, and dainty little coves full of the bluest water and rimmed with the whitest sand. After threading our way through various islands, we passed between El Morro and the craggy islet of Borracha, and cast anchor opposite Barcelona, another State capital. The place was not attractive, and I was glad to be able to answer no when a Venezuelan asked me if I was not going to visit the great English paper-manufactory which is established in the town.

The district is interesting, for here commence the great "llanuras" which stretch away to the Orinoco, and whose inhabitants are veritable free children of the desert. The "Llanero" will not live in towns, and is only happy when with his horse for a companion he roams over the boundless grassy plains tending his cattle. Brave, hardy, athletic, and eminently patriotic, the "Llanero" is a power in the land, and has played an important part in the establishment of national independence.

Inexpressibly sombre was the vast brown savanna extending to the purple horizon, relieved only at intervals by a few hills or a flat-topped mountain. Even the sea seemed to have caught the cheerless tint

T

of the land, and instead of sparkling blue, we tossed in dull water of a leaden grey. By degrees the level shore gave place to undulating ground, this to rounded hills, and the hills to a mountain range, above which towered La Silla, one of the highest peaks—in the State of Bolivar—of the northern Cordillera of the Andes.* Then we knew we were approaching La Guaira.

* In the mountainous district of Mérida—another of the States of Venezuela—the Sierra Nevada peak attains an altitude of nearly 14,000 feet above the sea.

CHAPTER XXV.

VIEW OF LA GUAIRA—PROJECTS IN VENEZUELA—LANDING—INDIAN
PATH TO CARACAS—BRILLIANT BEETLES—VIEW FROM CERRO DE
AVILA—DESCENT TO CITY—CLIMATE—AN EARTHQUAKE ALARM
—SAD ASPECT OF THE CITY—MYSTERIOUS POWER OF THE MOON
—PERIHELION AND PESTILENCE.

VIEWED from the open roadstead where vessels
anchor, La Guaira is picturesque. Almost
from the very edge of the water the land begins to
rise, so that the houses, with the exception of those
that line the curved shore, are perched on the various
spurs and knolls in a gradually ascending scale. The
depth of the little town is only a few hundred yards,
and straight up behind it rises the rocky wall of the
Cerro de Avila, which terminates in the peaks of
Naiguatá and La Silla. The height of the former is
8,800 feet above the level of the sea. On the right,
the cliffs which shut in the town end in an abrupt
white promontory, enclosing a low stretch of cultivated
ground dotted with palm groves and strips of forest;
and on the left the coast range extends away, casting
down long spurs and spits of palm-covered land which
shoot out far into the sea. On all sides there is a
blending of green hills, rugged and barren precipices,
cactus-clad rocks, fertile plains, and white houses.

To the right of the town may be traced the carriage

road to Carácas, which after endless zig-zags disappears round a mountain corner Of the mule or Indian path to the same place nothing can be seen, except the general direction indicated by a steep ravine which cuts into the face of the Silla immediately behind the town. Near this ravine, at a height of about fifteen hundred feet, a fort holds a commanding position, and a battery on the shore completes the defence—such as it is—of La Guaira. Landing here is effected with considerable difficulty, owing to the tremendous swell, against which there is no protection.

Many projects have been formed to convert this roadstead into a port, but like all other good intentions in Venezuela, they remain projects. For some years a small breakwater has been in course of construction, but the sea demolishes it as fast as it is made. Lighters are used for the conveyance of passengers from the vessels, and from one of these we were jerked on to the jetty dripping like river-gods, as the wave which had carried us on its crest to the landing was followed by another which broke over the boat. A capsize in these waters would probably be fatal, owing to the number of sharks which here lie in wait for victims. Not long ago a young negro was bathing near the jetty and was attacked by a shark, which snapped off his right hand. He did not lose his presence of mind, but by beating the water with his left arm hoped to frighten away the monster. But he was again attacked, and before the boat which had put off from shore to his assistance reached him, his left hand had been cut off. The shark was harpooned and captured, and on opening the stomach of the animal, there were the two little black hands. The boy recovered, and now earns a living by showing his hands, which he has preserved in spirits, to compassionate strangers. If the sea-sharks are bad, the land-sharks are equally so, and it requires an hour's hard bargaining to have your luggage carried from the Custom House to the hotel—a distance of a hundred yards—even for the exorbitant sum laid down in the official tariff.

The Hotel Delfino is in keeping with the wretched town, and rather than sleep there I determined to start at once to Carácas. Having made arrangements that my heavy luggage should arrive there early next morning by coach, I hired a mule for three pesos—dollars—and set off for the capital by the famed Indian path. The distance from La Guaira to Carácas by the new coach-road is over twenty miles, and as the crow flies about nine, but then the great Silla has to be crossed. At the end of a narrow ill-paved street we reached the ravine, down in whose depths several swarthy washer-women were dabbling in about two inches of water, which was all that remained of the usual mountain torrent. This we followed for a short distance, and then turned off to the right, up an excessively steep and stony path.

From the fort, the view over the town and the neighbouring village of Maquetia towards Cape Blanco was charming, and it was a relief to have left behind the insufferably hot streets. I do not think my steed was accustomed to extend his walks farther than this fort, as henceforth my time was fully occupied in persuading him to move. Before starting I had remarked to his owner that he hardly seemed up to my weight, but the reply was that, in spite of his appearance, he had many good points and his indomitable spirit atoned for all imperfections. His points certainly were numerous, but unfortunately they were all physical, as a more angular creature I had never seen—in fact he was all points, and I soon discovered that his indomitable spirit was unquestionable. After repeated efforts to make the saddle stay in its proper place, I at last fastened the girths so tightly that I was sure nothing could move it. In this endeavour I had been aided by the animal, who very kindly, as I thought, drew himself into the smallest possible compass. Hardly was I again seated when he commenced to swell, and in a second the girths were in shreds and the saddle and its occupant slid to the ground. In Guiana, tapirs are said to rid themselves of boa-constrictors in the same manner. With the assistance of cord and boot-laces I managed to patch up the broken tackle, but my futture progress was necessarily very slow.

The path was ever winding up and up, and pretty scenes were continually opening. Here was a bold rock sparsely covered with prickly pears or magueys, and there in a deep ravine, through which a mountain torrent ran in many leaps and falls, the light green plantain fields were ruffled by the breeze into waves of frosted silver. Plantations of coffee and bananas fringed the path, and at the hill corners, where the ground fell steeply to the valley below, were perched the owners' houses, with their clean white walled drying grounds, which looked like little forts. Over the large gateway of one of these, which was particularly neat and flourishing, was the inscription. "Rio Grande," Señr. Pacheco, 1877. The proprietor, or perhaps the superintendent, was sunning himself on the door-step, whilst his old wife improved the opportunity by a searching examination of his head.

From the back of his rancho there was a delightful view looking towards the sea. On all sides the forest was gradually giving place to cultivation, and even the steepest of the rocky angles were in many places blackened by the destroying fire. Occasionally, where the woods were thick brilliant cotingas flew in and out, and amongst the coffee trees glossy green jacamars darted about like giant humming-birds. There were only a few bright butterflies, but a great variety of gorgeous beetles. Some of the latter were of great size, and most of wonderfully metallic hue. Others were of satiny green with black spots, silvery white with red lines, black with crimson bands, brown with yellow bands; there were blues, greens and velvety browns, all touched with rich bronze, and as different in shape as in colour. Here was one clouded like a goatsucker, there another in maroon velvet ornamented with black hieroglyphics, some with antennæ three inches in length, others with only a horn.*

Afterwards in Carácas I had an opportunity of inspecting a private collection of Coleoptera, and I was astonished at the amazing variety of species belonging to Venezuela, and their extraordinary shapes and strange proportions :

> "Their shape would make them, had they bulk and size,
> More hideous foes than fancy can devise,
> With helmet heads and dragon scales adorned,
> The mighty myriads, now securely scorned,
> Would mock the majesty of man's high birth,
> Despise his bulwarks, and unpeople earth."

---

* Amongst the few coleoptera that I recognised were those of the curious genus Brentus and the giant Prionus. There were also brilliant

The only four-legged animals that we saw were small donkeys, so laden that the legs and ears were the only parts visible, and their great bulk made it a difficult matter to avoid collision.

At last we reached the top of the ridge of Avila, on one side of which were ravines and cultivated slopes and hill spurs trending away to the blue sea, and on the other rounded hill-spurs that half concealed the city of Carácas, which was situated in the valley below. The south-western limit of the valley was bounded by the strangest range of hills ever seen ; hundreds of sharp skeleton ribs formed the base, and these were of all shades of brown, green, yellow, and red. Above them rose the grey and arid slopes, cut into endless clefts and chasms, and over their summit range after range of mountain stretched away to the horizon. Soon we left the Indian path, and descended by the old military road, half-paved, steep, and winding towards the city. The descent seemed almost as long as the ascent, and I began to wonder how so low an elevation—for Carácas is less than 3,000 feet above the level of the sea—could possess a climate which has been designated that of " perpetual spring."

When we entered the city limits it was night, as instead of the usual four hours, our journey had occupied nearly eight. Trusting to my mule to find its way to its stable in the hotel, for none of the few people who were still abroad could give me any direction, we at last arrived opposite a spacious building, the Legislative Palace, which was surrounded

silver green Curculios, golden green and coppery Buprestidæ, steel blue Scarabœi glossed with purple, and a few specimens of Phaucus lancifer, whose golden body was tinged with green and violet.

with sleeping soldiers. There they lay in companies
and detachments across the roads, on the side walks,
and under the porticoes. Could a revolution have
suddenly broken out? Strange that they should not
have known anything about it at La Guaira! A sentry
opposed my progress by pointing his musket at me,
but the mule was in a hurry for the first time, and
could not stop. Soon after it walked through an open
gateway on the opposite side of the Palace, and I found
myself in the courtyard of the hotel. There I heard
that there was no revolution at present, but the military
and most of the inhabitants slept out of doors, for fear
of another earthquake similar to that which a few days
previously had destroyed the neighbouring town of
Cúa.

For a Spanish American city the Hôtel Saint Amand
had fair accommodation and good living. The former
was limited, as the best rooms were occupied by the
English Minister, but to partake of the latter all the
non-resident inhabitants of the town and the members
of the Legislature used to assemble. Still there was
plenty of room for improvement in the establishment,
and the new hotel which is about to be built will
probably supersede the old one.

From the accounts I had heard of Carácas, I had
expected to find a bracing atmosphere after the heat of
Guiana, but I was doomed to be disappointed. From
the time I arrived until I left, neither the days nor the
nights were enjoyable. No breeze tempered the heat,
the air was dull and heavy, the sun was as hot as at
La Guaira—which is said to be one of the hottest
places in the world—and the general feeling was one
of depression. Of course, I was told, it was an excep-

tional season, that the heat was unusual, and that the oldest inhabitant—that unfailing encyclopedia of dates and events—could not remember such weather. Where can one go in the present day without finding exceptional weather, and changes that are always astonishing to the oldest inhabitant?

After leaving Bermuda—and, indeed, whilst we were there—we had met with nothing but exceptional seasons. At St. Thomas it was said to be exceptionally cool with the thermometer at 89.° At Martinique such rain had never been known. At Trinidad it was extraordinarily dry. In Demerara there was an unheard of drought, and here in Carácas weather-prophets foretold dire phenomena from the unusual state of the atmosphere and its unwonted sultriness.

Since the destruction of Cúa—of which I shall speak in another chapter—the alarm had increased in Carácas; nor, after two severe shocks on the 13th, was it at all diminished by a printed warning issued on the 15th of April by Señor Briceño, a scientific gentleman of the city, who had made the study of earthquakes one of his principal pursuits. In it he wrote to this effect: " Be watchful! humanity compels me to place the inhabitants of Carácas on their guard, for I believe there are causes for fear, and the situation is alarming." He then showed how in former earthquakes the shocks corresponded with the different phases of the moon, and affirmed that " it was much to be feared that at full moon on Wednesday the 17th of the month (April), at 1° 29′ 0″ at night, a tremendous shock would be experienced." It was in vain that men of great scientific attainments refuted the arguments of Señor Briceño, in vain that they asserted that all the com-

bined intellect of the world could not foretell earthquakes, and that regarding such phenomena nothing
could be affirmed and nothing denied, a panic had
seized the people of Carácas, which increased as the
prophesied time approached. To have turned a river
with a book, or have stayed an avalanche with a wise
saying, would have been as easy as to have stemmed
the tide of the general alarm by scientific discussion.

It was Holy Week, but for fear of a catastrophe the
religious ceremonies did not take place, and the churches
were closed. The weather was damp and changeable.
A painful silence reigned in the deserted streets, and
scarcely a house gave signs of being inhabited. An
immense number of people had left the city and gone
into the country, taking their household effects with
them. Carriages and conveyances of all sorts demanded exorbitant prices for transportation, and received
them. The great square—La Plaza Bolivar—was
like an encampment. From its trees hundreds of
hammocks were suspended, its avenues and gardens
were covered with picturesque tents, its benches and
seats were turned into couches, and every available spot
was occupied with camp bedsteads, canvas stretchers,
or sofas. To avoid a similar fate to that which befell
a regiment of 800 soldiers who perished in the great
earthquake of 1812, when Carácas was destroyed, all
the military had left their barracks and slept in the
open air. The other plazas, and even the Calvario,
presented a similar appearance to that of the principal
square.

To add to the sad scene which the city presented,
the neighbouring heights and woods were on fire, and
the heavy smoke thickened the dense atmospheric

vapours. The day previous to the expected fatality passed slowly and mournfully away. As night advanced, anxiety increased. It was intensely still, the only sounds were those of coughing and crying children, and the moans of frightened women. One o'clock sounded from the cathedral, and then the quarter. Heads appeared at tent doors, pale faces grew paler, watches were examined, there was an extraordinary air of expectancy, and people only listened. The clock struck the half hour. Everyone breathed again, a confused murmur arose simultaneously, the name of Briceño was received with jeers and laughter, some women fainted and others fell into hysterics now that the tension was removed, and the panic was over. None, except the experienced, can appreciate the intense dread inspired by earthquakes; some may say they are too accustomed to them to care for them, but it is not those who live in South America, where the terrible shocks level houses, villages, and towns in a few seconds.

In 1812, there was a roar as of cannon firing, then a silence; this was followed by a tremulous motion, which increased until the ground seemed to roll in great waves, and in a moment the city of Carácas was in ruins and 12,000 people perished. Of late years there have been an extraordinary number of tidal waves, devastating storms, and earthquakes in Peru, Chili, and Ecuador; the direction of the convulsions has been more and more northerly, and since the destruction of Cúcuta in 1874 the north of South America has been widely shaken. The wise men of the south have paid much attention to the causes of these convulsions of nature, and numerous theories have been indulged in. By some they

have been attributed to luni-solar attraction, by others
to the transits of Venus and Mercury, to comets, and
to different electric influences. Quite lately, a sensation
has been created in Europe by the prediction that we
are rapidly approaching one of the most pestilential
periods of the earth's history. And why? Because in
1880, or soon after, the perihelia of the four great
planets—Jupiter, Uranus, Saturn, and Neptune—will
be coincident. The theory is that, when one or more
of the largest planets is nearest the sun, the temperature
and condition of our atmosphere are so disturbed as to
cause injurious vicissitudes, terrible rains, and prolonged
droughts &c., resulting in the destruction of crops
and pestilence among human beings and domestic
animals. Soon, for the first time in 2,000 years,
four planets are to be against us, and we are warned
that every living thing will be put to a severe and
trying ordeal.

Various prophets have arisen who have foretold the
advent of great convulsions within certain dates, but I
think the Caraqueñan astronomer alone has been bold
enough to predict the destruction of a city by an earthquake, at a given hour and minute, taking for his
data the changes of the moon. It is strange that, for
so long a period, a mysterious power should have been
attributed to the cold, peaceful moon, or its phases.
Superstition has assigned to it great influence over
health, over the weather, over the tides, over the
ascent of sap in trees, over vegetation, &c., and we
all know how dangerous it is said to be to sleep with
the moon's rays falling on the face. Eminent men of
science have declared that these ideas have no foundation whatever, and that neither theoretically nor practic-

ally have they ever been proved true in the smallest particle. Yet on account of their antiquity and the firm hold they have established on public belief, it is probable they will exist for a much longer time yet. Regarding the periods at which earthquakes occur, Humboldt has said that, if it were possible to notice the daily state of the earth's superficies, one would soon be convinced that the earth was always being shaken at some point or other. For the inhabitants of Venezuela, it is an alarming fact that the intervals of time between the great earthquakes are growing less and less. In 1766, a great earthquake occurred at Carácas, and in 1812, Carácas was totally destroyed, as were Cumaná in 1853, Tocuyo in 1868, Cúenta in 1874, and Cúa in 1878.

CHAPTER XXVI.

FOR a view of Carácas and its neighbourhood, no better point can be chosen than the summit of the "Calvario," or, as it is now called, the "Paseo-Guzman Blanco." The hill lies to the west of the city, and has been changed from a barren waste into a very pretty garden, with winding carriage-drive and walks. It has an historical renown, as it was here that the old Indian rulers of the country made their last fight against the Spanish invaders, and from its summit, where now stands the statue of the late President, the Cacique Paramaconi defied to single combat the leader of the Spanish host.

On the side nearest to the town the slopes are laid out with flower-beds, rockeries, fountains and miniature cascades. The shrubs and plants are of hot, temperate and cold climes ; there are lichens and ferns, lilies, sunflowers, two or three kinds of hybiscus, gardenias, dahlias, verbenas, sago palms, roses, heliotropes, lantanas, honeysuckles, and various brilliant creepers. In the centre of the beds on the summit were two

magnificent clusters of one of the commonest yet
showiest orchids—Cattleya mossix—in Venezuela. The
large flowers were of a rich rose colour and the lip
delicately spotted; in each cluster I counted over two
hundred blossoms, and they formed most attractive
centre-pieces Near by are the reservoirs which supply
the city with water from the river Macarao. They
are cut out of the solid rock and are of fine proportions; the distributing pipes are of iron, but it seems a
mistake that the aqueduct itself should have been made
by open trench-work instead of by piping.

    From our elevation, Carácas looks like all other
Spanish American towns; low houses with brown and
red roofs, among which stand out conspicuously numerous cupolas, domes, spires, towers and the white façades
of the churches. The city divides the valley of Chacao
into two parts, that towards the east looking fresh
and green with coffee and sugar plantations, thick
groves and forest; and the other, towards the south-
west, fertile and cultivated but without the rich woodland which marks the opposite side. Winding about
through rows of poplars and willows, the river Guaire
flows through the valley in a south-easterly direction,
being joined in its course by three little streams called
respectively El Caroata, El Catuche, and El Anauco.
These three streams divide the town into four parts
and have broad, deep beds, but in the dry season would
hardly rank above gutters; yet a national writer,
taking them, I suppose at the flood, has recognised
in them—together with El Guaire—the four rivers of
Paradise, and taking into consideration its climate of
perpetual spring, has compared the situation of Carácas
to that of Eden.

Still, small as these streams may be, their green banks clothed with orange, quince and avocata trees with here and there plantain, or sugar and coffee estates, give a bright smiling aspect to the valley which contrasts with the arid range of the southern hills.

The northern sierra, with its domed Silla, is also barren and grim for a considerable portion of its lower half, but above it is crowned with fine trees and foliage. I tried hard to be impressed with the scenery so highly praised by Humboldt, but I failed. Perhaps it was because I could not shake off the remembrance of another valley view, viz: that of Mexico from the hill of Chapultepec, which I had seen the previous year. In the two panoramas, there were just sufficient points of resemblance to cause a comparison. The green plain, the poplar rows, the magueys, the weeping willows, the cypresses, the ruined habitations, the white city and the mountain frame were in both pictures, but the view of modern Carácas was only a diminutive shadow that faded almost out of sight with the memory of the Mexican landscape. In the latter, everything is on so magnificent a scale, and all is enshrouded in the glamour of history.

From Chapultepec, with its giant cypresses and sad associations, the eye wanders over the garden, villages, cultivated-fields and swamps, avenues of poplars, and great aqueducts to the city itself, with its innumerable churches and convents. Beyond it sparkles a silver lake and canal, and the whole is enclosed by lofty mountains, above which tower the snow-covered heights of Popocatapetl and Iztaccihuatl, the volcanic guardians of the city of Montezuma. Though externally Carácas presents a similar appearance to other Spanish American towns, yet internally it is far brighter and more cheerful. Its streets, which intersect one another at right angles, are broad and clean, the houses are well-built, the merchants' stores and the shop-windows are quite attractive, and what with flowers, fountains and statues, the Paris of South America—as the inhabitants love to call their little town—at certain seasons looks gay and animated.

In the centre of the city is the chief Plaza—Plaza de Bolivar—which is flanked by the Cathedral, the President's or the Yellow House (Casa amarilla) as it is called out of compliment to the White House at Washington, the Archbishop's Palace, and the usual collection of small shops and " palperias " that abound in all plazas. The trees and flowers are carefully tended, and the benches and chairs are not only numerous, but, strange to say, comfortable. When there is no moon the Plaza is well lighted by pretty clusters of oil-lamps. Once the city was lighted by gas, but the company—like other Venezuelan projects —failed, and now oil is used.

The middle of the Plaza is occupied by a magnificent equestrian statue of Simon Bolivar the Liberator. It is a work of art that must be deemed fully worthy of the great man, even by his most ardent admirers. An unprejudiced observer might ask whether the man was worthy of the statue. It is doubtful whether the true life and character of Bolivar will be known or at least acknowledged. I have lately read his memoirs by General Holstein, who was chief of the Staff of the President Liberator, and with whom he claims great intimacy. The author here says, " The dominant traits in the character of General Bolivar are ambition, vanity, thirst for absolute, undivided power, and profound dissimulation. . . . . Paez was heard to tell Bolivar, after the action at Villa del Cura, that he would move off his own troops and act no more with him in command; adding, 'I never lost a battle wherein I acted by myself, or in a separate command, and I have always been defeated when acting in concert with you and under your orders.' . . . . To these brave men (here a number of men are named) Colombia and Bolivar himself owe the expulsion of the Spaniards, and the salvation of the country, if their present expulsion may be called so. The brightest deeds of all these Generals were performed in the absence of Bolivar. Abroad they were attributed to his military skill and heroism, while in fact he was a fugitive a thousand miles from the scenes of their bravery, and never dreaming of their successes. . . . . . General Bolivar, moreover, has never in person commanded a regiment, nor four soldiers. He has never made a charge of cavalry, nor with a bayonet. On the contrary, he has ever been careful to keep himself out of danger. . . . . Bolivar has several times offered his resignation, but never unless he knew beforehand that no one would dare appear in favour of accepting it. . . . . . The great mass of the people are ignorant, bigoted and rude, to a degree not easily conceived by one educated in almost any Protestant country. Hence it is that Bolivar's speeches, proclamations, promises, conversations, are thought of so highly. These people, once getting a notion into their heads, keep it fast. They think Bolivar a great man, and believe that his monstrous faults are in fact the faults of others, because he tells them so."

Colonel Hippisly in his " Narrative of the Expedition
to the Rivers Orinoco and Apure, in South America,"
says :—

" Bolivar would ape the great man.   He aspires to
be a second Bonaparte in South America, without possessing a single talent for the duties of the field or the
cabinet. . . . . He has neither talents nor abilities for
a general, and especially for a commander-in-chief. . . .
Tactics, movements, and manœuvres are as unknown
to him as to the lowest of his troops.   All idea of
regularity, system, or the common routine of an army,
or even a regiment, he is totally unacquainted with.
Hence arises all the disasters he meets, the defeats he
suffers, and his constant obligations to retreat whenever
opposed to the foe."

Certainly his life was one of extraordinary vicissitudes;
he was perpetually flying from, or returning to, his
country.   At one moment an outcast, at the next
making a glorious entry into Carácas.   In reference to
one of these returns the author I first quoted, says :—

" The entry of General Bolivar into Carácas (August
4th, 1813) was the most gratifying event of his whole
military career.   But here I cannot omit to mention a singular and characteristic trait of that vanity
of which I have already spoken.   Previous to his entry
into Carácas, a kind of triumphal car was prepared,
like that which the Roman consuls used on returning
from a campaign after an important victory.   Theirs
was drawn by horses; but Bolivar's car was drawn by
twelve fine young ladies, very elegantly dressed in
white, adorned with the national colours, and all
selected from the first families in Carácas.   They drew
him in about half-an-hour from the entrance of the

city to his residence; he standing on the car, bareheaded and in full uniform, with a small wand of command in his hand. To do this was surely extraordinary on their part; to suffer it was surely much more so on his. Many thousands were eye-witnesses of the scene."

The same year Bolivar was again a fugitive. Once more, in December 1842, the inhabitants of Carácas flocked in immense throngs with banners, pennants, oriflammes, and trophies of war, to do honour to Bolivar. But this time it was a funeral procession, as the remains of the Liberator were being brought for interment in the city. In a poem on Simon Bolivar, Whittier has written :—

" How died that victor? In the field with banners o'er him thrown,
   With trumpets to his falling ear, by charging squadrons blown,
   With scattered foemen flying fast and fearfully before him,
   With shouts of triumph swelling round, and brave men bending o'er him?
   Not on his fields of victory, nor in his council hall,
   The worn and sorrowful leader hears the inevitable call,
   Alone he perished in the land he saved from slavery's ban,
   Maligned, and doubted, and denied, a broken-hearted man."

But the question naturally arises, how is it possible that Bolivar should have liberated his country, and preserved in himself the supreme power, without superior talents? To this General Holstein replies :—
" If by ' liberating his country ' it be meant that he has given his country a free government, I answer, that he has not done so. If it be meant that he has driven out the Spaniards, I answer that he has done little, or nothing, towards this; far less, certainly, than the meanest of the subordinate chieftains. To the question, how he can have retained his power without superior talents, I answer, in the first

place, that the reputation of superior talents goes a great way. . . . . The stupid management of the Spanish authorities has facilitated all the operations of the patriots. The grievous faults of Bolivar and some of his generals have been exceeded by those of his adversaries. It is not strange, therefore, that Bolivar should have been able to do all that he has done with very limited talents."

A late writer on Venezuela—Señor Miguel Tejera —has thus summed up the character of Bolivar.

" Bold and fortunate as Alexander, a patriot like Hannibal, brave and clement like Cæsar, a great captain and profound statesman like Napoleon, honourable as Washington, a sublime poet, a versatile orator, such was Bolivar, who united in his own mind all the vast multiplicity of the elements of genius. His glory will shine in the heaven of history, not as a meteor that passes and is lost in the bosom of space, but as a heavenly body whose radiance is ever increasing."

Between two such extremes of blame and praise as those I have quoted, a middle line may perhaps give a true estimate of the character of the Liberator; and, though his fame may not have been spotless, though he may have been neither a great warrior nor a statesman, yet he was a patriot, and above all, successful. Alive, he was by turns a demi-god and an impostor; dead, his beautiful monument in the Cathedral of Carácas testifies to the reverence of the nation.

CHAPTER XXVII.

FROM the Plaza Bolivar you pass at once into the square where stands the Legislative Palace. This edifice of Doric architecture is graceful and imposing, but does not impress one with the idea of the necessary solidity in so earthquaky a country. A handsome court with a large fountain (fine as regards its material, but feeble in its water-jets) divides it into two parts, one of which is surmounted by a huge dome—another compliment to the city of Washington —that will probably fall at the first severe shock. The most solid portions of the building are the iron pillars of the corridors which came from England.

The history of the building of this edifice is singular. The original site was occupied by the Convent of La Concepcion. One morning the convent was missing; it had been swept away during the night by the order of the President, and already hundreds of workmen were busily engaged erecting a new structure. Such were the activity and enthusiasm displayed in this work,

that within ninety days the Chambers destined for the
Legislature were ready for occupation. Whenever one
of the numerous arches was finished, the event was
celebrated with music and fireworks, and when the last
sound of the hammer was heard, previous to its occupation, the occasion was made one of general rejoicing.
A pretty little garden plaza runs down one of the sides
of the Palace, and in the centre is another equestrian
statue of heroic proportions, which has been raised in
honour of Guzman Blanco, " the illustrious American
and Regenerator of Venezuela," who built the palace
and the aqueduct. I do not think his successor, General
Alcántara, the present President, has built anything, but,
if he would introduce ice into the Paris of South
America, a niche might be found for him in the
Temple of Fame.

On the opposite side of the little garden, and running
parallel with the Palace, stands the University and the
Museum, both of which have a modern rococo façade
in semi-gothic style, that contrasts strangely with the
arched cloisters and great stone patios in the interior
of the ancient building. The exterior decoration is
perhaps too suggestive of the educational system that
is carried on inside. Yet in spite of teaching a somewhat superficial character, public instruction received
a great impetus during the Presidency of Guzman
Blanco, and the great increase in the number of schools
and scholars promises favourably for the progress of
this Republic, whose chief city has earned from some
writers the cognomen of the " American Athens." It
must be admitted that the Museum is not a credit to
the city; its eminent director—Dr. Ernst—has laboured
long and arduously in its cause, and has hitherto vainly

implored the Government to support the institution. Promises are made, but only to be broken, projects are inaugurated, but never carried out; and at present there can be no better example of a "whited sepulchre" than the Museum of Carácas.

With the exception of the cathedral, none of the numerous churches offer much interest to a visitor. That of San Felipe Neri is a fine edifice, and its exterior presents a curious appearance on account of the numerous cupolas which adorn it. Already four generations have contributed largely towards its completion, and it is still unfinished.

One day when wandering near the Pantheon I passed through an ancient doorway, and found myself in a little wilderness, in which stood ruined walls and rooms open to the sky. Trees thrust themselves through the broken pavement, moss and grasses grew on the fissured stones, vines twisted themselves about the empty window spaces, and lizards and butterflies were the only living creatures to be seen. It resembled many other of the fragments that alone recall the terrible earthquake of 1812, but it possessed a special interest, for it was once the home of Humboldt when he visited Carácas in 1800. Another relic of Humboldt is to be seen in the market-place, where, on a brick pillar, stands a sun-dial which he is said to have erected, although the inscribed date (1803) hardly corresponds with the time of his visit. The market differed in no particular from the usual Spanish American market. The geography of arrangement was just the same; stalls with imported goods, calicoes, cloths, hardware, &c.; then cordage, baskets, and native manufactures; then fruit and vegetables, poultry in eel-pot cages, and turkeys tied by the leg. Last of all, the meat-market. Here and there were some small parrots, cardinals, and mocking-birds, but not a specimen of the lovely "siete colores,"* a bird I was very anxious to obtain. On the Orinoco I was told I should be able to obtain them at Carácas, here they said I should only find them on the Orinoco. There was very little beauty and a great amount of ugliness amongst the market women; a few pensive Indians, with their mahogany babes slung across their backs, carrying off the palm in both instances. The most curious sight, and at the same time the most repulsive, was that of a negro who was literally covered with large round knobs from head to foot. I was told the name of the terrible disease, but have forgotten it.

To gain an idea of the celebrated Caraqueñan beauty, neither the market, nor even the Plaza Bolivar on band nights, must be visited. On Sundays it is the rude fashion for the youth of Carácas to congregate round the door of the favourite church, near the University, and there to feast their eyes on the lovely figures that have been attending mass. That it is worth their while to do so is evident from the never-failing throng of admirers. The prevailing type of beauty has very distinct characteristics. The expression of the face is spirituelle, and, in colour, white as alabaster, but tinged with a healthy glow. The eyes are dark and lustrous as the hair, and the teeth perfect. But occasionally one sees types similar to the "rubias" or "morenas" of Mexico; the former with gold or auburn hair and soft eyes of the deepest blue, and the latter with delicate olive complexion, black, poetic

* Tanagra septicolor.

eyes, and brown-black hair. These beauties are by no
means numerous, and beauty tinted by nature is rare,
but altogether I do not think anyone could deny
that the women of Carácas are worthy of their reputation.

The environs of the town are neither picturesque
nor interesting; the roads are unshaded and dusty,
that to Sabana Grande—a favourite drive—particularly
so. On the way there, and just within the city limits,
may be seen another of Venezuela's failures. This
time it is a railway, which was intended to connect
Carácas with Petaré. The station is there, and a short
distance of grass-covered rails, but they, together with
a broken engine and a mouldy carriage, alone represent
the projected means of communication. Harbour improvements, railroads, gas and ice companies, and all
advances in civilization seem to fail in Venezuela ;
nothing succeeds except revolutions and statues. And
yet the lemon—which those in authority call country—
is squeezed to the last drop !

Near the station is a plantation—La Guiana—whose
owner must have been disgusted with the repeated
failures of the city, as over his gateway is inscribed
the legend,* "Dost thou love liberty? then live in
the country." Beyond Petaré is the curious Cave of
Encantado, which contains bats, stalactites, quaint rock
formations, and the usual accessories of a well-appointed
cavern. In the valley of the Tuy are some pretty
villages, and as it was there that the severest shocks
of the late earthquake had been felt, it was of more
interest than usual. In the neighbourhood of Cúa,
and for some miles before reaching that town by the

* "Amais la libertad ? pues—vivais en la campagna."

Charayave road, the signs of desolation were especially apparent. Houses in ruins, fallen church towers, tottering walls, and deep chasms in the earth, all betokened the excessive violence of the earthquake.

For days previous to the great catastrophe of the 12th of April, the inhabitants of Cúa had suffered from the intense heat. The air was heavy with a yellow vapour, and chairs and pieces of furniture felt as if they had been exposed to the sun. Slight shocks were continually felt, and repeated detonations like distant musketry shots were heard. On the 12th the church bells were agitated by a movement, a low, rumbling sound, as of thunder, brought the frightened people from their houses, then all was quiet again. Sand of a leaden colour burst up from the streets and patios. Hours of complete calm ensued, and it was anticipated that the worst was over. At 8.40 p.m. Cúa was a pretty, flourishing town; at 8.41 it was a cemetery. From east to west ran the earthquake wave, and this was instantly followed by perpendicular oscillations which left no house standing. There was no time for escape, and beneath the ruins four hundred people were buried. Very few who were indoors at the moment of the shock were saved. The wife of one of the principal merchants was standing near her doorway, when suddenly she saw the walls open, and she was buried beneath the *débris;* she was not crushed, however, as a great quantity of tobacco and piles of skins prevented the mass from touching her. With her freed hand she saved herself from suffocation, and all through that terrible night she heard the groans of her husband who was buried near her. He died, but she was dug out alive.

Three days later a soldier, who was passing a ruin, heard a small voice call out " I am hungry." Search was made, and in an aperture formed by three large stones was found a child, the only one saved out of a large household. A singular circumstance occurred in one of the houses whose owner had for many years been accustomed to prepare and decorate the sacred image of the Tomb, which was carried in procession during Holy Week. This casket was in one of the largest rooms, when two of the walls fell outwards leaving the ceiling poised in equilibrium by a single beam. In this position it remained until the image was removed in safety, and shortly afterwards another shock dislodged it.

At daybreak, when the disinterment of those who had been overwhelmed commenced, the most heartrending scenes were witnessed. Mothers sought children only to find disfigured corpses ; husbands discovered their dead wives pressing their babies in their arms. In many cases features could not be recognised, for fire had completed the work commenced by the falling habitations. Some lives were taken away in sleep, others when employed in various occupations. Here a hammock formed a shroud, and there an open book lay by the side of its reader. For days after the destruction of the town, shocks of earthquakes were felt and subterraneous rumblings heard, but at length these died out, and a troubled peace rested with the survivors of unhappy Cúa.

Perhaps I visited Carácas at an unfortunate time, but it certainly seemed to me to be the most stupid town I had ever seen. There was very little to see, and no amusements of anykind, unless a weekly lottery

and the continual firing of rockets can be classed as
such.   Of   the   latter,   the   people   were   never
tired, and day and night they were thus comme-
morating some civil or religious event.   The perpetual
hissing and explosions reminded me of the conversation
once held by Ferdinand, King of Spain, and a Mexican
courtier, when the news had arrived of a successful
revolution.

" What do you suppose the Mexicans will be doing
now ?" said the King.

" Letting off rockets, your Majesty."

" Well—I wonder what they are doing now in
Mexico ?" said the King in the afternoon.

" Letting of rockets, your Majesty."

" What will your countrymen be doing at this time ;"
said the King in the evening.

" Letting of rockets, your Majesty."

Day after day I attended the demure and uninteresting debates of the Legislature, and once witnessed the
official presentation of the new American Minister to
the President.   This ceremony, which took place in
the handsome state-room of the palace, was brilliantly
attended by the élite of Carácas, and was simply but
imposingly conducted.   The Minister was an agreeable,
well-read gentleman but, unfortunately, neither he nor
any of his family understood a single word of Spanish,
and of all towns Carácas is the least entertaining for a
foreigner who does not speak the language.   I think
that, after arriving, they never ceased to regret that they
had left their home in the valley of the Mississippi.
To a very dry manner the Minister added great quaint-
ness and humour of expression, and his society made
a very pleasant change in the dulness of the hotel life.

He was fond of exaggerating his natural American intonation and quaint pronunciation, and when with grave and rather pompous air he slowly uttered his long carefully worded sentences, the effect was irresistibly comic. " My young English friend," he said one day to me, in the course of conversation, " we look upon your best men as Americans ; John Bright, Cobden, Dickens and Gladstone: they air Americans. Our recent visitors, the Emperor of Brazil, ought to be an American, he had quite an outfit of intelligence, and, Sir, if Dom Pedro would come over to the States and settle, mind — I say and settle, we would make a senator of him."

On another occasion he said, " Sir, you air a traveller, if you've been to Florida you air a traveller ; out of a thousand people you may meet not five have visited Florida ; and even in the great American nation, which stretches from the Atlantic to the Pacific and from 49° north to the confines of Mexico, though ten may have been to Paris hardly one will have seen Florida. Sir, you air a traveller."

My only regret in leaving Carácas was bidding good-bye to my kind-hearted friend. It had been my intention to proceed overland to Valencia and Puerto Cabello from Carácas for the purpose of seeing the beautiful lake and some of the most fertile parts of Venezuela. As the steamers which touch at the different ports only remain a few hours, and are liable to arrive twenty-fours before or after their appointed time, it is necessary for passengers to anticipate them. Not wishing to remain on the coast longer than I could avoid, I had timed my departure from Carácas so as to catch the French Mail at Puerto Cabello, allowing myself four days for the journey.　　Inland travel is very limited, the charge for carriages or mules is most exorbitant. After much trouble I at last hired some animals at a price which ought to have bought them and the guide. However, as they did not appear at the appointed time, I suppose their owner repented his bargain, and as it would have been too late to seek others, I was obliged to return to La Guaira.

CHAPTER XXVIII.

IN the dry season the carriage-road between Carácas
and La Guaira is by no means a pleasant one.
The ricketty old coaches which perform the journey
have leather flaps instead of windows ; if these are
down you are stifled with the heat, and if they are
open you are suffocated with dust. On account of the
bad springs and deep ruts, you are little better than an
animated shuttle-cock for a great part of the drive,
and the exercise you undergo is of the most severe
description.

The scenery is wild and romantic, but when I passed
through it was dry and barren. Only here and there,
in the deep valley on the left, were there patches of
green and cultivated spots, whilst the hills on the right
were rugged and aloe-clad. For the first two hours we
wound up the hill-side, and then commenced a long
zig-zag descent. Every now and then we had to halt,
to allow the numerous pack-trains of donkeys and
oxen to pass, the poor animals toiling painfully in

x

such clouds of dust that breathing must have been difficult.

Not far from the station where we changed horses, I left the road to visit a cow-tree*—Palo de vaca. It was about eighty feet in height with long, thick leaves of a deep, shining green. The milk, which is said to be wholesome, is thick and glutinous and of a yellower tinge than that of a cow. A few of these wooden cows would be valuable acquisitions in many grassless regions, but I do not think any attempt to acclimatize them has ever been made.

The first view of La Guaira and the coast recalls the "Corniche" road. Below lie green fields edged with palms, groves, and white cottages standing in gardens ; and beyond the clustering houses of the town the land runs out in numberless promontories into the blue sea. Truly this is a land of projects and projections! On the right and above rise steep mountains specked with the white flowers of the Frangipanni, and its ravines green with coffee plantations, mangos and bananas. A glimpse of white houses, and the Fort of San Carlos perched above the Quebrada de Tipe, add to the picturesque element of the scene. At the pretty little village of Maiquetia they were firing off rockets, as they had not yet finished the celebration of a great event in Venezuela, viz., the completion during the past week of a single-line tramway, connecting the village with La Guaira, a distance of about a mile. And thus the contemplated railroad between the coast and the capital has ended in a one-horse car with a mile run, and even that enterprise will probably have failed in a few months. By the advice of the agent I

* Bersimum glactodendron.

arrived in La Guaira one day before the French mail steamer was due; as a natural consequence it was a day late. Those three days I will pass over in silence, so utterly wretched were they on account of the heat, the bad hotel, and the squalid town.

When at last the steamer arrived, the port-captain kept the passengers waiting on the wharf for about three hours before he would allow the boats to take them off. The first remark that greeted us on board was from the afore-mentioned agent.

" Show your permits, please."

" I have no permit," I replied.

" Monsieur," said the Agent, " must be good enough to return to land, and get a permit from the port-captain."

" You must really excuse me," I remonstrated, " it is too far to return, and when I bought my ticket I ought to have been informed that it was necessary to obtain a permit."

" The steamer cannot leave until you have received your permit," insisted the agent.

" Then the steamer must remain," I said coolly.

A whispered conference between the agent and his myrmidon now ensued.

" If Monsieur will not leave, the captain will be appealed to," resumed the agent.

" Appeal to the captain," was my calm but firm rejoinder.

" Monsieur must go at once," said the agent with firmness, a decision which his myrmidon seemed ready to applaud.

" Monsieur will not go," replied the passenger with

equal firmness, which was greeted with applause by the other passengers.

"Once for all, will Monsieur leave?" exclaimed the agent, now furious.

"Once for all, he will not," I replied, rather angrily.

At this moment another delinquent came on board without a permit, and as I turned on my heel to look after my baggage I heard, "Monsieur must be good enough, &c." Whether this one returned to shore I do not know; if he did, he must have lost his passage, as a few minutes afterwards the anchor was lifted and we were off.

In the saloon I heard an animated discussion between the new passengers and the stewards. I think the port-captain and the head-steward must have had an arrangement between them, not to allow the passengers to come on board until after dinner. Dinner was over, and we were refused anything to eat until tea time. Now, as none of us had dined, we were hungry and did not wish to wait for another three hours. Expostulation was useless, so I sought the captain, and as he was just going to dinner, he requested me to join him, and I fared extremely well. The others, who would not go to the fountain-head, growled angrily until tea-time. I never had been glad to get on board ship before, but after the land heat and the utter impossibility of procuring anything cold to drink, the sea breeze and ice were both refreshing.

The steamer was a fine vessel, built to carry the countless hordes who were expected to visit the Paris Exhibition, *via* Panama. On no mail-steamer have I ever seen better attendance or such good living. The cooking was perfection, and the viands were

just suited to the tropics. Abundance of cool salads
—that of the cabbage-palm being particularly well
made—delicious bread and coffee, really good butter,
appetizing dishes, and very fair white and red wines,
ad lib., were items on the daily bill of fare not often
found on board ship. The price of the passage was undoubtedly high, but so it was with the other lines of
steamers that touched at these ports.

Close along shore we glided past the green plains
around ·Maiquetia and the white cape, beneath which
sat a row of pelicans with the most solemn physiog-
nomies. The high coast range was broken and ribbed,
deep ravines backed stretches of white sand, and the
only signs of habitation were in the few canoes which
floated near the shore. The next day we were still
in view of the mountains of Ocumare, and soon
sighted Puerto Cabello. From a distance the town
appeared to be far inland, but mingled with towers
and red roofs were the tall masts of vessels. Low,
bush-covered islets and white sandy beaches, on which
the surf broke heavily, lay between us and the town.
We rounded a long point of land, and saw the Golfo
Triste curving away to the north ; then we entered
the strangest little harbour in the world. Passing
close alongside an island fort and lighthouse, we
gradually drifted into a deep, narrow channel, and
were soon moored to the wharf. This inside bay
affords admirable shelter for shipping, but it is small,
and the islets and mangrove banks on its eastern
limits seem to indicate a gradual shallowing of its still
waters. It is like a small swampy lake protected from
the sea by sand-bars, rocks, and bushes. The town is
quaint and pretty ; palms, minarets, and pagoda-like

towers giving it an oriental aspect.   The high mountain back-ground is crowned by two peaks, the " Tetas
de Hilaria," and on the hill of the " Vigia" is an old
and useless fort.   To the east is Fort Mirador del
Solano, on which vast sums have been spent, and
which now, when nearly completed, is discovered to
be of no use whatever.

Up in the mountains is the picturesque village of
San Estéban, famed for its feather flowers, and also as
a health resort for the fevered dwellers on the coast.
In the olden days, when Puerto Cabello was the refuge
for pirates, smugglers, and criminals, it was considered
the most unhealthy spot in northern South America ; the
terrible " vómito negro" devastated the region.   It has
always maintained its bad reputation with the outside
world, but in reality it is comparatively salubrious at
the present day.   Its military history eclipses that of
other Venezuelan towns, as in 1743 it was attacked by
an English fleet, which was repulsed with great loss,
and in 1824 its capture by Generals Padilla and
Paez ended the war of emancipation.   Since then it
has undergone three sieges.   Altogether, Puerto
Cabello and its environs are interesting, but the heat
is too great to render a prolonged sojourn enjoyable.

Soon after leaving, we sighted the Dutch island of
Curaçoa, which, during the revolution, had been the
head-quarters of the Spaniards, as, although its people
were with the patriots, yet the Government and the
rich merchants were in favour of Spain.   As we proceeded, the high main-land grew fainter, and presently
we crossed the entrance of the deep gulf of Maracaïbo.
Then great rocks of a ghostly whiteness started up
near the ship's course, and long reaches of sand

bordered the yellow green sea which surged heavily on the hot coast of Colombia. The land scenery was flat and sombre ; the coast hills dwindled away to a vanishing point, and grey savannas reached to the horizon. It was dull and sad-looking and intensely hot, too hot, apparently, for the traditional dolphins which, on the previous day, had never ceased racing with the steamer, and had entertained us by the marvellous unanimity with which long lines of them would appear and disappear, taking their graceful leaps like trained steeplechasers who had disposed of their riders, but were still determined to complete the course.

Forty hours after leaving Puerto Cabello we reached Savanilla, and anchored in a large bay at a great distance from shore, where we could see only a few cottages and a lighthouse, standing in an amphitheatre of undulating green hills. It had been my intention to disembark here and proceed up the Magdalena River to Bogotá, but when the little tug came alongside to take passengers for Barranquilla, I heard that the river was too low at present even for the small steamers that run on it. This was a great disappointment, as I had been anxious to visit the emerald mines of Muzo, not only for the sake of seeing the mines themselves, but in order to obtain some specimens of the rare " Morpho Cyprio." Afterwards, at Panama, I saw two of these wonderful butterflies, and was not astonished at the belief of the miners of Muzo that the splendid insects feed on the emeralds, and so obtain their brillant hue. Anything more exquisite than the colour and sheen it is impossible to imagine. Unfortunately for me their owner appreciated them as highly as I did, and though I was by no means illiberal in my offer, I could not tempt him to part with one of them.

Whilst we were at Savanilla great swarms of a single species of butterfly — *Danaidæ* — hovered over the vessel, and many of them rested on the deck and rigging. They appeared to be outward bound, and flew north-east in delicate clouds.   As there was no breeze to blow them from the land, it must have been their own wish to migrate   If their destination was one of the islands, I am afraid the poor emigrants never could have reached it, as before we left Savanilla a strong north-easterly wind sprang up, against which they could not have sailed onwards.   The heavens were already sprinkled with silver stars when we steamed out of the bay ; and where only a few minutes before, in the direction of our course, there had been a bank of rainbow-coloured clouds, there was now only a pale silvery vapour that gradually diffused itself over land and sea.

CHAPTER XXIX.

THE dream of Clarence has occupied the waking
thoughts of many since Shakespeare's time, and
in the West Indies, as well as off our own coast, it has
been the ambition of treasure-hunters to find the
Spanish gold which here and there paves the sea.
Near Carthagena we passed a vessel engaged on a
diving expedition, and not far from Cumaná we had
seen another ship, which was said to be in search of
the vast treasure sunk in the San Pedro Alcántara.

The history of this unfortunate vessel is an interesting one. In 1815, Ferdinand VIII. of Spain, dispatched
from Cadiz a number of transports with men, money,
and provisions, for the supply of the fleet, which was
then stationed in the Caribbean Sea. These ships
sailed under the convoy of the San Pedro Alcántara,
a three-decked line of battle-ship mounting seventy-
four guns. On board were 1,400 soldiers, under the
command of General Morillo, and in the treasure-chests
were between three and four million dollars. When
the San Pedro Alcántara arrived at La Guaira, the

revolution had so far progressed that the Spanish citizens of that town and of Carácas, fearing the loss of their personal property, transferred their gold and jewels to the man-of-war. This act was soon imitated by the convents and churches of Venezuela, and the vessel was laden with an immense treasure of jewels, gold and silver altar plate, valuable pictures, coin, and costly ornaments. The jewelled tiara of the Virgin of Guadaloupe, which was sent from Valencia, was alone of almost priceless value.

From La Guaira the San Pedro Alcántara sailed up the coast to the island of Margarita—now known as Nueva Esparta—where the troops disembarked and defeated the Venezuelan forces stationed there. The brave Margaritans, who, during the War of Independence, proved themselves to be as truly patriotic as the Llaneros, retired to the hills and inaugurated a guerilla warfare which harassed the Spaniards beyond measure. Still their towns were open to attack, and Asuncion, Pampatar, Norte, and others, were sacked and destroyed by the invaders. Thus the wealth of the San Pedro was again added to, and, as there was much treasure in these towns, it is supposed that little was saved from the sudden descent of the conquerors.

After the plundering of the last town, orders were received that the San Pedro should sail at once to Cumaná. To celebrate their successes a grand revel was held on board one night; casks of wine and spirits were broached, and success to the ensuing expedition was so eagerly drunk that it is doubtful whether there was a single sober man in the vessel. Then arose an alarm of fire. How the fire originated is unknown, but it speedily reached a cask of brandy,

which burst, and the deck was instantly deluged with
liquid fire. The flames were soon darting through the
hatchways and lapping the sails, and so quickly did the
conflagration spread that nothing could have checked
it, even if sober men had tried to stem the danger.
As it was, the wild mob, mad with drink and fear,
thought only of flight. With difficulty the boats were
lowered, and men sought to reach them, either by
jumping into them from the deck, or battling with each
other in the water to clutch their sides. Of the few
boats that there were, all except one were either capsized
or stove in.

In the meantime the fire made its way to the
powder-magazine. Suddenly a tremendous explosion
rent the air, a lucid light hung for a moment over the
doomed vessel, and the air was filled with mangled
corpses and fragments of the ship. The after-half of
the San Pedro Alcántara had been blown to pieces, and
the forward half quickly sank beneath the waves.
Over a thousand men perished in the fire and ocean
on that night. The magazine had been situated beneath the strong chambers wherein were stored the
Spanish treasure-chests, the riches of the people and
churches of Venezuela and the plunder of the towns.
All was now scattered and buried in the sea.

In a paper describing this disaster, it is said that
in 1816 an American Captain visited the scene of the
wreck, one mile from the island of Cuagua, and succeeded in securing about 30,000 dollars in silver.
Again in 1845 a company was organized in Baltimore
for the purpose of seeking the lost treasure. The
remnant of the wreck was easily found, but owing
to the lack of proper diving apparatus the attempt

proved a failure. A few months later the same company sent out another expedition. This search was prosecuted under an agreement with the government of Venezuela. During the first three months quantities of copper, huge rusty anchors and guns, were dragged up, but only about 1,500 dollars in silver coin were recovered. The search had been confined to the immediate vicinity of the sunken wreck, and the divers became so dissatisfied by the ill results of their labour that they refused to continue unless those in charge of the explorations would test the theory they formed, which was that the force of the explosion had hurled the treasure-chests some distance away from the spot where the ship went down. They were humoured, and the vessel was anchored in another place. The first time the diving bell went down on the new ground, 750 dollars were picked up in two hours, and this success continued so well that in six months about 200,000 dollars in silver had been recovered. Then the major portion of the divers and crew having surreptitiously possesssed themselves of such portions of the treasure as they could secrete, stole a boat and set sail for La Guaira. The remainder of the party returned to Baltimore, having been unable to pursue the exploration for want of divers.

In 1849 another American barque recovered several thousand dollars in silver, but how much is not known, as the Captain suddenly hauled his anchor on board and set sail for the Horn, bound for the new El Dorado on the Pacific coast. In 1856, 28,000 dollars were recovered, and, in 1858, 30,000 more. In April, 1877, a Captain Folingsby went to Venezuela to obtain permission from the government to search for the lost millions, and effected a contract whereby, in consideration of the payment of five per cent on all sums he might recover, he was granted the exclusive right to drag, dredge, and dive for the sunken treasures of the San Pedro Alcántara for the period of six years. Armed with this contract, Captain Folingsby organized an expedition for the thorough and exhaustive exploration of all the ocean bed over which the treasure might have been scattered by the explosion of the ship. He has had extensive experience as a diver, and having been in the employ of the Baltimore company in 1845 and 1846 in their searches, is thoroughly familiar with the ground on which he is to work. He believes that the strong boxes which held the gold, jewels, and church plate were not burst by the explosion, but simply tossed away to a greater distance than seekers have hitherto deemed it worth while to go from the wreck. No gold has as yet been found, but simply silver, and this he accepts as evidence of the correctness of his theory. He thinks that he can go over all the ground in about eight months. His dredges and drags are of the most approved patterns, fitted with special appliances such as chair-nettings, to let sand escape, but to hold everything else, As 500,000 dollars are about all that have hitherto been recovered, he has the hope of finding at least four or five millions and, with every requisite that knowledge and unrestricted capital can supply, he confidently expects to achieve success. As he was to sail from New York early in 1878, the vessel we saw near Cumana must have been his. With that idea we cordially wished a prosperous finale to the ocean-mining of the enterprising Captain.

From Savanilla onwards to Panama the little we saw

of the coast was uninteresting. We were seldom near enough to appreciate the colour-chords on beach, hill and savanna, and the sombre monotone of the land seemed but an extension of the yellow green sea. The nights were calm and beautiful, and as we sailed on and on through the great star-chamber, the vessel appeared to plunge through a sea of fire. Long gleams of blue, green and purple crested the waves that were only raised by the vessel's bow, and the teeming phosphorescent life made the starry waters more brilliant even than the sky. But pleasant as the nights were, the French Mail Company interfered with our entire enjoyment of them, by a silly order which forbade passengers to take their pillows on deck. They might sleep there if they chose—and everyone did choose—but under no circumstances were pillows allowed. Various were the devices made use of to disguise the forbidden articles, but those who indulged in them were generally awakened by a polite reminder from one of the officers or stewards that the pillows must be taken below. Then the different *ruses* had to be repeated. The pillow-prohibition was the only fault that could be found with this comfortable vessel.

Our little voyage along the Spanish Main had been slow and deliberate, but as the old Spanish proverb says "step by step goes a long way," and at last we entered a pretty horse-shoe bay surrounded by low misty hills, and were presently moored alongside one of the fine wharfs at Colon. Here we were at the narrowest point of that narrow isthmus, to cross which by water has been a problem to the great nations of the world for three centuries and a half. The project of connecting the Atlantic and Pacific Oceans by a canal is a scheme of such vast commercial importance that it may be interesting to take a rapid glance at a few of the numerous surveys made with a view to inter-oceanic communication. As early as 1513 the Spanish explorers believed in the existence of a narrow strait leading across to the Pacific. In the following year, the Spanish Government gave a secret order for the preparation of a coast-chart to determine whether such a strait really existed. In the hope of finding such a passage, Cortez sent out his expeditions and prepared a map of the Gulf of Mexico, which he sent to Spain in 1524. Then the European Powers explored and searched the whole coast-line of the New World, and at length realized the fact that from Colon the continent extended uninterruptedly north and south. Just as the Suez Canal is only an enlargement of the plan conceived and executed by the Pharaohs 4,000 years ago, so the Panama or Darien route, when completed, will be the practical result of a project contemplated as far back as three centuries and a half.

In 1551, a Spaniard of the name of Gomara proposed that a canal should be constructed to connect the oceans, and suggested three of the same routes that have been under the consideration of modern engineers. " It is true," said the proud Castilian, " that mountains obstruct the passes, but if there are mountains there are also hands; let but the resolve be made, and there will be no want of means; the Indies, to which the passage will be made, will supply them. To a King of Spain, with the wealth of the Indies at his command, when the object to be attained is the spice trade, what is possible is easy." But soon Spain fell from her high estate, religious intolerance benumbed her energies, and the project of the canal became at last a mere legend.

In 1780 the Nicaragua route was first projected, and Captain—afterwards Lord—Nelson conveyed a force of 2,000 men to San Juan de Nicaragua for the conquest of the country, and in one of his despatches said, "In order to give facility to the great object of Government, I intend to possess the great lake of Nicaragua, which at the present may be looked upon as the inland Gibraltar of Spanish America. As it commands the only water-pass between the oceans, its situation must ever render it a principal port to ensure passage to the Southern Ocean, and by our possession of it Spanish America is severed in two." The expedition was a failure, however, and nothing came of Nelson's project.

In 1814, the Spanish Cortes decreed the opening of a canal, but the matter was deferred and the decree never executed. In 1825, after the Central American States had secured their independence, they asked the co-operation of the United States in constructing a canal. In 1828, the King of the Netherlands proposed to undertake the work, and sent over General Verveer with instructions to build the canal. The General found Central America engaged in one of its regular half-yearly revolutions, and the matter was deferred until 1830, when the revolution in his own country put an end to the plans. In 1836, Mr. John Bailey made some preliminary surveys for a route across Nicaragua, which were brought to a close by the dissolution of the " Confederation of the Centre." In 1850, under appointment from the Atlantic and Pacific Ship-canal Company, Mr. Childs, of Philadelphia, began a survey on the Pacific side, and after examining several routes chose the line which terminated in Brito Harbour, giving very strong reasons against the Lake Managua route, which have been confirmed by every subsequent survey. British capitalists were interested in this route, and would have adopted Mr. Child's plans if favourable arrangements could have been made with Nicaragua. But the Nicaraguan Government finally killed the scheme, as far as British capital was concerned, by demanding twenty-five per cent of profits.

In 1873, President Grant appointed an Inter-oceanic Canal Commission, to examine the various proposed routes and report on the most feasible. The Commission considered the following surveys : the Isthmus of Tehuantepec ; the Nicaragua route, *vid* Lake Nicaragua ; the Isthmus of Panama ; the San Blas and Chepo route ; the Caledonian and North routes ; the Caledonian and Sucubti route ; the Cacarica and Tuyra route ; the Atrato and Truando route ; and the Atrato-Napip route. The Commission unanimously reported that the Nicaragua route possessed, both for construction and maintenance of a canal, greater advantages, and offered fewer difficulties from engineering, commercial, and economic points of view, than any one of the routes shown by surveys to be practicable. This route, beginning on the Atlantic side, at or near Greytown, would run by canal to the San Juan River, thence following its left bank to the mouth of the San Carlos River, at which point navigation of the San Juan begins, and by the aid of three short canals of an aggregate length of three and a half miles reach Lake Nicaragua. Thence across the lake and through the valleys of the Rio del Medio and the Rio Grande to what is known as the Port of Brito, on the Pacific coast. No doubt exists as to the entire practicability of constructing this canal, the cost of which, with all the necessary adjuncts—locks 400 feet in length and 26 feet depth of water—may be set down as at least twenty million pounds sterling.

The last survey of the several routes has very lately been completed by Lieutenant Commander Wyse of the French Navy. After an exhaustive survey, he judges that the best route for a canal is what he describes as the Acanti-Tupisa route. This starts from the Gulf of Darien on the Atlantic side, following the Atrato River for a short distance and passing through the valley of the Tupisa to the Tuyra River, which flows into the Gulf of San Miguel. Commander Wyse has proposed that M. de Lesseps should be President of an International Commission that shall assemble before long to examine the different lines that have been surveyed, and to select whichever will be, in their judgment, the easiest and most desirable to construct. It is probable that the choice of routes will rest between the Acanti-Tupisa and that of Nicaragua, but when work will actually be commenced on either is doubtful. Before the Atlantic and Pacific join hands across the Isthmus another century may elapse, and the problem propounded four hundred and fifty years before may still be unsolved.

CHAPTER XXX.

COLON—DEPARTURE—COLUMBUS AND MR. ASPINWALL—RAILWAY
ACROSS ISTHMUS—SCENES ON THE ISTHMUS—TELEGRAPH POSTS
—HOLY GHOST ORCHID—PANAMA HATS—PARADISE—MOUNT
ANCON—PACIFIC MAIL STEAMER—ON THE WHARF AT PANAMA
—PANAMA FROM THE SEA—LAST LOOKS.

FROM the sea Colon had looked pretty and mysterious; gauzy vapours floated over the town, and all we could see were the outlines of palms, a few roofs, and behind the surrounding forest the dim shadows of the distant hills. We landed, and with the vanished mists all romance disappeared. We stepped from the shelter of the roofed wharf, and in the dirty, decayed village that lay before us beheld Colon, or the city of Aspinwall as it is called by the Americans.

The principal street runs along the shore, and its shambling frame-houses with verandahs and balconies are of the most tumble-down description. Drinking saloons predominate, and the various stores and shops are stocked with a miscellaneous assortment of goods, such as shells, calico, coral, toilet articles, parrots, hats, pale ale, boots, oranges, bananas, and ready-made clothing. The untidy tenement houses, the dirty lanes, the swamps, and the apparent effort to make life in the tropics as uncomfortable as possible, give an impression of squalid poverty. Nor are the inhabitants un-

suited to their dwellings ; from the sallow German Jew
who dispenses iced drinks across a dirty counter, to
the slippered negro who beats a gong at meal time
in front of a wretched eating-house, all are unkempt
and unclean. The officials and their houses are too
few in number to counteract the general atmosphere
of unpicturesque decay, and both they and their well-
appointed offices render the native unsightliness more
conspicuous by contrast.

After arriving in Colon the principal aim is to get
away as soon as possible. " Thank goodness it is'nt
a full stop," was remarked by a perspiring passenger,
whose extreme heat must account for the want of
brilliancy in his joke. The Panama Railroad Company
facilitates this object by starting a train for Panama as
soon as the passengers' luggage has arrived from the
steamer. As the main street is the terminus of the
railway, the entire population assembles to bid farewell to their only source of income. Then may be
seen a motley crowd, each member of which is endeavouring to extract some coin or other from the
pockets of their late guests. Black porters appear
at the last moment with some trifling article that they
have taken care their employer should forget ; jet-
black Africans, Jamaica negroes, half-castes, yellow
Peruvians, naked children, both black and brown, all
endeavour to sell some article or other, either cakes,
fruit and sweetmeats, or fans, coral, and smoking-caps
of palm-fibre. Nor are the passengers themselves of
less varied nationalities, as the steamers from New
York and St. Thomas have brought emigrants, business
men, pleasure-seekers, fortune-hunters, and travellers
from all parts of the world.

Here is an entire German family, from the grandmother to the baby in arms, and not one of them
can speak other language than their own; there are
some Mexicans carrying on a rapid conversation in
mixed French, English, and Spanish, with the negro
fruit-sellers, and those five ladies, who have paid such
a tender adieu to the captain of the American Mail
Steamer, are tourists—probably you will learn that
they are not travelling *viá* Panama on account of its
cheapness, but for the sake of the sea-voyage. Then
there are several commercial travellers, each of whom
thinks it correct to wear one of the fibre smoking-
caps and chaff the crowd in " h-less " English. Those
rosy-cheeked damsels, with flower-decked hats and
general gaudy aspect, are Irish servant-girls who have
left New York to seek a fortune in San Francisco.
On leaving the wharf I had passed two of these
maidens, who were looking at the beautiful statue—
the only beautiful thing in Colon—of Columbus and
the Indian. Said one to the other, " Sure an' its
Mr. Aspinwall himself, the man who built the
town."

At last, amid a faint cheer, or rather a hoot of deri-
sion, the train moves slowly off, and we pass almost
at once from the so called civilization into the primeval
forest. Perhaps we were a very ignorant set of passengers, but strange to say none of us—and some had
crossed the Isthmus before—knew to whom the railroad or the land belonged. Some said both land and
road belonged to England, others to America, and a
few that both belonged to Colombia, who leased it to
the United States. Afterwards we found out that the
Panama Railway is American, by contract with the

Government of New Granada,* to whom the land belongs.

With the history of the survey, and the building of the road, the world is familiar from the time when in 1850, " two American citizens leapt, axe in hand, from a native canoe upon a wild and desolate island, (Manzanilla), their retinue consisting of half-a-dozen Indians, who clear the path with rude knives," up to the 27th of January, 1855, when, " at midnight in darkness and rain, the last rail was laid, and on the following day a locomotive passed from ocean to ocean." The undertaking was intrepid, the expense enormous, and the loss of life tremendous. Pestilential vapours, reptiles, poisonous insects, fevers, incessant rains, working waist deep in water, insufficient food and shelter, all combined to sweep off thousands of the labourers. Americans, English, Irish, French, Germans, Austrians, natives of India, South America and the West Indies fell victims to the malarious climate, but misery and suffering seems to have fallen most heavily on the Chinese. Of these, one thousand had been

---

* Mr. Otis says : " Among the most important concessions by the terms of this contract was one guaranteeing that all public lands lying on the line of the road were to be used gratuitously by the Company, also a gift of 250,000 acres of land, to be selected by the grantees from any public lands on the Isthmus. Two ports, one on the Atlantic and the other on the Pacific (which were to be the termini of the road) were to be free ports; and the privilege was granted of establishing such tolls as the Company might think proper. The contract was to continue in force for forty-nine years, subject to the right of New Granada to take possession of the road at the expiration of twenty years after its completion, on payment of five millions of dollars ; on the expiration of thirty years on payment of four millions ; and at the expiration of forty years on payment of two millions. Three per cent was to be paid to the New Granada government upon all dividends declared. The entire work was to be completed within eight years.

brought to the Isthmus by the Company, and though as much care as was possible was taken with their health and comfort, yet before a month had elapsed almost the whole of them became affected with a suicidal tendency, and scores ended their existence by their own hands. The memory of these sad details throws a shadow over the interesting journey of forty-seven miles from ocean to ocean, where each advancing step has only been gained by the sacrifice of a human life.

The traveller will gain some idea of the deadly swamps directly the train· has crossed the artificial isthmus—(for Colon is situated on the little island of Manzanilla)—which connects the island with the mainland. Dense mangrove thickets border the waters, both of the sea and swamp, the stems of those near the sea being loaded with clusters of small oysters. White egrets and an occasional roseate spoon-bill grace the banks with their presence, and the black forbidding water of the marshes is redeemed by the starry crinums and aquatic plants which grow in great luxuriance.

After passing Mount Hope, where the cemetery of Colon is situated, we are deep in the forest jungle. Cassias, pleromas, and all kinds of feathery-leaved shrubs mingle with giant cedros, ceibas, and locusts, and all are knitted together by the purple convolvulus, or by the chains of some thick-stemmed liane. Most conspicuous are the palms with their crimson clusters of fruit hanging like tassels below the green crown, and the red and yellow blossoms of the helianthus. Fleet-winged heliconias dart among the shrubs at the forest edge, and in the shady glades, which sometimes break the monotony of the jungle, silver-blue morphos

and yellow and orange pieridæ flit heavily along.   Now
and then a flock of parroquets wheels rapidly in the
air, or a black and yellow troupial pipes from a high
tree top, but birds are not numerous, with the exception of the ugly " black witches,"* that treat the
passing train with the utmost contempt.   To those
who have been accustomed to travel through tropical
forests only, after toilsome journeys on foot or on mule-
back, it is an agreeable sensation to glide—although
there certainly is a good deal of jolting—swiftly
through the luxuriant vegetation in a comfortable
railway carriage.   And yet it was strange, in the trip
I have been speaking of, to witness the indifference
with which most of the passengers viewed the many
pretty scenes.   Some did not see them at all, but
played whist during the whole journey, others slept,
and not a few improved the occasion by deliberately
drawing up the wooden blinds, so that nothing outside
should disturb their attention whilst they read.   " Look
at the grave-stones !" screamed one of the passengers,
who hitherto had been impervious to the novel scenery.
When the information was gently broken to her that
the small stone-like columns were not grave-stones,
but merely pillars to support the wires of the telegraph,†
she was quite disappointed.

* Crotophaga.

† Owing to the rapid decay of the wooden poles which were formerly
used, the chief engineer (Colonel Totten) conceived the idea of moulding
a support of concrete. A small scantling of pitch pine was placed upright and surrounded by a jointed wooden mould, fifteen inches in diameter
at base, tapering to about eight inches at the top and sunk into the earth
sufficiently for support ; this was filled with concrete. When the mould
was removed, it was found firm and strong and well adapted to the purpose, being perfectly weather and insect proof. These posts have the
appearance of hewn stone.

Near the stream called the Mindee, we saw patches of cultivated ground, and perched on the high knolls were a few picturesque wattled and thatched cottages, with clumps of bananas, mango-trees and palms. Gradually the ground became less swampy, and by the time we reached Gatun Station, situated on the eastern bank of the Chagres River, had given place to dry savanna land that stretched to the hill range. Almost immediately after leaving the station we crossed the Rio Gatun, and again entered a region of swamp and jungle. On the left rose the twin peaks known as the "Lion" and the "Tiger," conical in shape and clad with thick forest. And thus we sped on through an ever-changing scene ; from marsh and swamp we passed to plain and forest hills, and from the silence of the wilderness to the life and cheerfulness of the little settlements that dot the road.

Here was a swamp covered with pretty aquatic plants, then a stream almost hidden by overhanging bamboos, then forest trees laden with orchids, and from whose branches the pendent nests of the orioles swayed to and fro, or a narrow country-lane walled in by petræa and convolvuli so dense and of such shapely growth that they appeared like old ruins over which time had thrown a mantle of verdure. One view of the Chagres River, which we crossed near Barbacoas over a fine wrought iron bridge, was very charming. There were wide stretches of meadow-land with cattle farms, and in the broad stream which curved off to the undulating hills cows stood knee-deep, and under the high banks groups of women wearing flowers in their black hair were hard at work clothes-washing. It formed a pretty picture in the happy blending of wild forest and rural

scenery. At a native village, composed of three rows
of picturesque huts, standing in an open glade surrounded by palm trees, we found much needed
refreshments, as breakfast that morning had been small
and early.

All the inhabitants vied with each other in their
efforts to secure customers, yet though the competition
was great, fixed prices prevailed. There was a rare
mixture of home and foreign productions; Bass's ale,
claret, sardines, biscuits and potted meats were carried
by some, whilst others bore trays of bread, cakes, native
sweet-meats, pine-apples, oranges, inga pods, mangoes,
and other fruits. Here was a little urchin with a
bottle of milk, and there was another with hard-boiled
eggs and neat little packets of pepper and salt. The
chief trade was in eggs, and though they were not sold
"four for a dollar" as in the ante-railroad days, yet the
charge was sufficiently remunerative. Probably, the
sellers agreed with the dairy-woman who said that a
smaller price than that at which she sold her eggs
"would not pay for the wear and tear of the hen."
Old travellers shook their heads ominously at the
quantity of mangoes, starapples, and granadillas that
were consumed, and hints of Panama fever were thrown
out; but the novel fruits here, and the magnificent
Guayaquil white pine-apples that afterwards tempted
us at Panama seemed to be irresistible. The latter
were not mere consolidated lumps of sugar and water
like the West Indian pine, but equalled in flavour, and
in size surpassed, those of our hot-houses. It was a
miracle that no one was harmed by the fruit-con-
sumption, as everybody appeared to follow the example
of Artemus Ward, who "took no thought as to his

food ; if he liked things he ate them, and then let
them fight it out among themselves." Some bulbs of the
beautiful orchid* known as the " Holy Ghost," on
account of the marvellous image of the dove that rests
within the exquisite flower-cap, were for sale, but none
of the plants were in bloom, as they seldom blossom
before July. They are numerous on the Isthmus, and
grow luxuriantly on the decayed trunks that abound
in the hot, damp, low-lying grounds.

Some of the natives wore straw hats of a crimson
tint, which colour is extracted from the leaves of a vine
called "china." As yet but little attention has been
paid to this dye as an article of commerce, but it must
be of considerable value, as neither sun nor rain alters
the colour which is said to be permanent. The vine
grows abundantly in the hill districts, and sheds its
leaves annually. Such a dye would be vastly superior
to those so-called "fast" colours, whose only "fastness"
consists in their tendency to run. The hats themselves
were coarse and very unlike the famed "Panama,"
specimens of which were only to be seen on the heads
of some of the passengers from the West Indies.
Although the plant—Carludovica palmata—from whose
young unexpanded leaves the "Panama hats"† are
made, grows on the Isthmus, yet the manufacture is
confined to Moyobamba, on the banks of the Amazon,
Guayaquil, and the Indian villages of Peru.

* Peristeria elata.

† The author of "Three Years in Chili," says, "The grass of which
they—Panama hats—are made is found chiefly in the neighbouring province of San Cristoval. They can be braided only in the night or early in
the morning, as the heat in the day-time renders the grass brittle. It
takes a native about three months to braid one of the finest quality, and
I saw some hats which looked like fine linen, and are valued at fifty dollars apiece even here."

After leaving the refreshment-station the grade makes a gentle ascent until the summit—260 feet above sea level—is reached, and then we descend the Pacific slope. Here the scenery is bolder than previously, but the vegetation is as luxuriant as ever. Quickly we rush through cuttings and across rocky spurs, the Rio Grande winding through the forest maze below us; the pretty valley of Paraiso, enclosed in high conical hills, is passed, then once more we enter alternate stretches of swamp and cultivated savanna land.

We see meadows and cottages lying at the base of Mount Ancon, from whose summit Balboa, in 1513, saw the Pacific, and thus proved the fallacy of the belief in which Columbus died, that the New World was part of India and China. Then groups of huts, chiefly composed of flattened tin cans and shingles, came in view, and beyond them rose the Cathedral towers and the red roofs of Panama. Through the groves of cocoa-nut palms we caught sight of the glittering sea, and in a few minutes we entered a commodious station close to the wharf, where a tug lies ready to take passengers to the ocean steamer bound for California.

From Panama I had intended to visit Quito, and to descend the Amazon, but on account of ill-health I was advised to postpone that journey for a time, and to hasten to a colder climate. Of the town I, therefore, saw but little, and after a short ramble went on board the Pacific mail-steamer. Regarding the vessel, I will only say that she was very comfortable, and the food and attendance were very bad, and the ice and liquor supply grossly insufficient. The poor table was ascribed to the cheap rate of passage-money

from New York to San Francisco, but when I pointed
out that the Company reimbursed themselves by
exorbitant coasting charges—a first-class ticket from
Colon to San Francisco costing several dollars more
than the entire passage money from New York to San
Francisco—a shrug of the shoulders was the only
answer. It is a misfortune for travellers that the
Pacific Mail Steamers have no competitors on this
line.

It might be imagined that in the great central hive
of commerce, the old features of Panama would have
been replaced by those of more modern date. But
it is not so. Once leave the bustling wharf and freight-
depôt, loaded with coffee, cacao, ivory nuts, pearl
shells, india-rubber, ores, hides, woods, balsams, quina
bales, sarsaparilla, wool, and other products collected
from the two great continents, and pass through the
quiet lanes into the narrow streets of the town, and the
active life of the present is forgotten in the all-pervading memories of the past. It is like passing from the
busy work-shops of the stone-cutters into the quiet
shadows of the adjoining cemetery. Convent ruins,
voiceless bell-towers, grass-grown walls, broken arches
and fallen pillars, all tell of the departed glory of
Panama. Mellow time-stains have tinged alike the
carved stone-work and the rich mouldings of the plas-
ter façades, and over the crumbling edifices and through
the window-piercings, passion-flowers and luxuriant
creepers twist and twine in the wildest confusion.

During my short ramble, I rested for a moment on
the ancient ramparts with their old-fashioned sentry
towers, at whose feet lay the waters of the Pacific; so
still and glaring in the intense heat, and reflecting so

many colours from the pink-brown walls and high
tiled roofs that it resembled a sea of old Bohemian
glass. The hot sun had caused the streets and walks
to be deserted, and the only signs of life were the
swinging hammocks in the heavy balconies, and the
turkey-buzzards,* which with out-stretched wings
sunned themselves on every roof and steeple. The
natives of Panama have an odd legend, which accounts
for the absence of feathers on the head and neck of
these birds—gallinazos, as they call them. It is said that
after the deluge, Noah, when opening the door of the
ark, thought it well to give a word of advice to the re-
leased animals. " My children," said he, " when you
see a man coming towards you and stooping down, go
away from him ; he is getting a stone to throw at you."
" Very good," said the gallinazo, " but what if he has
one already in his pocket?" Noah was taken aback
at this, but finally decided that in future the gallinazo
should be born bald in token of its remarkable
sagacity.

   And now, before bidding farewell to the reader who
may have glanced through these pages, let me record
one more scene. Our vessel lay at anchor far out in
the bay, as owing to the reef and the great rise and fall
of the tide—between twelve and twenty feet—no ships
of heavy tonnage can anchor within two miles of the
wharf. Close to us were the pretty green islands of
Perico and Flamenco, and through a quivering haze,
which gave additional charm to the lovely panorama,
we saw the bold and rocky promontory on which
stands the city of Panama. Behind it rose the volcanic
peak Ancon, crowned by a signal-station—La Vigia—

---

* Cathartes aura.

forming the centre of the coronet of undulating hills that encircle the land. On either side were glimpses of white beach, palm groves and valleys, and away to the south-east, in a tangled wilderness of forest and brush-work, a solitary tower—at least we were told it was a tower—marked the site of the "ancient city of Panama." In the surrounding silver-green haze the town stood out like a dainty mosaic, whose tints of red, pearl, and brown flashed brightly in the warm sunlight. And in harmony with the tender beauty of the scene was the stillness which rested on all around; save the creaking of the anchor which was being weighed, and the distant notes of a song from some shore-returning boat, no other sound broke the silence.

Suddenly, some startled birds flew shrieking overhead, the water lost its sparkle and the colours faded; a rush of footsteps forward made us look to windward for the cause. Close to us, and rapidly approaching, was a long white line of foam which was driven along under a dense curtain of mist and rain. In a second the squall struck the vessel; the awning which the crew had hurried forward to save was torn to shreds, with a loud crash one of the ship's-boats was dashed against the hurricane deck, and for a moment the ship quivered and careened over from the extraordinary force of the wind. As quickly as it came, so quickly it passed, but the land was hidden from view by the grey mist, and before it had dispersed we had steamed out into the open sea, and Panama was soon left far behind.

APPENDIX.

NATIONAL BOUNDARIES

WITH

BRITISH GUIANA.

Articles Published in "La Opinion Nacional," by the Lawyer, Francisco J. Marmol.

Official Edition.
Caracas: National Printing Office.
1878.
(Translation.)

z

APPENDIX.

THE tracing of territorial limits has always been considered of the highest importance, not only because it determines and consolidates rights which constitute the welfare of the present, but also because it frees nations from conflicts in the future.

Guided by such considerations, we propose seriously to call the attention of our National Government towards the establishment (fixing) of our boundaries with British Guiana, as we consider that survey of the greatest public interest and of the highest transcendency. The importance of the territory of the State of Guiana, under the diverse phases that it may be considered, is beyond all doubt and discussion. It notably attracted attention since the times of the Spanish Government, and since then by the frequent invasions and controversies about boundaries, between Spaniards, Dutchmen, and Englishmen.

Our Republic began to fix, with marked interest, its consideration upon that territory since 1841, in consequence of the deeds of Schomburgh upon the Barima, always in pursuit of the great mouth of the Orinoco. Those deeds gave rise to the preliminaries of a Boundary Treaty, initiated in London in 1841, and which did not merit the approval of our Government. When in 1857, we found ourselves managing the Government of the Province of Guiana, we had occasion to confront new and more exaggerated pretensions consummated by the Governor of Demerara, at the time when the discovery of the mines of Tupuquen powerfully attracted public attention. It even got to be officially maintained that those auriferous lands were within the limits of British Guiana; and in so false an idea, expeditions were authorized and exploring licenses granted to Engineers, who might carry them out in the name of the Government of Great Britain. We opposed ourselves vigorously to all this in fulfilment of our official duty ; we maintained the exclusive right of the Republic over those lands, in controversy with the English Vice-Consul, and we gave a documentary account of everything to our National Government.

Such a number of acts reveals undoubtedly the marked tendency of our neighbours for those regions, to invade progressively our territory, induced to it without doubt by the indecision of our boundary lines, and the easy and frequent communication between both territories. There are later acts of noteworthy significance, and we believe it is our duty to place them clearly before public consideration, and very specially before the National Government, for the purpose of inspiring the profound conviction of the importance of the demarcation about which we are discoursing.

In the vicinity of the river Amacuro—a navigable and important affluent of the Orinoco, which empties to the west of Barima—there exists an Indian village belonging to the district Curiapo, Department of Zea. On taking our last census, in 1874, some British subjects from Demerara, who trade with those Indians, claimed the non-incorporation of that village in the census of the Republic, with the pretext that it is under the jurisdiction of the Government of Demerara. Fortunately our Commissioner for taking the census energetically opposed that design, and the Indian village was incorporated in it. Still further : an Indian (of the tribes of the Moroco, a river which undoubtedly belongs to us, as it rises and empties in our territory) having committed a murder, was taken to Demerara to be judged. The defendant's lawyer demurred on the ground of the incompetency of that tribunal, because the crime had been committed in Venezuelan territory, and to that nation belonged also the indictment. The controversy being carried to the superior tribunals, it was declared that there was competency to continue the suit, because the territory as well as the accused were under the jurisdiction of the English nationality, and this opinion was printed in the official newspaper of Demerara.

The acts which we have already narrated and others still which we omit, not to be prolix, demonstrate the great necessity of fixing definitely on boundary lines with the neighbouring British Guiana. The want of that demarcation, the proximity of the territories, and their easy and frequent communication by diverse ways are the causes why they continue slowly, but progressively, to invade us; an invasion that may be perfected by the great distance of our capital cities, and without the public authorities being able to be warned. For example, by the Yuruari, an affluent of the Cuyuni, which runs navigably close up to Tupuquen. By the Batonamo, an affluent of the same river, and which is situated in the neighbourhood of Tumeremo. By the road of the Palmar seeking the waters of the channels of the Toro, which communicate interiorily with those of the eastern Delta of our Orinoco till they descend to the currents of the Moroco.

Still further and of graver consideration. There exists the tradition of a land communication between the mouths of the Essequibo and the interior of our Guiana—a communication which is not at all unlikely, since it is well known that the sources of the Pumaron and of the Moroco descend from the hill country of Imataca, which penetrates considerably into our Guiana territory. The facility of such communications being allowed, and the proper industrial interests of both territories, the consequences of an unsettled state of boundary are as obvious as grave, and worthy of consideration by the high national powers. It should be known and kept well in remembrance that there exists a constant and frequent commercial traffic between the English establishments of Demerara and the interior of our channels of the eastern Delta of the Orinoco, that the Indian inhabitants of these districts are found provided with all kinds of goods for their clothing, with powder and arms for their hunting, effects which they obtain either from the English colonists who come to trade with them, or get for themselves when travelling to Demerara ; that some of these traders fix their residence among our Indians, and come to establish families. And what will be the result of that proceeding in no distant time? that in lands situated on the banks of our rivers, tributaries of the Orinoco, populations will be formed whose instincts, whose interests will not be those of Venezuela ; a prediction that is not exaggerated if we bear in mind the ignorance and simple disposition of those Indians, and the little interest with which past governments have unfortunately regarded the immense advantages and the vast future of that territory.

Grave, very grave conflicts will arise for the Republic the day in which these Indians, ours to day, influenced by whatever suggestions, become inclined to invoke British Nationality. We understand that the English language is no longer unknown to many of those Indians. We do not exaggerate upon vain hypotheses. It is indisputable that our boundaries extend beyond the Essequibo. Such was the insurmountable domination of Spain, such is ours as their legitimate successors. Every occupation from the western bank of the Essequibo towards the mouths of the Orinoco has not been, neither is it in fact, anything but an occupation always opposed by Spain, never accepted by us, and which no legitimate right can consolidate. Well then, if by occupying, in fact, part of the western banks of the Essequibo and of the mouths of the Pumaron, they aspire to the domination of those rivers and the territory which they occupy, will there be no foundation for believing that when that occupation is consummated upon the interior tributaries of the Orinoco, the same pretensions will be unfolded?

Nobody at present disputes with the Republic the exclusive domination over that river which involves the vastest and grandest future. The day in which it must be divided with any other nation, it will decline under all its aspects, principally if we treat with a foreign power with institutions contrary to ours. Its internal and external security will be in a great measure compromised, the first military line of its defence exposed. Under a commercial aspect it seems superfluous, writing in Venezuela, to call to mind the advantages of the navigation of the Orinoco. It will be sufficient to consider it from the western confines of our territory, serving as a base to the future prosperity of these districts, and carrying its waters to the provident Casiquiari to open a way for us to the regions of the Amazon. To descend then in its course to receive from the territory of Granada powerful affluents like the Meta, the Arauca and others that put us in communication with the industrious States of Colombia, so effectually helping to the prosperity of both nations. Later, by its right bank to promote with astonishing facility the industrial and mercantile development of the extensive State Guiana—one might say maritime at the same time as continental—very fecund in natural wealth. By the left bank, and by numerous affluents that form an immense network of water communications, to foment the agricultural and commercial growth of important States to the South and West of the Republic—Apure, Guárico, Zamora, Portuguesa Cojedes y Záchira. Afterwards to run over the Eastern States where all its banks have easy and secure ports, with navigable tributaries that penetrate extensively into those same States running over immense belts as suitable for agriculture as for stock-raising. Then to descend majestically to the ocean by an infinity of canals that fertilize the fruitful lands of its beautiful Delta.

Such is in a general way the course of the Orinoco, such is

that immense water-way of four hundred leagues of navigation, whose exclusive domination the Republic must never share with any other nation. And it is not that we are partisans of that selfish and retrograde policy that Rosas maintained in Buenos Ayres, nor that we aspire for our Orinoco, to the restrictions which Brazil maintains over the Amazon. No, ours are other designs. What we do not want, is that our territory upon that river should be invaded as by alluvion, slowly but surely, for the want of a settlement by boundaries.

What we do not want is that on those banks populations should be encouraged that may have another spirit, other interests and other tendencies that are not essentially Venezuelan. What we do want is that no nation may be able to allege any right, of whatsoever nature it may be, over the banks of that river that may disturb our exclusive domination, and give rise sooner or later to questions about territorial limits, nor about any regulations restrictive of our free traffic and commerce like those which disturbed Paraguay and the Argentine Republic—whose inhabitants live on the banks of the La Plata —and which served as a pretext for a prolonged as well as a disastrous and bloody war. We wish that our maritime ports, like our interior rivers, may be open as they are to all the nations of the world, as becomes a civilized people ; but we wish also above all that the territory of the Republic may remain integral, and that its rights may be properly respected.

Entering now into the question of boundaries, we maintain the following conclusions :—First : Our limits extend beyond the Essequibo up to the limits of French Guiana. Second : Spain, as the first discoverer and first occupier, and of whose rights we are the legitimate successors, always maintained her boundary lines beyond that river. Third : The occupation in fact, first by the Dutch and afterwards by the English does not give a right to the exclusive domination of the Essequibo. Fourth : The Dutch possessions never went beyond Cape Nassau. Fifth : The boundaries proposed by the British Minister must be rejected as invasory of our Guiana territory.

For greater clearness let us invert the order of these propositions. That Spain, as the first occupant, always maintained her boundaries beyond the Essequibo, in spite of the Dutch possession, which it always considered but as an occupation in fact, different documents of indisputable authority evidently prove. In the general map of the province of Cumaná sent to Spain by the Governor Don José Dibuja in 1761, and which was properly approved, it said that the province of Guiana is bounded on the East by all the coast in which are found situated the Dutch colonies of Essequibo, Berbice, Demerara, Corentin and Surinam ; from which it is clearly deduced that Spain considered these possessions as Dutch colonies established on territory belonging to her. So certain is this, that on tracing in the same map the Southern boundaries, it says : by the South the dominions of the very faithful King of Brazil. Here exists a true acknowledgment of territorial domination which does not occur with the Dutch possessions.

With such boundaries was erected the province of Guiana by Royal Decree, June 4, 1762, under the command of Don Joaquin Moreno de Mendoza. In proof of this right, always maintained by Spain, may be cited the Royal Decree of May 5, 1768, confirming the arrangement that the Upper and Lower Orinoco and Rio Negro should remain in charge of the Governor of the province of Guiana, in which is given, as the Eastern boundary of this province, the Atlantic Ocean. It may also be adduced, in proof of the assertion, that we are maintaining the Royal Decree of September 19, 1777, describing the boundaries of the province of Guiana incorporated already, as was also Upper and Lower Orinoco. In it is also given as the Eastern limit, the Atlantic Ocean. From these antecedents, deduced from official and authentic documents, the truth of what we have stated is evidenced, that Spain, as discoverer and first occupant, maintained her boundaries beyond the Essequibo, and did not consider the Dutch possessions but as an occupation in fact. Such was undoubtedly the character of the Dutch colonies to which we are referring.

Two acts came afterwards to modify that occupation. The Treaty of Munster, ratified in 1648, and that of Aranjuez in 1791. By the first, Philip IV. recognised the sovereignty and independence of the Netherlands, and agreed that the high contracting parties should remain in possession of the countries, forts and factories which they occupied in the East and West Indies. By the second, bases and conditions were established for the extradition of the deserters and fugitives in the American colonies. These agreements considered in the light of the principles of the Law of Nations, it cannot be put in doubt that Spain recognised the possession of the Dutch colonies, since, in regard to them, she undertook to treat with Holland as one power with another. However, if this is true, if that possession was recognized, it is also true that Holland, by virtue of those very treaties, was subject to the common condition of conterminous and subordinate nations, in consequence of the established rules and prescriptions of the Law of Nations for the territorial division between bordering nations.

It is not in accordance with the principles of that Law, neither has it ever been so, nor will it ever be, that the occupation of the mouth of rivers in undivided territories between conterminous nations, should confer any right for acquiring the exclusive domination of those rivers, or of the territories which surround them. Such a principle would be equivalent to a justification of the invasions, and to proclaiming the right of force as a legitimate title to territorial property. The Law of Nations prescribes the contrary. It establishes that for the demarcation of boundaries between nations who are joint holders, natural boundaries are to be preferred, such as rivers, mountain chains, &c., and that if those rivers have great volumes of water, each one of the contiguous nations has the domination over the half of the breadth of the river, or all the bank which it occupies. Such are the conditions of the Essequibo.

The territories of our Guiana and of British Guiana are naturally of curved boundaries. So that even raising the right of Holland to the height of that of Spain, which is ours, there is no kind of reason whatever for the supremacy which is claimed over the Essequibo. In almost all its course we dwell on the bank, and it may be said to rise in our territory. We have then, at least, an indisputable right to the domination of one half of its width and to its free navigation. The doctrine that we have explained is so generally acknowledged and accepted that we think ourselves that we can dispense with the production of the authorities on which it is supported. It is among those points on which there is no divergence in the Law of Nations. The occupation in fact, then, first by the Dutch, and lately by the English, does not give any right to the exclusive domination which is claimed over the Essequibo. That the Dutch possessions never passed beyond Cape Nassau, and that Spain repulsed with force every invasion toward the Orinoco, among other and conclusive proofs, the Royal Order of October 1st, 1780, clearly demonstrates. In it instructions are given to Don José F. Inciarte to destroy a fort which the Dutch had constructed on the right bank of the Moroco. Incontrovertible as is the right of the Republic to maintain its boundary beyond the Essequibo, it cannot forego that line without exposing itself to grave perturbations in future. Every other demarcation compromises the integrity of our territory which should be defended on its Eastern flank with the basin of that river. The demarcation proposed by the British Minister since 1841, offers the gravest difficulties besides injustice.

First.—Leaving out the Essequibo, it begins in the Moroco, and comes to compromise, in great part, the course of the Cuyuni. It should be borne in mind, as of the highest importance in the fixing of our boundaries with British Guiana, to preserve entire the course of the Moroco and of the Cuyuni, which belong to us exclusively, as they rise and empty in our territory. The first serves as boundary to our Eastern Delta of the Orinoco, it communicates with all its channels, is of extraordinary importance to the internal security of the Republic, and may serve as a vehicle of clandestine commerce. The second runs extensively into the mainland of our Guiana, and navigable rivers that encircle its interior are tributaries to it. To permit part of its course as a boundary would be the same as to permit foreign navigation in our Guiana territory.

Second.—The mountain ranges and the rivers to which the alluded demarcation refers not being fixed astronomically, it is exposed to further invasions and exaggerated pretensions that may compromise the tranquillity of the Republic.

Third.—The English possessions which may be established on this side of the Essequibo will open a passage to the North in order to be on the banks of the Orinoco, and then will arise complications of immeasurable magnitude. They must then reject the limits proposed by the British Ministry as invasive of our territory. Our general conclusion then may be formulated in the following terms : The question of boundaries between ourselves and Great Britain is reduced purely to a question of fact, viz. Up to where did the Dutch establishments, recognized by Spain, extend ? and whose domination was transmitted to Great Britain by her treaty with the Sovereign of the Netherlands in 1814 ; setting out from the principle that our interior limits, founded on authentic documents, extended beyond the Essequibo up to the borders of French Guiana.

Some will say that we have lost time, that England is a powerful nation, of eminent rank among the Powers of Europe, and will not abdicate her claims upon the Essequibo, and on the territory of Guiana to which she aspires. No, we reply, the question is not of cannons or of squadrons ; it is of International Right, of principles consecrated by eyes before which all civilized peoples of the world bow respectfully. Nor do we believe that Great Britain, whose historical precedents in the splendours of our Independence, give her titles to our consideration and high esteem, and who boasts of her respect and importance to the other nations, would found the solution of her boundaries with us on the preponderance of her force. But if, unfortunately, it should be so, we are in possession of indirect and legitimate means to make the rights which with such evident justice we maintain, be respected.

The importance of the demarcation of our limits with British Guiana brings us again to the arena of discussion. Supported by official documents of absolute authenticity, we have proved the most important of our conclusions in our former explanation ; that Spain, as the discoverer and first occupier, had always maintained her boundaries beyond the Essequibo, that she had repelled with force every invasion from the banks of that river toward the Orinoco. We reproduce now those documents entire, no longer to prove an argument, but to demonstrate that the question of our boundaries with Great Britain is not situated—nor ought to be—in the region of controversies, but in that of consummated acts.

Let us enter into the matter. Among those authentic documents, two, above others, surpass, and are of the highest transcendency, if they be not decisive. The instruction of the Intendente-General of Venezuela to people the province of Guiana, and the exploration of the Eastern Delta of the Orinoco by virtue of that very instruction ; documents corroborated by the authority of the Sovereign of Spain, who was then the Sovereign of that territory ; documents that are in the fullest harmony and consequence, and are completed the one by the other.

Respecting the first, it is to be observed that, with indisputable right, Spain made her limits beyond the Essequibo up to the frontier of French Guiana. As regards the second, it is evidently proved that the Dutch possessions occupied, in that epoch, only the banks of the rivers near the sea, without penetrating far into the interior of the country. We will occupy ourselves later, in this same writing, with the legitimate consequences that emanate from those acts authentically proved. We think also of the highest importance the exploration of the Eastern part of the Lower Orinoco, carried out by the Spanish engineer, Felipe de Inciarte, and more important still the Royal approbation of March 9th, 1780, which gives to that instruction, to those traced boundaries, to that exploration, the seal of the national sovereignty which indisputably Spain was competent to do in those times in which those acts were consummated, and it conferred on them irrevocable authority within and without the Peninsular dominions.

One of the most important results of the commission confided to Inciarte is that exploration of the Eastern Delta of the Orinoco in which were comprehended the Barima, the Guaima, the Moroco, and the Pumaron the latter is designed under the authority of Bauruma. The exploration of the rivers is an act of authority of national sovereignty ; so the Law of Nations has recognized it. Spain exercised that right exclusively over that territory and over those rivers without any kind of obstacle, and without the participation of any other nationality. We may then allege in all time the exercise of that right with certain and indubitable success in the question of boundaries, with Great Britian principally, as she has not desisted in her claims over the Barima. However, let us raise the question to its true height. Let us fix it in its proper place, analyzing at length the documents adduced, in order to give it its genuine significance. From this analysis will result, undoubtedly constituted on a solid foundation, the right of Spain, which is our own.

The instruction of the Intendente-General of Venezuela— in order to occupy in the province of Guiana, for its object, for the genius and character of its dispositions by the faculties with which that functionary was invested, and by the Royal appro- bation which it received in 1780—is not after all anything else than a Government order to occupy a territory in the posses- sion of Spain ; and as a consequence of the occupation which was ordered, the boundaries of that territory were traced. Let us demonstrate this. The instruction says : "The commissioners shall try to occupy said lands, as belonging to Spain, their first discoverer, and not ceded afterwards nor occupied at the time by any other Power, nor have they any title for it—advancing in the occupation by the eastern side as much as may be possible until they reach French Guiana." And what were those lands which the Intendente of Venezuela was commanded to occupy as belonging to Spain ? The Intendente had surveyed them before. "At the back of the Essequibo and other Dutch pos- sessions, running east up to French Guiana and south up to the river Amazon is situated the territory, unoccupied on this part, and only occupied by Pagan Indians and a large number of fugitive negroes, slaves of the Dutch, and also from the plan- tations of Guiana."

The Intendente of Venezuela speaking from Carácas, says that the phrase, "at the back of the Essequibo" means "beyond the Essequibo." Here then in the clearest manner, in the most explicit way, is the authority of the Spanish sovereign fixing his national limits, with just and unimpeachable titles, in land of his own. Every nation has a right to trace the boundaries of the territory which it occupies, and it is the duty of the other nations to respect these boundaries, as long as they are not disputed by others with better titles. That Spain was sovereign of the territory which now belongs to us in Guiana, and that she had the right to trace its boundary lines, are asseverations placed beyond all doubt and controversy. We should rather say they are true acts consummated. And in truth, it would be superfluous, except for the claims of Great Britain, to open a discussion to sustain the titles of Spain in the disputed territory, after that for more than three centuries they were recognized by all the Powers of Europe; after having been recognized by Holland—the very one from whom England derived her right—in public treaties like those of Munster and Aranjuez; after having been recognized also in public treaties by Portugal, the only Power of Europe that could have been able, as discoverer, to compete with Spain in the regions of Guiana, but that never dared, respecting those agreements, to overpass the boundaries of what now constitutes French Guiana.

To discuss the titles of Spain after they have been solemnly recognised by England herself in the Treaty of Utrecht! And no one less than Great Britain has a right to dispute territories acquired by Spain with the title of discoverer and first occupant, she that has made use of these same titles and same rights. If not, what right had she—Great Britain—to cede to the North Americans by the Treaty of 1783, in which she recognised their independence, the territory which constituted the primitive Confederation of the North? No other right except that of discoverer and first occupier. And why deny to Spain, and to us now, her legitimate successors, equal rights to those which Great Britain has exercised by public treaties.

Returning again to the document which we are analyzing, we find in it, by explicit acts, the exercise of the public power, by means of a magistrate, who, with full conscience of the rights of the Sovereign whom he represents, orders the occupation of Spanish Guiana, and traces its boundary lines.

Paragraph II.—" The Commissioners shall endeavour to occupy said lands, as belonging to Spain, their first discoverer, and not ceded afterwards, nor occupied at this time by any power, neither have they any title for it."

Paragraph I.—" The principal and greatest importance of this business being, not to work uselessly the securing the said boundaries of the said Province of Guiana, that begins on the Eastern part of it at a point where the Orinoco empties into the sea, called Barlovento, on the border of the Dutch colony of Essequibo "

Paragraph XXX.—" The principal object is the occupation and security of the boundaries of the Province of Guiana, on the East of Essequibo and French Guiana."

Such Government acts, sanctioned by the authority of the
Sovereign of Spain, give to this document the character of a
direct and unimpeachable proof in the question of boundaries
that we are elucidating. And will Great Britain be able to
present documents of equal nature and with equal titles? Has
she presented them up to now?

As a result of the preparations of the Intendente-General
of Venezuela, they proceeded to the exploration of the lower
Delta of the Orinoco. The official Report of Inciarte which
contains it, is an important document of high significance under
various aspects. In the first place, it confirms the idea which
the instructions of the Intendente give in respect to the nature
and true position of the Dutch colonies in the times to which it
refers—1779—situated on the banks of the rivers near the sea,
and without penetrating far into the interior of the country.
Inciarte explored all the territory embraced between the Orinoco and the Essequibo, and finds no establishments, nor
buildings of any kind with the exception of the small fort of
Moroco, whose insignificant nature he describes, and that he
was ordered to destroy it by express order of the King of
Spain.

And where is the act of our national sovereignty in virtue
of which we may have abdicated the right that we have to the
immense extent of territory which extends from the Essequibo
to French Guiana? Who has marked for us the limits of
those possessions? Who has marked those boundaries? Great
Britain, intercepting us by means of the Essequibo. And still
more is claimed; they deny us all share in that river, and
limits are proposed invasive of our territory. And we must not
cede any more. It is not just, neither politic nor convenient.
Every foreign invasion on this side of the Essequibo ruins our
territory. The British possessions which might commence on
that flank, increasing themselves towards the North, would
become part of the banks of the Orinoco; while advancing
towards the south, they have a speedy way to the auriferous
zone of our interior. Lord Aberdeen well understood this
when he proposed to our Minister in London—Fortique—
according to official data that we have before us, that the
English Government would cede territory in Barima, provided
that of Venezuela would yield on the Cuyuni. That Great
Britain ought not to consider herself exclusive mistress of the
Essequibo, she herself has said in the most solemn and explicit
manner.

There exists in our Ministry of Foreign Relations a communication which she made by means of the public Minister, in

1840, of the commission which she had given to Schomburgh to explore the Essequibo, and mark its limits. Certainly Great Britain would not have made such a communication if she had considered herself possessed of the exclusive predominance which she now claims over the Essequibo. Neither is the object conceived of informing our Government of the establishment of their boundaries on that river, if they did not consider the Republic joint possessors of its waters. That communication involves an explicit acknowledgment of our right. The vacillation of Great Britain certainly contradicts her claims over Guiana. Before the exploration of Schomburgh, she communicates officially to our Government, giving public testimony that she considered the Republic joint holder in the waters of the Essequibo. But after the exploration, and when the intelligent English engineer had, without doubt, revealed the immense advantages of that water-way, by its prolonged extension, by its numerous affluents, by its ramifications that extend to the Amazon, then they deny us all right in the Essequibo, and they propose to us boundaries which extravagantly invade our Guiana territory.

We wish now to enter into a new kind of argument, either for greater clearness of our right, or to reply to some observations which have already been made on the part of the Government of Great Britain, and others that may be made in future. The explanation of our Plenipotentiary Fortique in London; the demarcations of Codazzi; the records of those eminent men, Messrs. Yones and Baralt; the diplomatic notes addressed to the British Government by our Minister of Foreign Relations in November 1876, so full of abundant reasoning on behalf of our right ; the statistics of Guiana published in 1876, and the annual statistics of 1877 ; in all these explanations and official data, the Essequibo is presented as the absolute Eastern limit of our territory with British Guiana. We believe that that boundary, so expressed, diminishes the territorial right of the Republic, and we are going to explain ourselves. The records of Messrs. Yones and Baralt, like the observations of Codazzi, which served as a base to our Plenipotentiary Fortique, for his explanation before the British Cabinet, and the said official data, rest on two foundations to which we do not lend the merit or the force which have been attributed to them. The opinions of geographers and historians, and the demarcation of the Missions were made by the Government of Spain. However valuable may be the opinions of wise men, of historians and geographers, they have no authority whatever where national boundaries are treated of, which are but legitimate acts of the Sovereigns in use of their natural prerogatives; so that in the present question, every opinion, however authorised it may be considered, is ineffectual and unable to exist before the Royal decrees of the King of Spain, which, drawing the boundary lines in Guiana places them beyond the Essequibo up to the borders of French Guiana. No asseveration, whatever its nature may be, can oppose itself to the authority of the official documents that we have analyzed.

The demarcation of the Missions has no more strength. Guided by its intentions of occupying their dominions, and of widening the civilization and culture of the Indians, Spain continued, in the course of time, to mark out Mission districts which it subordinated to the different religious orders; but such demarcation was made within its territory and national boundaries, it was an eternal economic act, purely administrative, and had no other object but order and regularity in the service of the Missions. And it is certain that the demarcation carried out in Venezuela was ordered by the Governor of Cumaná, in agreement with the " padres" in charge of the Mission, who had to make their residence in Guiana. There is then no truth, no reason for confounding the demarcation of Missions with the national boundaries of Spain. From that confusion of boundaries, which we oppose, it would be reasonably deduced that Spain did not possess in Venezuela any other territory than that marked out by its Missions; an assertion very far from the truth, and which fails in every legal and rational foundation. Such an assertion leads us evidently to the maintenance of the theory which establishes that the material occupation of the whole of the territory of a nation is necessary in order to found exclusive domination over it, or it may be right of property. Such a theory that recognises, as a principle, only an erroneous idea about the nature of the possession which serves as a title to acquire, by the Law of Nations, cannot be sustained, cannot be accepted, without confusing and shaking the territorial domination of all nations, because none of them occupies materially all the territory which they have declared in their possession. That theory, inadmissible under all aspects, would be extremely disastrous to all the nationalities of South America.

More than this—Great Britain can produce no argument favourable to her right as emanating from the explanations and data to which we have referred. Of whatsoever nature may have been the asseverations of our Minister-Plenipotentiary Fortique in London, they are null, and of no value, since our Government denied its approbation to the preliminaries of the boundary treaty initiated by him, and they cannot be the object of any reasonable pretension. As regards Codazzi, it is certain that Lord Aberdeen replied to Señor Fortique, in a diplomatic note, denying the Essequibo for the dividing line, and supporting himself on the demarcation of Codazzi, that presents the Moroco. Such an agreement has no value whatever. The map of Codazzi is not an official map. There is no act of competent authority which declares it such ; on the contrary, our Government has lately rejected claims from the Government of New Granada for possessions on the bank of the Orinoco, founded on his demarcation. Great Britain cannot constitute an exception.

The records and official data to which reference has been made, are opinions of citizens and public fenctionaries which in nowise compromise, or diminish, the rights of the Republic. It is certainly strange that our Government, being in possession of the documents that we have analyzed—the Instruction of the Intendente of Venezuela, and the Exploration of the Delta—it being allowed that Messrs. Baralt and Fortique refer to them, they should have been presented to demonstrate our boundaries by the Essequibo, when they prove most abundantly that they extended beyond that river. There not existing then any act of our National Sovereignty which defines our boundaries with Great Britain in detriment of what we are sustaining, the rights of the Republic continue to have unalterable force.

We have demonstrated that since 1810, we find ourselves in legal possession of the territory which constituted the ancient Captaincy-General of Venezuela with its legitimate boundaries, and it was only in 1814 that Great Britain obtained possession of some Dutch colonies which the Sovereign of the Netherlands transmitted. Well, what were the boundaries of that transmission ? What the boundary lines traced by Holland in the ceded territory ? None, because Holland herself was without them. Her possession was only in fact. She only held in Guiana what Spain, the discoverer and first occupier, had seen fit to permit her. And for that reason, with the good faith which ought to distinguish nations in their treaties, in the Third Article in which she ceded to Great Britain some of her colonies in Guiana, she does not mark out any kind of boundaries whatever. It is to be noticed that that treaty was an agreement between Holland and Great Britain, without the intervention of Spain ; that it establishes bonds and obligations between the contracting parties, but in no way can it bind Spain, that no longer legally possessed that territory, nor her legitimate successors, in all that may prejudice them.

We have founded our right to the territory which constituted the ancient Captaincy-General of Venezuela on the "*uti
possidetis*" of 1810. We are going to make clear that right
beyond all controversy. Nobody has ever put in doubt, not
only in Venezuela, but in all the sections of South America,
that by virtue of the political transformation that gave rise to
our new nationalities, these were substituted respectively for
the territorial Seignory of Spain in all her former dominions.
Brazil herself, in spite of the diversity of her institutions, has
recognized that principle, and could not proceed differently
without grave inconsequence, because, in short, what other
right did the new empire represent but the one proceeding from
the old kingdom of Portugal? If she has maintained controversies about boundaries with adjacent nations, it has not
been in denial of the principle cited, but rather confirming it,
for having believed herself helped to rights which she could
enforce before Spain herself by virtue of old treaties. Our
succession to the seignorial rights of Spain in all the territory of
the ancient Captaincy-General of Venezuela was constant
prescription, and an infallible arrangement of all our consti-
tuent bodies-politic, even in the midst of our great struggle for
independence.

The Liberator, in incorporating the Province of Guiana in
1817 with the territory conquered by the Republican arms,
traced its boundaries after the tenor of the Royal Decrees of
Spain which he expressly mentions. The first Congress
assembled in Angostura, which sanctioned the Fundamental
Law of Colombia, established in its Second Article: "Its territory shall be that embraced in the old Captaincy-General of
Venezuela and the Vice-royalty of the new kingdom of Granada." The "Constituyente" of Cúcuta in 1821, ratifies the
former Fundamental Law by that of July 12th, whose Fifth
Article reads: "The territory of the Republic of Colombia
will be comprehended within the limits of the old Captaincy-
General of Venezuela and the Vice-royalty and Captaincy-
General of the new kingdom of Granada, but the assignment
of its exact boundaries will be reserved for a more opportune
occasion."

The same "Constituyente" sanctioned, at last, the Constitution of the New Colombian nationality, and ratified the
former prescriptions in its Articles 6th and 7th.—7th. "The
towns of the said extension still under the Spanish yoke, at
whatever time they may free themselves, will form part of the
Republic with rights and representation equal to all the others
that compose it."

6th.—" The territory of Colombia is the same that comprised the old Viceroyalty of New Granada and the Captaincy-General of Venezuela." As is seen from Article 7, the right sanctioned by the " Constituyente" of Colombia referred not only to the towns that had already gained their independence and liberty, but also to all those that remained under the rule of the Spanish Government. It was not only to the territory of which the founders of our nationality were already in possession, but also to all that which they believed themselves to have the right to possess.

Venezuela, which separated from the Colombian Union, and constituted her nationality independently, in 1830, sanctioned the same right in her fundamental agreement. Article 5th. " The territory of Venezuela comprehends that which, before the political transformation of 1810, was denominated the Captaincy-General of Venezuela." And this canon has been essentially reproduced in all the Constitutions that afterwards have been given to the Republic. In that of 1857, 1858 and 1864. " Article 3rd. The territory of Venezuela comprises all that before the political transformation of 1810, was denominated the Captaincy, &c., &c."

Such is the canon which has reproduced itself in all our fundamental institutions since the birth of our nationality, in the glorious splendours of Colombia; the same which is found sanctioned in all the Constitutions of our sister Republics. Its appearance as constant as universal has elevated it to a dogma of the Public International Law of South America. It could not happen in any other way, because the existence of such a precept is not a creation of that public right, but a natural and legitimate consequence of the political transformation which the different sections that constitute the dominion of Spain have experienced. In truth, political forms are variable, are purely accidental, in conformity with the times; at the wish of the radical sovereignty of the people; yet those same people, in society congregated, have by the I aw of Nations the eminent domination of the territory which they occupy with the demarcations which they have assigned to them for their special use.

Such is, in short, the radical foundation of the " *uti possidetis*" of 1810. The existence of that right, as far as we are concerned, is solemnly sanctioned by the public treaty with Spain upon recognition of our Independence.

" Article I. In consequence of this renouncement and cession, His Christian Majesty recognizes as a free Sovereign and Independent Nation, the Republic of Venezuela, com-

posed of the provinces and territories expressed in its Constitution, and other later laws, viz. : Margarita, Guiana,
Cumará, Barcelona, Carácas."

Separation being made of the renouncement and transfer of
rights on the part of Spain, which are but diplomatic formulæ
that do not embody any modification of the treaty, the truths
which in it appear as a relief, are, the recognition of our Independence, the legitimate succession of our right in the right
of Spain, and that the territory of the old Captaincy-General
of Venezuela came to constitute that of the Republic of the
same name, traced out in its Constitution and in its laws.
Such understanding Spain has lately confirmed by an act of
her own, extremely solemn. A controversy being raised by
the Netherlands about the ownership of the island of Aves,
the Court of Spain was designated as arbitrator by the con-
tending parties, and in 1865 declared that the said island
belonged to Venezuela in right and possession, basing its decision especially on the fact that all the islands of the Caribbean
sea, among which is found the aforesaid—were discovered
by Spain, and on Venezuela being established with the territory of the old Captaincy-General of Carácas, she had succeeded to Spain in all her territorial rights.

There exists a public act emanating from our Government
which we judge worthy of being commemorated in this writing, because it strikes the heart of the question which we
are sustaining. About the middle of 1822, Señor J. Rafael
Ravenga was accredited as Plenipotentary to His Britannic
Majesty, and in the instructions sent by the Secretary of
Foreign Relations is found the following paragraph :—

" May I be permitted, however, to call your attention
particularly to Article 2nd of the projected treaty about
boundaries. Agree as exactly as may be possible about fixing
the dividing line of both territories, according to the last
treaties with Spain and Holland. The colonists of Demerara
and Berbice have usurped a great portion of land, which
according to them belongs to us, from the side of the river
Essequibo. It is absolutely necessary that said colonists either
put themselves under the protection and obedience of our laws,
or that they retire to their former possessions. In short, the
necessary time will be given them, as is set forth in the project."*

The conscientiousness of the Government of Colombia—
which was ours then—expressed in the preceding instructions,

* " Historical Record upon the Boundaries between the Republic of
Colombia and the Empire of Brazil." By José M. Quijano Otero.

has two important phases; the usurpation of our territory on the Essequibo by English colonists, such as exists now, and the possession of the *uti possidetis* of 1810, which is nothing else than the guaranteeing of our rights in the treaties celebrated between Holland and Spain, and to which the Colombian minutes refer.

Again, in order to carry to the highest evidence the demonstration of our right in the present question we will say that Great Britian has virtually recognized the *uti possidetis* of 1810, in public Convention in the Treaty of 1783, in which it recognized the independence of the United States of the North. Let us prove it. The Articles 1st and 2nd of that Treaty are the following :

" Article 1st.—His Britannic Majesty recognizes as free, sovereign, and independent the States of New Hampshire, Massachusetts, Rhode Island, &c., agreeing to recognize them as such, and renouncing for himself, his heirs, and successors all claim against the rights of their government and territory.

" Article 2nd.—In order to avoid all discussions and differences that may arise in future about the question of the boundaries of the said United States, it is declared and agreed that those shall be the following, namely, from the Northwest angle of Nova Scotia, &c."

Well then ; what difference exists between those articles and those of our treaty with Spain upon the identical object of recognizing our independence, which we have reproduced ? Essentially none. In one, as much as in the other, the national sovereignty of a people is recognized that proclaims its independence and effects it. In the one, as much as in the other, the right which it has as a sovereign nation to all the territory which they occupied as colonies is recognized. And what else is the *uti possidetis* of 1810 ? On what principle of the Law of Nations, on what practice of civilized nations will Great Britain be able to found the difference which she claims, between the national sovereignty of the United States and the national sovereignty of the people of Venezuela ? No difference exists which can be founded on reason, and if any could be adduced it would undoubtedly be in our favour, because no chain of former subordination linked us to the government of Great Britain.

From the mass of reasoning which we have brought forward, we can deduce the following conclusions. 1st.—Spain, as a sovereign nation, traced the boundaries which belonged to her in Guiana. 2nd.—On establishing herself, the Republic or Venezuela succeeded Spain in the domination and ownership of that territory, under its legitimate boundaries, either by virtue of the *uti possidetis* of 1810—recognized by all the nationalities of South America—or as a national prerogative of its national sovereignty. 3rd.—Great Britain has no right to annul the legitimate exercise of two national sovereignties. 4th.—As a European Power, possessor of territory on our continent, she is incorporated in the great family of nationalities of South America, and has no right to violate a principle recognized and sanctioned by all other nationalities, as that of the *uti possidetis* of 1810.

From these affirmations that we have deduced from authentic official documents, and from indisputable principles of the Law of Nations, we may conclude definitely that the question of our boundaries with Great Britain does not present, in its solution, such grave difficulties as we supposed. That it should not be placed in the region of controversies but in the district of accomplished facts, allowing that Spain of whom we are the legitimate successors, traced its boundaries. That by the priority of our right, and the nature and origin of the titles that confirm it, we are rather in the position to grant concessions than under the necessity of accepting conditions which it may be wished to impose upon us. Above all, we wish to inspire the profound conviction, as a result of this writing, which is extremely important to the Republic, *viz.*, the necessity of a speedy solution of this controversy, that its delay prejudices immensely its gravest and most transcendental interests in various respects. Thus, it betters the conditions of Great Britain ; time, our silence and indifference give margin that they may effect invasions, which are afterwards alleged as accomplished facts, as bases of acquired rights, which is the formula hitherto adopted. Lord Aberdeen well judged it so, when in a diplomatic note he said to our Plenipotentiary Fortique, in London, that he did not understand the interest of Venezuela in the urgency of the question of boundaries, and that he should be satisfied that things should remain as before.

Our Government has officially addressed that of Great Britain proposing a speedy solution of the controversy. We understand that no satisfactory answer has been given, and it is probable that it will not be given, because, thus, it suits the interests of Great Britain. We think that it would be convenient to reiterate that effort in explicit and peremptory terms, by proposing the arbitration of a third Power, in case of negation to a direct convention. We have all the data sufficient to accept, without any kind of fear, an absolute decision ; and as far as principles are concerned, all of them are also in favour of our right.

Lifting the question to its highest, it will be understood easily that these interests are not purely Venezuelan. The position of the Orinoco in the hands of a friendly power, that fraternizes in institutions, is a question eminently American and of the highest transcendency. The day in which this is not so, the day in which a European Power of political institutions adverse to ours dominates on the Orinoco, or makes its influence felt as a possessor on its banks, and in any other respect with the water communication of that river, with the Amazon, or the numerous navigable affluents of either. then not only the political and commercial interests of Venezuela would be in a great measure compromised, but also those of New Granada, Ecuador, Peru, and Bolivia, and even those of Brazil herself. Under these circumstances, the navigation of the Orinoco may become a grave international question of South America. (Here, follow a few paragraphs relating to the ruptured intercourse between Colombia and Venezuela, which I omit.)

In continuation :—We offered to discuss the demarcation proposed by the British Government. We are going to comply with that promise as a summary of our former observations. At once we maintain that that demarcation is inadmissible, because it compromises and prejudices in the highest degree the interests of the Republic, in the present and in the future. In short, every dividing line between us and British Guiana that is not in the Essequibo, ruins the territory of the Republic. In the first place it is extremely difficult to fix that dividing line, making it correspond with mountain chains and rivers of the second class, geographically unknown ; to trace meridians in unexplored and perhaps unexplorable lands without exposing our territory to new invasions and dangerous controversies, and of uncertain success, which have always to be sustained with powerful nations accustomed to impose their will by using force. The Essequibo being free and only under British domination, our territory may be invaded and dominated with impunity. It being ‘allowed that that river communicates by means of the channels of the Orinoco, which are difficult to be watched and guarded, so also it communicates with our territory of the Amazon by its upper part. These ways of communication would be free, rapid, and without power of being restricted, as long as the Essequibo

remains under the exclusive domination of Great Britain.
The demarcation proposed by the British Minister is the
following :—

"A line that should go from the mouth of the Moroco to
the point at which the river Barama unites with the Guaima ;
thence by the Barama up the stream as far as the Aunama,
which would be ascended up to the place where this stream
approaches nearest to the Acarabici, and following this river
to its confluence with the Cuyuni ; then continuing by this
last up stream till it arrives at the high lands in contact with
the Roraima range, in which are divided the waters that
flow into the Essequibo from those which run into the Rio
Blanco."

This line has inconveniences and most prejudicial disadvant-
ages for the Republic. As is seen, it begins at the mouth of
the Moroco, it runs by insignificant rivers, almost geographically
unknown, and mountain-chains of the same kind, till it arrives
at the waters of the Cuyuni ; it follows then the course of this
river up to the Roraima range.* The explanation of that line
is the following ; as a point of departure and continuation
it takes the secondary mountain ranges and rivers of our
continent, subject to controversies and invasions, till it arrives
at the Cuyuni, an affluent of the Essequibo, which belongs to
us integrally : it runs all its course, attaching great part of the
territory of our State Guiana, up to the Roraima range, where
rises our Caroni. That is to say, England marks herself
boundaries within our territory, imprisoning us within a line
of circumvallation from the ocean up to the sources of one
of our most important interior rivers. And with what right
can Great Britain claim from us the abrogation of incontrovertible principles of the universal Law of Nations? Even
laying aside our original titles from Spain, which prove,
evidently, that our interior boundaries passed beyond the
Essequibo up to the borders of French Guiana, even laying
aside, we say, those titles which we have analyzed over-
abundantly, England has no right to take possession of the
Essequibo and to declare it her exclusive property.

It is an invariable law and constant practice of the Law of
Nations that in order to divide nations, possessors of common
territories, the rivers and mountain ranges of consideration and

---

* It seems to have slipped the notice both of the proposers and those
to whom it was proposed, that by no possible means could a line following
the Cuyuni river reach the Roraima range or anywhere near it —
J.W.B.W.

importance are preferred as boundaries. In these conditions is found the Essequibo, which is a natural curved boundary between us and British Guiana. And what right has Great Britain not only to declare that the Essequibo is her exclusive property, but also to pass beyond its banks and penetrate into our territory and leave her boundaries? It is also an invariable law of the Law of Nations that when a broad river divides the territories of two conterminous nations, each one of them has a right to the domination of the half of that river in all the bank which it occupies. And with what right can Great Britain claim from us the abrogation of that incontrovertible prescription of the Universal Law of Nations? Besides the line which we have traced and which was proposed by Great Britain, there was also the dishonourable condition that Venezuela should engage herself not to alienate that territory to any other foreign power.

The Government of Great Britain well understood the importance of that territory under diverse phases, and that it would not suit for it to pass into the power of a nation that might be able to repel force by force with equal advantages and conditions. Guided by the design of putting an end to this question of boundaries, our Government Council, in 1844, submitted for disscussion a proposal for a dividing line that should be offered to Great Britain. It humoured sufficiently the exactions of Great Britain, but that dividing line was not so onerous as that which had been proposed by that nation. It began at the mouth of Moroco, following the course of that river up to its source. Thence it drew a meridian, which crossing the Cuyuni went up to the Pacaraima range, which divides the waters of the Essequibo from those of the Rio Blanco. If not so prejudicial as that proposed by Great Britain, it comprises, in a great measure, the gravest transcendental interests of the Republic in the present as much as in the future. All that may be cut off from the Essequibo, as our eastern boundary with British Guiana, is to ruin the territory of the Republic; it is to cause that British subjects, that the foreigner may travel and navigate through our territory without our being able to impede it. Having the exclusive domination of the Essequibo, they have the free navigation of that river and of its most important affluents, which penetrate extensively into our territory, and among others the Cuyuni and the Mazaruni.

Besides this, the nation has already given forth its judgment, has already expressed its will respecting the territorial rights by that flank in the most solemn manner, and it is not possible to contradict itself without great indignity, besides grave prejudices, under different respects and considerations.

The 1st Article of our Boundary Treaty with Brazil, in its 3rd division, speaks thus :—" The line will continue through the most elevated points of the Pacaraima range, so that the waters which go to the Rio Blanco may remain belonging to Brazil, and those which run to the Essequibo, Cuyuni, and Caroni to Venezuela, up to where the territories of the two States reach on their eastern part." From this boundary convention with Brazil, the only nation that could dispute with us original titles in Guiana, is deduced that the Republic stretches its territorial dominion on the south as far as the Pacaraima range, a continuation of the Parima and which divides the waters of the Rio Blanco from those which run to the Essequibo ; that it has declared and maintained its dominion over that territory, and over the Essequibo and its affluents in those regions, and, what is more important, that it is bounded on the east by Brazil. Comparing this demarcation with Brazil with the line proposed by the English Government, it results that the latter is going to terminate in the Roraima range, which is in the interior of our State Guiana, and which is a ramification of that of Pacaraima. In short this line with our Brazilian division comes to form an immense angle in our Guiana territory. If it is cut off then from the Essequibo the following absurdities result, in which grave prejudice and national indignity dispute the palm.

1st.—That we lose not only the territory that belongs to us, from the Essequibo to the boundaries of French Guiana, but that comprehended to the east between that river and the line proposed by Great Britain, which amounts to a multitude of square leagues.

2nd.—This nation taking possession of the Essequibo, she bounds herself in fact and divides us from Brazil, by which we are bounded on the east according to the public treaty with that nation.

There is then in the usurpation of the Essequibo, a usurpation of territory and a usurpation of national sovereignty.

We terminate these articles, recommending as we have already done in several places, the importance of putting, as soon as possible, an end to the question of our boundaries with Great Britain, and the necessity and justice of maintaining the Essequibo as the limit of our concessions, as the natural boundary of our territory, as much by the original authentic titles which we have from Spain as by the principles of the Law of Nations, which we have discussed and analyzed in these writings.

Francisco J. Marmol.

Caracas, February 18th, 1878.

(Here follow copies of the original documents from which these arguments have been deduced, but it is unnecessary to re-produce them, as their substance is contained in the above writings.—J.W.B.W.)

THE END.

London: Printed by, A. Schulze, 13 Poland Street.

MESSRS. HURST AND BLACKETT'S
LIST OF NEW WORKS.

ROYAL WINDSOR. By W. HEPWORTH DIXON.
SECOND EDITION. Volumes I. and II. Demy 8vo. 30s. To be completed in 2 more volumes.

CONTENTS OF VOLS. I. AND II.—Castle Hill, Norman Keep, First King's House, Lion Heart, Kingless Windsor, Windsor Won, Geoffrey Plantagenet, Windsor Lost, The Fallen Deputy, The Queen Mother, Maud de Braose, The Barons' War, Second King's House, Edward of Carnarvon, Perot de Gaveston, Isabel de France, Edward of Windsor, Crecy, Patron Saints, St. George, Society of St. George, Lady Salisbury, David King of Scots, Third King's House, Ballad Windsor, The Fair Countess, Richard of Bordeaux, Court Parties, Royal Favourites, Rehearsing for Windsor, In the Great Hall, Simon de Burley, Radcote Bridge, A Feast of Death, Geoffrey Chaucer, At Winchester Tower, St. George's Chapel, The Little Queen, At Windsor, Duchess Philippote, The Windsor Plot, Bolingbroke, Court of Chivalry, Wager of Battle, Deserted Little Queen, Captive Little Queen, A New Year's Plot, Night of the Kings, Exit Little Queen, Dona Juana, Constance of York, The Norman Tower, The Legal Heir, Prince Hal, The Devil's Tower, In Captivity Captive, Attempt at Rescue, Agincourt, Kaiser Sigismund, The Witch Queen, Sweet Kate, The Maid of Honour, Lady Jane, Henry of Windsor, Richard of York, Two Duchesses, York and Lancaster, Union of the Roses.

"'Royal Windsor' follows in the same lines as 'Her Majesty's Tower,' and aims at weaving a series of popular sketches of striking events which centre round Windsor Castle. Mr. Dixon makes everything vivid and picturesque. Those who liked 'Her Majesty's Tower' will find these volumes equally pleasant reading."—*Athenæum.*

"A truly fine and interesting book. It is a valuable contribution to English history; worthy of Mr. Dixon's fame, worthy of its grand subject."—*Morning Post.*

"Mr. Dixon has supplied us with a highly entertaining book. 'Royal Windsor' is eminently a popular work, bristling with anecdotes and amusing sketches of historical characters. It is carefully written, and is exceedingly pleasant reading. The story is brightly told; not a dull page can be found. Mr. Dixon is to be congratulated on having put so much information into so agreeable a shape."—*Examiner.*

"These volumes will quickly find favour with the widest and most inclusive circle of readers. From the first days of Norman Windsor to the Plantagenet period Mr. Dixon tells the story of this famous castle in his own picturesque, bright, and vigorous way."—*Daily Telegraph.*

"Mr. Hepworth Dixon has found a congenial subject in 'Royal Windsor.' His exploration of the Tower of London for a similar purpose, and the curious and careful researches which his study of that fatal fortress occasioned, had furnished him with an abundance and variety of materials for his present monograph on an ancient keep and palace of the English Monarchy. Under the sanction of the Queen, he has enjoyed exceptional opportunities of most searching and complete investigation of the Royal House and every other part of Windsor Castle, in and out, above ground and below ground."—*Daily News.*

"'Royal Windsor' is a worthy companion to 'Her Majesty's Tower.' It brings before the reader with no less fidelity the splendid pageants of history, and it gives an animated series of tableaux, the characters in which are so life-like that they seem again in very flesh and blood before our eyes."—*Sunday Times.*

"In 'Royal Windsor' Mr. Dixon has found a subject most rich in opportunities for the gorgeous word-painting and the dramatic power of which he has unquestionable command. The Royal dwelling in its various phases—Saxon hunting-lodge, Norman keep, and Palace-Castle, altered, enriched, and added to by king after king—supplies in vulgar phrase the peg on which to hang the storied chronicle of the kings and captives who all these years have tenanted its walls. The work is pre-eminently one for the general public."—*Graphic.*

MESSRS. HURST AND BLACKETT'S

LIST OF NEW WORKS.

ROYAL WINDSOR. By W. HEPWORTH DIXON.

SECOND EDITION. Volumes I. and II. Demy 8vo. 30s. To be completed in 2 more volumes.

CONTENTS OF VOLS. I AND II.—Castle Hill, Norman Keep, First King's House, Lion Heart, Kingless Windsor, Windsor Won, Geoffrey Plantagenet, Windsor Lost, The Fallen Deputy, The Queen Mother, Maud de Braose, The Barons' War, Second King's House, Edward of Carnarvon, Perot de Gaveston, Isabel de France, Edward of Windsor, Crecy, Patron Saints. St. George, Society of St. George, Lady Salisbury, David King of Scots, Third King's House, Ballad Windsor, The Fair Countess, Richard of Bordeaux, Court Parties, Royal Favourites, Rehearsing for Windsor, In the Great Hall, Simon de Burley, Radcote Bridge, A Feast of Death, Geoffrey Chaucer, At Winchester Tower, St. George's Chapel, The Little Queen, At Windsor, Duchess Philippote, The Windsor Plot, Bolingbroke, Court of Chivalry, Wager of Battle, Deserted Little Queen, Captive Little Queen, A New Year's Plot, Night of the Kings, Exit Little Queen, Dona Juana, Constance of York, The Norman Tower, The Legal Heir, Prince Hal, The Devil's Tower, In Captivity Captive, Attempt at Rescue, Agincourt, Kaiser Sigismund, The Witch Queen, Sweet Kate, The Maid of Honour, Lady Jane, Henry of Windsor, Richard of York, Two Duchesses, York and Lancaster, Union of the Roses.

"'Royal Windsor' follows in the same lines as 'Her Majesty's Tower,' and aims at weaving a series of popular sketches of striking events which centre round Windsor Castle. Mr. Dixon makes everything vivid and picturesque. Those who liked 'Her Majesty's Tower' will find these volumes equally pleasant reading."—*Athenæum.*

"A truly fine and interesting book. It is a valuable contribution to English history; worthy of Mr. Dixon's fame, worthy of its grand subject."—*Morning Post.*

"Mr. Dixon has supplied us with a highly entertaining book. 'Royal Windsor' is eminently a popular work, bristling with anecdotes and amusing sketches of historical characters. It is carefully written, and is exceedingly pleasant reading. The story is brightly told; not a dull page can be found. Mr. Dixon is to be congratulated on having put so much information into so agreeable a shape."—*Examiner.*

"These volumes will quickly find favour with the widest and most inclusive circle of readers. From the first days of Norman Windsor to the Plantagenet period Mr. Dixon tells the story of this famous castle in his own picturesque, bright, and vigorous way."—*Daily Telegraph.*

"Mr. Hepworth Dixon has found a congenial subject in 'Royal Windsor.' His exploration of the Tower of London for a similar purpose, and the curious and careful researches which his study of that fatal fortress occasioned, had furnished him with an abundance and variety of materials for his present monograph on an ancient keep and palace of the English Monarchy. Under the sanction of the Queen, he has enjoyed exceptional opportunities of most searching and complete investigation of the Royal House and every other part of Windsor Castle, in and out, above ground and below ground."—*Daily News.*

"'Royal Windsor' is a worthy companion to 'Her Majesty's Tower.' It brings before the reader with no less fidelity the splendid pageants of history, and it gives an animated series of tableaux, the characters in which are so life-like that they seem again to pass in very flesh and blood before our eyes."—*Sunday Times.*

"In 'Royal Windsor' Mr. Dixon has found a subject most rich in opportunities for the gorgeous word-painting and the dramatic power of which he has unquestionable command. The Royal dwelling in its various phases—Saxon hunting-lodge, Norman keep, and Palace-Castle, altered, enriched, and added to by king after king—supplies in vulgar phrase the peg on which to hang the storied chronicle of the kings and captives who all these years have tenanted its walls. The work is pre-eminently one for the general public."—*Graphic.*

MESSRS. HURST AND BLACKETT'S
NEW WORKS—*Continued.*

A LEGACY: Being the Life and Remains of John Martin, Schoolmaster and Poet. Written and Edited by the Author of "John Halifax." 2 vols. crown 8vo. With Portrait. 21s.

"This is, in many respects, a remarkable book. It records the life, work, aspirations, and death of a schoolmaster and poet, of lowly birth but high-strung and ambitious soul. His writings brim with vivid thought, keen analysis of feeling, touches of poetic sentiment, and trenchant criticism of men and books, expressed in scholarly language."—*Guardian.*

"Mrs. Craik has related a beautiful and pathetic story—a story of faith and courage and untiring energy on the part of a young and gifted man, who might under other circumstances have won a place in literature. The story is one worth reading."—*Pall Mall Gazette.*

"In these volumes a well-known novelist presents us with a history so touching, so marvellous, and so simple, as no invention could produce. Few more pathetic or more instructive volumes have fallen in our way."—*Morning Post.*

"We strongly recommend our readers to procure this charming book, not only because it is a gem of beautiful writing, showing the finished style and graceful heart of the talented authoress, but because the subject matter in itself is of absorbing interest."—*Church Review.*

A YOUNG SQUIRE OF THE SEVENTEENTH CENTURY, from the Papers of Christopher Jeaffreson, of Dullingham House, Cambridgeshire. Edited by John Cordy Jeaffreson, Author of "A Book about Doctors," &c. 2 vols. crown 8vo. 21s.

"Two volumes of very attractive matter:—letters which illustrate agriculture, commerce, war, love, and social manners, accounts of passing public events, and details which are not to be found in the Gazettes, and which come with singular freshness from private letters."—*Athenæum.*

"Two agreeable and important volumes. They deserve to be placed on library shelves with Pepys, Evelyn, and Reresby."—*Notes and Queries.*

"In the interests of history a publication such as the present is of almost incalculable value. Every historical student ought to make himself acquainted with these two very delightful volumes."—*Morning Post.*

HISTORY OF ENGLISH HUMOUR. By the Rev. A. G. L'Estrange, Author of "The Life of the Rev. W. Harness," &c. 2 vols. crown 8vo. 21s.

"This work contains a large and varied amount of information. It is impossible to give any idea of the wealth of anecdote and epigram in its pages, and for anything like a proper appreciation of its value we must refer our readers to the book itself."—*John Bull.*

"This work gives evidence of a vast deal of industry and study of the subject, and is distinguished by considerable analytical power, and contains many pleasant anecdotes."—*Morning Post.*

"A book of the highest mark and character. The literary man, the antiquarian, and the historian will combine in pronouncing it worthy of admission into every well selected library."—*Messenger.*

MY LIFE, FROM 1815 TO 1849. By Charles Loftus, formerly of the Royal Navy, late of the Coldstream Guards. Author of "My Youth by Sea and Land." 2 vols. crown 8vo. 21s.

"The praise which the *Athenæum* gave to the first portion of Major Loftus's work, may be fairly awarded to the second. These reminiscences are pleasantly told. There is a cheerfulness about them which communicates itself to the reader."—*Athenæum.*

"A thoroughly interesting and readable book, which we heartily recommend as one of the most characteristic autobiographies we ever read."—*Standard.*

MESSRS. HURST AND BLACKETT'S
PUBLICATIONS—*Continued.*

THE THEATRE FRANCAIS IN THE REIGN
OF LOUIS XV. By ALEXANDER BAILLIE COCHRANE, M.P. 1 vol. demy 8vo. 15s.

CONVERSATIONS WITH M. THIERS, M. GUIZOT,
and other Distinguished Persons, during the Second Empire. By the Late NASSAU W. SENIOR. Edited by his Daughter, M. C. M. SIMPSON. 2 vols. demy 8vo. 30s.

Among other persons whose conversations are recorded in these volumes are King Leopold; the Duc de Broglie; Lord Cowley; Counts Arrivabene, Corcelle, Daru, Flahault, Kergolay, Montalembert; Generals Lamoricière and Chrzanowski; Sir Henry Ellis; Messieurs Ampère, Beaumont, Blanchard, Bouffet, Auguste Chevalier, Victor Cousin, De Witt, Duchâtel, Ducpetiaux, Dumon, Dussard, Duvergier de Hauranne, Léon Faucher, Frère-Orban, Grimblot, Guizot, Laffitte, Labaume, Lamartine, Lanjuinais, Mallac, Manin, Mérimée, Mignet, Jules Mohl, Montanelli, Odillon-Barrot, Quételet, Rémusat, Rogier, Rivet, Rossini, Horace Say, Thiers, Trouvé-Chauvel, Villemain, Wolowski; Mesdames Circourt, Cornu, Ristori, &c.

"This new series of Mr. Senior's 'Conversations' has been for some years past known in manuscript to his more intimate friends, and it has always been felt that no former series would prove more valuable or important. Mr. Senior had a social position which gave him admission into the best literary and political circles of Paris. He was a cultivated and sensible man, who knew how to take full advantage of such an opening. And above all, he had by long practice so trained his memory as to enable it to recall all the substance, and often the words, of the long conversations which he was always holding. These conversations he wrote down with a surprising accuracy, and then handed the manuscript to his friends, that they might correct or modify his report of what they had said. This book thus contains the opinions of eminent men given in the freedom of conversation, and afterwards carefully revised. Of their value there cannot be a question. The book is one of permanent historical interest. There is scarcely a page without some memorable statement by some memorable man. Politics and society and literature —the three great interests that make up life—are all discussed in turn, and there is no discussion which is unproductive of weighty thought or striking fact."—*Athenæum.*

"The present selection of Mr. Senior's Journals, edited with remarkable skill and judgment by Mrs. Simpson, is extraordinarily full and interesting. Although the unreserved and original communications of Thiers are especially fascinating, the book would be abundantly interesting if it consisted only of the reports of conversations with Guizot, Montalembert, Cousin, Lamartine, and other persons of celebrity and eminence."—*Saturday Review.*

"These conversations extend from the year 1852 to 1860, and will be found to refer to some of the most interesting public events of our time—the Revolution of 1848, the Crimean War, the French Alliance, the attempt on the life of Louis Napoleon, the Indian Mutiny, and the Italian campaign of 1859. Besides these great public occurrences of European celebrity, we have many very curious and piquant anecdotes of a private character, and expressions of opinion on men and things by persons of eminence. All that is said in these volumes of France, England, and Russia, is as interesting now as when it was first uttered."—*Standard.*

"The two new volumes of the late Mr. Nassau Senior's most interesting conversations give us the ideas of some eminent foreign statesmen on the Eastern Question. They embrace the eventful years from 1852 to 1860, during which Mr. Senior paid prolonged visits to Paris, and conversed on the most confidential terms with some of the shrewdest men of the time. They set forth the opinions of those who had the best means of informing themselves on Russian objects and English interests. They abound, besides, in most interesting details as to the personal character of the Emperor Nicholas and his successor; as to the relations of Russia and Austria; as to the social condition and resources of the two empires; as to the considerations that govern their policy, and their respective capabilities as fighting Powers."—*Blackwood's Magazine.*

MESSRS. HURST AND BLACKETT'S
NEW WORKS—*Continued.*

HISTORY OF TWO QUEENS: CATHARINE
OF ARAGON and ANNE BOLEYN. By W. HEPWORTH DIXON.
Second Edition. Vols. 1 & 2. Demy 8vo. 30s.

"In two handsome volumes Mr. Dixon here gives us the first instalment of a
new historical work on a most attractive subject. The book is in many respects a
favourable specimen of Mr. Dixon's powers. It is the most painstaking and
elaborate that he has yet written. . . . . On the whole, we may say that the book
is one which will sustain the reputation of its author as a writer of great power
and versatility, that it gives a new aspect to many an old subject, and presents in
a very striking light some of the most recent discoveries in English history."—
Athenæum.

"In these volumes the author exhibits in a signal manner his special powers
and finest endowments. It is obvious that the historian has been at especial pains
to justify his reputation, to strengthen his hold upon the learned, and also to
extend his sway over the many who prize an attractive style and interesting narrative more highly than laborious research and philosophic insight."—*Morning Post.*

"The thanks of all students of English history are due to Mr. Hepworth Dixon
for his clever and original work, 'History of two Queens.' The book is a valuable
contribution to English history. The author has consulted a number of original
sources of information—in particular the archives at Simancas, Alcala, and Venice.
Mr. Dixon is a skilful writer. His style, singularly vivid, graphic, and dramatic—
is alive with human and artistic interest. Some of the incidental descriptions
reach a very high level of picturesque power."—*Daily News.*

VOLS. III. & IV. OF THE HISTORY OF TWO
QUEENS: CATHARINE OF ARAGON and ANNE BOLEYN.
By W. HEPWORTH DIXON. *Second Edition.* Demy 8vo. Price 30s.
Completing the Work.

"These concluding volumes of Mr. Dixon's 'History of two Queens' will be per-
used with keen interest by thousands of readers. Whilst no less valuable to the
student, they will be far more enthralling to the general reader than the earlier
half of the history. Every page of what may be termed Anne Boleyn's story affords
a happy illustration of the author's vivid and picturesque style. The work should
be found in every library."—*Post.*

"Mr. Dixon has pre-eminently the art of interesting his readers. He has produced a narrative of considerable value, conceived in a spirit of fairness, and
written with power and picturesque effect."—*Daily News.*

HISTORY OF WILLIAM PENN, Founder of
Pennsylvania. By W. HEPWORTH DIXON. A NEW LIBRARY EDITION.
1 vol. demy 8vo, with Portrait. 12s.

"Mr. Dixon's 'William Penn' is, perhaps, the best of his books. He has now revised and issued it with the addition of much fresh matter. It is now offered in a
sumptuous volume, matching with Mr. Dixon's recent books, to a new generation of
readers, who will thank Mr. Dixon for his interesting and instructive memoir of
one of the worthies of England."—*Examiner.*

FREE RUSSIA. By W. HEPWORTH DIXON. *Third*
Edition. 2 vols. 8vo, with Coloured Illustrations. 30s.

"Mr. Dixon's book will be certain not only to interest but to please its readers
and it deserves to do so. It contains a great deal that is worthy of attention, and
is likely to produce a very useful effect."—*Saturday Review.*

THE SWITZERS. By W. HEPWORTH DIXON.
Third Edition. 1 vol. demy 8vo. 15s.

"A lively, interesting, and altogether novel book on Switzerland. It is full of
valuable information on social, political, and ecclesiastical questions, and, like all
Mr. Dixon's books, is eminently readable."—*Daily News.*

4

MESSRS. HURST AND BLACKETT'S
NEW WORKS—*Continued*.

MEMOIRS OF GEORGIANA, LADY CHATTERTON; With some Passages from HER DIARY. By E. HENEAGE DERING. 1 vol. demy 8vo. 15s.

Among other persons mentioned in this work are Lords Lansdowne, Brougham, Macaulay, Lytton, Houghton; Messrs. Wilberforce, Wordsworth, Hallam, Rogers, Moore, Sydney Smith, Landor, Lockhart, Fonblanque, Warburton, Harness, Chantrey; Count Montalembert, Dr. Ullathorne, Dr. Newman, Joanna Baillie, Lady Gifford, Lady Cork, Mrs. Somerville, Mrs. Norton, &c.

"Lady Chatterton's Diary gives a sketch of society during a well known but over-interesting period. Mr. Dering may be congratulated on having furnished a graceful epilogue to the story of an interesting life."—*Athenæum.*

"In this work we have the pleasant picture of a literary artist and an amiable lady, and some interesting anecdotes which give value to the volume."—*John Bull.*

"In this agreeable volume Mr. Dering has succeeded in bringing before us in vivid colours the portrait of a very remarkable, talented, and excellent lady. Her Diary is full of charming reminiscences."—*The Tablet.*

HISTORIC CHATEAUX: BLOIS, FONTAINEBLEAU, VINCENNES. By ALEXANDER BAILLIE COCHRANE, M.P. 1 vol. 8vo. 15s.

"A very interesting volume."—*Times.*

"A lively and agreeable book, full of action and colour."—*Athenæum.*

"This book is bright, pleasant reading."—*British Quarterly Review.*

"A most valuable addition to the historical works of the time. It is full of life and colour."—*Morning Post.*

"A well executed book by a polished and vigorous writer."—*The World.*

THE SEA OF MOUNTAINS: AN ACCOUNT OF LORD DUFFERIN'S TOUR THROUGH BRITISH COLUMBIA IN 1876. By MOLYNEUX ST. JOHN. 2 vols. crown 8vo. With Portrait of Lord Dufferin. 21s.

"Mr. St. John has given us in these pages a record of all that was seen and done in a very successful visit. His book is instructive, and it should be interesting to the general reader."—*Times.*

"Mr. St. John is a shrewd and lively writer. The reader will find ample variety in his book, which is well worth perusal."—*Pall Mall Gazette.*

"These volumes are amusing, interesting, and even valuable. They give us a very clear idea of the great quarrel between British Columbia and the Dominion of Canada; and they contain a full report of Lord Dufferin's great speech at Victoria. Then there are some graphic sketches of social life and scenery, and some entertaining stories.'—*Spectator.*

A MAN OF OTHER DAYS: Recollections of the MARQUIS DE BEAUREGARD. Edited, from the French, by CHARLOTTE M. YONGE, Author of "The Heir of Redclyffe," &c. 2 vols. 21s.

"The 'man of former times' whose biography is now introduced to our notice, will be remembered by all who have read the correspondence of Count Joseph de Maistre. A Savoyard by birth, M. Costa de Beauregard lived long enough to see the last years of the Monarchy, the Revolution, and the early promise of General Bonaparte. The opening chapters of the work introduce us to Paris society at the time when it was perhaps the most brilliant; and it is amusing to accompany our hero to Mme. Geoffrin's salon, where Marmontel, Rochefoucauld, Greuze, Diderot, Cochin, and many others, discourse literature, art, and philosophy. Sent off to Paris for the purpose of finishing his education by mixing with all the choice spirits of the day, young Costa writes home brilliant descriptions of the sights he has seen and the company to which he has been introduced. The variety of scenes described in these pleasant memoirs, the historical personages crowded on the canvas, and the account of the noble struggle of Savoy against the French Republic, give to the whole work a dramatic interest which derives additional charm from the character of the Marquis himself—a character in which high principle, genuine wit, and patriotism are happily blended together."—*Saturday Review.*

MESSRS. HURST AND BLACKETT'S
NEW WORKS—*Continued.*

VOLS. I. & II. OF HER MAJESTY'S TOWER.
By W. HEPWORTH DIXON. DEDICATED BY EXPRESS PERMISSION TO THE QUEEN. *Sixth Edition.* 8vo. 30s.

FROM THE TIMES:—"All the civilized world—English, Continental, and American—takes an interest in the Tower of London. The Tower is the stage upon which has been enacted some of the grandest dramas and saddest tragedies in our national annals. If, in imagination, we take our stand on those time-worn walls, and let century after century flit past us, we shall see in due succession the majority of the most famous men and lovely women of England in the olden time. We shall see them jesting, jousting, love-making, plotting, and then anon, perhaps, commending their souls to God in the presence of a hideous masked figure, bearing an axe in his hands. It is such pictures as these that Mr. Dixon, with considerable skill as an historical limner, has set before us in these volumes. Mr. Dixon dashes off the scenes of Tower history with great spirit. His descriptions are given with such terseness and vigour that we should spoil them by any attempt at condensation. In conclusion, we may congratulate the author on this work. Both volumes are decidedly attractive, and throw much light on our national history."

VOLS. III. & IV. OF HER MAJESTY'S TOWER.
By W. HEPWORTH DIXON. DEDICATED BY EXPRESS PERMISSION TO THE QUEEN. Completing the Work. *Third Edition.* Demy 8vo. 30s.

"These volumes are two galleries of richly painted portraits of the noblest men and most brilliant women, besides others, commemorated by English history. The grand old Royal Keep, palace and prison by turns, is revivified in these volumes, which close the narrative, extending from the era of Sir John Eliot, who saw Raleigh die in Palace Yard, to that of Thistlewood, the last prisoner immured in the Tower. Few works are given to us, in these days, so abundant in originality and research as Mr. Dixon's."—*Standard.*

RECOLLECTIONS OF COLONEL DE GONNE-
VILLE. Edited from the French by CHARLOTTE M. YONGE, Author of the "Heir of Redclyffe," &c. 2 vols. crown 8vo. 21s.

"This very interesting memoir brings us within the presence of Napoleon I., and some of the chiefs who upheld the fortunes of the First Empire, and its anecdotes about that extraordinary man are evidently genuine and very characteristic. It introduces us to the inner life and real state of the Grand Army, and lays bare the causes of its strength and weakness. The work discloses a variety of details of interest connected with Napoleon's escape from Elba, the Hundred Days, the Bourbon Restoration, and the Revolution of July, 1830. We have dwelt at length on this instructive record of the experiences of a memorable age, and can commend it cordially to our readers."—*The Times.*

MY YOUTH, BY SEA AND LAND, FROM 1809 TO
1816. By CHARLES LOFTUS, formerly of the Royal Navy, late of the Coldstream Guards. 2 vols. crown 8vo. 21s.

"It was a happy thought that impelled Major Loftus to give us these reminiscences of 'the old war,' which still retains so strong a hold on our sympathies. Every word from an intelligent actor in these stirring scenes is now valuable. Major Loftus played the part allotted to him with honour and ability, and he relates the story of his sea life with spirit and vigour. Some of his sea stories are as laughable as anything in 'Peter Simple,' while many of his adventures on shore remind us of Charles Lever in his freshest days. During his sea life Major Loftus became acquainted with many distinguished persons. Besides the Duke of Wellington, the Prince Regent, and William IV., he was brought into personal relation with the allied Sovereigns, the Duc D'Angoulême, Lord William Bentinck, and Sir Hudson Lowe. A more genial, pleasant, wholesome book we have not often read."—*Standard.*

MESSRS. HURST AND BLACKETT'S
NEW WORKS—*Continued.*

CELEBRITIES I HAVE KNOWN. By Lord
William Pitt Lennox. Second Series. 2 volumes demy 8vo. 30s.

Among other persons mentioned in the Second Series of this work are—The Princess Charlotte and Prince Leopold; the Dukes of Wellington and Beaufort; the Earls of **Durham** and Carlisle; Lords Byron, Clyde, Adolphus Fitzclarence, and Cockburn; Sirs Walter Scott, G. Wombwell, A. Barnard, John Elley, Sidney, Harry, and C. F. Smith; Count D'Orsay; Dr. Dodd; Messrs. Thomas Moore, Theodore Hook, Leigh Hunt, Jerdan, James, Horace, and Albert Smith, Beazley, Tattersall, Hudson, Ude, George Colman, The Kembles, G. F. Cooke, Charles Young, Edmund and Charles Kean, Yates, Harley; Miss Foote; Mrs. Nisbet; Mesdames Catalani, Grassini, Rachel, &c.

"This new series of Lord William Lennox's reminiscences is fully as entertaining as the preceding one. Lord William makes good use of an excellent memory, and he writes easily and pleasantly."—*Pall Mall Gazette.*

"One of the best books of the season. Pleasant anecdotes, exciting episodes, smart sayings, witticisms, and repartees are to be found on every page."—*Court Journal.*

COACHING; With Anecdotes of the Road. By
Lord William Pitt Lennox, Author of "Celebrities I have Known," &c. Dedicated to His Grace the Duke of Beaufort, K.G., President, and the Members of the Coaching Club. 1 vol. demy 8vo. 15s.

"Lord William's book is genial, discursive, and gossipy. We are indebted to the author's personal recollections for some lively stories, and pleasant sketches of some of the more famous dragsmen. Nor does Lord William by any means limit himself to the English roads, and English coaches. Bianconi's Irish cars, the continental diligences, with anecdotes of His Grace of Wellington, when Lord William was acting as his aide-de-camp during the occupation of Paris, with many other matters more or less germane to his subject, are all brought in more or less naturally. Altogether his volume, with the variety of its contents, will be found pleasant reading."—*Pall Mall Gazette.*

LIFE OF MOSCHELES; with Selections from
HIS DIARIES AND CORRESPONDENCE. By His Wife. 2 vols. large post 8vo, with Portrait. 24s.

"This life of Moscheles will be a valuable book of reference for the musical historian, for the contents extend over a period of threescore years, commencing with 1794, and ending at 1870. We need scarcely state that all the portions of Moscheles' diary which refer to his intercourse with Beethoven, Hummel, Weber, Czerny, Spontini, Rossini, Auber, Halévy, Schumann, Cherubini, Spohr, Mendelssohn, F David, Chopin, J B. Cramer, Clementi, John Field, Habeneck, Hauptmann, Kalkbrenner, Kiesewetter, C. Klingemann, Lablache, Dragonetti, Sontag, Persiani, Malibran, Paganini, Rachel, Ronzi de Begnis, De Beriot, Ernst, Donzelli, Cinti-Damoreau, Chelard, Bochsa, Laporte, Charles Kemble, Paton (Mrs. Wood), Schröder-Devrient, Mrs. Siddons, Sir H. Bishop, Sir G. Smart, Staudigl, Thalberg, Berlioz, Velluti, C. Young, Balfe, Braham, and many other artists of note in their time, will recall a flood of recollections. It was a delicate task for Madame Moscheles to select from the diaries in reference to living persons, but her extracts have been judiciously made. Moscheles writes fairly of what is called the 'Music of the Future' and its disciples, and his judgments on Herr Wagner, Dr. Liszt, Rubenstein, Dr. von Bülow, Litolff, &c., whether as composers or executants, are in a liberal spirit. He recognizes cheerfully the talents of our native artists, Sir Sterndale Bennett, Mr. Macfarren, Madame Arabella Goddard, Mr. John Barnett, Mr. Hullah, Mrs. Shaw, Mr. A. Sullivan, &c. The celebrities with whom Moscheles came in contact, include Sir Walter Scott, Sir Robert Peel, the late Duke of Cambridge, the Bunsens, Louis Philippe, Napoleon the Third, Humboldt, Henry Heine, Thomas More, Count Nesselrode, the Duchess of Orleans, Prof. Wolf, &c. Indeed, the two volumes are full of amusing anecdotes."—*Athenæum.*

7

MESSRS. HURST AND BLACKETT'S
NEW WORKS—*Continued.*

WORDS OF HOPE AND COMFORT TO
THOSE IN SORROW. Dedicated by Permission to THE QUEEN. *Fourth Edition.* 1 vol. small 4to, 5s. bound.

"These letters, the work of a pure and devout spirit, deserve to find many readers. They are greatly superior to the average of what is called religious literature."—*Athenæum.*

"The writer of the tenderly-conceived letters in this volume was Mrs. Julius Hare, a sister of Mr. Maurice. They are instinct with the devout submissiveness and fine sympathy which we associate with the name of Maurice; but in her there is added a winningness of tact, and sometimes, too, a directness of language, which we hardly find even in the brother. The letters were privately printed and circulated, and were found to be the source of much comfort, which they cannot fail to afford now to a wide circle. A sweetly-conceived memorial poem, bearing the well-known initials, 'E. H. P.', gives a very faithful outline of the life."—*British Quarterly Review.*

"This touching and most comforting work is dedicated to THE QUEEN, who took a gracious interest in its first appearance, when printed for private circulation, and found comfort in its pages, and has now commanded its publication, that the world in general may profit by it. A more practical and heart-stirring appeal to the afflicted we have never examined."—*Standard.*

"These letters are exceptionally graceful and touching, and may be read with profit."—*Graphic.*

OUR BISHOPS AND DEANS. By the Rev. F.
ARNOLD, B.A., late of Christ Church, Oxford. 2 vols. 8vo. 30s.

"This work is good in conception and cleverly executed, and as thoroughly honest and earnest as it is interesting and able. The style is original, the thought vigorous, the information wide, and the portrait-painting artistic."—*John Bull.*

LIFE OF THE RT. HON. SPENCER PERCEVAL;
Including His Correspondence. By His Grandson, SPENCER WALPOLE. 2 vols. 8vo, with Portrait. 30s.

"Mr. Walpole's work reflects credit not only on his industry in compiling an important biography from authentic material, but also on his eloquence, power of interpreting political change, and general literary address. The biography will take rank in our literature, both as a faithful reflection of the statesman and his period, as also for its philosophic, logical, and dramatic completeness."—*Morning Post.*

MY YEAR IN AN INDIAN FORT. By Mrs.
GUTHRIE. 2 vols. crown 8vo. With Illustrations. 21s.

"Written with intelligence and ability."—*Pall Mall Gazette.*

"A pleasantly written book. Mrs. Guthrie appears to have enjoyed her visit to the Fort of Belgaum, in the Deccan, immensely. Those who know India, and those who do not, may read her work with pleasure and profit."—*Standard.*

"Mrs. Guthrie's charming book affords a truthful and agreeable picture of an English lady's life in India."—*Globe.*

ACROSS CENTRAL AMERICA. By J. W. BOD-
DAM-WHETHAM, Author of "Pearls of the Pacific," &c. 8vo, with Illustrations. 15s.

"Mr. Boddam-Whetham writes easily and agreeably."—*Pall Mall Gazette.*

"Mr. Whetham's new volume contains the story of his journey by land and river from San José de Guatemala to Carmen on the Mexican Gulf. This journey is so interesting in many ways, that Mr. Whetham's sprightly work may fairly rank as one of those rarer books of travel which tell us something that is really new and quite worth telling. It has enabled him to present us with some charming pictures of a curious country."—*Graphic.*

"A bright and lively account of interesting travel. We have not met anywhere a truer picture of Central American scenery and surroundings."—*Globe.*

MESSRS. HURST AND BLACKETT'S
PUBLICATIONS—*Continued.*

THROUGH FRANCE AND BELGIUM, BY
RIVER AND CANAL, IN THE STEAM YACHT "YTENE."
By W. J. C. MOENS, R.V.Y.C. 1 vol. 8vo. With Illustrations. 15s.
"This book is pleasantly written, the descriptions of the scenery and objects of
interest are fresh and lively, and are interspersed with entertaining anecdote. Mr.
Moens gives very valuable information to his yachting readers."—*Sporting Gazette.*

A BOOK ABOUT THE TABLE. By J. C.
JEAFFRESON. 2 vols. 8vo. 30s.
"This book is readable and amusing from first to last. No one ought to be
without it. Racy anecdotes coruscate on every page."—*Morning Post.*

COSITAS ESPANOLAS; OR, EVERY-DAY LIFE IN
SPAIN. By Mrs. HARVEY, of Ickwell-Bury, Author of "Turkish
Harems and Circassian Homes." *Second Edition.* 1 vol. 8vo. 15s.

RAMBLES IN ISTRIA, DALMATIA, AND MON-
TENEGRO. By R. H. R. 1 vol. 8vo. 14s.

PEARLS OF THE PACIFIC. By J. W. BODDAM-
WHETHAM 1 vol. Demy 8vo, with 8 Illustrations. 15s.
"The literary merits of Mr. Whetham's work are of a very high order. His
descriptions are vivid, the comments upon what he saw judicious, and there is an
occasional dash of humour and of pathos which stirs our sympathies."—*Athenæum.*

NOTES OF TRAVEL IN SOUTH AFRICA.
By C. J. ANDERSSON, Author of "Lake Ngami," &c. Edited by
L. LLOYD, Author of "Field Sports of the North." 1 volume
demy 8vo. With Portrait of the Author. 15s. bound.

WILD LIFE IN FLORIDA ; With a Visit to Cuba.
By Captain F. T. TOWNSHEND, F.R.G.S., 2nd Life Guards. 1 vol.
8vo, with Map and Illustrations. 15s.

SPAIN AND THE SPANIARDS. By AZAMAT
BATUK. 2 vols. crown 8vo. 21s.

TURKISH HAREMS & CIRCASSIAN HOMES.
By MRS. HARVEY, of Ickwell-Bury. 8vo. *Second Edition.* 15s.

MEMOIRS OF QUEEN HORTENSE, MOTHER
OF NAPOLEON III. Cheaper Edition, in 1 vol. 6s.
"A biography of the beautiful and unhappy Queen, more satisfactory than any we
have yet met with."—*Daily News.*

RECOLLECTIONS OF SOCIETY IN FRANCE
AND ENGLAND. By LADY CLEMENTINA DAVIES. 2nd Edition. 2 v.
"Two charming volumes, full of the most interesting matter."—*Post.*

ON THE WING ; A SOUTHERN FLIGHT. By the
Hon. Mrs. ALFRED MONTGOMERY. 1 vol. 8vo. 14s.

THE EXILES AT ST. GERMAINS. By the
Author of "The Ladye Shakerley." 1 vol. 7s. 6d. bound.

THE NEW AND POPULAR NOVELS.

PUBLISHED BY HURST & BLACKETT.

THE LAST OF HER LINE. By the Author of "St. Olave's," &c. 3 vols.

THE GRAHAMS OF INVERMOY. By M. C. STIRLING, Author of "A True Man," &c. 3 vols.

PAUL FABER, SURGEON. By GEORGE MAC DONALD, LL.D., Author of "David Elginbrod," "Robert Falconer," "Alec Forbes," &c. 3 vols.

"A powerful story, It is impossible to do justice to its lofty purpose and its rare merits in the limits of a review."—*John Bull.*

"In 'Paul Faber' Dr. Mac Donald adds to his high reputation. The plot is deeply interesting, the characters are life-like, and the incidents remarkably striking."—*Court Journal.*

KELVERDALE. By the EARL OF DESART. 3 vols.

"Lord Desart's book is agreeable and amusing. It is a spirited novel, pleasantly written, and full of clever pictures of the society of to-day, evidently sketched from life."—*Morning Post.*

"Lord Desart lays bare the impostures of the various classes of society with unsparing directness and with a good deal of humour."—*Athenæum.*

A YOUNG MAN'S FANCY. By Mrs. FORRESTER, Author of "Viva," "Mignon," &c. *Second Edition.* 3 vols.

"We hail with pleasure another novel from the pen of Mrs. Forrester. Her book has all the natural interest and tact which distinguish a work of a clever woman."—*Court Journal.*

"These volumes are brightly written, and are of varied interest."—*John Bull.*

LOVE LOYAL. By MARY C. ROWSELL. 3 vols.

A BROKEN FAITH. By IZA DUFFUS-HARDY, Author of "Only a Love-Story," "Glencairn," &c. 3 vols.

"An exceedingly interesting story, of considerable power. Miss Hardy is to be congratulated on having added to her reputation by this fascinating and clever novel."—*Morning Post.*

"A well-written story, with occasional touches of effective humour. The plot is well imagined and well worked out."—*Academy.*

MICHELLE AND LITTLE JACK. By FRANCES MARTIN, Author of "The Life of Angélique Arnauld." 1 vol. 10s. 6d.

"These stories are masterpieces. The stamp of genius is apparent in every page."—*Examiner.*

"Far above the average of novels in literary merit, greatly above in moral tone and purpose, and equal in interest to any novel of the season, is the volume which contains the tales of Michelle and Little Jack."—*John Bull.*

A TRUE MARRIAGE. By EMILY SPENDER, Author of "Restored," "Son and Heir," &c. 3 vols.

"A thoroughly pleasant and satisfactory book. It is a genuine story of human concerns and interests such as are met with in the world of every-day experience, rather than in the world of fancy or of fiction."—*Athenæum.*

"A very pleasant and clever novel."—*Post.*

UNDER TEMPTATION. By the Author of "Ursula's Love Story," "Beautiful Edith," &c. 3 vols.

"An extremely clever story, remarkably well told."—*Morning Post.*

MRS. GREY'S REMINISCENCES. By LADY BLAKE, Author of "Claude," "Ruth Maxwell," &c. 3 vols.

"A satisfactory, amusing, and attractive book."—*Examiner.*

THE NEW AND POPULAR NOVELS.
PUBLISHED BY HURST & BLACKETT.

THE PRIMROSE PATH. By Mrs. OLIPHANT, Author of "Chronicles of Carlingford," &c. 3 vols.

"Mrs. Oliphant's last novel has merits which will recommend it to the general public, and it should be hailed with something like enthusiasm by all who happen to have, like Sir Ludovic Leslie, 'a warm heart for Fife.' A prettier Scotch story it would be hard to find, and the refinement of its humour and picturesqueness of its descriptive setting cannot fail to be appreciated. There is not a character without individuality from one end of the book to the other."—*Athenæum.*

A CHEQUERED LIFE. By Mrs. DAY, Author of "From Birth to Bridal," &c. 3 vols.

"A genuine story, of well sustained interest."—*Spectator.*
"We have seldom seen a more taking novel, or one that better commands the attention and interest of its reader."—*Post.*

WOOD ANEMONE. By Mrs. RANDOLPH, Author of "Gentianella," "Wild Hyacinth," &c. 3 vols.

"A charming novel. The characters are natural and life-like. It is written in Mrs. Randolph's very best manner."—*John Bull.*

MARGERY TRAVERS. By Miss BEWICKE, Author of "Onwards, but Whither?" &c. 3 vols.

"An excellent novel: fresh, interesting, and entertaining."—*Sunday Times.*

THE BUBBLE REPUTATION. By KATHARINE KING, Author of "The Queen of the Regiment," &c. 3 vols.

"Miss King is favourably known as the author of several novels of a more or less military character. 'The Bubble Reputation' is quite equal to its predecessors. The plot is ingenious, and the interest sustained to the last."—*Athenæum.*

HATHERCOURT RECTORY. By Mrs. MOLESWORTH (ENNIS GRAHAM), Author of "The Cuckoo Clock," &c. *Second Edition.* 3 vols.

"We have read 'Hathercourt Rectory' with not a little pleasure. The tone of the book is healthy throughout."—*Saturday Review.*

RUBY GREY. By W. HEPWORTH DIXON. *Third Edition.* 3 vols.

"This novel is one which everyone fond of an exciting story, with a good deal of human interest in it, should read, and upon which it is pleasant to congratulate the author."—*Morning Post.*

HIS LAST STAKE. By SHIRLEY SMITH, Author of "All for Herself," &c. 3 vols.

"An extremely interesting story, written in a style much above the average of contemporary works of fiction. An excellent novel, abounding throughout with striking episodes. It is well worth reading."—*Morning Post.*

BROTHER GABRIEL. By M. BETHAM-EDWARDS, Author of "Kitty," "Bridget," &c. 3 vols.

"This book may be read with pleasure. It is carefully written, and contains very pleasant sketches of character."—*Academy.*

CALEB BOOTH'S CLERK. By Mrs. G. LINNÆUS BANKS, Author of "The Manchester Man," &c. 3 vols.

"This book is written with power and is a capital story, which we found it difficult to lay down."—*Spectator.*

11

Under the Especial Patronage of Her Majesty.

*Published annually, in One Vol., royal 8vo, **with the Arms beautifully
engraved**, handsomely bound, with gilt edges, price 31s. 6d.*

LODGE'S PEERAGE
AND BARONETAGE,
CORRECTED BY THE NOBILITY.

THE FORTY-EIGHTH EDITION FOR 1879 IS NOW READY.

LODGE'S PEERAGE AND BARONETAGE is acknowledged to be the most
complete, as well as the most elegant, work of the kind. As an established and authentic authority on all questions respecting the family
histories, honours, and connections of the titled aristocracy, no work has
ever stood so high. It is published under the especial patronage of Her
Majesty, and is annually corrected throughout, from the personal communications of the Nobility. It is the only work of its class in which, *the
type being kept constantly standing*, every correction is made in its proper
place to the date of publication, an advantage which gives it supremacy
over all its competitors. Independently of its full and authentic information respecting the existing Peers and Baronets of the realm, the most
sedulous attention is given in its pages to the collateral branches of the
various noble families, and the names of many thousand individuals are
introduced, which do not appear in other records of the titled classes. For
its authority, correctness, and facility of arrangement, and the beauty of
its typography and binding, the work is justly entitled to the place it
occupies on the tables of Her Majesty and the Nobility.

LIST OF THE PRINCIPAL CONTENTS.

Historical View of the Peerage.
Parliamentary Roll of the House of Lords.
English, Scotch, and Irish Peers, in their
orders of Precedence.
Alphabetical List of Peers of Great Britain
and the United Kingdom, holding supe-
rior rank in the Scotch or Irish Peerage.
Alphabetical list of Scotch and Irish Peers,
holding superior titles in the Peerage of
Great Britain and the United Kingdom.
A Collective list of Peers, in their order of
Precedence.
Table of Precedency among Men.
Table of Precedency among Women.
The Queen and the Royal Family.
Peers of the Blood Royal.
The Peerage, alphabetically arranged.
Families of such Extinct Peers as have left
Widows or Issue.
Alphabetical List of the Surnames of all the
Peers.

The Archbishops and Bishops of England,
Ireland, and the Colonies.
The Baronetage alphabetically arranged.
Alphabetical List of Surnames assumed by
members of Noble Families.
Alphabetical List of the Second Titles of
Peers, usually borne by their Eldest
Sons.
Alphabetical Index to the Daughters of
Dukes, Marquises, and Earls, who, hav-
ing married Commoners, retain the title
of Lady before their own Christian and
their Husband's Surnames.
Alphabetical Index to the Daughters of
Viscounts and Barons, who, having
married Commoners, are styled Honour-
able Mrs.; and, in case of the husband
being a Baronet or Knight, Honourable
Lady.
Mottoes alphabetically arranged and trans-
lated.

"This work is the most perfect and elaborate record of the living and recently deceased members of the Peerage of the Three Kingdoms as it stands at this day. It is
a most useful publication. We are happy to bear testimony to the fact that scrupulous
accuracy is a distinguishing feature of this book."—*Times.*

"Lodge's Peerage must supersede all other works of the kind, for two reasons: first, it
is on a better plan; and secondly, it is better executed. We can safely pronounce it to be
the readiest, the most useful, and exactest of modern works on the subject."—*Spectator.*

"A work of great value. It is the most faithful record we possess of the aristocracy of the day."—*Post.*

"The best existing, and, we believe, the best possible Peerage. It is the standard
authority on the subject."—*Standard.*

HURST & BLACKETT'S STANDARD LIBRARY

OF CHEAP EDITIONS OF

POPULAR MODERN WORKS,

ILLUSTRATED BY SIR J. GILBERT, MILLAIS, HUNT, LEECH, FOSTER, POYNTER, TENNIEL, SANDYS, HUGHES, SAMBOURNE, &c.

Each in a Single Volume, elegantly printed, bound, and illustrated, price 5s.

1. SAM SLICK'S NATURE AND HUMAN NATURE.

"The first volume of Messrs. Hurst and Blackett's Standard Library of Cheap Editions forms a very good beginning to what will doubtless be a very successful undertaking. 'Nature and Human Nature' is one of the best of Sam Slick's witty and humorous productions, and is well entitled to the large circulation which it cannot fail to obtain in its present convenient and cheap shape. The volume combines with the great recommendations of a clear, bold type, and good paper, the lesser but attractive merits of being well illustrated and elegantly bound."—*Post*.

2. JOHN HALIFAX, GENTLEMAN.

"This is a very good and a very interesting work. It is designed to trace the career from boyhood to age of a perfect man—a Christian gentleman; and it abounds in incident both well and highly wrought. Throughout it is conceived in a high spirit, and written with great ability. This cheap and handsome new edition is worthy to pass freely from hand to hand as a gift book in many households."—*Examiner*.

3. THE CRESCENT AND THE CROSS.

BY ELIOT WARBURTON.

"Independent of its value as an original narrative, and its useful and interesting information, this work is remarkable for the colouring power and play of fancy with which its descriptions are enlivened. Among its greatest and most lasting charms is its reverent and serious spirit."—*Quarterly Review*.

4. NATHALIE. By JULIA KAVANAGH.

"'Nathalie' is Miss Kavanagh's best imaginative effort. Its manner is gracious and attractive. Its matter is good. A sentiment, a tenderness, are commanded by her which are as individual as they are elegant."—*Athenæum*.

5. A WOMAN'S THOUGHTS ABOUT WOMEN.

BY THE AUTHOR OF "JOHN HALIFAX, GENTLEMAN."

"A book of sound counsel. It is one of the most sensible works of its kind, well-written, true-hearted, and altogether practical. Whoever wishes to give advice to a young lady may thank the author for means of doing so."—*Examiner*.

6. ADAM GRAEME. By MRS. OLIPHANT.

"A story awakening genuine emotions of interest and delight by its admirable pictures of Scottish life and scenery. The author sets before us the essential attributes of Christian virtue, with a delicacy, power, and truth which can hardly be surpassed."—*Post*.

7. SAM SLICK'S WISE SAWS AND MODERN INSTANCES.

"The reputation of this book will stand as long as that of Scott's or Bulwer's Novels. Its remarkable originality and happy descriptions of American life still continue the subject of universal admiration."—*Messenger*.

8. CARDINAL WISEMAN'S RECOLLECTIONS OF THE LAST FOUR POPES.

"A picturesque book on Rome and its ecclesiastical sovereigns, by an eloquent Roman Catholic. Cardinal Wiseman has treated a special subject with so much geniality, that his recollections will excite no ill-feeling in those who are most conscientiously opposed to every idea of human infallibility represented in Papal domination."—*Athenæum*.

9. A LIFE FOR A LIFE.

BY THE AUTHOR OF "JOHN HALIFAX, GENTLEMAN."

"In 'A Life for a Life' the author is fortunate in a good subject, and has produced a work of strong effect."—*Athenæum*.

HURST & BLACKETT'S STANDARD LIBRARY

10. THE OLD COURT SUBURB. By LEIGH HUNT.

"A delightful book, that will be welcome to all readers, and most welcome to those who have a love for the best kinds of reading."—*Examiner.*

11. MARGARET AND HER BRIDESMAIDS.

"We recommend all who are in search of a fascinating novel to read this work for themselves. They will find it well worth their while. There are a freshness and originality about it quite charming."—*Athenæum.*

12. THE OLD JUDGE. By SAM SLICK.

"The publications included in this Library have all been of good quality; many give information while they entertain, and of that class the book before us is a specimen. The manner in which the Cheap Editions forming the series is produced, deserves especial mention. The paper and print are unexceptionable; there is a steel engraving in each volume, and the outsides of them will satisfy the purchaser who likes to see books in handsome uniform."—*Examiner.*

13. DARIEN. By ELIOT WARBURTON.

"This last production of the author of 'The Crescent and the Cross' has the same elements of a very wide popularity. It will please its thousands."—*Globe.*

14. FAMILY ROMANCE.
BY SIR BERNARD BURKE, ULSTER KING OF ARMS.
"It were impossible to praise too highly this most interesting book."—*Standard.*

15. THE LAIRD OF NORLAW. By MRS. OLIPHANT.
"The 'Laird of Norlaw' fully sustains the author's high reputation."—*Sunday Times.*

16. THE ENGLISHWOMAN IN ITALY.
"Mrs. Gretton's book is interesting, and full of opportune instruction."—*Times.*

17. NOTHING NEW.
BY THE AUTHOR OF "JOHN HALIFAX, GENTLEMAN."
"'Nothing New' displays all those superior merits which have made 'John Halifax' one of the most popular works of the day."—*Post.*

18. FREER'S LIFE OF JEANNE D'ALBRET.
"Nothing can be more interesting than Miss Freer's story of the life of Jeanne D'Albret, and the narrative is as trustworthy as it is attractive."—*Post.*

19. THE VALLEY OF A HUNDRED FIRES.
BY THE AUTHOR OF "MARGARET AND HER BRIDESMAIDS."
"If asked to classify this work, we should give it a place between 'John Halifax' and The Caxtons.'"—*Standard.*

20. THE ROMANCE OF THE FORUM.
BY PETER BURKE, SERGEANT AT LAW.
"A work of singular interest, which can never fail to charm."—*Illustrated News.*

21. ADELE. By JULIA KAVANAGH.
"'Adele' is the best work we have read by Miss Kavanagh; it is a charming story full of delicate character-painting."—*Athenæum.*

22. STUDIES FROM LIFE.
BY THE AUTHOR OF "JOHN HALIFAX, GENTLEMAN."
"These 'Studies from Life' are remarkable for graphic power and observation. The book will not diminish the reputation of the accomplished author."—*Saturday Review.*

23. GRANDMOTHER'S MONEY.
"We commend 'Grandmother's Money' to readers in search of a good novel. The characters are true to human nature, and the story is interesting."—*Athenæum.*

HURST & BLACKETT'S STANDARD LIBRARY

24. A BOOK ABOUT DOCTORS.
BY J. C. JEAFFRESON.
"A delightful book."—*Athenæum*. "A book to be read and re-read; fit for the study as well as the drawing-room table and the circulating library."—*Lancet*.

25. NO CHURCH.
"We advise all who have the opportunity to read this book."—*Athenæum*.

26. MISTRESS AND MAID.
BY THE AUTHOR OF "JOHN HALIFAX, GENTLEMAN."
"A good wholesome book, gracefully written, and as pleasant to read as it is instructive."—*Athenæum*. "A charming tale charmingly told."—*Standard*.

27. LOST AND SAVED. By HON. MRS. NORTON.
"'Lost and Saved' will be read with eager interest. It is a vigorous novel."—*Times*. "A novel of rare excellence. It is Mrs. Norton's best prose work."—*Examiner*.

28. LES MISERABLES. By VICTOR HUGO.
AUTHORISED COPYRIGHT ENGLISH TRANSLATION.
"The merits of 'Les Miserables' do not merely consist in the conception of it as a whole; it abounds with details of unequalled beauty. M.Victor Hugo has stamped upon every page the hall-mark of genius."—*Quarterly Review*.

29. BARBARA'S HISTORY. By AMELIA B. EDWARDS.
"It is not often that we light upon a novel of so much merit and interest as 'Barbara's History.' It is a work conspicuous for taste and literary culture. It is a very graceful and charming book, with a well-managed story, clearly-cut characters, and sentiments expressed with an exquisite elocution. It is a book which the world will like."—*Times*.

30. LIFE OF THE REV. EDWARD IRVING.
BY MRS. OLIPHANT.
"A good book on a most interesting theme."—*Times*.
"A truly interesting and most affecting memoir. Irving's Life ought to have a niche in every gallery of religious biography. There are few lives that will be fuller of instruction, interest, and consolation."—*Saturday Review*.

31. ST. OLAVE'S.
"This charming novel is the work of one who possesses a great talent for writing, as well as experience and knowledge of the world."—*Athenæum*.

32. SAM SLICK'S AMERICAN HUMOUR.
"Dip where you will into this lottery of fun, you are sure to draw out a prize."—*Post*.

33. CHRISTIAN'S MISTAKE.
BY THE AUTHOR OF "JOHN HALIFAX, GENTLEMAN."
"A more charming story has rarely been written. Even if tried by the standard of the Archbishop of York, we should expect that even he would pronounce 'Christian's Mistake' a novel without a fault."—*Times*.

34. ALEC FORBES OF HOWGLEN.
BY GEORGE MAC DONALD, LL.D.
"No account of this story would give any idea of the profound interest that pervades the work from the first page to the last."—*Athenæum*.

35. AGNES. By MRS. OLIPHANT.
"'Agnes' is a novel superior to any of Mrs. Oliphant's former works."—*Athenæum*. "A story whose pathetic beauty will appeal irresistibly to all readers."—*Post*.

36. A NOBLE LIFE.
BY THE AUTHOR OF "JOHN HALIFAX, GENTLEMAN."
"This is one of those pleasant tales in which the author of 'John Halifax' speaks out of a generous heart the purest truths of life."—*Examiner*.

HURST & BLACKETT'S STANDARD LIBRARY

37. NEW AMERICA. By HEPWORTH DIXON.

"A very interesting book. Mr. Dixon has written thoughtfully and well."—*Times.*
"We recommend every one who feels any interest in human nature to read Mr. Dixon's very interesting book."—*Saturday Review.*

38. ROBERT FALCONER.
BY GEORGE MAC DONALD, LL.D.

"'Robert Falconer' is a work brimful of life and humour and of the deepest human interest. It is a book to be returned to again and again for the deep and searching knowledge it evinces of human thoughts and feelings."—*Athenæum.*

39. THE WOMAN'S KINGDOM.
BY THE AUTHOR OF "JOHN HALIFAX, GENTLEMAN."

"'The Woman's Kingdom' sustains the author's reputation as a writer of the purest and noblest kind of domestic stories.—*Athenæum.*

40. ANNALS OF AN EVENTFUL LIFE.
BY GEORGE WEBBE DASENT, D.C.L.

"A racy, well-written, and original novel. The interest never flags. The whole work sparkles with wit and humour."—*Quarterly Review.*

41. DAVID ELGINBROD. By GEORGE MAC DONALD.

"The work of a man of genius. It will attract the highest class of readers."—*Times.*

42. A BRAVE LADY.
BY THE AUTHOR OF "JOHN HALIFAX, GENTLEMAN."

"A very good novel; a thoughtful, well-written book, showing a tender sympathy with human nature, and permeated by a pure and noble spirit."—*Examiner.*

43. HANNAH.
BY THE AUTHOR OF "JOHN HALIFAX, GENTLEMAN."

"A very pleasant, healthy story, well and artistically told. The book is sure of a wide circle of readers. The character of Hannah is one of rare beauty."—*Standard.*

44. SAM SLICK'S AMERICANS AT HOME.

"This is one of the most amusing books that we ever read."—*Standard.*

45. THE UNKIND WORD.
BY THE AUTHOR OF "JOHN HALIFAX, GENTLEMAN."

"The author of 'John Halifax' has written many fascinating stories, but we can call to mind nothing from her pen that has a more enduring charm than the graceful sketches in this work."—*United Service Magazine.*

46. A ROSE IN JUNE. By MRS. OLIPHANT.

"'A Rose in June' is as pretty as its title. The story is one of the best and most touching which we owe to the industry and talent of Mrs. Oliphant, and may hold its own with even 'The Chronicles of Carlingford.'"—*Times.*

47. MY LITTLE LADY. By E. F. POYNTER.

"There is a great deal of fascination about this book. The author writes in a clear, unaffected style; she has a decided gift for depicting character, while the descriptions of scenery convey a distinct pictorial impression to the reader."—*Times.*

48. PHŒBE, JUNIOR. By MRS. OLIPHANT.

"This novel shows great knowledge of human nature. The interest goes on growing to the end. Phœbe is excellently drawn."—*Times.*

49. LIFE OF MARIE ANTOINETTE.
BY PROFESSOR CHARLES DUKE YONGE.

"A work of remarkable merit and interest, which will, we doubt not, become the most popular English history of Marie Antoinette."—*Spectator.*
"This book is well written, and of thrilling interest."—*Academy.*